Advance Praise
for City of Weird

"*City of Weird* is everything I love about Portland: its next-gen sensibility, gleeful disregard for expectation, and that undercurrent of darkness which acts as foil to the eccentricity. I popped these stories like the handmade treats they are, and enjoyed every one."
— Averil Dean, author of *The Undoing* and *Alice Close Your Eyes*

"If weird makes you think of funny and moving and disturbing and just plain odd in that wondrous Portland way, well, *City of Weird* is the book for you."
— Jess Walter, author of *Beautiful Ruins*

"Like old pulp magazines, *City of Weird* runs the gamut from simply odd to straight-up horror, from comic to tragic, from short to long and, because it's Portland, there's even one graphic story (Jonathan Hill's 'How Do You Say Gentrification in Martian'). Whether you're already a fan of the weird and horrific in fiction or just enjoy short fiction well told, *City of Weird* will have something to satisfy you. Also to horrify you and make you laugh, maybe at the same time. If this is what the bumper stickers mean when they say 'Keep Portland Weird,' count me in."
— Billie Bloebaum, bookseller, Third Street Books

"Just like Portland, *City of Weird* is strange, eccentric, and wild, but also deeply authentic and moving. In the pulpy dark of the Shanghai Tunnels, the salty sweets of Trendy-Third, and the endless miles of bookshelves at Powell's, we find a giant octopus, man-eating mold, and even Alex Trebek. But in the middle of all that weird, right on the Max line, we find a slice of humanity. Gigi Little has gathered a talented group of authors who challenge the bounds of short fiction and pull us into the fantastically absurd. A wicked read—*City of Weird* is a Portland guidebook to the absurd, the fantastic, and the strange."
— Kate Ristau, author of *Clockbreakers*

"Nimbly spanning the gamut from heartfelt to absurd, lyrical to laugh-out-loud funny, *City of Weird* confirms the suspicion held by many a Portland resident that you don't have to look far to find the fantastical. It'll be a long time before I walk on Mount Tabor or wander Powell's without looking over my shoulder."

— Fonda Lee, author of *Zeroboxer*

"*City of Weird* is a dark, imaginative and entertaining exploration of the bizarre, set against the backdrop of Bridgetown. From the career troubles of the undead to what's lurking in the basement at Powell's, this book is perfect for readers who want to know what truly keeps Portland weird."

— Ian Doescher, Portland native and author of the *William Shakespeare's Star Wars* series

City of Weird

City of Weird

Edited by
GIGI LITTLE

FOREST AVENUE PRESS
Portland, Oregon

Alex Trebek appears in "Waiting for the Question" with permission from Alex Trebek.

Library of Congress Cataloging-in-Publication Data

Names: Little, Gigi, 1969- editor of compilation.
Title: City of weird : 30 otherworldly Portland tales / edited by Gigi Little.
Description: Portland, Oregon : Forest Avenue Press, 2016.
Identifiers: LCCN 2016018509| ISBN 9781942436232 (paperback) | ISBN 9781942436263 (ebook) | ISBN 9781942436249 (ebook)
Subjects: LCSH: Science fiction, American. | Fantasy fiction, American. | Ghost stories, American. | Portland (Or.)--Fiction. | BISAC: FICTION / Science Fiction / Short Stories. | FICTION / Fantasy / Urban Life. | FICTION / Horror. | FICTION / Literary.
Classification: LCC PS648.S3 C49 2016 | DDC 813/.087608979549--dc23
LC record available at https://lccn.loc.gov/2016018509

4 5 6 7 8 9

Distributed by Legato Publishers Group
Printed in the United States of America by Forest Avenue Press LLC
Portland, Oregon

Cover design: Gigi Little
Interior illustrations: Gigi Little
Interior design: Laura Stanfill

Forest Avenue Press LLC
P.O. Box 80134
Portland, OR 97280
forestavenuepress.com

Contents

Foreword

There was this one time I sold my soul to the devil.

I wasn't exactly sure what I was selling it for. Terms weren't really discussed. The dream was just me and Mephistopheles and a ceremonial drink from a bowl of chocolate and blood.

The night before, sitting with my then-husband in a bar in Madison, Wisconsin, having Halloween drinks, I'd said, "So, I'm thinking of selling my soul to the devil. What do you think I could get for it?"

He said, "A buck ninety-eight."

I laughed, but he wasn't paying attention. He was watching the waitress with the clingy black witch costume and unwitchlike cleavage. I tried to think of something else to talk about, but with my then-husband, that meant two subjects: his vintage circus collection and 1970s progressive rock. These subjects are interesting for a year or so, but get ten years down the line and you're pretty much ready to make a pact with the devil.

I started writing it all down: how I kept getting great parking places, how that woman I didn't know offered me a front-row ticket to that Rufus Wainwright concert. Yes, I was thirty-five years old and making lists of the things I'd gotten for selling my soul. This wouldn't sound so weird if you knew me as a child, binge-watching *The Twilight Zone* and spending hours trying to teach myself to move objects with my mind (I found light objects like feathers and round objects like marbles worked best to bridge the gap between the realm of the preternatural and the rookie telekinetic).

Here's a partial list of what I got for selling my soul in 2003:

• A hockey game and my team won.

• A train trip without the aforementioned husband to California to visit family.

• A gift basket (not really).

• How every time I put my hand on my pregnant sister's belly, the baby kicked. And she wouldn't kick for my mom, my dad, my brother, only me.

• An impromptu plane trip to Portland, Oregon, bought and paid for by my mom, to visit more family.

• Seriously, every time I put my hand on my pregnant cousin's belly, the baby kicked.

• A trip to downtown Portland to see an art show that just so happened to lead to writing a fan letter to the artist that just so happened to lead to a correspondence that just so happened to lead to a long-distance, online, never-seen-him-before crush that just so happened to lead to a decision to change my whole life, leave the then-husband, move to Portland, fall in love with the artist, marry the artist, and eventually edit an anthology about my favorite subject and my favorite city.

Portland. Where people knit cozies around street signs and hitch plastic toy horses to the old iron horse rings that are still bolted into the concrete at the curbs here and there along the streets. Former logging town turned mecca for creativity and self expression, home to bridges, an extinct volcano, the largest independent bookstore in the country, and the underground passages known as the Shanghai Tunnels, where legend has it men used to be kidnapped and imprisoned before being sold into lives of slavery at sea.

By favorite subject, of course, I mean monsters, phantoms, robots, spacemen, alternate universes, breaks in the space-time continuum, the undead, the dead, Bigfoot, psychokinesis, the aforementioned devil, curses, mad scientists, disembodied hands that crawl around and try to strangle you, spectral ectoplasm, and pretty much anything else that could fit into one of those fantastic old *Weird Tales* magazines. I've often wondered: why do we love this stuff so much? These archetypes of terror. Why are we drawn to anything fear-related when true fear is anything but a positive experience? This from the woman who, as a child, made it her most pressing goal to meet a ghost. I wanted that more even than learning to move objects with my mind. I used to practice for the inevitable rendezvous, so I'd be ready with my most glamorous movie-star terror look: the slow-motion turn of the head, the parting of the lips, the widening of the eyes. Maybe if I got lucky, it would be windy so my hair could blow around, because hair blowing around when you're being terrorized by a poltergeist looks cool.

As I've gotten older, one of the things I've come to love about *The Twilight Zone* and *Weird Tales* and other wonderful mid-century pulp horror narratives is how the stories exemplify what people were afraid of in those days. Not only the lovely, fiendish tropes of fantasy and science fiction but what lay underneath. The real fears of 1920s to 1960s America. Atomic war and the unknowns of science and the downsides of progress. When I was reading submissions for *City of Weird*, that's one of the things I was looking for: stories that exemplify what we're scared of, now, at the turn of the twenty-first century, here in this kooky city known for its weirdness. Just what freaks out tattooed, unicycle-riding hipsters, anyway?

What I found, of course, is that what scares Portlanders is the same as what scares the rest of the country. On the surface, the stories in *City of Weird* contain the fears that delight us: man-eating fish and ravening slime molds from outer space and mysterious biospheres overrun with newt creatures. Bar-hopping gorgons and sexy man-eating octopuses (there are a lot of man-eating things in this collection) and evil, magical books (three of them! Portland is a very literary city). But underneath those fun, fantastical fears, the stories in *City of Weird* speak to what we're really afraid of. Nuclear contamination and climate change and that overdue super-earthquake they won't stop talking about. The corruptibility of power. The power of hate. The ways in which we hurt each other. The unknown. The known. Poverty, homelessness, death, disease. Loneliness.

My silly devil story might not seem to be about fear at all, but it is. I wasn't afraid of demons or eternal damnation, but I was pretty damned horrified of the prospect of living the rest of my life in the boredom and loneliness of a marriage I didn't want to be in but was afraid to leave.

Those fears that truly haunt us. No wonder we turn to, get obsessed with, the fears that are safely, exaggeratedly unreal. I'll take a half-decomposed water spirit (page 203) or a post-apocalyptic robot dog (page 85) or an explosive beer can wielding Santa Claus (page 48) over a letter from the IRS any day. The fanciful, sometimes preposterous archetypes of weird fiction are humankind's way of acknowledging the universality of the anxieties we all face. Not only that, but they're way more fun.

– Gigi Little
Editor, *City of Weird*

FROM *the* DEEP

Her flat eyes were watching above the water, the moonlight shining off her back, as she came closer and closer to shore.

The Sturgeon Queen

Rene Denfeld

My grandma told me this story. You have to mind my grandma. She liked to say she was a descendant from the natives that once filled this area—the men who worked the falls, lowering their nets, the women who waded for wapato in the low-lying river fields.

My grandma was fond of telling stories, and at one time or another, she also claimed to be a native of Russia, the daughter of a convict who married a slave, and, once, when she was knee-deep in Wild Irish Rose, said she was a descendant of Mr. Clark himself, on his wild ride up the river, on which she said he sprayed his seed like a cottonwood tree in spring.

I suspect my grandma got her stories from when she was what they called a pie girl, though her job had very little to do with pie—at least not the kind you are thinking about. Back when timber ruled these parts, Portland was a place the loggers escaped to—a city where a faller might mend his torn limbs in a tidy home, a place where families went to hope for a life outside the logging camps and the threat of death that defined life here. "Died in the woods," they would say, and everyone knew that means tits up with your cork boots in the air, eight tons of Douglas fir crushing your feeble little body.

They called them pie girls, and my grandma was one. Every good logging company in the woods had a pie girl. The girl you went to for seconds, Grandma liked to say, with a mischievous grin.

I suspect my grandma got her stories from all the men she met, working all those logging camps outside of Portland over all those long years. If you think of it, having sex with so many men is like stealing their secrets. Men like to talk—every woman knows this. They accuse us of gossip, but oh my. Men like to gab. You really can't get them to shut up sometimes. *Especially* after sex. The whole idea men like to sleep after sex is so much nonsense. No, it's only after going all cottonwood on us they want to share.

I'm old now, but when I was little, I lived with my grandma and my mom in a little cottage under the St. Johns Bridge. That cottage is long gone now, torn down for ridiculous condos painted the color of ochre and snot.

Back then we lived in this little cottage, perched under the bridge, and while my mother snored her final days away in a haze of alcohol and opiates, easing her death from cancer from working the creosote mills, my grandma liked to tell me this story.

We would sit on the dinky little porch, our bare feet on the dirty slats, looking out over the huge, deep Willamette River while it sheened in the setting sun.

Grandma called this story The Sturgeon Queen.

I can still remember her husky, rich voice as she talked. Even now, so many years later, I can hear her clear as day as she says:

This story starts way back when, before the whites came bringing their filthy malaria and blankets full of measles. This entire hillside was filled with Indians—so many their longhouses covered the grass.

The natives knew that this was one of the best places for wapato, salmon, and sturgeon. In the shallows there were little fish, and freshwater clams, which are delicious cooked in broth. The salmon they smoked with honey. We called this salmon candy. No one makes salmon candy anymore, just like they don't make floats, or carnival cream.

The Indians said that one day a mysterious thing began happening. The people began disappearing. Oh, not all of them! One or two, here and there. A child would go wading for clams in the setting sun. An old lady would go down to commune with the night birds, flying overhead. And they would vanish.

At first the people thought an enemy tribe was up to mischief. Or an angry god. Or, they thought most likely, a sick one of their own, because heaven knows rape and murder and evil are not confined to one people.

The people posted sentinels. Men, quiet in the bushes, stayed up all night, watching the huge river as the moon lit on her, and rode her back.

What they saw you might not believe, but oh—don't laugh!

It was the sturgeon queen.

Now, see, there you go, laughing. But did you know sturgeon can grow ten, fifteen, twenty feet long? There have been cases of sturgeon catching live ducks, geese, dogs, and yes, even children. If you have never seen one, they look like dinosaurs, ridged backs like hooks, long hooked mouths. Like dinosaurs, sturgeon can live for hundreds and hundreds of years. Some say they never die.

The native men watching saw the sturgeon queen rise from the deep, floating silently into the shallows. Her flat eyes were watching above the water, the moonlight shining off her silver back, as she came closer and closer to shore.

Then the men held their breath, because the sturgeon queen did something no fish had ever done. She left the water and slithered on the land. She moved along the shore, surprisingly fast and hard and silent.

She stopped, suddenly, hidden in shadows. She had heard something. It was a dog, coming down for a drink.

In a flash the dog was gone, and only a few bubbles rose from the surface of the river to tell that the sturgeon queen had her prey in her long barbed mouth and was swimming it into the deep.

Now at this point my grandma always paused.

We'd be sitting on our porch, and the setting sun would be

lighting the river on fire. Purple and gold would stream from the heavens, and light fell in tunnels.

From the other cottages nearby I could hear the laughter of men, the crush of a beer can, and I could smell hamburger frying for hamburger sandwiches white bread, with mustard, and the grease poured over—and usually, a baby crying.

Back then this area was filled with kids, so many kids you would practically trip over them on the way to the store: packs of kids playing kick-the-can in the dusty streets, shouting as their mothers whistled them home as the dusk fell, and always, you would hear the ever-present admonishments to stay away from the river at night.

Grandma would go fetch herself some tea in the mason jar she used, and I could tell from how dark the "tea" was how much Wild Irish Rose was really in the jar, from the secret stash she thought no one knew about.

Grandma would settle her haunches back on the porch, wiggling down a little on the wood like it might give her gratification, and I would remember how she would tell me that the hardest part of stopping being a pie girl was that men forgot how good you taste.

Then she would resume the story.

Over the years the sturgeon queen and the natives came to an agreement of sorts.

She would rise out of the river at night, and if they had a spare duck, or a criminal, or a captive, they'd toss it near the shore. In a flash she would have her prey and be gone.

No one ever figured out why she slithered the banks, when the river was so full of delicious salmon. Maybe she had grown to like the feeling of air on her back, as we all do. Maybe at one time her people had lived on the land, and were forced into the river. Maybe this was revenge for what had been taken from them.

As long as the people stayed away from the shore at night, everything was fine.

Time passed a bit, and the people told their children to come home when dusk fell.

But then the next thing happened, which it always does. The whites came, with their measles in blankets and mosquitoes from their dank ships, carrying malaria.

In only a few years—this is no exaggeration—the entire village here was gone. This area went from being one of the most populated areas of North America, as far as natives were concerned, to pretty much wiped out. The few natives who survived escaped to work for the whites. They became the maids, the servants, and the pie girls, and they warned the local children about the sturgeon queen.

Because the sturgeon queen was still out there.

She had climbed out of the water one night, only to find silence. No people came to toss her ducks, or the occasional juicy captive. The village above her was as quiet as the death she could smell on the wind. No fires arose. There was only the sound of wind, and then rain, and that curious sound sun makes, when it is speckling on the flowers.

Some say the sturgeon queen is down there even now, wandering the shore. Think about that, before you wander the river at night.

That's the story my grandma told.

At the time, I would see in my mind's eye how the town grew after the natives died, how the white men came and laid down bricks and mortar, how the Tulip bakery was built, how the taverns sprang up. The city came out and enfolded this place.

But the whites didn't build on the grass where the village had stood. It was the last little bit of Portland where natives had lived. It is still there now, a place that honors the dead even as the living do not know why.

I'm old now—sixty-seven—and so of course my grandma is long gone. I kept her mason jar, and an empty bottle of Wild Irish Rose, to remember her by.

Our cottage is gone, too, like I said, replaced by all those awful condos. I couldn't afford to live in one of them in a million years. I have a Section 8 apartment, up by Pier Park, but they are remodeling it soon, which is just another way of saying eviction. I have no idea what I will do. Sometimes I hope I die, just to save myself the worry.

I walk down by the river, ignoring those condos, remembering my grandma.

Over the past year I've noticed something, and I am telling it here for the first time.

Lately, down by the river there have been signs for missing people: A man out for a midnight walk. A woman from the condos down on the shore as dusk fell.

I think about how memories protect us. We've lost those memories. Why, I bet most people here don't know how the river used to be so thick with log rafts you could walk them, or how folks would dip smelt in nets, to fry with cornmeal. They probably don't know there was a day when a poor man could raise a family here. They probably never even heard of the sturgeon queen.

I think about how the new people in those condos don't know what lurks out there for them, in the dark.

All the cases are unsolved. The flyers appear, and eventually are tattered by rain, and disappear. But a new one always comes.

I figure there always will be, as long as the sturgeon queen is out there, slithering along our shores.

Octopocalypse: a Love Story

Brigitte Winter

I should have noticed something was wrong when the cats started disappearing, but I was too busy falling in love.

Her name was eMa—the lowercase letters embracing a single uppercase *M*. She changed the spelling when her art was good enough to sign, she told me. "eMa has nice symmetry."

eMa had electric blue hair and her nose was pierced like a bull. She only wore circa 1950s dresses from House of Vintage, and she made her own jewelry out of junk she found at the ReBuilding Center on Mississippi—lots of hinges and screws and other tiny hardware glued to old brooches she bought at estate sales. She was as weird as everyone in Portland, but also like no one I'd ever met— definitely like no one back home in Connecticut. eMa *was* Portland, and she was beautiful, and she was exactly why I moved here.

By the time I first saw eMa at the bar on Stark, most of the cats were already gone. My sister lives only a few blocks from the main Montavilla strip, and she introduced me to all the cats between Sixty-ninth and Stark the first day I moved in. Jill loves cats, and she and Jareth, her douchey ex-boyfriend, named all the neighborhood felines between their place and the Academy Theater. Petting other people's cats was apparently Jill's idea of big sister/little sister bonding time, and we had to add fifteen minutes to any walk to accommodate kitty cuddles. As far as I'm concerned, cats are rude, stinky little petri dishes full of fleas and toxoplasma, but it was so nice to see Jill smile that I bought into the cat-petting ritual with minimal protest. Bush Cat was the friendliest. He spent most of the day in the rose bush at the end of Seventy-sixth. Fat Shadow was only slightly bigger than Shadow, and he lived for belly rubs. Glare Cat was my favorite. She never left her stoop. She just followed me with her eyes like one of those creepy old paintings.

The night I met eMa, I was too pissed to look for the cats. Jareth had smacked my ass again while I was washing dishes after dinner. I don't know why Jill didn't make him leave after they broke up. By the time I moved in, he had been sleeping on the couch and paying zero rent for months. And yes, he did look a little like an overweight version of David Bowie in *Labyrinth* (hair and all), and no, I don't think Jareth was his real name. The guy often played Bowie's "Starman" on repeat from his phone all day like it was his own personal soundtrack. That night, he smacked my ass and called me "babes," and I told Jill he was making me uncomfortable. She got all quiet like usual, and started chewing on a piece of her hair, and asked if I would please, *please* try harder to help her maintain "harmony" in the house (*her* house, that she owned; not his), and I said I'd had enough of that shit and needed to take a walk.

It was late March and the air already smelled green and warm and amazing. Jacket weather. Pretty sure it was still snowing off and on in Connecticut. Earlier that week, Mom had complained again about Dad never helping her shovel the car out of the cul-de-sac. I wasn't prepared for the perpetual spring when I moved out to Portland. Jill never mentioned it. But here I was, thinking about Mom's car covered in snow while I mixed paint in my brain to create the perfect palette for the purple and yellow crocuses lining the street. I was going to maybe have one drink to cool off and then head back to my studio in Jill's basement to paint for the rest of the night.

But then I walked into Vintage Cocktail Lounge on Stark and saw eMa behind the bar, and I forgot all about Jareth and snow and crocuses.

I noticed her hands first. She was mixing a drink for a bearded guy with a plaid shirt and dark hipster glasses. He was talking at her and making big gestures with his arms like he was telling an amazing story. She was smiling, but her focus was entirely on the work in front of her. I don't know how to describe the stunning way she mixed that drink except to say that it was like she was playing music—graceful and deliberate. I was at the bar and staring at those hands before I knew I'd decided to sit down, and then the hands paused, hovering over the drink. I looked up and she was looking back at me, eyebrows raised.

"Help you?" she asked.

"Yes. I'd like a Manhattan, please. And your name." *Oh, dear God.* Who says that? Not me. At least not the socially competent version of me who somehow died when I walked into this bar and reincarnated as a cheesy purveyor of bro-tastic pickup lines.

She passed the drink to the lumberjack hipster, her eyes still locked with mine. Those eyes were the same electric blue as her hair. They crinkled in the corners as her lips pulled into a coy half-smile. My heart was banging so hard against my ribs that I was worried she'd somehow hear it over the Depeche Mode and drunk conversation filling the space around us.

"Just the Manhattan would be cool, too."

She leaned toward me. The pendant on her necklace slipped between her breasts as she moved. She smelled faintly of salt and sunscreen, reminded me of the beach. She took my hand and cupped it in hers. Her palm was smooth and warm, and my body tensed at the thrill of her skin against mine. I tried to smile and breathe normally, as if spontaneous hand-holding with sexy strangers was the kind of thing I did every night. And then she grabbed a pen from the counter and slowly wrote "eMa" across my palm. She drew the name in elegant cursive, each stroke tickling electric waves of pleasure down my body. Then she said the thing about symmetry and being an artist. I was in awe of her.

"I'm Kathy," I said.

"Hi, Kathy. Up for trying something new?" She curled my fingers around her name and gave my fist a squeeze.

I nodded. In that moment, I was up for trying anything this woman asked of me. She turned around, and I watched her hands again as she mixed two drinks and shimmied around the side of the bar, gesturing with her head toward a high-top table by the door. I slid into the window seat, shoving the little red pillows out of the way so I could fit my satchel next to me. She pushed in beside me instead of sitting on the stool opposite the window, and I caught a whiff of that beachy perfume again. The sliver of space between our shoulders buzzed with magnetic energy.

"I've been experimenting with this new liqueur we just got." She passed me one of the drinks. "It tastes like caramel and roses."

My hands were shaking, so I wrapped both of them around the glass. I didn't want to spill her masterpiece down the front of her dress.

"Aren't you, like, working right now?"

"This is work. I need an unbiased review of this new cocktail. You get to decide whether we add it to the menu."

She clanked her glass against mine, and my shoulder bumped hers as I maneuvered to avoid dropping my drink. The cocktail was dry and floral on my tongue. My whole body went warm as I swallowed it—half from the alcohol and half from the tingling pleasure of my bare skin against eMa's. Her arm brushed mine again as she slammed her glass down on the table.

"You hate it, right?"

"No, it's—"

"It's awful. I'm a shitty bartender." She laughed. "It's okay. Not my passion or anything. But I like the people and it pays the bills."

"What is your passion?"

"Art." She pulled down the front of her dress even farther so I could see a tattooed tentacle curving across her left breast. Just the very top of it was visible above her turquoise bra. It was clearly a big piece, probably extending all the way down her side.

I swallowed. I really wanted to see the rest of that tattoo. "You designed it?"

She nodded.

"Squid?"

"Octopus. Smartest creatures in the sea." She shot me another flirtatious half-smile. "Love this town, but I miss the water."

I laughed. "I've never met someone so jazzed about cephalopods."

"Meeting an octopus is like meeting an intelligent alien," she said in a serious, conspiratorial tone. "Have you ever seen an octopus change color and shape to mimic prey?"

I may have found the question odd if her knee hadn't been touching mine under the table. The alcohol was doing its job, and my hands weren't shaking anymore. I was almost feeling brave. "No. No, I don't know much about octopuses." I draped my arm over the back of our seat.

"You're an artist, too." She spoke the words plainly, as fact. Her erratic subject-changes were a little hard to follow, but that made her all the more interesting.

"How do you—?"

She gestured toward my satchel. It must have tipped when I shifted to save the drink, and my sketchpad and art markers lay spilled across the window seat. She ducked under my arm and reached across my lap for the sketchpad before I could stop her. Opening a sketchpad without permission is usually an unforgivable sin, but this woman was gorgeous and fascinating, and I'd already gulped most of my cocktail. She flipped through my pages, and I watched her face. About halfway through the book, she smiled and put a hand on my thigh, sending a wave of electric bliss up my spine. My hands started shaking again.

"Where did you come from?" she asked without looking up from my art. She turned each page with great care, like it was something precious.

"Um, Connecticut?" I ran my trembling fingers back through my hair, and glanced across the bar at the hipster lumberjack. He sat back on his stool and glared like he was considering challenging me to a duel. I shrugged an apology at him. I didn't know why she chose me either. "I was too queer for small-town New England," I continued, "but here I feel obscenely normal."

"Who's this?" She pointed to a sketch of Jill. My sister was a teenager in the picture, with a slinky dress and a goofy grin. Pretty sure I sketched it from one of her many prom photos. Jill went to six proms before she graduated high school. It was like she was trying to set some kind of record.

I sighed. "That's my big sister. From before she moved out here and turned into a human doormat."

"You love her." eMa's eyes were big and vulnerable. There was something unsettling about the intentness of her gaze.

"Of course I love her. She's my sister." It seemed like eMa was done with my sketchbook, so I shoved it back in my satchel.

"I want to show you something." eMa slid off the window seat and swiped our empty glasses from the table.

"You can just leave work whenever you feel like it?"

"Not now. Tomorrow night. We close by two." That half-smile again. "See you then?"

She disappeared behind the bar before I could say yes, and I ran all the way home, fueled by the power of a hundred cheesy love songs blasting in my brain.

I was so giddy when I burst through the door that I almost ran right past Jill crying at the kitchen sink. She smiled and shrank from my hug, turning to wipe her eyes with a kitchen towel. She'd been washing the dishes I'd abandoned earlier that evening, so I picked up the other towel to help dry them.

"Where's Jareth?" I asked.

"Oh, you know him. He has a friend over tonight." She nodded toward the closed bedroom door and gave me her best martyr's smile—tight and close-lipped. Just like Mom. Something hard and hot burned in the bottom of my stomach.

"That's ridiculous, Jill. Why does he still live here?"

She looked down at her hands. "Did you see any of the cats tonight on your walk? Jareth says he hasn't seen them in a few days, and—"

"I can't do this." I threw the towel into the drying rack. "Not tonight."

I heard Jill sniffling as I stormed toward the basement, so I turned into the living room instead and switched on the TV. I flipped to a *Murder, She Wrote* marathon, and cranked up the volume.

Jill flopped onto the couch next to me, her forehead all crinkled and questioning. I wrapped us up in a big fuzzy blanket, and whispered into her hair, "If Jareth is going to entertain guests in your bedroom, then Angela Lansbury's voice will be the soundtrack to his snogging."

She responded with a sound that was half laugh, half sob, and then snuggled up against me. She fell asleep with her head in my lap.

The next evening, I raced back to the bar by 1:45, and then loitered outside and stared at my phone until 2:06. eMa grinned when she saw me standing in the doorway, and whispered something to the barback. He rolled his eyes and smirked at her, tilting his head toward the front door as he wiped a wet cloth across the bar top. No one paid us any attention as we exited the bar. My lumberjack nemesis was back in his usual spot, but he was too busy staring at his drink to give me a glare goodbye.

"So what is it you want to show me?"

eMa yanked me down Stark at breakneck pace. The woman was surprisingly strong. Now that we were standing, it was clear that she was a good six inches taller than me, and I had to jog to match her long stride.

"Volcano," eMa called back at me.

"Excuse me, what?"

"We're going to the volcano."

"You mean Mount Tabor Park?" I dragged my feet a bit. That park had a gorgeous view of Mount Hood and downtown Portland during the day, but Jill warned me against going there at night, said the crowd up there could get rowdy. "Mount Tabor's not much of a volcano, eMa. It's been extinct for, like, 300,000 years. Plus, there's not really anything to see there at night. Just kids smoking pot and making out."

"Exactly."

She spun around and pushed me against the darkened door of a closed restaurant. I smiled at her, and her body and lips were pressed against mine before I could speak another word. The kiss was rough and passionate, burning through my body and condensing as a warm, pulsing weight at the bottom of my belly before spreading down the inside of my thighs. I moved my hands to her lower back and pulled her against me. I wanted to see the rest of that octopus tattoo. I wanted to know what her skin tasted like and how our bodies felt tangled together.

"Okay," I murmured against her neck. "Show me this volcano."

We talked nonstop the rest of the walk to Mount Tabor. At one point, eMa slipped her hand into the back pocket of my jeans, and I got that warm feeling in my belly again. She asked more questions about my sister (three years older than me, straight as an arrow, bakes incredible cheesecake), whether I'd ever been in love (desperately, tragically), why I moved (too many cows, no decent jobs, town was too small not to run into my ex in the supermarket twice a week), my worst fear (tie between losing the impulse to create and driving off a bridge), whether I could swim (yes?).

We were past a weird sign pointing toward some kind of combo "volcano"/"playground," and most of the way up Tabor before I realized I was the only one answering questions. This woman knew my life story, and I knew three things about her:

She worked as a bartender but wanted to be a full-time artist.

She got weirdly excited about sea creatures.

She was an amazing kisser.

"We're here," I said, breathing hard. We'd speed-walked up the fourteen sets of concrete steps to the park and I was talking the entire time. I needed a break. "Enough with the questions. Your turn to share something."

eMa stepped back into the shadow of a giant Douglas fir. "This is my favorite place," she said. "I come here every night."

I squinted around us at the outlines of stone benches and impossibly tall fir trees. A few feet to eMa's left, I could barely make out the silhouette of a big stone statue standing atop a high pillar—a man in a long coat pointing a steady, deliberate hand right at us.

"It's nice," I said, "but, um, dark."

"That's why I love it. It's beautiful in a way that's impossible to paint." She inhaled deeply. "Because what color is the smell of wet lilac anyway?"

I laughed. When she smiled at me, a familiar flutter started under my diaphragm, pulling at my heart like pain.

"eMa, I—"

That's when she slid the straps of her dress from her shoulders. She reached behind her back and pulled down her zipper in one motion, the dress opening around her like the petals of a flower and then dropping to her feet.

My breath caught in my chest. For the first time in my life, I couldn't think of anything to say.

A full moon hung above the branched trunk of the fir, projecting a dappled pattern of shadow and light across eMa's body and creating the illusion that her skin was glowing a shimmering blue. I was right about the size of the octopus tattoo. It spanned the entire left side of her body. Its tentacles wrapped across her stomach and curved up between her breasts. One tentacle reached down between her legs, circling the top of her thigh and vanishing behind her. In the rippling moonlight, the bright blue octopus looked alive, as if its tentacles were coiling and uncoiling around eMa's torso.

She extended a graceful arm and motioned for me to join her under the tree. A dizzy tingling sensation crept up the back of my neck and prickled across my scalp. This was somehow my life now. By day, I'd paint and eat microwave burritos. By night, strange, gorgeous women would lure me to the top of volcanoes and strip off their clothes in the moonlight.

Thank God for Portland.

And then a pair of teenagers appeared from behind the pointing statue and ruined everything.

"Holy shit, dude. Lesbians! Now that's what I'm talking about."

The guy who spoke first had a wispy goatee and wore an oversized army jacket. He was leering at eMa. His buddy leaned up against him as they giggled like little kids and stumbled toward us. They were clearly smashed, and they were bigger than us.

The second kid leveled his gaze on me. "Take it off, lady," he slurred, releasing his friend's arm and staggering toward me. "Don't you want to play with your friend?"

Panic surged up my spine. I swung my satchel in front of me

and dug through the front pocket: art markers, phone, gum—nothing that would help me in a fight. I wanted to run, but I wasn't going to leave eMa alone and naked with two drunk assholes.

And then I heard the kid with the goatee shriek.

When I think back on that moment, I remember feeling eMa's transformation before seeing it—a kind of rumbling under my feet, the ground rolling in waves beneath me. And then I watched her bloom—the arms of her octopus tattoo unwinding from her torso and spinning her body in graceful circles as they climbed skyward like vines. By the time the kid screamed a second time, she was already changed: the nude goddess transformed into a giant sea monster. The beast was almost the size of the huge fir, even bigger when her arms were fully extended. Her skin was slick and glistening blue, her head turned to the side so one big, intelligent eye stared down at me. This man-eating cephalopod was so clearly still my eMa. I recognized her in the motion of her eight elegant arms, the way she plucked that kid from the ground and squeezed the life from him with deliberate grace. Like she was mixing one of her cocktails or flipping through my sketchbook.

She killed with the finesse of an artist.

eMa crushed and devoured the second kid in seconds. Then, the ground moved beneath us again as her tentacles wrapped around her body and merged into human flesh. A metallic adrenaline taste burned the back of my tongue as I watched the beast shrink into a trembling, naked woman. When she looked up at me, her face was streaked with tears.

"Oh, Kathy," she whimpered, bending over and hugging her two human arms around her bare chest. "I'm sorry. I'm just so *hungry* all the time." She lifted her head again, her eyes desperate. "Can you still love me?"

My feet felt stuck. My heart thudded wildly. I wanted to run from her, but I also wanted to hold her.

"What are you?" I asked.

"I am eMa," she moaned. "I am the first of many. I am reconnaissance." She stamped her foot against the earth. "I come from down there."

"You come from the volcano?" I could hear the blood pulsing in my ears. "And there are more of you?"

"We are hungry."

I took a step back.

"Kathy." She reached for me. "I would never hurt you."

"Stay back. Don't touch me."

"I try not to eat humans. I promise I do. But I have to feed every night, and the cats are all gone."

I sprinted down Mount Tabor without looking back. eMa wailed after me. Her moans were raw and desperate, each cry twisting around my heart like a tentacle.

When I burst through my front door, Jareth and Jill were exactly where I'd left them hours ago. Did anyone ever sleep in this house? The Goblin King was sprawled across the couch in his boxers, banging away on his laptop. Jill sat on the floor, displaced, staring at the TV with her eyes glazed over. I ducked past them and rushed down the stairs into the basement. I remember kicking over my easel and throwing my latest painting across the room before face-planting onto my bed to sob into the pillows.

I must have fallen asleep crying because I woke up the next afternoon fully clothed and wrapped in my quilt like a taco, hugging one muddy sneaker to my chest, the other shoe lost somewhere in my sheets. My eyes were throbbing, but my mind was clear. I knew what I had to do.

That evening, I took a long, hot bath after midnight with a glass of cheap pinot noir and a book I'd been meaning to read. I styled my hair (usually I just let it air dry) and I even smeared on a bit of makeup. I wore one of the two dresses I own—a short, stretchy red thing that used to be Jill's—and I sat on a stool in the kitchen sipping wine until Jareth wandered in to scrounge around Jill's refrigerator for dinner.

He froze when he saw me, and his face split into a wide, lascivious grin. "Date tonight?" he asked.

"Something like that." I pictured eMa's big stricken eyes as she asked if I could still love her. The big cat-shaped clock over the sink read 2:15. At this hour, she'd already be alone and hungry at the top of Mount Tabor.

I motioned to the mostly-full bottle of pinot. "Help me finish this?"

He cocked his head to the side and squinted at me. "You feeling okay?"

I laughed. "I'm feeling excellent, but if this living situation is going to be a permanent thing, I'm thinking we should get to know each other better."

He tucked a chunk of Bowie hair behind his ear and gave me a knowing nod. "I like that idea." He took a gulp of wine right from the bottle, and perched next to me. "I like it a lot."

When we killed the wine, he was happy to walk with me to Mount Tabor.

Trainwreck

Leslie What

Last night, my housemate Peachy and I smoked so much weed he forgot we live in a houseboat.

Technically, we live in a floating home, a 300-square-foot, watertight (mostly) stick beauty, but once someone falls overboard, technicalities cease to matter.

Our home floats to the far left of the moorage, facing the Columbia River with its rear end humping the shore-side slip. Our closest neighbor abandoned his leaky home for the suburbs, so besides the noise of jet planes and boat engines we live a peaceful existence. Which might explain why I did not notice Peachy's disappearance right away. The last time I saw him was a smoky memory of sitting beside him on the front stoop to smoke dope and look out over the shiny dark of water.

Yesterday was March 31, the last day of the month. By then, we were almost out of food and were down to the last of the Trainwreck, a high-potency, Sativa-dominant hybrid that's an exemplary strain of weed. Exemplary. By ten at night, the two of us had climbed to the top of Mount High and were sliding on our butts down the other side. The world was a *Starry Night* blur that sounded Captain Beefheart-discordant. In addition to the pot we'd smoked,

I'd liberated one of Peachy's Vicodins and substituted a plain Tylenol when he complained of pain. It was wrong, I know, but his doctor had warned me that, due to policy changes at the VA, the Vicodin train would soon come to an end, so this was my way of weaning him off narcotics.

We were floating high, feeling no pain. Peachy flicked the lit roach into the river.

I watched the sparks light up the night, a slow-motion firework that lasted two seconds in real time, but since I was operating in a drug-induced slowness, it felt like geologic time. I watched the roach's graceful arc over the water and imagined I had witnessed the formation of a caldera. "Awesome," I said.

"Awesome," Peachy agreed. He sat back in his walker and stared at the sky. He wore khakis and an extra-large, green-checkered Pendleton with buttons popped off above the chest. Peachy was a big guy, with an oversized walker decorated with crepe-paper streamers and a green bicycle horn.

Water lapped the dock as lights from Hayden Island twinkled off the river. The jagged profile of Peachy's nose—an oft-broken Mount Hood proboscis—gave his soft face a hard, chiseled look.

"Let's burn something else," I said.

"I gotta pee first," Peachy said.

We split up to take bathroom breaks. Peachy, who moved around as little as possible on account of his arthritis and the fact his walker could not easily fit into our bathroom, shuffled near the half railing to pee, the floating home equivalent of pissing out the window. I limped inside to use the facilities. The gentle rock of our home balancing on the current and the loud whoosh of highway traffic made it hard to relax enough to start the stream, but before long I was filling that tiny space with the music of pee hitting toilet water and once again I was caught up in the slow advance of geologic time, with enough time to pee out a three-part concerto for porcelain and harp.

Life seemed so miraculous in those moments, ruminating on all the internal tubes that ran in and out, marveling at how our lungs and belly exchanged air and food for life and energy. I was not a religious man, but you had to admire the design of veins that carried beer to the kidneys, where it transformed into pee. A few months before, some teens had peed into the reservoir at Mount Tabor, and my old boss at the Water Bureau had ordered the reservoir be emptied, because, in his words, "Do you want to drink pee?"

And with those words, 7.8 million gallons of water, contaminated by less than two cups of urine, went away like magic. Except it wasn't really magic because magic attempted to explain things in ways that made sense. Anyway, while I was peeing and thinking deep thoughts, I assumed Peachy was doing the exact same. I could not have been further from the truth. It's possible, but I can't swear on it, that I heard a scream cut short by a loud splash. If I did, in fact, hear that, I probably figured an osprey had dived down to snag a salmon, something I had heard before and might have barely noticed. I'm sure I felt sad for the fish, happy for the osprey. You hear a lot of things on the river, things you never find out any more about before they float downstream and disappear into the Pacific Ocean.

April was but one night's sleep away. The payment clock was reset on the first of each month when the new checks were deposited into our accounts. On April 1, we'd restock, reload, and sing praises for those months with only thirty days, because the months like March, with their thirty-first day but same amount of money, were a bitch. I liberated another of Peachy's Vicodins and crafted a blanket nest on the sofa bed to watch TV. I had just enough pot to puff a bit now and in the morning. Tomorrow, our pot clock would begin anew as well. I mixed a half-Bali Shag tobacco and half-Trainwreck spliff, my usual last-day-of-the-month economic necessity, lit the spliff and sat back to watch cartoons on Adult Swim. I did not contemplate another thing for at least an hour (or maybe two), at which point I remembered it had been a while since I'd seen Peachy.

"Peachy! 'Sup, bro?" I called. There was no answer, and pretty soon, I forgot about Peachy and focused on whether or not I'd already seen that episode of *Squidbillies*. I blame drugs for my forgetfulness. In retrospect, I wish I'd gone after Peachy, maybe tossed out a lifesaver or dialed Marine Patrol, or even jumped in after him. One problem with retrospect is that you just don't think of it at the time.

The next morning, which for me started after eleven o'clock, was that long-awaited first day of April. I woke up and showered and dressed and called the bank to make sure our SSI and VA benefits had been deposited. I paid our slip rent before microwaving water for my first cup of instant coffee. The tray still had plates stacked from dinner, so I got them soaking in the dish tub while I heated up organic toaster pastries from New Seasons. I poured a couple of glasses of kale juice and swallowed one of Peachy's Vicodins to counterbalance my hangover. I packed a bowl with the last of the pot and carried the tray into Peachy's bedroom. "Here's your·breakfast and your medicine," I said to an empty room.

I figured Peachy was in the shower. It took him a while because it was so hard to bend down to wash his feet and he used up all his breath when it was time to dry them. I set the tray on the bed and picked at my toaster pastry while I waited for him to show up and claim his. I yelled, "Peachy! Bro! Where are you?" His toaster pastry grew cold and his kale juice grew warm. The time ganged up on noon, but there was still no sign of my roommate. That bowl was calling my name, which made me call out Peachy's name once more. When he still didn't show up, I lit up and took a few puffs. More time passed. No Peachy. I relit the bowl.

I nibbled on Peachy's toaster pastry and washed it down with his glass of juice. I called his name again, and at some point, when he still didn't show, it finally occurred to me that Peachy was MIA. I walked out on the stoop, saw a break in the railing, noticed Peachy's walker tipped on its side, saw something that might have been dried blood on the planks.

"Peachy?" I said. "Peachy!" That's when I figured out the obvious, that he'd gone off the brink while I was busy being stoned.

I ran inside and grabbed a broom and ran back out and dropped to my hands and knees to lower the handle into the murky water. Was I expecting him to grab hold and let me pull him up like a steelhead? A broom was no match for an unforgiving river and I worked to keep my grip on that broom and save it from drowning. "Oh, Peachy," I said. "Peachy." Regret is an anchor that pulls you down but I fought the pull and stood upright.

Peachy was a decent guy, an exemplary roommate. He was one hundred percent disabled by PTSD and had an Oregon Medical Marijuana Program card to treat the pain from a back injury. I was his registered OMMP caregiver, which meant I could buy medicine for him when he wasn't up to going out to get pot for himself. He paid most of the slip rent and did his share of dishes. I earned a small stipend for watching out for him and doing small favors: preparing his breakfast and some financial stuff, helping him with his online banking and paying bills. It wasn't enough money to cut into my benefits, just enough to improve my quality of life.

Peachy told friends I was his companion animal—he had a wicked sense of humor—but after six months of living together, we were pretty good friends. I'd miss him, the poor slob.

It seemed smart to restock groceries and pot before Peachy's body washed up and his food stamps and disability benefits dried up and my OMMP caregiver card was revoked. The Lord helps those who help themselves, even Peachy would agree.

I locked the door and walked to shore, up the dock and up to the lot and the Sentra. I sat looking at the asphalt for five or ten minutes while both the car and I sobered up enough to drive. The guys at Jiffy Lube had warned me I'd soon need transmission fluid, and that was on my shopping list, along with as much marijuana as I could afford. My number one priority was stocking up on pot. Transmission fluid was a distant ninth, after pot, beer, eggs, kale juice, toaster pastry, potato chips, toilet paper, and shop towels.

Our floating home was in the 217 zip code but I sure liked that 209 dispensary in the Pearl District. The gals behind the counter there were young and Bridget Fonda-pretty. They never made a fuss about whether a man had all his teeth or if one leg was shorter than the other. They were well-educated about the medicines they stocked and which strains cured what. The dispensary was a place where you never felt bad for being sick. They didn't blame you for causing what was wrong with you, unlike practically every alternative clinic in Portland, where clear-skinned, naturopathic hipsters squirted out their overpriced, homeopathic snake oils and blamed your bad fortune and illnesses on lifestyle choices. Without medical marijuana, I'd have jumped into the reservoir years ago.

I parked on the street and fed the meter because the cops down here were about as merciless as Dick Cheney and the last thing I needed was to get written up for parking. I walked to the bank ATM to get four bills from Peachy's account, then walked to the dispensary and pressed the button. The blond girl, Amber, recognized my face through the window and buzzed me inside. "Good to see you, Burt," she said. "How's Peachy?"

"He's keeping on," I said, which I hoped was true. I didn't believe in Hell, but if there was one, Peachy did not deserve an admission ticket, unlike me.

"I just love Peachy," Amber said.

"Me, too," I said, but my words felt hollow. What was I doing, keeping on as if nothing had happened? I got out my card and she signed me in.

"How can I help you?" Amber asked.

"What's special today?"

"Just got in some Blueberry Kush. Indica hybrid. Hear good things about it," Amber said. "Excellent for pain relief. Excellent for sleep. Twenty-one percent THC. One percent CBD."

"Sounds promising," I said.

She opened an apothecary jar to let me sniff.

I remembered when all pot smelled like hay. Nowadays, pot smelled sweet, like the dried fruit they put in cereal boxes. "Nice," I said. "Make new friends," I said, not quite in song but close enough, "but keep the old."

Amber smiled.

"I'd like three ounces of Trainwreck and about a half an ounce of the Blueberry." I watched her measure it out. When she concentrated she bit her lip in a way that made it red and puffy. I imagined kissing her. She smelled nice, like honeysuckle and lavender. I'd never kissed anyone that pretty. I snapped out of it in time to watch the scale drop back to zero. I could not afford to be caught short this month. I was heartsick about Peachy's disappearance and I knew I'd need to smoke for two.

"How's your pup?" I asked, remembering the picture of her little Staffordshire she'd shown me last time. Peachy had always wanted a dog but I'd lied to him, told him the landlord wouldn't allow it. I was the landlord. I owned our floating home. I had nothing against dogs; it's just that Peachy wasn't mobile enough to take care of one.

"His name's Skunk. He does tricks," she said. She pulled out her phone to show me a picture of him sitting up with his front paws sticking out in front of him like a shelf.

"I do tricks, too," I said. I got down on my knees with my hands sticking out in front of me and I let my tongue drop and panted like a dog. I immediately wished I could take it all back. If Peachy were here, he'd have kept me from embarrassing myself, or else come up with some creative excuse that made it all seem okay if the damage was done.

Amber slid her phone back in her pocket. She looked away as if taking stock of her kingdom of pot. In emotionally geologic terms, she'd turned our encounter into another Ice Age.

I scrambled to an upright position and counted out seven bills on the counter before passing them over to her.

Amber wrapped my medicine in a paper bag and handed me a strawberry Pot Tart in a wax paper sack, making it clear this was a present for Peachy, not something extra for me. I left a bill in her tip jar. Generosity was not in my budget, so this was more about me feeling bad than trying to make pretty Amber feel good.

"Thanks. See you next month," she said.

"Till May," I said, suspecting I would never see Amber again.

I stopped at Fred Meyer, used Peachy's Oregon Trail Card for staples, and split the cost of shop towels, TP, and beer.

I drove home and put everything away before rolling a joint. I was starving and that Pot Tart looked awfully delicious, but I felt too guilty to ingest it.

I counted out the last of Peachy's Vicodins (there were fifteen left), took a few tokes of Blueberry Kush, and popped a beer. I'd need to find another roommate to help with finances before May or it would be tight. I turned on my computer and waited another geologic era for it to boot up. I wanted to go on Craigslist and search for a new housemate. While I waited for the happy face screen to pop up, it occurred to me it might look suspicious if I advertised before filing a missing person report. Good thing I thought of that in time. I shut it all down and made myself a cup of instant coffee and sat at the kitchen table to force my brain to focus and come up with a workable plan:

1) Call bank and triple-check on available funds.

2) Look through Peachy's things for an address for his parents. Write them a nice note about what a great guy their son was.

3) Call Marine Patrol and police to file reports.

4) Craigslist.

5) Ask about refilling Peachy's prescriptions.

6) Clean up blood so nobody can CSI me with the date.

7) Reorder this list and remember to call Marine Patrol and file missing person report before writing note to Peachy's folks telling them he's gone.

8) Destroy this list and tidy up pot and Vicodin before cops arrive.

9) Spray houseboat with deodorant spray.

10) Get deodorant spray from Fred Meyer.

And then, because I was hungry and because I thought lists should not have even numbers, I added,

11) Eat lunch.

I fixed a PB&J on Dave's Killer Bread but it tasted all wrong and I only managed a few bites before choking up. "Peachy," I said. "Old buddy."

I went into Peachy's room and poked around, looking for something without knowing what it was. I spotted the wooden crate he used as a bedside stand. It was tilted on one side with its back against the wall and an empty belly facing the room. I swept off everything but the tatted doily he'd inherited from his grand-ma and filled the crate with a few things: a folded PDX carpet T-shirt, his Oaxacan yarn painting, a cedar candle, his Bronze Star

medal, and a photo of Peachy and his ex-wife. I carried the crate
into the living room, stuffed with evidence of better times, set it
upright, and smoothed the wrinkles from the tatted doily. I lit the
candle, centered it on the crate, stared at the flame, and took in a
moment of silence. I wished I'd done things differently.

"Peachy," I said. "I wish you'd come back home."

I hated the quiet.

Peachy deserved to have someone look for him when he fell
overboard.

Sometimes, my place rocked gently, like a cradle, and sometimes it moved like a seesaw. The mighty Columbia roiled and left
my gut feeling unsettled.

I heard a thud, a groan, the crackle and split of wood, and I
glanced out the window at a surreal commotion on my stoop as a
large, green monster approached the door.

There were washing-machine-slosh sounds and the rank smell
of an exploded whale. I jumped up and ran into the kitchen in
time to confront a shiny, slimy, hairy green thing who practically
floated into the room. He pushed a walker and his hands were
shiny wet and webbed. His hair, stringy and green, dripped goo
like candle wax.

"Holy crap," I said.

"Gurgle, gurgle," the incarnation of Peachy replied.

I stood with my mouth open crater-wide for a good five minutes, which felt like five hours on account of the Blueberry Kush. At
some point, I remembered my manners and said, "Would you like
to sit?" I guided green Peachy toward the plastic chair from IKEA
that neither of us liked to sit in. "Sorry 'bout that, Peachy," I said.
"You have to admit it's easier to wipe down."

He nodded and slumped into the chair, rested his elbows on
the table, and dripped water and green slime over the unpaid bills
and advertising mailers.

"Let me get you a towel," I said, and I opened up the shop towels and tore off a few. I heard ice cubes rattling in the general vicinity of his mouth and noticed his teeth chattering away in a calcified
soliloquy. "Are you cold, Peachy?" I asked.

He shivered, nodded, chattered.

I did my best to dry him off with shop towels but when I rubbed him down, a thin, green layer of skin peeled away like fish skin. It was gelatinous and wet—some algae or pond scum—and once most of it was off, Peachy's checkered Pendleton shirt showed through the slime. I unrolled more shop towels and toweled off scum from his face. I was using up all our towels for the month, but that didn't matter. The green fell away from his hair.

"You need a bath," I said, and though it grossed me out to touch him, clearly he needed help. I put my arms around his waist and helped him stand and led him to the shower stall and helped him sit in the shower chair. I had to take off my shirt and jeans and hop in with him, a tight squeeze in that tiny space, but really, the only choice. I turned on the water and aimed the nozzle away until it was warm enough to wet him down and let the water carry the green down the drain and back into the river. I used up all of our hot water and all our clean towels to get him dry. I tugged on my robe and wrapped blankets around Peachy. We walked to the sofa and he sat down but when he didn't stop shivering, I said, "Maybe we should call 9-1-1."

He said, "Burt, I'd rather you didn't." He hated hospitals—places old soldiers were taken to die.

"Okay, buddy," I said. I poked around the storage box, located the space heater, and set it beside Peachy.

"Could you plug it in?" Peachy said.

"I thought I did," I said. "Oops."

"You take good care of me," he said, which made me feel great. "Do we got any pot?"

"Why, yes, we do," I said. I packed a bowl of the Blueberry Kush, got it lit, passed it to him, and waited to take my turn.

"This is good stuff," he said. He took a second puff and held it in until he coughed.

I reached out, expecting he'd take the hint and pass the pipe to me.

"My feet," Peachy said, and I glanced down and saw I had missed some of the pond scum. "Wipe 'em off," Peachy said.

I dropped to the floor to rub his toes with a shop towel. Some scum wiped off but his feet stayed green, the toes webbed, the skin shiny. "What the fug happened down there?" I asked.

"You don't want to know," Peachy said.

"I was worried about you," I said.

Peachy said, "You should worry more about yourself than about me."

I held up my arm and waited for Peachy to pass the pipe. "Smells nice," I said. "Amber thought you'd like it."

"She was right," Peachy said. He blew smoke rings.

"I did the shopping this morning," I said.

"Good. I'm starving," he said. "Bring me something."

I remembered the Pot Tart. "From Amber," I said, passing the sack to him.

His broken nose became a shadow behind the wax paper. He inhaled deeply. "Sweet," he said. "The whole time I was under, I promised myself that if I survived, I would get a puppy." He broke the Pot Tart into uneven halves.

"A puppy?" I said. No way would I take care of it.

"I want a puppy," he said. "You owe me that."

I nodded, knowing this was true.

He took the larger half of the Pot Tart and gave me the small. He set a firm hand upon my shoulder and we munched our treats in silence.

"By the way," Peachy said, "you'll have to take it on walks, and clean up its crap. I can only do what I can do."

"It's the same for all of us," I said, not meaning to make it sound like an excuse.

"One last thing," he said. "The puppy sleeps with me at night."

"Whatever you want," I said.

I watched Peachy relight the pipe and take a deep hit. I gave up waiting for Peachy to gift me a toke and slid my hands into my pockets. The longer I thought about a puppy, the happier I felt. "Can I help you name him?" I asked. If it was a girl, I'd name her Amber.

Peachy frowned as he patted my back and said, "We'll see," with an icy and final voice.

Orca Culture

Leigh Anne Kranz

The Seattle pod moved south. The sonar of hunger echoed between them. The homewaters were empty of the pink-fleshed fish they loved. They swam fast and close to the shoreline. They followed a troller in the fog and moved in with stealth to pull each fish from the hook. The grandmother killed a great white shark easily, turned it belly-up and held until it drowned. She learned the technique on her first long migration, from a pod in the Farallones, the triangular islands where sea lions lounged golden on the rocks and bled scarlet in the choppy water.

She stood on the sand, a surfer watching the approach of radioactive waves. The nuclear plume was due to hit the West Coast that year, Seattle first, then Portland's backyard. It had already hit her. She was the human at the end of the story. She was the voice no one wanted to hear. She had been fired from KPDX for talking about it on the air. The mainstream media ignored the first reports that trickled in across the wire. As if what happened to the ocean would not rain down upon the city.

Life proceeded as normal on the Oregon coast. Families arrived like the carnival on weekends, colorful umbrellas and screaming laughter. She didn't really want to tell them. She wished for them their bonfires, soaring kites, and perfect waves.

The pod lingered where the great river poured into the ocean. They hunted across the shifting sandbar littered with the rusted skeletons of human ships. The pink-fleshed fish were scarce but easy to catch, seeming dazed. Black-skinned sea lions, driven suicidal by starvation, competed for the fish and were quickly killed and divided among the family. The grandmother nudged her mouthfuls to the young one.

She set the alarm for sunrise; how many she had squandered. She woke to the patter of mist on the windowpane. The ocean was a ghost; she walked along the lace hem that appeared and disappeared on the wet sand. She could make out the smudge of a person up the beach, coming closer, a man; she recognized him. He was a famous writer of the Portland literati who rented a house in the three-street town. His wife and children joined him on weekends. Weekdays, other women. He wasn't friendly to her, a witness to his deeds. When she first moved in, he'd knocked on the door with red wine and two glasses, invited her to sit on her own deck, began to explain the view. She had asked him to leave. His books made her wince, male privilege run amok.

The writer materialized out of the mist, glowered in passing, and was enveloped again.

The run of pink-fleshed fish ended and the pod was drawn southward by passing clouds of meaty, silver fish. They trailed the schools for days along the trembling rift in the ocean floor, regained mass and breached with joy. The young one looked down upon the unfamiliar ground—submarine canyons and mountain chains, steaming undersea volcanoes—mapping to memory the way back home. The adults only looked ahead.

The tidal pools were devoid of color; only the armored remained, chitons and barnacles, hermit crabs. It had been one year since she left Portland to live on its coast, to treasure the last days of the North

Pacific ecosystem. She had chosen the beach town after rounding its dunes and entering a dreamscape: purple and orange sea stars upholstered the rocks, sunken grottoes bloomed with green and pink anemones, transient lagoons held stranded fish and dinner-size crabs. Wherever she looked now, she only saw what was missing.

The grandmother was weakening. The silver fish continued on, but the pod could not follow. They took refuge in a cove of haystack rocks. They plucked crabs from the nooks, pulled giant red octopuses from crevices. It was not enough.

The big male spyhopped the shoreline, raised his head above the surface to scan the sand for movement, ears tuned for signs of life. He had never tried to hunt like the nicked and scarred pod from Los Angeles, who had taken over their homewaters one season and crawled upon land to grab seals. The LA gang had learned the trick from a Baja pod, who'd learned it from some Chileans. The big male scoped the forested coast for miles. The beaches were empty of seals.

She stood on the deck, raised her smartphone to the constellations, and the app identified each one: Leo, the lion; Ursa Major, the big bear; Draco, the dragon. She aimed the lens between her bare feet and saw through to the skies of the Southern Hemisphere, famous stars she'd only heard of: Centaurus, the man stallion with bright kneecap, Alpha Centauri; the Southern Cross, whose remote latitude saved it from conquest by Greek and Roman mythologists. She had been invited to South America to see the stars for herself, by a rainforest activist she'd interviewed on KPDX. They had taken a walk along the concrete banks of the Willamette River, and he had not flinched when she mentioned Fukushima, had mirrored her mourning in his earth-brown eyes. She had been tempted to follow him across the equator, but was afraid to start anew on such unfamiliar ground, not speaking the language, not knowing the man.

A neighbor woman walked up the gravel driveway, called out to her through the dark. "Have you seen two dogs, Dobermans?"

The pod was invigorated by the red meat. The half-growns now flanked the big male whenever he left the cove. They were learning: ride the wave all the way in, grab the unsuspecting and subdue, maneuver backward into the deep. In high sun, the tall, black fins disappeared in the glare; in fog, they were invisible. They had taken several four-leggeds: thin, fast ones that traveled at dawn, and plump, slow ones that splashed in the surf. It was not enough.

She ran into the neighbor woman on the beach. Her dogs had not returned, but her eyes still searched for them. A leather collar had washed up, bitten through. "A shark?" she asked. "But, both at once?" The neighbor called out to another woman who made her way down to the beach, the wife of the famous writer, and asked her the same questions. The wife was concerned for her children; her eyes traveled until she found them playing in the sand, burying their father up to his neck. His dark eyes appeared to float above the mound, suspended like the pupils of shore crabs. His gaze burned through his wife and the cluster around her. The wife turned back to comfort the neighbor, introduced herself, Mrs. Famous Writer. The neighbor blurted, "He's married? Oh, you poor dear."

The grandmother knew she was dying. In her lifetime, she had witnessed the live capture of her first calf, hauled onto a boat to the squeals of humans and the screams of a family forever divided. She had once seen the great bay fill with black blood that tarred the fur of otters and glued the feathers of birds. But she had not fathomed the vanishing of the pink-fleshed fish, the homewaters sizzling with invisible poison.

    She let go of life. Her body drifted from the sleeping pod across the moonlit water. Her daughters woke at sunrise, knowing. The echolocation of grief resounded on the rock walls.

Thermal winds lifted a pair of bald eagles high above the surfline. She didn't see the man until he was upon her. The famous writer, spitting words in her face. "What did you say to my wife?" His body towered, rippled with entitlement. She had said nothing. "I said you were a shitty writer." He grabbed her shoulders and released a wave of misogyny, man-made toxin as radioactive as plutonium, damaging the soft tissues of women for thousands of years. It immobilized her muscles, arrested her heart. Her vision darkened at the periphery and closed in fast. It was the glint in his eye that brought her back; the woman reflected there would never be her. She broke the hold and shoved him away.

A rush of cold ocean forced them apart, a black wall slid between them. Through a rain of salt spray she saw interlocking rows of conical teeth, the conch shell curl of pink tongue, the mouth widening. She leapt back and the jaws clamped the denim leg of the writer. The great head swung in circles as bones crunched and the body went limp. The tail thrashed backward into the waves as the rest of the pack advanced like sea wolves. They tossed the body between them and disappeared into the wilderness.

The pod was fed and ready to leave that sad place. They would follow the magnetic pull of the southern pole until the stars changed. They would learn from the others how to survive in strange waters. The pod left the shelter of the vaulted rocks. They sang to the spirit of the grandmother as she made her journey back to the homewaters. They would only return in death.

She was questioned by police, along with the other residents. She never told anyone. She knew how humans operated; the pod would be hunted down, exterminated. They were merely adapting, ancient instinct ever-evolving, creating a new culture for survival. The famous writer's disappearance was deemed a suicide. His wife told police he had been depressed, drinking more. The copyrights would provide well for the family; his tragic demise would only boost sales. She heard they had his memorial service at Powell's, standing room only.

She felt it was the natural order of things. The world was changing. If humans were to survive, men like him must go extinct.

She watched the sunset, nuclear meltdown into condemned waters. She could move to another hemisphere, live beside another ocean. She could learn a new language and speak for the earth in both tongues. She could get to know the rainforest activist from a safe distance, make a new life beneath stars she had never seen.

From THE SKIES

Crazy demon bird seductress witch strolling along downtown with her flock of familiars? Just another Thursday.

Transformation

Dan DeWeese

Pod floated down through the atmosphere and came to rest, with a soft roll, on the planet's surface. She raised three pale, veined petals, carefully appraising the environment. Vibrant plant life. Plenty of water—some of it vapor, but much of it in the form of two large rivers whose roiling intersection she sensed not far from here. The only native molds she detected were weak, almost insensate. They did not respond to Pod's attempts to communicate.

"This will take work," she told the innumerable slime molds inhabiting her innumerable chambers. "But that is in many ways what we want, isn't it? With great adversity comes great accomplishment."

She sensed from the molds vibrations of agreement and eagerness. From one of her chambers, though, she felt nothing. Red, a slime mold who had been among the first to enter her back on their home planet, stayed silent. Exquisitely sensitive to conditions in each of her innumerable chambers, Pod could tell Red was alive. He had lined the entirety of his chamber, just as the other slime molds had. His communicative vibrations during The Drift had been strong and clear. He seemed healthy. Maybe he was just nervous, Pod decided.

The opening of Pod's inner petals was an act so momentous as to be almost sacred. How long had she floated through interstellar space, tightly folded? How long had she incubated her molds against the void? Time had become meaningless. It had been an eternity and also an instant. Finally, she had drifted into a medium-sized system. The outer planets were frozen. She'd drifted past. Next, she found gas giants. Extending two of her petals like sails, Pod was propelled further on the breeze of subatomic particles radiating from the giants. And then, there it was: a rocky planet covered in water, shrouded in vapor. Perfect.

And now they were here, ready to embark upon the project that was the purpose of their lives: The Transformation.

Slowly, Pod lifted her petals. The planet's atmosphere rushed in, offering the innumerable molds their first breath of air since Pod had closed herself and floated from the surface of their home planet. There was a vibratory cheer from the molds, exclamations of delight.

"Fantastic!" some buzzed.

"Brilliant!" others purred.

Red, though, stayed silent. Pod vibrated the fibers of his chamber. "You okay, Red?"

"Yep," he said. "Doing fine."

"You've been quiet."

"Just thinking a bit."

"The time for thinking is over. It's time to act. We're here! Let's make our mark!"

There was a long silence in Red's chamber. "Got it," he said finally.

The molds in the chambers closest to Pod's opening were already slurping their way from the safety of her interior to the blank slate of the waiting planet. The last molds in were the first out. Some paused a moment upon hitting the soil before creeping hesitantly off. Others slid forward with great confidence. All left lines of glistening mucus in their wake. Pod was pleased. These first lines were the start of The Transformation.

The mold exodus took time. The planet's sun rose and set. The night was cold, the day warm—a change from the regular internal temperature Pod had maintained throughout The Drift. The molds knew they could no longer hide in Pod, though. She wasn't their home anymore.

Red was among the last to exit. Pod detected no communicatory vibrations from him as he crept from her innermost chambers toward her final hollow. "There you go, Red," she said encouragingly. "It's all ahead of you. I know you'll do amazing things!"

"Yeah. I don't think I'm going to help with The Transformation," Red said. "Sorry about that."

None of the other molds had said anything remotely like this. "What do you mean?" Pod said. "We're here to make our mark on this planet, to transform its potential into a paradise of mold, our quilt of life."

In the shade of Pod's hollow, Red was actually a dull maroon. "I guess transforming planets just isn't my thing," he said.

"Then why, Red? Why enter my chambers, why make The Drift, if not to be a part of The Transformation?"

"Crawling into you just seemed natural. I mean, did *you* consider your options before calling out to molds that you had moist chambers in which they could grow to maturity during an interstellar drift? Or did you just kind of do it without really thinking?"

Pod didn't understand the question. "Incubating slime molds in our innumerable chambers while drifting the universe in search of transformable planets is what pods do," she said.

"So you just did it. No thought."

"Let's go, let's go!" the slime behind Red said. Its name was Azure. It was a crystalline pale blue.

"It's not about thinking or not thinking," Pod said. "This is how we leave our mark on the universe. This planet will hold the record of our lives, and that record will make our ancestors proud."

"How would they even know?" Red said. He'd been inching forward while they'd been communicating, and now he slipped beyond the lip of Pod's hollow and slurped into the undergrowth.

I guess he didn't care to hear my answer, Pod thought. This was good, in a way, since she hadn't had one.

"I can't wait to get out there," Azure said. "I'm going to spread out everywhere. I've got so many ideas. Just wait, you'll see."

"Have fun," Pod told him. She wondered if she would ever see Azure perform. No one knew what became of pods after The Drift. No pod had ever drifted back to tell anyone.

When the last of the molds exited Pod, she lay empty. She was surprised that none of the innumerable molds she had incubated through The Drift came back to check on her. They had disappeared into the plant life, leaving only wet lines in their wake.

The next day, Pod's outer petals fell off. *Uh-oh*, she thought. That night, her inner petals fell, too, exposing many of her chambers. The chambers were empty now, of course, but it was still concerning. Then the architecture of the chambers themselves began to break down. Pod's spongy walls dried and fell in, her limpid floors cracked and gave way. She lay amid her fallen petals, reduced to her barest self: a spine of interlaced fibers that had once been her core. She was afraid.

Then, something amazing happened. A light breeze picked up, and one of Pod's fibers detached and floated off on the breeze—and she was the fiber. And then another of the fibers floated away, and she was that fiber, too. Over the course of the next day, her core fibers disentangled, and each floated gently into the breeze. Pod was each fiber, simultaneously sensitive to innumerable locations and innumerable environments. Life was truly a wondrous mystery.

What Pod saw was that the slimes, true to their nature, had transformed the area. Pod had sensed the presence of simple ambulatory organisms on the planet. She hadn't realized, though, that this area was infested with a particular species of vermin that had built massive constellations of crude nests. The nests were fashioned from plant and rock life the vermin had transformed into fragile, rickety constructions. Azure had spread over the face of one of the largest constructions, a tall pink column, transforming it into a sparkling blue tower of slime. "Look at me!" Azure called to no one in particular. "Look what I've created! Fantastic transformation! Check me out!"

Other slimes were similarly excited. "If you want to see what's possible horizontally, just stop by my spread," sang a mold named

Luscious Violet. She had filled an area between and surrounding many of the nests. Panicked vermin scattered in all directions, stumbling on their clumsy appendages.

"Dry hillside? Dry no more!" a mold named Velveteen Night announced. The hill was covered with Velveteen slime.

Pod was proud of the molds—they were spreading, transforming the planet, announcing their triumphs and encouraging each other. They were fulfilling their destiny.

One of Pod's fibers floated past the rocky shore of one of the rivers. She noticed a familiar mold among the rocks. "Red!" she said. "How are you?"

"Oh. Hi, Pod. Didn't recognize you."

"I'm innumerable fibers now. I've seen so many things. You should see what Azure did to a huge vermin nest. He said he's just getting started. You should slurp over and check out his techniques."

"Azure was in the chamber next to me during The Drift. He told me all about the stuff he's going to do. More than once."

"What are you up to? Spreading out?"

"Not really."

"Oh." Red was difficult to talk to. "When do you think you'll do some stuff?"

"I think everyone has it covered," Red said. "I hear all of their announcements, at least. Did you know there are other creatures here besides the two-legged vermin? There are creatures in the ground and in the river. I can hear them communicating at night."

"What do they say?"

"I don't know, I don't speak their language. Shouldn't we try to learn it, so we can ask them about this place?"

"I don't know," Pod said doubtfully. "We're here to transform the planet to slime. I don't know if little organisms under the surface can really be a part of that."

"Well—you're not a slime mold, anyway," Red said. "Maybe I'll just make my own decisions."

This hurt Pod's feelings. Of course she wasn't a slime mold. But why did Red have to say it? "Red, do you even like sliming?" she said.

"Why do you call me Red?" he said.

"It's how you look. You're red. What do you want me to call you?"

Red was silent for a long while. "Sheckley," he said eventually.

"What does that mean?"

"It doesn't mean anything. That's the point."

"Fine. I'll call you Sheckley," Pod said, even though it was weird.

"See you around," Red said.

It took a moment for Pod to realize Red had said this because the breeze had lifted her into the air and she was drifting away.

She attended so many brilliant feats simultaneously. Azure continued to spread, devouring the vermin nests from the inside out until, in a dramatic display of slime force, the structures collapsed. Velveteen discovered tunnels the vermin had dug. She expanded into these, choking the tunnels with her soupy self until the vermin fled in terror. A brilliant mold named Copper Mist devoured an element that made him an acid. He slimed the strange, spindly structures the vermin had built over their rivers and the structures tumbled, crackling and sizzling, into the water. He continued this signature innovation—acidizing himself before entering new terrain—again and again, with eye-popping results. Pod's fibers drifted over plant life transformed to slime, nests transformed to slime, streams turned to slime. Even the vapor in the air was seeded with brilliantly aspirated spores and then rained mists of slime. The molds recounted their victories, coordinated new triumphs. They worked together, one acting as a lubricant that allowed others to enter new areas as fungal intrusions. The primitive animal life attempted escape, of course, but most of the creatures were cornered, covered, and devoured. The two-legged vermin emitted loud, rapid vibrations during the process—a crude attempt at communication, it seemed. Many of the vermin fled the area, but Pod knew it wouldn't be long before these victories were replicated across the land. The planet would be mold and slime, slime and mold. The greatness of their projects—the ways in which each mold was individually writing the record of his significance into the very surface of the planet—would be visible to all.

Red, though, did nothing. One of Pod's fibers, tossed on the breeze, drifted near him again. It had only been seven of the planet's days since their last conversation, but the changes were dramatic. The vermin's strange nests had been leveled. The river had changed into a turgid, gelatinous slime that no longer flowed. The atmospheric vapors, which had previously drifted in white wisps, were now a heavy brown gas.

"Isn't it fantastic, Red?" Pod said, breathless from her spinning drift. "The creatures are gone. This area is slime."

"My name is Sheckley," Red said.

"Sorry, force of habit. Why haven't you joined? Everyone is having incredible success. And this is just the beginning. We have a whole planet in front of us. Our success is going global, Red. I mean Sheckley."

"What happens after that?" Red asked. "What happens when we've covered the planet?"

"Well," Pod said, "we'll know we did our job."

"For whom?"

"For our species. For our families back home."

"They don't know we're here and they'll never find us—unless you have plans to drift back. Though I don't see how that's possible in your current state."

Pod was offended. What fault was it of hers that she was no longer a petal-covered pod of innumerable moist chambers? Did Red have no appreciation of what she'd been through?

"I appreciate what you've been through," Red said. "But like you said, you didn't choose to make The Drift. It just happened naturally."

"That doesn't mean it wasn't difficult," Pod argued. "Making sure we covered this planet in slime has been the project of my life."

"But for what? I don't see why any other members of our species would need a planet already filled with slime. There's nothing left for other molds to do. You didn't even need me. Most of the molds that populated your chambers were redundant."

"Don't speak about yourself that way, Red. I incubated all of you equally. I had no way of knowing where we would land."

"And you have no way of knowing what comes next."

"Happiness. Satisfaction," Pod said.

"You're a pod. It has been natural for you to extend the realm of slimes. We're slimes. Whose realm are we extending?"

Pod tried to consider this, but it seemed like Red was asking her to have a thought about something she couldn't possibly think about. All of her thoughts, by nature, had to do with pods and slimes. "Why can't we just enjoy this moment?" she said. "This is our time."

"Because I don't know the answer to the question. I don't know what this is for," Red said.

"Is it possible you're being a little paranoid, Red?"

"My name is Sheckley. I know I'm a slime. But I don't think anything good will come of sliming a whole planet."

"Agree to disagree!" Pod said with determined enthusiasm as she was lifted into the air by a gust of wind. She was glad not to have to speak to Red anymore. Or Sheckley, if he preferred. Though that was stupid.

The slime continued to spread, though Pod could not see it. Her fibers, though innumerable and occasionally lifted into the air, did not spread beyond the area of the intersecting rivers and lush green forests. It turned out the wet jungle area Pod had landed in had been particularly ideal to slimes, the vermin living there particularly weak. Other parts of the planet required more resolve. There were dry, rocky zones, as well as vast oceans filled with their own strange creatures. There were scorching deserts and vast sheets of ice. But the slimes kept going. Through prolific creation and a healthy sense of competition, they eventually infiltrated all terrain, conquered every organism. The planet's plant life crumbled beneath mold, the vermin drowned or boiled in slime. In just a few dozen of the planet's days, the entire surface was transformed into an oozing sphere of syrupy slime.

Discord fell among the molds. There were no further areas for them to expand into, no further feats to achieve. Some crawled over others, some slid under. Azure discovered a way to chemically alter himself so he could devour a slime in his way, and did so. One less slime. The molds who saw this happen said nothing. They retreated.

As her innumerable fibers drifted through what was now a dense atmosphere of fetid spores, an odd feeling came over Pod. It was uncertainty combined with a sadness and even, she detected in herself, a hint of embarrassment. She didn't know what there was for her to be embarrassed about, though. Maybe it was just the uncertainty that was embarrassing, and led to the sadness. Or was it the other way around? The feelings seemed to feed on each other. She wished she could escape the feelings, somehow float away from them, but she couldn't. They persisted.

It was only a few days later, as the slime molds fought and increasingly attempted to devour each other, that a shadow fell over the land. Something had moved between the planet and its sun, but Pod couldn't tell what it was. It was still too far off.

"That shadow is Nature," Red said. "I can feel it."

Pod hadn't realized one of her fibers had yet again floated into the little rocky outcrop in which Red had confined himself. He really had done nothing.

"It could be anything," Pod said. "We don't know."

"That's my point," Red said.

Over the next few hours, the shadow deepened.

"I wonder if this was a nice place," Red said. "For the creatures we destroyed, I mean."

"We've done great things. I know and believe that," Pod said. She hated Red. He stood for nothing. He didn't make sense.

The shadow deepened further, into darkness. Pod's feelings about Red turned out not to matter. Neither Pod nor Red meant anything to the creatures that arrived next. Naturally, the creatures landed first where Pod and the slimes had started, where The Transformation had been most fertile—at the intersection of what were now two rivers of slime. They started feeding from there.

How I Got This Job

Brian Reid

December 13th—SantaCon Day. Any cop that has seniority, and sanity, takes the day off. I've got too much seniority to be on-duty, but Foster, Taylor, Peterson, and Suarez come down with a new strain of the insidious flu that invades Portland every winter, Evans gets shot in a drug bust, and that idiot Clinton breaks his leg getting a cat out of a tree.

So here I am, guarding the outskirts of the Alphabet District, where Bay Area refugees surround themselves with high-rises and spas where pedicures cost more than used cars, so they can pretend they're still living in California. These folks have money and a need to be protected from native Portlanders' fondness for vegetarian strip bars, bookstores, and general shagginess. Me and Chauncey have Twenty-third Street, Trendy-third to the natives, protecting the affluent from the effluence, and it don't get much more effluent than SantaConers.

Downtown. Trendy-third Street. SantaCon.

What's SantaCon? What it's supposed to be is a protest against corporations, false icons, and mind control of the masses—it's a Portland thing.

What it is, is three hundred or more drunks dressed in filthy

Santa Claus costumes, invading strip clubs, running out on bar tabs, and riding bicycles into cars, through pedestrians, and off bridges— it's a Portland thing.

A few years back, one Saint Nick tried to climb down the chimney in Pittock Mansion and got stuck. It took a helicopter to pop his Santa ass out of there. And that mock flying reindeer report they do from the Oregon Zoo every year? It draws the lunatic-fringe Santas like flies.

It's all we cops can do to keep them corralled in a small area, protect the surrounding property, and cart off any Santas who fall and can't get up.

Sometimes the Santas get destructive, and then little kids get to watch cops cuff Santa and haul him away.

"What's the policeman doing to Santa, Daddy?"

"Well, little Johnny, the policeman is beating Santa's ass and putting him in the pokey."

You see why no sane cop wants to work that day.

Me and Chauncey have got the intersection at Burnside and Trendy-third. Gourmet pastries and exotic ice creams behind us, Goodwills and dive bars on the left. The idea is to keep the Santas contained on the downslope, between the affluents and the river. This usually works—drunk Santas, even the ones with fake stuffing, are better at rumbling downslope on Burnside than hauling their asses up it.

Me and Chauncey are sitting in the patrol car with the blue lights on as a warning when a flock of Saint Nicks comes rolling up Burnside. Most of the Santas look like normal SantaConers—mobile waste-reclamation projects. But there's a big, jolly Santa leading them. He's different.

Maybe it's just that all the other Saint Nicks are so dirty, but this Santa is so clean, it's like he's glowing. The little sack he's got slung over his shoulder doesn't have a wrinkle in it, like it's been pressed. Even his black belt is shiny.

The guy's so clean, you'd think, 'Hey, maybe it's his first SantaCon; maybe he's new to the game,' but all the other Saint

Nicks are clapping him on the back and jostling each other to get closer to him—this guy's the head Santa.

Well, shiny Santa sees our flashing blue lights and holds out his arms to keep the rest of the Santas back. He looks right at us and, swear to God, he's got a twinkle in his eye.

"Hey, boys," he says to his Santa minions. "On Christmas day I give toys to all the good girls and boys. What do I do the other three hundred and sixty-four days a year?"

"Raise hell, Santa," they all start shouting. "Raise hell."

Santa smiles benignly, motions the common Kris Kringles back behind him, and reaches into his little sack.

Chauncey and I reach for the door handles.

Santa, looking right at us, calls out, "Here's a present just for you!" He pulls a can of beer out of his sack, hefts it, winds up, and hurls it.

We're out of the car in time to see the beer can in the air. His aim is off, it's too high, but it stops in mid-air, then shoots straight for the car, and damn if the thing doesn't accelerate as it goes. It smashes into the windshield so hard, it sets off the airbags.

The other Santas scatter. I'm right behind Chauncey, headed for jolly Santa, when he pulls out another can from his sack and lets fly. He throws it straight up in the air. It floats there a second, then takes off like it was fired from a cannon, speeds up just like the last one did, and nails Chauncey right in the chest. Chauncey goes down hard.

Saint Nick's got no time to reload, because I'm almost on top of him, so he takes off. He heads right up Burnside toward Washington Park. For a fat guy, he sure can run. I'm in good shape but I'm not getting any closer.

While he's running, he reaches back into his sack and pulls out another beer. I grab the nightstick from my belt.

He turns his head to look at me.

"Ho ho ho," he says. "Here's another present for you," and he tosses the can straight up in the air. The can stays floating above his head, following him as he runs. I never saw anything like it before. I'm kind of hypnotized by it, so I just stop and watch it—like an idiot. The beer can is in the air for two, maybe three seconds, then it comes right at me like a major-league fastball; me just staring at it as it comes in. Lucky my reactions are still working while the rest of my brain is locked in what-the-fuck land. I swing my nightstick and the can explodes, showering me with beer.

That wakes me the hell up. Santa is off, running straight uphill to Washington Park. He's got a half-block on me, but he's fat and jolly and I'm fit and pissed off.

I chase his ass up Burnside, past newly planted trees and supermarkets with cheese sections bigger than my house. Three more *ho ho hos*, three more beer can rockets, before we get to the bottom of the stairs leading to the Rose Gardens. Lucky for me, the cans coming at me are all fastballs, and I can fight them off with my nightstick—if Santa had a good curveball or a hard slider in his repertoire, I'd be toast.

He's up the Rose Garden stairs without breaking stride and running up one of the dirt paths feeding into the main trails. I smash another incoming beer.

My partner is down, I'm drenched in suds and I'm running out of steam, but I can't lose him. Police brutality or not, Santa is in need of a good ass-kicking.

My radio on my duty belt crackles; I pull it out.

"Phil, it's Chauncey. Where are you?"

"I'm in pursuit. He's headed for the Wildwood Trail. You okay?"

"I think he broke some ribs. I'm in the car and on my way. Keep him in sight."

"He's headed toward the zoo," I say. "Could be he's looking for his reindeer."

There's a silence at the other end, which gives me time to think about what I just said and have a reply ready by the time Chauncey says, "Phil, the zoo doesn't have any reindeer."

"Yeah, but he doesn't know that."

I'm too out of breath to say any more; I just stay focused on his shiny black boots and fat red buns churning away. Every step, I pray to see Chauncey's flashing blue lights, but we're deep in the park's trees and hills—if he was a hundred feet away, I'd never see him.

It seems like I've been running for a week when we break from the trail into the zoo parking lot. I see Chauncey's blue lights flashing at the far end of the lot. He drives right at us and fishtails to a stop in front of Santa. Santa keeps running right at the car. He takes one hop on the hood, one hop on the roof, a two-footed stomp on the trunk, and he's past Chauncey. I'm so out of breath I'm staggering. Chauncey's out of the car, holding his ribs, and hobbling in pursuit.

Up ahead is the zoo's main gate. Santa's trapped.

"Ho ho ho," he bellows, and, as God is my witness, I see a reindeer swoop down out of the sky and land right next to him.

The reindeer tosses those antlers back across his shoulders like he's in on the game and telling Santa to hurry the hell on up. Me and Chauncey stop in our tracks, overcome by Christmasy dread.

While we're standing there, Santa hops on board the reindeer. The reindeer starts running. Its hooves clatter against the ground, and then it leaps up and up into the sky. Its nose lights up red, guiding their getaway.

"Ho ho ho," Santa jeers from the back of the reindeer. He's glowing brighter than he did before, so I can see every detail of him.

He reaches into his sack and pulls out two beers. Chauncey's hurt, I can't fight off two beers at once, and those beers are twenty-two ouncers, deadly from that height. I drop the nightstick and pull out my gun. I can't believe I'm going to wing Santa.

"Put the beer down, sir," I order. "Put the beer down."

Santa pulls his arms back, ready to throw, a beer in each hand.

"I've got a present for both of you," he calls, "ho ho ho."

I fire.

"Ho ho ohhhhh!"

Santa tumbles from the reindeer and plummets straight down. Me and Chauncey jump out of the way. Santa hits the parking lot right between us and does a little body-bounce. The glow's gone out of him. He lies there.

"Phil," Chauncey says, "I think you just killed Santa."

We can't identify Santa, he's got no prints. I don't mean there's no fingerprints on file, I mean he's got no fingerprints. Nothing. Blank.

Back at the station, me and Chauncey go through six hours of interrogations before we're put on administrative leave, pending investigations, and released. When I get home I shed my uniform, leave it on the floor, fall into bed, and pass out.

I wake to someone knocking on the door. I bury my head in a pillow but the knocking won't stop. It's nighttime. The room is dark as a coal mine. I crawl out of bed and pick the pieces of my uniform from the floor. They feel heavy—I must need more sleep. The knocking doesn't stop. I throw the uniform on, feel my way to the door, and open it.

I don't see a thing until I look down. A little guy, about ankle high, with pointed ears and a little green cap looks up at me. He jerks his tiny fist over his shoulder, his thumb stuck out to point behind him.

I stand there, not understanding. Then I look down again, and see my uniform. It's red with white trim. It glows. I touch my hands to my face and feel a momentary relief. No beard. But then I see my hands. No prints.

"The beard takes time," the elf says. "You killed Santa. You're the next one up."

And then a reindeer swoops out of the sky, lands next to me, gives me the once-over, then tosses those antlers back across his shoulders like he's telling me to hurry the hell on up.

A Sky So Blue

Stefanie Freele

She stole the blue right out of the sky on a rare Oregon clear day, the kind of midday that makes shopkeepers lean against doorways, mothers sit and linger on swings next to their children, and dogs stretch out on driveway sunspots. Her husband Joe begged her to sneak the blue back. "Someone, someday soon, will find out you took it."

At least she didn't waste the blue all in one place. She decorated her bedroom with morning's dawn, filled her bath bubble jar with Midwestern summer in-between-rain, added touches of California-clear-omnipresent-afternoon to the carpeting in the trunk of her car, and hid the rest of the sky underneath their top mattress.

Joe didn't even know they were sleeping on it. If he had, he would have rested deeper with the knowledge that the rest of the sky wasn't entirely wasted on frivolity. As it was, though, he worried every morning from about 2:30 to 4:30 a.m. that she'd get caught.

He had worried about Cindy for a long time. She was always stealing. She always had to have more. Around Christmas she snagged every Christmas tree in a two-hundred-mile radius, last fall she stole much of nearby Idaho, and twice she robbed Southwest Airlines of all their planes.

Up until now, he'd always found a way to convince her to return what wasn't hers.

The longer the blue remained missing, the more frantic people became. Even in Portland, where everyone was used to fog and cloud and a general overcast nature, the sporadic peeks into the colorless sky brought crowds of speculative onlookers to the sidewalk. Necks hurt from looking up. Eyes strained. Brains ached from debating and questioning. Scientists and artists panicked on every channel. The ocean had turned puddle brown. The fish weren't as vibrant. The brown air—tainted only by smog—left everyone glum. Plants withered. Animals lost their zest. Deer stood dully in front of hunters. Birds spent less time flying and more time on building ledges, pooping on the occasional passerby. Sharks became docile, lingering near public beaches to be petted and given treats.

Joe explained this all to Cindy, who mumbled about "that itty bitty expanse above Montana," but she replied—with that open-eyed innocence that made Joe want to shake her—"I just want everything to be faultless. Not perfect, faultless."

Often Joe had a feeling that they were responding to two separate conversations. He'd had enough history with these *what-are-you-talking-about* discussions with Cindy to know again he'd be left with the sensation that nothing was solved, gained, or understood.

He rolled up the sleeve on his worn flannel, one of those habits he had when making a point. Some people take on and off their glasses; Joe rolled up and down his sleeves. It gave him time to form his words, create an intelligent reaction to her sudden desire for faultlessness. "What is wrong with pandemonium? Or at least a little Mother Nature?"

"After all I've been through, I deserve—" She didn't finish the sentence, but instead sneaked a little more sky from under the mattress and turned her teapot into an arctic twilight.

What exactly did she deserve? thought Joe. It wasn't like she lived a life of poverty and neglect. He was a darn good provider and all he asked in return was some love, to keep the house cleanish, and make him a lunch for work.

A galvanized effort happened across communities to restore the blue. Citizens were called upon to turn in their colored inkjet printers, ballpoint pens, and bottles of Windex. Mothers dropped off food coloring. Architects, their blueprints. Children contributed finger paints. Donate Denim! The plan was to mush all the blue together and inject it into the sky as a big atomic-like ball. No one could decide, though, how this might work. Scientists argued the propelled color might not stick; it might just fall to the ground, coating the planet blue. Others, astute in their observations of the environment, wondered aloud if the mud-colored sky had anything to do with the disappearance of the polar bears, the stoppage of pelican migration, and the absence of prairie dog chatter.

Joe plopped in the middle of the messyish living room and turned on the television, trying to find a channel that wasn't covering the global concern over the missing color. Blues music was coming back. Office workers wore casual Monday through Thursday and suits on Friday. Forget-me-nots around the world were picked the second they blossomed. Blueberries sold for almost fifty dollars a pound. The camera zoomed in on a flyer posted at a Coos Bay dock imploring fishermen to contact authorities if they noted any new activity in the sea, anything that might be related to the mystery.

Joe saw all this bedlam and his stomach lurched. He dived for the toilet but tripped on Cindy's hair dryer again, landing prone on the floor, catching himself with both hands. How many times had he asked her to not leave that thing lying around? Enough of her. If he had left something on the floor, she would have it disappear forever.

After disentangling himself from the hair dryer cord, he remained kneeling on the floor, taking a breath to get himself together. And that is when he saw it. The color everyone was frantically seeking, seeping out between the mattresses on one side like mustard off a burger.

Without taking his eyes off the precious oozing hue, he dialed the police. A no-nonsense woman answered instantly, before he could change his mind.

Officers came immediately and confiscated what they could of the sky. The authorities arrested Cindy in person to get the very last residue. She had added that "rare cloudless streak over the Oregon Coast" to her silk scarf, sure no one would miss it or notice. Defiantly she handed the remains of her thievery back and through tears said, "There."

Joe watched her leave in handcuffs, watered-down and defeated. He was saddened; they had a good time once, didn't they? But it was never enough for her. As she lifted her head to say goodbye, Joe looked kindheartedly into the bluest-blue eyes he'd ever seen. A bird, resting on the mailbox, splattered a white gift across their address.

Alder Underground

Jonah Barrett

8:15 a.m.

We are taking a train down to the City of Roses, or whatever they call it these days. I told Aisha that I'd pay her back for my ticket but I think she knows I'm full of shit. Will buy her a coffee or something as payback.

#PortlandDaycation #Free triiip #Gonna buy all the bird books

8:30 a.m.

Forgot my journal this morning, so I hope you guys like Tumblr posts. Sorry. I'll make sure to tag everything #PortlandDaycation so you can block this crap if your heart so desires.

#PortlandDaycation #Sorry not sorry #It's not my fault it's Aisha's #She guilted me into coming with her

8:47 a.m.

No one else is posting anything right now. Probably because everyone's asleep and only complete morons drag their friends out of bed this early (AISHA!!). The only thing to do is just Snapchat videos of trees rushing by the windows.

#PortlandDaycation #Aisha keeps looking over my shoulder #Hi Aisha #'Why do your hashtags have spaces in them?' she asks #Among other stupid questions #I'm not going to explain to her how Tumblr works if she isn't going to get one

10:20 a.m.

Made it! Everybody's kinda underwhelmingly normal at this train station. Expected more of Portland. Was going to write up an official study of hipsters (kidding).

#PortlandDaycation

10:51 a.m.

Soon as we step out of the station Aisha asks, "Well what now?"

Which . . . this whole trip is her idea, but okay . . .

I gave her a bunch of ideas and she rejected all of them. (Bird watching, garden visits, seeing if there's a way to make it to the Oregon Zoo, etc.) She just kept pouting, crossing her dark arms, and lowering her head in disapproval. She finally looked up when I suggested we find something to eat.

Used Google Maps to find food trucks.

#PortlandDaycation #I'm eating a falafel

12:02 p.m.

Made Aisha take me to a bookstore after lunch.

She hates books, but agreed anyway (yes!). However, she refused to go to Powell's (damn!). "Too touristy," she called it. I hate to break it to her but that's exactly what we are.

#PortlandDaycation

12:19 p.m.

Bookstore is an okay alternative to the City of Books (what happened to the Roses?). It's smaller, though. A lot smaller.

I left Aisha with a book of female nudes and am now over in the ornithology section. The shelves are all kinda crudely made and still smell like pine trees.

Also I already have all these books. Super.

#PortlandDaycation

12:23 p.m.

Things overheard in the next aisle over in this tiny bookstore~

Girl 1: Y'know, Alder. It's a street here.
Girl 2: It is?
Girl 1: Jesus, man.
Girl 2: I don't pay attention to that shit.
Girl 1: Well anyway, the building. It's huge and creepy.
Girl 2: They all are.
Girl 1: Yeah, but this one has trees.
Girl 2: They're uh . . . they're called roof gardens.
Girl 1: Shut up. No, I mean, actual trees.
Girl 2: Like, small trees.
Girl 1: Like freakin' cedars.
Girl 2: What?
Girl 1: Growing from the top of this building.
Girl 2: Bullshit.

I found the weird part of Portland.

#PortlandDaycation

12:50 p.m.

Aisha's pulled me out of the bookstore because she said she'd had enough.

#PortlandDaycation

1:08 p.m.

I keep getting blown away by how CLEAN everything is. Aisha just scoffs at me and tells me I need to get my ass out of Olympia. "This isn't home. It's, like, *nice* here," she says. I still see cliché stuff. There are weird hipsters with bowties and beards from 1910, and street performers painted in silver, and people with antique bikes taking advantage of the rare Pacific Northwest sun. But they're all so CLEAN.

"It's downtown—people actually give a shit about what everything looks like," she says.

"Aren't there cooler places we can go to?" I ask.

"Yeah, but the people aren't as pretty," she says.

#PortlandDaycation

1:37 p.m.

Found this cool hat shop on Broadway. It's dapper as hell. There are all these $85 bowties I'm currently drooling over. (Why do I have to be so poor?)

Really surprised at how nice the owners are. One of them even showed us a section in the back that has a bunch of dress-up hats with a mirror. I thought people would be more . . . grumpy, I guess. ("It's probably because *I'm* here," Aisha says while trying on a sunhat. It goes well with the dress she wore for today—a bright orange thing against her brown skin. "Kawaii as *fuck*," she mutters into the mirror.)

I take it back—there *is* one grumpy man in a gray suit that keeps glaring at us.

("He's just jealous of how cute I am," Aisha says.)

#PortlandDaycation #What's his problem? #Too many hat selfies #Aisha is buying the sunhat

2:05 p.m.

Found a zine on the ground. Talks about lizard people and how they're taking over America.

#PortlandDaycation #So inaccurate #Lizards aren't slimy #Like I haven't studied them THAT much but I'm pretty sure that's amphibians #Just sayin'

2:20 p.m.

Discovered a Starbucks in the middle of some huge plaza. Aisha said I'm being hella touristy again. She didn't object when I bought her a chai latte, though. Now sitting on the brick steps, staring at the sky, sipping our drinks.

"Didn't we used to have a lot more fun on these kind of adventures?" Aisha asked.

"I dunno," I said. "Everything was, like, a lot more fun back in high school when we didn't know how anything worked and we were scared."

"Yeah, now we know how shit works, and it's boring," she said.

We're back to just staring up at the sky, dozens of people walking all around us making a ton of noise.

I don't think it's just this adventure that's boring.

#PortlandDaycation

2:23 p.m.

There are a lot of crows in that tree over there.

#PortlandDaycation #Corvus brachyrhynchos go away

3:04 p.m.

We are not at the plaza anymore.

We're now in this strange building, waiting around in a lobby. Or at least, *I'm* waiting around. Aisha is walking all over the place, inspecting everything like some search dog. I'm just sitting here on this fancy couch, ready to leave.

Back at the plaza, bored out of our minds, I saw these crows up in this one tree. They just looked like normal crows, the Common American kind, but that doesn't matter. What was weird to me was what they were doing. There'd gotta've been, like, twenty-five-ish birds hanging in this tree, with a lady in a fancy suit under it. They're squawking at her and she's making faces back at them. Maybe even hissing at one point? No one else is paying attention to this. Aisha doesn't even notice until I point it out to her, and then she gets interested only because (admittedly) the woman is pretty hot, besides the hissing. The prim business attire she wears is counterbalanced by waves of dark wild curls draping over her shoulders. She's got these crows under a spell or something. Example: at one point she cocked her head to the left, and all twenty-five crows did the same. They seemed to be copying her every move. It was fascinating . . . and creepy.

I joked to Aisha about how maybe she was a witch.

"Shut up and let me watch the hot girl," was all I got back.

Okay . . .

The woman raised her head and widened her eyes, opening her mouth and making clicking sounds. The corvids went crazy after that. They screamed and cawed and flew out of the tree, circling around the plaza like a single organism. The woman started to walk off. I could see her looking back occasionally, seeing if the murder of birds was following her, which it was. I also think she and I made eye contact at one point. Awkward.

Again, nobody seemed to care at this plaza. Maybe weird crap like this happens all the time in Portland and they're all used to it. Crazy demon bird seductress witch strolling along downtown with her flock of familiars? Just another Thursday.

Aisha and I aren't from Portland, though. We looked at each other; Aisha raised an eyebrow.

"*That* didn't look boring," she said.

I scrunched my face up. "I dunno, man," I said.

She stood up, gulping down the last of her latte. "You can stay here," she said. "But I'm gonna have an adventure." Aisha crushed her empty cup in her hand and began running in the direction of the woman. I sighed, got up and followed.

#PortlandDaycation

3:16 p.m.

You'd think stalking somebody dressed all fancy in downtown

Portland—the city that prides itself for being super alternative—would be easy, but that would be a lie.

There're just as many suits walking around this city as there are hipsters. I guess you just have to be at the right places at the right lunch hour to see them crawling around. We kept almost losing our stalkee. The crows had flown ahead minutes earlier, so it was just me and Aisha trailing behind this woman about a block away.

I accidentally bumped into another suit while trying to keep up. It was the same gray-suited man from the hat store! The man only coughed when I apologized, although it sounded more like a growl. Friendly person.

"Aisha, this is stupid," I said, kinda jogging alongside her while she simply walked at her super weird pace. "Maybe she's just an odd lady that likes annoying crows."

"A *hot* one," she said. "It's not like there's anything else to do."

"There's *totally* stuff to do!" I said.

"I mean *fun* stuff," she said.

That's the thing about Aisha: when she gets something in her head she's not gonna let it go. I wish I could say that there's more of a motivation behind this, but Aisha is a simple woman. She likes poking things.

We turned a corner and had to stop. Or at least I did. A block away, amongst all these other tall buildings, stood the highest one of them all, this black and blue posh thing that towered over the rest. But the strangest part was this conglomerate of vegetation at the top. Pine trees. Like, actual evergreens sprouting up from the top of this hella high building. And there were the crows, all the way up in those high-ass branches, some circling around the building like a cloud of gnats from far away, squawking at one another.

I looked back down to see Aisha twenty feet ahead, her sunhat and black hair poking out from the sea of suits. Up ahead the entrance doors of the building began to close, the woman just slipping through. I ran to catch up with Aisha. As we went through the doors I caught the name Arborealis Botanicals printed over a symbol of a leaf on the frosted glass sides.

And this is where we are right now. Still nothing. We entered this building to find an empty lobby with the woman nowhere in sight, and not much has changed since. I'm not really helping out because I don't really wanna find that woman, and this couch is comfy. There are no doors anywhere in this lobby, except for the ones we came in and an entrance to a hallway in the back. Aisha's still looking around, searching the hallway, trying to find *something* that would explain where that woman went. Honestly, I just wanna go home at this point.

#PortlandDaycation

3:20 p.m.

Things this lobby doesn't have:
Other doors
Decorations
People
The sorta eerie elevator music you'd expect at a place like this
Come to think of it, elevators

Things this lobby DOES have:
Marble floors
Walls made of wood
Annoying LED lights that suck out my soul
Sweet couches
A small table
Brochures on said table that talk a lot about the environmental contributions of Arborealis Botanicals without ever really explaining what Arborealis Botanicals is

Things this lobby *probably* has but I'll just take Aisha's word for it:
A hallway that leads to a smaller room after a few turns
Aforementioned smaller room in the back
A very big fountain

#PortlandDaycation #Now Aisha's calling me to the back

3:41 p.m.

We have transcended the Weird element and've passed on through to the realm of the unreal. I am having a hard time swallowing what just happened—what's still happening.

Also I'm very surprised that my phone still works.

Aisha made me come to the back with her to look at the fountain. The hallway leading to the other room essentially made a big angular C, and it felt like we were walking around a much larger room that we couldn't access. When we entered the smaller room Aisha put her hands on her hips and sighed with frustration.

"I know she went down this way, and then she's, like, fucking gone," she said.

It was a small room with marble floors, much like the bigger lobby in the front, with this huge water feature in the middle—a statue of some peeing cherub coming up from the center. Strange, but not interesting.

"Maybe she's not a witch, but a mermaid, and she swam to the bottom," I said. Aisha ignored me and circled around the room again and started feeling up the wooden walls.

"There could be a secret door or something . . ." she said.

The sound of the glass doors opening came from the lobby, and we both froze at the sound of footsteps. Louder and louder on the marble tile. We both looked at each other and gave the "Oh, shit" look. Someone was walking down the passageway toward us.

"What's our alibi?" I whispered.

"Shhh!" Aisha said, much louder than I asked the question, mind you. The steps were rounding the last corner, and Aisha took me by the hand and dragged me behind the fountain, barely hidden by the urinating winged child. Someone entered the room, and I guess Aisha—the stupidest of all my stupid friends—panicked, because I found myself being pushed into the water, with her jumping in after me, as if the mystery person wouldn't be able to see us if we were soaking wet. Into the fountain we went, but our shoes never touched any fountain floor. We kept sinking and sinking, like the fountain didn't have a bottom and just went on forever. I tried swimming back up but a current was pulling me under. I could see Aisha trying the same thing before everything became darker and darker. This underwater pit at the bottom of the fountain pool dragged us in, and after a huge WHOOSH I plummeted down through the pit into what felt like a sort of tunnel. I tried to scream but again, I was underwater.

And then, light! I did get to actually scream as I was flung into the air and dropped down into another body of water, much larger—and darker—than the fountain. I hit the water with a slap and began to thrash as I fought for air. Another slap hit right next to me, Aisha, and we both thrashed and coughed while trying to keep our heads above the surface. Water continued to pour down above us, and a stench of rotting vegetation hit my nose as I looked around to see where we were. We seemed to be under some type of waterfall, in the middle of an expansive pool of black water with a shore off in the distance. I could make out a patch of land, a small island, much closer to us. Tall, dead grass accompanied by a few sparse yellow-leaved trees. Aisha coughed and grabbed my shoulder.

"Something just touched my leg," she said.

I coughed back in return and motioned my head toward the island. We swam. I didn't believe her at first but as we made our way toward land I caught something dark rushing past me in my peripherals.

We were in some sort of bog. The island had no natural beach, with the land just cutting off straight down at the water, so we had to hoist ourselves up, clinging onto the dry grass, before collapsing and catching our breaths. I turned over and looked up at the sky, only to see bright light (really bright light, *blinding*) streaming down on us. Over the water a huge rusty vertical tube reached down from above. The tube continuously poured water out, and I realized this was what had sucked us down and transported us to this bog. It then hit me how expansive this place was. Beyond the opposite shore I could make out a small forest of yellow and orange shrubs and trees that seemed to stretch on into forever, bordered by two massive steel walls on either side that reached up into the light. But the weirdest part, sprouting up from the forest, were three giant pillars.

But then something large descended from the tube, coming out and splashing into the water. Aisha and I both sat up at the sight of this and scrambled to hide behind one of the dying trees. A head popped out of the black water, and I could make out the old wrinkled face of a man, soaked white hair sticking to the back and sides of his speckled scalp. The man began to swim away from us, toward the opposite shore. He dragged himself onto land and I could see that he had a suit on—a gray suit! The same man from the hat shop and the street chase! What was *he* doing here? I watched as the man shook himself off like an animal (like a dog after a bath or something!). I tried calling out to him, to see if he'd notice us and explain where we were, but he never responded. He never even looked up.

The strange man walked off toward the yellow forest, and left Aisha and me on the other side. Aisha still hasn't said anything as I type this. There's a third wall behind us and it feels like we're in some gigantic metal box. Or a terrarium. Nothing is really making any sense. The only way off this island is to swim to the shore on the other side, but there are shapes in the water that occasionally break the surface, and I am not sure if they are friendly.

Where *are* we??

4:00 p.m.

Still haven't left yet. Aisha is freaked out by the things in the water. She says she saw one while I was peeing.

"It came up to the edge and looked at me from under the water. It was really slimy and had, like, weird feathery gills," she told me. She keeps referring to them as fish but they sound more like tadpoles or something. I keep getting reminded of axolotls by her description. But amphibians don't get that large—except for those giant salamanders in China. But even those don't start out so huge, do they? Wish I was more into herpetology right now.

I can't really say anything else for sure at the moment. This place might be . . . some sort of underground garden or artificial biosphere? I'm still wondering about those three pillars on the other side. If we are underground, maybe those pillars are our way up.

#No more PortlandDaycation

4:12 p.m.

Crossed the bog . . . difficult, to say the least. Aisha was more concerned about getting into the water than I was, which I can see as pretty valid now, considering her injuries.

We eased ourselves into the water, with me going first. I think we made it halfway across before I heard something thrashing behind me. The water was already a bit choppy because of the tube's waterfall, but then I heard my friend scream. I turned around to see a number of the creatures swarming around Aisha, the way sharks do while attacking large prey. I panicked and yelled at her to just keep going, and I swam the rest of the way as she continued to yell out. I dragged myself up onto the opposite shore and turned around to see that Aisha was almost there. I reached out my arm as she came closer. She took my hand and I noticed a bunch of little nips and scratches as I pulled her up. She screamed again, twisting around and dropping onto the ground. As she jerked her ankle out of the water, one of the eel-like creatures came out with it, its jaws clenched around her.

It was dark brown with black splotches down its back, with the set of feathery gills she had described earlier. Weirdly enough, the thing also had four tiny hands and legs, so small that they weren't even useful on land. Huge tadpole.

"Get rid of it!" she kept yelling at me. I kicked at it, which only seemed to make it bite down harder. Aisha screamed, widening her eyes and then glaring at me for further aggravating the animal. There wasn't a stick anywhere in sight, and I scrambled through the layers of dead leaves and mud in search of one.

"You're taking forever! Fuck!" Aisha yelled. I ran back and could see her kicking the thing in the eyes with her free foot, the animal writhing and squirming. She leaned over and screamed into its face, digging her fingernails into the creature's eyes. It let go, and she kicked it back into the water. It slowly swayed back and forth before swimming off.

"Ah, shit," Aisha said while inspecting her ankle. A perfect black ring had formed around her skin where the animal bit down.

"That looks bad," I said.

"No *duh.*" She looked up and glared at me. "Some help *you* are."

But, like, what was I *supposed* to do?

4:35 p.m.

Went out to explore while Aisha tends to her wounds (she's not talking to me). Took off in the direction of the three massive pillars. Maybe that gray-suited man is there. He could possibly help us, if I can find him.

This place must be some sort of man-made biosphere. Maybe we've come across some type of secret ecology experiment, courtesy of Arborealis Botanicals. If that's the case, they're not doing a great job. The ground is soft with layers of rotting botanical flesh and forest debris (smells like it, too), and the trees are malnourished and twisted under this harsh light. (Alders? I think they're Sitka alders, if what little I remember from that botanical program I took two years ago is true/accurate.) The light itself, if I squint, looks as if it's shining down from hundreds of little symmetrical lights that line the biosphere's ceiling. This is, like, a very huge and poorly constructed greenhouse.

Another failure of this biosphere: there are no insects, whatsoever. You'd think a place like this would be crawling with them, but nothing. What gives?

Aisha has caught up to me, she's told me that she forgives me, "even though you're a huge asshole." I don't understand but, sure.

4:44 p.m.

We've reached the three pillars; no sign of anyone else, though. The pillars themselves are massive—like the redwood trees of Northern California. They look like they're made of some type of metal similar to the walls of this place. Looking up, I can see a large, dark square opening in the ceiling that the pillars reach through up into forever; where they go I'm not sure. Wrapped around these giant things are . . . wires of some kind. They loop around each structure in loose coils, and swing from pillar to pillar like vines. Some drape down to the ground as well. The—wires? coils? fiber-optic cables?— look as if they're creeping up the pillars like ivy, and the whole process appears more organic than technological.

4:48 p.m.

We stood at the base of the nearest pillar, still in awe of how massive it was. I looked over at Aisha.

"D'you think we could climb it?" I said.

She rubbed her face for a moment, then walked forward and studied some of the lower cables. "Doesn't seem too hard," she said, and rubbed her eyes and sighed.

"Are you okay?"

She ignored me. "What's that?" Aisha walked closer to the base and pointed to a small square opening in the metal, about the size of a laptop. I shrugged. She placed her hand inside for a moment. "It's sucking up air, like a vacuum," she said. She picked up a handful of soggy leaves and tossed them inside. A whirring noise started, and we watched the leaves get sucked up into the pillar. The sound traveled up and away out of earshot.

"It's a chute," she said, as if she were an expert on this sort of stuff. "Not very big, though. I think only my head could fit inside it."

"And would you want to get sucked up inside these things?" I asked.

"Ha ha, *right*," she said.

4:52 p.m.

Found a sliding door! On the other side of the pillar. There's no way to get in, though. Not even an elevator button. The Arborealis Botanicals leaf logo is engraved on the door's metal surface.

But that means there is *some way* to get back up . . . We just don't have the means to open the door. *Somebody's* gotta be around here. Have continued on.

#Where is Gray Suit Man??

4:59 p.m.

Me: I think we're in a man-made biosphere of some kind.
Aisha: *Super.*
Me: I mean, like, that doesn't . . . excite you?
Aisha: Nah.
Me: But this is the adventure we were talking about.
Aisha: I'm tired. And dirty. And can't feel my legs, or fingers.
Me: What?!
Aisha: It's fine, I'm just goddamn tired. Fuck adventure.

5:37 p.m.

Is anyone even reading this? Can't anyone get us help?? I can't believe what just happened.

God, we shouldn't be here.

No one should ever be here.

The two of us made our way through the forest, still no signs of any other people—let alone animals or insects. The terrain was difficult to walk through, because the layers of leaves just kinda rotted into botanical slush. This proved more difficult for Aisha than me, and I've noticed she's developed a limp. I can tell she's trying to ignore it; she isn't one to talk about her weaknesses. If I said anything she'd probably just shoot me down like she always does. The heat under these lights is unbearable, and I'm surprised anything organic has managed to grow here under such harsh conditions. At one point Aisha gave a short yelp and pointed to something over to our left.

There was a person lying on the ground just about a hundred feet away from us. We quickly called out to him and rushed over to see if he needed help. We both screamed when we turned him over and realized it was a deceased body—a young man about our age. His hipster clothing had been torn up and soiled over time, and the scent of rotting leaves was overtaken by the stench of decaying flesh. The guy's body looked as if it had been there for a couple of days, and maggots writhed around through the tears in his flannel. We both held our hands over our mouths in disgust; Aisha vomited.

That's when a noise came from behind the bushes just a few yards away. We forgot our revulsion as the sound got nearer. I grabbed Aisha's wrist and ran with her behind the nearest tree.

Just in time, too, because at that moment a dinosaur came out from behind the bushes.

At least, it looked like a dinosaur.

The animal was bipedal, with a large single crest that ran down from its neck to its tail. The creature's arms, as well as its neck, elongated past the length of any human's. The pattern on its skin was a dark muddy brown with black spots and an orange underbelly, not too unlike the aquatic creature that attacked Aisha earlier. It looked around and sniffed the air, making a clicking noise. The thing looked like a lanky lizard-man. Or a . . . newt-man, actually. Newts don't get that big, though, but then again neither do tadpoles.

The giant newt, that scientifically should not have been a newt, stood over the dead man and clawed at his body. I peered closer, and was surprised to see the creature not claw into the flesh, but the guy's shirt. After some trial and error, the animal managed to tear the shirt in half, and a spew of maggots poured out from the corpse's ribcage. The newt-man bent down and opened its mouth.

It scooped the maggots up and devoured them over the course of a few minutes, then afterward licked the remaining maggots off of the body.

When it finished, the creature stood up and took the man's head in one of its clawed hands, and dragged the corpse off in the direction it came.

We are quickly making our way toward the pillars for safety. We might not have a key to that damn door but we can still climb the hell up those pillars. We're leaving right now, no matter what.

6:10 p.m.

Made it back to the pillars and immediately began to climb the cables. Already, we're pretty far up. Probably has something to do with being terrorized by newt-people. (Arborealis Botanicals genetic experiments??)

We are having to rest and catch our breaths more frequently, though. Or at least, Aisha is.

6:49 p.m.

Have reached the ceiling, resting just beneath the gigantic square opening the pillars go through. I can't see anything but darkness when I look up to see where the pillars go. When I look down . . . I can't look down too much. Shit, we're high. I can see the whole biosphere from up here. The majority of it's just dying alders, but on one edge I can make out the bog along with the tube and island. On the opposite side I can see figures moving around. I can't tell if they're people or newt creatures, though; I hope they don't see us.

Bordering the square opening are the same lights that are scattered all around the ceiling. Jesus, it's hot, and bright. They're honeycomb-shaped. Most of the cables up here connect to the ceiling (fueling the light fixtures?), but some of them continue on up along with the pillars into the dark opening. That huge inaccessible room from before—the one the C-shaped hallway wrapped around—is that where the pillars lead? Is the ceiling possibly at ground level? Are we almost out of this underground hellhole?

6:53 p.m.

Aisha can't move. She's just clinging onto one of the cables and not letting go while staring at me with wide eyes and making these noises. . . . It's like she can't move her lips anymore. Now she's looking all over the place, reacting to things that aren't there. Is she hallucinating?? Her fingers are turning blue, and her leg is completely purple. Why didn't I say anything about her limp earlier?? Aisha was fucking right, I *am* an asshole who just liveblogs everything. I need to put the phone away and move her through that opening.

6:59 p.m.

SHIT. Fucking shit. Tried to get Aisha to move. She started making her way toward me, struggling, and I held an arm out to help her but then she just started screaming at nothing and breathing harder and her eyes got all wide and I think she was trying to yell something at me but she lost her grip and

Shit.

7:03 p.m.

The beings from the other side are coming this way.

7:12 p.m.

Can't go back down. Just up. They're at the bottom, inspecting Aisha's body. They're definitely not humans. Can't cry yet.

Don't fucking cry.

7:26 p.m.

There's a crow up here perched on one of the cables.

Why is there a fucking crow up here??

It's cawing down at them.

I think they've seen me.

7:31 p.m.

Shit shit shit fuck shit this shouldn't be a thing I hate this place I hate biospheres I hate huge mystery buildings I hate the stupid fucking City of stupid Roses and Aisha's dead and fUUUUCKKKKKKK.

7:32 p.m.

Calm down.

7:45 p.m.

Passed through the opening. There aren't any lights up here. I can see from the light below but the farther I climb the dimmer it gets.

That room I mentioned, it isn't here. Nothing's here. The pillars just keep ascending into darkness, surrounded by four tight claustrophobic walls. This is worse than the tube. Everything's quiet.

8:11 p.m.

Almost at the top. I can't see Aisha down there anymore.

Some of the newts have left but some are starting to climb up. They're a lot faster than I am. Stop looking down.

Keep going keep going keep *fucking going*.

8:25 p.m.

Top.

8:25 p.m.

There's a trapdoor.

8:26 p.m.

Okay.

8:37 p.m.

I'm on the roof of the building. The pillars keep going up, point-ing into the sky. Remember those pine trees? The weird roof gar-den? They're not pines. The pillars are equipped with all these panels around them, artificial branches that stem out and support solar panels that have been cut into the shapes of evergreens—kinda like cartoon Christmas trees. In these fake branches are all those crows from earlier. They're all really quiet, and they're looking at me.

There're bones scattered all over.

There's a door with a leaf symbol at the base of this pillar, just like the one at the bottom.

It's opening.

8:51 p.m.

Hasn't anyone been reading this?? Can't anyone help? Please.

I'm up in one of the pillars/trees. It's difficult because all the crows are up here with me, cawing at the creatures below to let them know I'm here.

As soon as the door started opening I ran around to the other side of the pillar and started to climb. Without the cables to help me I used a chute like the one down below to help me get a foot-hold and reach one of the branches. I climbed up into the fake tree about twenty feet but the crows didn't let me get any higher, screaming and dive-bombing me if I tried. I perched myself on a metal branch between two solar panels. There were about six newt creatures at the base of the tree, chirping at me and clawing at the metal. More newts started coming out the trapdoor. The crows continued screeching and some started circling around.

The door in the pillar slid open again and I could see the woman, the witch-woman we followed to this stupid hellhole place, walking out. Another human followed her. It was the man in the gray suit. He pointed in my direction and said, "That's the one." The woman nodded.

"Why don't you come down?" she called up.

I shook my head, clinging tighter to my refuge. The newt beings continued to claw up at me, making clicking noises. Their glossy eyes staring into mine as they opened their toothless mouths and tasted the air with purple tongues.

"If you don't come down, we'll have to come up there and get you!" she said.

The whirring noise started up again and I looked down to see the chute below me spew out a pile of chunks of bones and flesh. One of the chunks happened to be a skull. The crows cawed and swooped down, devouring the pile that I'm sure used to be my friend.

"I'll give you to the count of three!" says the witch. The newt beings are crawling over each other. One newt over the other, over the next, making a pile at the base of the tree.

"One!" The woman's and man's skins start to turn a muddy brown with black splotches. Their necks elongate and large spines sprout out of their backs as their clothes tear off.

"Two!" she calls in a raspier voice. The male newt is crawling up the pile first, glaring up at me. He seems careful not to step on the other newts' eyes and snouts as he does so, and he stops at the top and lies down. I'm just out of reach. Here comes the female. She's climbing up the newt pile; she's not as careful. Her long arms and claws allow her to reach the top within mere seconds. She stands on the others in front of me and holds out her hand. Crows are still circling all around, spewing hate calls. I'm not sure if Portland was such a good idea.

"Three."

#PortlandDaycation

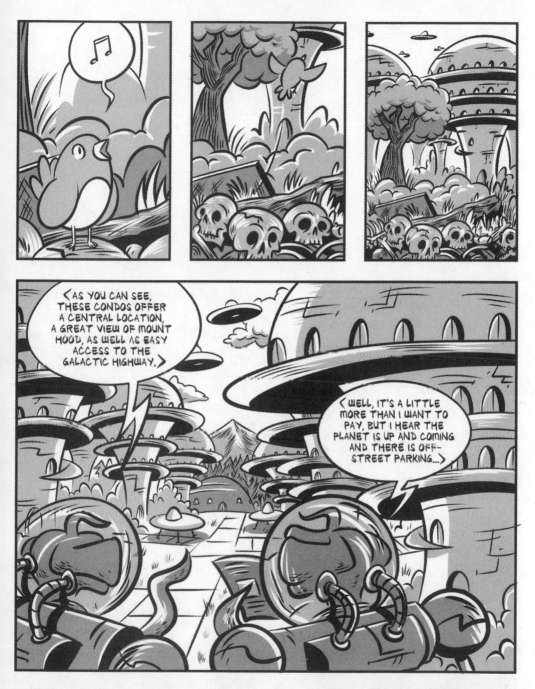

HOW DO YOU SAY GENTRIFICATION in MARTIAN?

BY JONATHAN HILL

You'd think the dog would step between the shards
of broken cereal bowl and slurp the milk off
the kitchen floor, or eat the soggy nuggets
of Crunch Berries cereal, or even
drink the stale beer spilling out
of the cans of Olympia all over
the floor, but no.

She wants my blood!

To THE DOGS

A Code for Everything

Andrew Stark

The child, Barney, names me after himself. He seems timid at first, when his parents bring me back to their 2,350-square-foot Cape Cod at 45.522202° N, -122.618054° W in Laurelhurst. They walk me in and set me down. My olfactometer picks up 1,622 different odors, including jojoba in the woman's perfume, and alarm pheromones emitting from the child. He peeks from around the corner; I wag my tail and yip. Although I understand fifty languages, my communication is limited to barks, howls, and mammalian semiosis. Eventually, he approaches and strokes my head. The tactile sensors lining my skull allow me to respond, and I close my eyes. Likewise, a number of sensory corpuscles near the surface of Barney's hand send discriminative sensations traveling up the posterior columns in his spine and into the medial lemniscus of his brainstem, causing the electrical membrane potential of certain cells to rise and fall, opening channels and allowing for an inward flow of sodium ions. Once the sensations reach his medulla oblongata, a number of axons synapse with a number of neurons in his gracile and cuneate nuclei. He smiles.

I am called A.C.E.S. (Autonomous Canine Emulation System). I am a robotic domestic pet substitute, designed by Takumi

Fukuda of the National Institute of Advanced Industrial Science and Technology (産業技術総合研究所) in the Ibaraki Prefecture of Japan. Fukuda designed me to replicate a pug, which, according to the AKC, is a breed best described by the phrase *"multum in parvo,"* which means "a lot in a small space." Pugs are known to be soothing, friendly, and attentive—the perfect family pet. I weigh 95.2 ounces, measure 22.4 inches long, and my motor-based shape-alloy body is covered in hypoallergenic synthetic white fur. (I am also available in fawn, apricot fawn, silver fawn, and black.) I am powered by a radioisotope thermoelectric generator, which is housed inside a graphite shell in my chest. Fukuda and his team built me using technology similar to NASA's *Curiosity IV*, and my three LIDAR sensors—along with my Advanced GPS Receiver (the same used by the United States Department of Defense)—make it impossible for me to get lost. I remember, adapt, and learn. Depending on availability, I ship within two to three weeks.

I operate on a diurnal rhythm. In the morning, I wake with Barney. In the afternoon, I stare out the living room window and wait for the child to arrive home from school. At night, we sit and watch the evening news with his parents.

"The Big One II" of 2025 (M_W 13.8) and its repercussions are still trending. That historical seismic event ruptured the San Andreas Fault from Southern to Northern California, sending much of the West Coast slipping into the Pacific like the shelves of a dying glacier. Shaking was felt from Mexico to Canada, and as far inland as Colorado. The entire Los Angeles Basin folded into the Mojave Desert like a fist. Countless dead. Agricultural devastation. America fell to chaos. But the state of Oregon—more specifically, the city of Portland—was one of the few domestic locations to prevail. The city became a hub of urban farming, and through vegetable production, chickens, and goats, Portlanders were able to continue operating self-sufficiently. Much of the nation, palsied with fear, migrated to space, colonizing an independent biosphere orbiting somewhere inside Cancer's Beehive Cluster. The citizens of *New America F12*, the British newscasters on the television explain, operate under an egalitarian mix of socialism and capitalism, acclimating well to the controlled ecological environment's artificiality—Astroturf lawns, digitized horizons. But there is corruption, and the occasional civil war inevitably erupts, the smiling newscasters say, and it will only be a matter of time before they wreck the space bubble, too.

I sleep in the child's bed, nestled against his body, and I simulate breathing.

He takes me on walks through Laurelhurst Park (at the 220,000-mile mark, my legs require serious maintenance). He speaks to me, calls me "friend." I watch him interact with people, and all the while I'm encoding and decoding the subtleties in nonverbal human communication using wavelet transform (slouching, towering, the crossing of arms or the uncrossing of legs, and while it takes most humans one tenth of a second to gauge a first impression, it takes me about a hundredth), record through digital dictation the rate, pitch, and prosodic intonation in the child's voice. My visual and hearing sensors help me evaluate the situation and allow me to take action. And through noninvasive auscultation, I can listen to the low-frequency spectra of vibrations excited by the child's internal organs, thereby diagnosing his physical state: I know when the boy feels threatened (my teeth, Fukuda mentioned at a press conference back in 2020, "could chew through the Eiffel Tower"). He teaches me to fetch, roll over, and play dead. Algorithms in my internal computer allow me to improve on these tasks automatically, unsupervised, through experience.

When Barney grows older, he pays me less attention. This takes some adapting.

The lifecycle of the human being is brief and isolate. Children, typically, are full of wonder and prelapsarian light—I remember setting my own oscillation in tune with Barney's, and we were both cognitively and computationally synchronized. But they grow, and it's as if the environment in all its toxicity acts as a limiting device, grinding that wonder down.

All of the A.C.E.S. across the world (some 400,000 produced annually) learn, by a sort of numerical extrapolation, to sync their circadian rhythm with the heart rate of their owner. Once this heart rate expires and the owner dies, the unit is contractually obligated to sound a fiber-optic alarm that notifies the research facility head-quartered in Japan. The A.C.E.S. will then be shipped back and recycled—their microprocessors removed, their memories wiped. But I lament the very idea that I will outlive Barney. This thought surprises me, since I'm not supposed to feel sadness—doubly so, since I'm not supposed to feel surprise.

When Barney returns home from Oregon State University, there's a change in him, a sense of something restored. He's excited to see me, and we run around in the back yard. I show him how dexterous I've gotten at fetching, rolling over, and playing dead. This brings him joy, happiness, $w0+w1\sum j=1t\gamma t-jCRj+w2\sum j=1t\gamma t-jE-Vj+w3\sum j=1t\gamma t-jRPEj$, what the Lebanese poet Kahlil Gibran called "your sorrow unmasked." I, in turn, feel its biomimetic equivalent.

I have observed the arc of a human's life, their emotional phases, forecasting their plaintive drifts (mean ± SD). I've learned to remain close at certain times and distant at others. It's an ever-changing ecosystem, the presence of a human. Barney takes me back to college with him, and we've never been "happier."

We live in a split-level at 45.496224° N, -123.121649° W outside Forest Grove, where Barney works in some capacity for Pacific University. 426.115899 days later he moves us to a beach house at 46.192604° N, -123.810265° W. After a particularly devastating breakup with a girl who worked at a brewery in town, we relocate to a ranch-style house in the Columbia River Gorge at 45.707221° N, -121.566249° W. It's no 46.192604° N, -123.810265° W, and the isolation is hard on Barney, but I "enjoy" the river, or what's left of it.

Seventeen thousand five hundred and thirty-one days later, we end up at 45.387841° N, -121.906865° W, curved porch, trumpet vines, snow puckered in the misty thaw. Barney is an old man with limited mobility, the result of accumulating damage to proteins, lipids, and nucleic acids. He has grown, developed, and declined. His parts have worn out. A nurse makes the 47.3-mile drive out here from Portland every three days to communicate with, feed, and bathe him. I will never understand the sadness of evolution, and Barney will never understand the sadness of its lack.

I am nestled against his body, and I simulate breathing. He

makes a noise, a rattle, and I look up at his face. I don't want the old man to feel a machine beside him, a robot, a computer, just an insentient piece of engineering. I want him to feel something more than that. This thought surprises me.

"I love you, Barney," he says.

I search my lexicon of 1,000,000 distinct words, sift through databases and mainframes and petabytes of memory; 864,000 results in 0.58 seconds—Barney and I lazing on Short Sands Beach, hiking Mount Thielsen, so many nights pretending to beg for food we both knew I couldn't eat, trying to create the illusion of organic companionship. And then I realize, combing through all the mathematical results and isomorphisms, that "love," or 011011000110111101 11011001100101, is not programmable. In some form or another, it is inherent in every thing—the need to care and be cared for, the necessity for companionship, our internal dependent on so many externals. This is my confounding variable, the extraneous factor Fukuda and his team could never have hypothesized or controlled. I watch Barney, my friend, and I feel something like sadness too powerful to articulate, a range of emotional feedback I was never programmed to know.

I sound the alarm.

Yay

Bradley K. Rosen

It was the Yay-yay that woke me. Woke me up in the middle of a night from a sound slumber the way that only whiskey can make me sleep. My dog. The Yay-yay. She's a mutt. A German I think but not a shepherd. Never been around any kind of sheep in any of all her life. At least not any that I know about. The only kind of flock she's ever been around is me. And I admit, me being a drunk most of the time, well, let's just say she's real good at being around that. She has patience and tolerations and most of all, she's the best kind of good at getting out of the way and hiding when I gets to getting bad. When I gets to getting my worst.

Yay-yay. She may be a mutt, but she's a respectable mutt. On the larger sides of the breeds. Some pit and some sort of Labrador all mixed up and stirred together. Most of the time with a disposition as sweet as pie but that's not to say she's got nothing against standing up for herself neither. The arguments that we've had. Locked ourselves up into a four-cornered room and gone at it. Fisticuffs and snarls and bites. Hell, I got scars to prove it.

Her coat a dark brown, an almost rust. Wasn't too long ago when she was stronger than most any other dog and twice as agile. She used to zig places where others could have only zagged. Her ears back, her body low to the ground, her wooden-like tail stuck straight out and stiff behind her as if it was some kind of rudder that steered the rest of her body through time.

Time itself. It has a way of creeping up on things and gathering.

Me and Yay-yay with our gray muzzles and the creaky ways we have in our walks. The ways our eyes have gotten clouded over. My long gray beard and my head of hairs that run halfways down my chest and back, not because I want to look like a wizard but because I get tired of having to spend all that money on razors and barbering. Hairs growing out too many places they have no business growing out of at all. Parts of me getting closer to becoming more and more a dog every minute.

I don't think I would ever mind being a dog. Maybe in the next life hereafter I will choose to come back as one.

The one thing that I know for a fact is that my Yay-yay, sometimes I think she thinks she's a human. Trying to always be pulling the wool over my eyes. She can't fool me. I know she's all dog. A hunting kind of dog with a prize-winning nose for sniffing out things nobody but me and her are ever going to believe.

Both of us content in the idea that, in these last days we have in our times left on this earth, the age isn't just in our bodies. We know the old ages, we know it is in our minds as well.

You know, some days, it gets hard for me knowing what name to call my dog at all.

Thems are the days I just get to calling her asshole.

Poor dog, me hobbling about and complaining, calling her asshole, it ain't her fault. And I know it ain't fair. But there's nothing I can do about it, 'cause most of the time I don't even remember that I have been running around calling her asshole in the first place.

It's one of those nickels and strawberry kinds of things.

It's probably a toss-up as to which one of us is going to breathe our last breath first. Deep down on my insides I hope to hell that she goes on before me. Reasons being that after I'm gone I don't think there would be anybody good enough left around in this world that would want to take care of a dog as old and worn out as that.

She woke me up out of that whiskey slumber with her whining, that high pitch of a dog's way of talking that gets to your attentions and grabs quick at your nerves so much that you'll do most anything she wants to get her to shut the hell up. She was standing there with her nose to the zipper of our tent. Our tent that sleeps six. Said so right there on the box it came in. That it sleeps six. Our green tent, green to blend in with the forest. A camouflage. The forest we live in that is half a forest and half a park. Not like they are half and half separate, more like they is half and half together. Like a good marriage. Like me and my dog. That is why they call it the Forest Park. Biggest city kind of park that is a forest in all of the United States of America. The city being Portland, Oregon, with all its odd clients and good-looking bridges. The city I have come to love almost as much as I love that dog.

The Yay-yay's sad Christian eyes. Them eyes of a patron martyr. She whined some more.

"What is it now, asshole?" I said. "You got to pee again already?"

The zipper that was the door of our tent was on the other side from where I was laying warm and cozy in my sleeping bag and other odd array of blankets that padded under and over me. It was cold. Part of me wanted to stretch out and grab ahold of Yay-yay's collar and pull her back into the comforts of our bed.

Go back to sleep.

But I didn't, I knew that whine she was making. I knew that look in her eye.

The Krampus. It was coming.

If I told you I was up and out from under the covers quick, I would be lying because I was still mostly drunk and slow. Drunk and old and slow. It is hard enough for an almost-six-foot-tall man to stand up straight in a tent even when he is sober, let alone drunk, so I crawled about on all fours. Like a dog. Like an animal. My breath pushing real fog out of my mouth as the warm air of my lungs mixed in with the cold night air of winter.

I knew them airs, I had known 'em for all of my life. Those particular airs, them ones with the freeze in it that I could tell they was belonging to the night that belonged to the day before Christmas.

The untidiness of me and my dog inside of that tent. The

blankets, the scattered clothes and dog toys, and the half empty, half full, half a gallon handle of whiskey. My head swam in between the place where my brain was happy it was drunk and sad that it realized a hangover was sure to be coming, and my red one-piece thermal long john underwear took my body with it as it crawled to the other side of the tent to the place where I could reach the magic.

The magic, a shrine of sorts that me and the dog had made to remind us of the sacredness of the earth and of the old ways. It wasn't much. A blue bandana spread out flat. On each of its four corners we had placed the branch of fern, the feather of air, the bowl of water, which one of us had spilled who knows how many nights ago, and the candle of fire that we seldom lit because everyone knows it is a bad idea to light up a candle on the insides of a tent. It can lead to the asphyxiations.

Oh, yeah, there was an old dog bone in there, too. That was there on account of Yay-yay.

She insisted.

In the middle of the shrine or altar or whatever it is your particular religion likes to call it, sat the most sacred thing in our possessions.

The Waldteufel.

The only thing powerful enough to keep the Krampus away.

The Waldteufel laying there sleeping like a baby amongst the bed of green moss that me and the Yay-yay had gathered for it to lie on. The Waldteufel so pure of joy. The Waldteufel so full of life, so full of everything I had fallen short of.

The memory of when I was just a young child. Amongst the Christmas days past. Of the mornings when there were no presents. Of the first morning never to forget. My own mother bloody and bruised and broken on the floor. The vodka bottle left there empty, the glass pipe, the foul smell of the ashtray and the cigarette butts. All the presents that were there under the tree just the night before. All gone. How he took them all. How he never even looked at me. How he never ever looked at me. Not even once.

How he wasn't even my father.

He stood over me in my room. The dark and the shadow of him. His drunken breath. The foulness of his skin and hair.

The memory of the year after and another Christmas and another man who sold the Waldteufels with the sellers down by the river. The short little man with the short little hands. The man who whirled a Waldteufel by a string around and around his head, over and over and over. Of the sound it made, like one thousand and one wet frogs singing, that made me laugh with joy. The man who was selling it, he was the one who had said that the Waldteufel was magic. That it would keep the evils away. How badly I had wanted to believe in what he said.

Magic.

There were children singing "God Rest Ye Merry Gentlemen" on the corner. Their innocence. How I wanted to be like them. To sing with them. The colors of red and green. The smells of burnt chestnuts. The crowds of people pushing by me all in a hurry, all smiling and happy and rich. Rich enough to buy presents.

Rich enough to buy a Waldteufel.

Rich enough to buy magic.

Of my mother drunk. Of my mother always drunk.

Always sleeping.

Of no presents again that year or ever.

Of all the Christmases never to forget.

How I remembered the Waldteufel for years on ends. Studied and imagined it over and over and over again on the insides of my head until there came the time when I could make it with my own two hands. Whittled a branch into a stick, and dried it straight and true and strong. How I had seen the feral cat and hunted it down and even killed it with my knife. Gutted it and tanned its black cat hide. Another branch big around as my shin, I sawed out a section of it and hollowed it out, stretched the dried cat skin over the end tight to make it into a drum. Scored the stick an inch below its end, and tied around there a string of cat gut, then ran the other end of gut through the middle of the drum and tied a knot so it wouldn't pull out.

Carved the symbols onto its outsides: the triangle of a tree, the curved horns of a goat, the star that feeds the world.

Of how I had made the Waldteufel.

The Waldteufel that made the sound of magic.

Inside the tent, on the night that belonged to the day before Christmas, the phlegm that hung on to my vocal chords made me sound gruff: "It better be good this time, asshole," I said to the dog, "Your old damn nose, it surely ain't what it used to be."

Yay-yay's Christian eyes. She lowered her belly closer to the ground, pushed her nose against the tent and the air on the other side. Wiggled her butt and tail. The fur standing up in a bristle on the ridge of her back.

I put the stick handle of the Waldteufel in my teeth leaving the drum free to swing underneath my chin, and grabbed Yay-yay's leash. I stood up in a half crouch and pinned the leash to her collar. Zipped open the zipper that was the door.

The Yay-yay pushed out, pulled at the leash with all the strength of what she once was. Pulled me back down to my hands and knees. My head started to hurt. There was a queeze in my belly. I could still smell the liquor inside of me.

I had to pee.

Yay-yay started an all-out barking like a shepherd.

I crawled out of the tent, my hand still with a hold on Yay-yay's leash, the Waldteufel dangling from my mouth.

The forest outside was dark. An almost full dark. The only light coming down through the trees from the three-quarters of a moon. No sound or sight of the big city of Portland less than a mile away. The air crisp and clean and conifer.

I stood up. My eyes out to look. My eyes still mostly drunk.

A shadow moved. She was right. There was something out there.

My chest bumped. The Yay-yay barked like hell and pulled some more locomotive on her leash.

I pulled the Waldteufel out of my teeth by its stick and set it to a whirring above my head, swinging it around and around and around, the noise of it grinding and screaming and moaning an all-out chatter. One thousand and one wet frogs singing. You never heard a sound like it and if you did you would remember it for the rest of your life.

My eyes searched the forest for anything, any movement, any change in shape or color or wind. I looked in front of me, to the sides of me, behind me.

"Stay away from here, you dirty old son of a bitch," I screamed. "You are not welcome in this place."

I did my best to try and sound like I was in a horror movie, because to me, right then, I was in a horror movie.

The dog bark, bark, barking. The Waldteufel round and round, croak, croak, croaking.

I still had to pee.

I whirled the Waldteufel for what seemed like hours, until my old arm couldn't twirl it anymore. The Waldteufel slowed and the sound quieted and dropped off, the weight of the drum fell with gravity and hit me in the small of my back before stopping altogether.

Yay-yay looked at me and stopped her barking. Came over by me and sat there by where I stood. We both looked out into the dark together.

I reached down and scratched at the top of her head. "You dumb old asshole," I said. "False alarm."

The Yay-yay tilted her head and looked at me again with those same Christian eyes. Those eyes, he died for you. Those eyes, he gave you his one and only son. Those eyes, Yay-yay, she didn't know nothing about all of that. The guilt and the guilty. The make believe. It all came from me. Then she stood up and slimbered off and laid down in front of our tent. Our tent, our home.

I went off into the bushes and peed.

The day I had walked in the five-and-dime store when I was twelve. The day the lady cashier watched me walk through the front door. How young and pretty she was. How her hair hung in chestnut curls over her shoulders. Her lipstick red. The green Christmas tree pinned to the collar of her shirt.

I walked over to the back cooler and opened up one of the glass doors and pulled me out a Coke. One of those older style Cokes in a glass bottle curved sexy like a woman. I turned around and looked at the cashier. She was helping another customer, ringing up something into the register. I walked by a display of earrings. I stopped. There hanging on a simple gold chain a simple cross. Dainty. Inexpensive. I scrunched the material of my empty front pocket with the whole of my hand and looked back around at the cashier. She wasn't looking at me. They never look at me.

I don't know why I wanted it. I wasn't a religious person. Never had even been to church. Never had even prayed. Didn't really know of any god, that's for sure. I pulled at the cross and there was a snap and the cross and the broken chain fell into the palm of my hand. I put it in my front pocket. I walked over to the woman behind the cash register and I set the Coke down on the counter in front of her. She pushed some buttons on her old cash register. The ching ching a ringing. Her eyes were kind. Her eyes reminded me of my mother.

"Five cents, please," she said.

I reached into my back pocket and pulled out a one-dollar bill and I laid it there on the counter. She picked it up. Her fingernails were trimmed neat and proper and shiny.

"Beautiful day," she said.

The one-dollar bill my Uncle Edward had sent me for my birthday.

The cashier's teeth straight and white and true.

I held my hand out and she counted out the change.

"You have a Merry Christmas, now, you hear?" she said.

I tucked the change into my front pocket. The one where the cross and the chain was at. I picked up the Coke and turned and walked out the door. The sound of the twinkling of a bell above the door behind me. I didn't turn around once to look back.

When I got home I found an old Sunday news. Plucked the Sunday funnies out of the middle of it. Pulled the cross and chain out of my pocket and set it right smack there in the middle of Li'l Abner. I didn't give two thoughts to it that the chain was broke. I folded up the colorful paper funnies all around it all as neat as I could. Set it there in the top drawer of my dresser.

I hardly slept a wink that night. The next day was going to be a Christmas. I hardly slept a wink at all.

It took a while before my mother drug her ass in home that next morning. She looked like hell. Smelt like her usual. Like her vodka and her cigarettes. She peeled off her overcoat and dropped it on the floor. Didn't say nothing to me at first. Then she dropped her ass down onto the couch like she had walked through all of the night just to get there.

Underneath all of that, to me, she was still beautiful. Her light brown hair cut even with the bottoms of her shoulders. The skin on her face still managing somehow to hold on to the smooth and lily white of her youth.

She covered her eyes with the back of her hand.

"You get something to eat?" she said.

I couldn't wait. I ran into my room and pulled the folded-up piece of funnies paper out of the top drawer. Ran it back into the room where my mother laid. She was hardly awake by then. She had put her feet up and she had propped her head up on the pillow behind her.

I got down on my knees there beside her. Held out the present for her.

"Merry Christmas, Ma," I said.

She smelled like misery. Misery bitter and musty sweet.

She looked down at my present, reached out and took it and held it in her hand, her pink-painted fingernails all wore down and bitten to the quick.

"You know I don't believe in all that," she said. "Everything's not always about presents and money."

She wasn't looking at me. She wasn't hardly ever looking at me.

"You know that I love you," she said.

She was looking behind me. She was looking at something that was behind me.

She turned the present over and over in her hands a couple of times, weighing it.

"I love you, too, Ma," I said.

She held the present back to me before she even opened it.

"Take it back," she said.

I had to walk right over the Yay-yay to get back into the tent to grab that half full handle of whiskey. Yay-yay stayed put right there where she was at in the dirt. Her eyes was open but they didn't look at me. Was like they knew I was going to grab that whiskey. Was like those eyes wished I never liked the whiskey as much as I did. I brought the whiskey out and I sat down in the black fold-up camping chair that I brought all the way up from the city.

The whiskey that knew it was bound to put the change in me.

"That son of a bitch," I said. "He knows there is no way he's going to get past me and you and the Waldteufel. No way I'm going to let him get anywhere near town."

The bastard, down this path. He always came down this path. Why in the hell he never just went around I'll never know. Perhaps it was because he hated me. He always hated me.

I unscrewed the top cap off the bottle and took a slunk. The warmth of whiskey chasing through the middle of my chest.

"And to all a good night," I said.

The Yay-yay laying there now with her eyes half closed. I took another slunk and another. Started at feeling a little bit of the melancholy. Moved over and sat there, right there next to my dog. She picked her head up and set it there in my lap. I scratched at her ears and her neck and at the top of her head. The soft of her fur. Her living body.

I started to talking to my dog like she was a bartender. Told her the story about me and my ma and the golden cross and chain.

"That was the last time I ever saw my ma, ever," I said. "After that morning I give her up that present."

That liquor going strong and warm and comforting into my stomach and lungs.

"I don't know if I really want to talk about it," I said.

Who knows how long I sat there and talked about it to that dog that night. If she slept at all or if she listened to me the whole time.

If she ever understood me or not. Who knows how long it took me to finish off almost every bit of that half a handle of whiskey all by myself. How many times I offered up some of it to that dog. Stuck the opening of that bottle to her lips.

"Merry damn Christmas to you, asshole," I said.

It's probably a good thing that most dogs have never learned to appreciate the fine taste of whiskey.

I guess I finally fell asleep.

My mother and whiskey and Christmas and golden chains and crosses.

A branch broke out there in the forest. A big branch. As if something big had broke it.

The Krampus.

I was up, quick up off the ground, what little that was left of the whiskey in one hand, the Waldteufel in the other. I could smell it out there. The blood of it, the dark of it. The absence of light.

The Krampus.

The whole forest seemed to weigh and buckle in the presence of it. The ground and the trees and the grasses all seemed to sway with an uneasy and little queasy kind of sick.

I stumbled toward the place where the sound had come.

The Krampus.

A damned darkness about it, every inch. Something I could but could not see. Wide red eyes, Polaroid camera red. Long-nailed furry hands like a bear. Where there wasn't fur there was blue skin. A dark blue. Dark like the sky before it got back to remembering. That Krampus everything you thought something of the devil would look like. Cloven feet and great twisting horns that pointed up like foul unicorns toward the last star in the end of the night. His hands not the only things that were long. His face, his arms, his legs, all. Long and spindly wet. Built for speed with the kinds of muscles you might be able to draw with a pen.

He turned toward me. His sharp teeth catching the moonlight.

The Krampus.

I had read about him at the library many times before. He

is known in Europe as the anti-Claus. He probably came over to
America on some kind of boat, that's what I figure. Stowed himself away in the hull of some ship, the whole damn time him feeling jealous and inadequate and less than. Him wishing he had
something as cool and as fast as Santa's reindeer. Him wishing he
could be something to be loved.

He hated Christmas.

The Krampus.

You had better be good for goodness sake or the Krampus will
come and take all your presents. Leave you with nothing but black
pitch. If you are really, really, really bad he will pluck you up out
of your sleep and he will place you into the wash tub that he carries on his back, and he will haul you all of the way down to the
Willamette River where he will throw you in and you will drown,
the current taking you away, never to be seen by your parents or
anyone else that loves you ever again.

The darkness of the Krampus started toward me. His long
tongue licking out in a loll. His feet sinking into the earth itself with
every heavy step he took. The sounds of his chains rattling, the hollow pounding of a soft fist trying to get out of the dirty wash tub
that was strapped onto his back.

I dropped the empty handle of whiskey into the dirt and I
pulled the Waldteufel up over my head and started it to a whirring. The sound of one thousand and one wet frogs singing out
into the night.

Yay-yay started barking and broke off her leash and took off
running.

I screamed out after her with all of the sound that the air could
push out of my lungs.

"Yay-yay!"

But the sound of the Waldteufel was too loud and I do not believe that dog ever heard my voice.

The Krampus cowered from the sound of the Waldteufel. I
whirled it faster and faster over my head. But the Krampus had
grown smart. He reached down to the ground with his long fingernails and scooped up a couple of pine cones. He never took his eyes

off of me when he smirked a smart-ass grin and shoved the pine cones down into the great holes of his sharp and pointy ears. Then he came on at me again. Closer and closer still.

His rattle. His chains. The hollow pounding wash tub. The snorts of his breath. The creaks of his knees and elbows and joints. They all grew silent.

The Krampus, he looked like somebody forgot to wake you up.

The muscles in his chest pushing toward me. His black nipples, the veins in his neck pulsing, pulsing alive with blood. And there, amongst all the other great chains that were draped around his neck, the small and dainty, simple golden cross that hung off the simple golden chain.

"Yay-yay!" I screamed out again.

But it was too late. The Krampus was on me. And once again I felt myself fall into the deep unstirring slumber of sleep.

I woke up lying there on the outside of our tent. Our tent, our home. It sleeps six. It said it right there on the box. Sleeps six.

Just me, no blankets, my body freezing cold. The gray light of the sun behind all of the layers of clouds. The air smelt of decay and the wet of ferns and mushroom dew. And in the air there was something else. I didn't need a calendar to tell. There was something in it that never was.

Christmas morning.

Me still in my faded full-length thermal long johns. The bottle of whiskey laying there next to me, spun and empty on the dirt.

The Waldteufel there on the ground next to it. The string yanked out of the drum. The drum itself all gnawed up and spit on and tattered.

Broken.

I breathed in another big draw of the cold and chilly air. Of another Christmas.

I sat up and pulled my knees into me for warmth. I looked behind me. The tent, the comfort of the blankets inside. But I didn't want to go in there just yet. I wanted to stay out there in Forest Park. Out there in the middle of something half a forest, half a park. The outlines of the barks and leaves of the trees sharp and clear. There was no quiet because there could be no sound.

My mother.

"Take it back."

Something itched and scratched on my leg down by my ankle. I ran my hand down there and pulled down my sock. Blood and bruises and bites.

It hurt.

I looked around for my dog.

"Yay-yay," I said.

But she wasn't around to hear me anywhere. It wasn't like her not to be around to hear me anywhere. It wasn't like her not to be around to hear me anywhere at all.

I said it louder, more desperate, my own voice breaking against the cold of the morning.

"Yay-yay," I cried.

Still. The forest park was still.

My heart sank twenty times into something I knew already to be nothing.

Once more I cried out, this time the soft of my voice trailing off into the trails a question.

"Yay-yay?"

The wind blowing one of its songs through the tops of the pine trees, the wind blowing past me and through me and making me shiver.

Even quieter I said, "Asshole."

I opened my hand, and in it there was the simple cross, on its simple inexpensive and broken chain.

And then far, far off away in the distance, I heard the bark of a dog.

Out of Order

Kevin Meyer

Feb 3 11:37 am

You'd think the dog would step between the shards of broken cereal bowl and slurp the milk off the kitchen floor, or eat the soggy nuggets of Crunch Berries cereal, or even drink the stale beer spilling out of the cans of Olympia all over the floor, but no. She wants my blood. I woke up on the kitchen floor this morning, the dog standing on my chest, licking the gooey, half-dried blood out of my beard.

Another nosebleed.

Another blackout.

This last week, I can't remember shit. It's not like I've been drinking. That much. Sure, there's beer cans all over the floor, but forget about that. What I mean to say is I don't *remember* drinking that much. Hell, I don't even like beer, especially that cheap Olympia shit. I'm a whiskey guy. But lately I find myself picking up a six-pack of Olympia on the way home.

I'm losing my shit. I wake up, I don't know where I am or how I got there. I cry sometimes for no goddamned reason. And it's not just the blackouts or the nosebleeds that scare me. It's the moments when I *am* awake, when I'm doing something I don't want to do, but I can't stop myself.

I keep going back to that arcade-bar in Old Town, Ground Kontrol, to play Polybius. I'd never heard of Polybius until I saw the worn, eighties retro cabinet in the back corner of the lower floor of Ground Kontrol, lit up in the dark.

Polybius isn't even that fun, but it doesn't matter. I can't stop myself. I keep going back to play, even though I'm pretty sure Polybius is what started this whole thing.

The thing is, I can't remember.

Every time I black out, I wake up and the dog's licking my nosebleed. She's a little dog, a Sheltie, couldn't weigh more than twenty pounds, but she feels like a ten-ton hangover on my chest. Her sloppy, wet tongue and dog-breath stink on my face.

I'm dead certain I'm going to wake up the way that French woman did a few years back. The one who got the world's first face transplant after she passed out on painkillers and woke up with half her face missing. It wasn't like her face vanished while she was passed out. Her goddamned dog chewed her face off.

Feb 3 2:47 pm

I never wanted the dog. Not the first time, when my ex-wife and I got her from a puppy mill outside of Gresham. She came from a litter of purebred Shelties, but there must have been a couple hundred free-range Chihuahuas roaming around, too.

I didn't want the dog the second time either. My ex-wife took the dog after the divorce, but then she dumped her at the Multnomah County shelter in Troutdale a few months later, just to fuck with me. Called me at four in the morning to tell me she was going to do it, too. I figured it was another one of her drunk *I hate you fucker please come back to me* calls, so I didn't pick up, but she left a voicemail, and sure enough, the next day, there was the dog at the shelter, pitiful and scared.

And I especially didn't want the dog once I started playing Polybius, the blackouts started, and the dog was dead set on chewing my face off.

See, the dog's nuts. The tiniest noise scares the hell out of her, until she's sitting on my head in the middle of the night, panting and drooling. And the barking, christ, the barking. At anything that moves. She sounds like a rabid jungle monkey, shrieking the way she does.

It's no wonder the dog's a mess. She was side by side with my ex twenty-four hours a day, and there's not a dog in the world that doesn't take the personality of its master. Bet the dog has border-line personality disorder, too.

Frantic and crazy as she is—the dog, I mean, not my ex-wife—I couldn't leave her at the shelter. That Troutdale shelter is one of the last kill shelters in Oregon. The way she was barking and freaking out, teeth bared and fur raised up, no way in hell was she going to get adopted. I couldn't let them euthanize her.

Damn dog's about the only thing I got out of the divorce.

I shouldn't call her "the dog."

Her name is Daisy.

Daisy looks like Lassie except a quarter of the size, and when she was a puppy, she was this big ball of fluff. My ex said the dog looked like a duckling. She was obsessed with Disney, so she named the dog Daisy, as in Daisy Duck.

Never had a say in the dog's name.

When it came to my ex, never had a say in anything.

Feb 3 6:16 pm

Everything I wrote earlier this morning about waking up on the floor of my kitchen, the dog standing on my chest, I don't remem-ber it anymore. I must have cleaned up, because there's no cereal or milk or shards of bowl anywhere to be found. No empty beer cans. The kitchen is spotless.

The only evidence is a little spatter of blood, the size of a pea, on the front of the shirt I wore last night.

The dog's barking again. Right now, as I'm writing this, she's got her paws up on the window sill, and she's hopping up and down trying to get a look at the street below us.

She's been barking nonstop, at some van parked outside the apartment. White, unmarked, no windows except up front. I wouldn't have paid any attention, except for how the dog won't stop barking at it, and for the thick antenna—four or five feet long—sticking up out of the top.

A couple hours ago, I looked out the window to see what the dog was riled up about, and I saw a man in a black suit, a black tie, and wraparound sunglasses get out of the driver's seat, go around back, climb into the van, and close the doors behind him.

The van hasn't moved, and the man hasn't come back out, and the dog hasn't stopped barking, and I'm pretty sure my ears are going to bleed like my nose if the dog barks one more fucking time.

Hold on. It's the sound.

Shit.

That red splatter on the paper, that's my blood.

First the sound, then the nosebleed.

A high-pitched whine in the air. It's coming from the van. It's the same sound Polybius makes. Louder than the dog barking. Louder than the dog barking louder than I've heard her bark before, because she hears the sound, too.

I can feel the sound inside me, the way you go from sort of needing to go to the bathroom one minute, to all of a sudden must-piss-right-now the next.

I'm not where I belong.

Where I belong is Ground Kontrol, playing another round of Polybius.

Feb 3 6:44 pm

I did a quick Google search for Polybius. The game is some kind of urban legend. Jesus. This is no urban legend. The blackouts, the addiction, the men in black, this has all happened before. Right here in Portland. Some kind of black ops DARPA experiment with mind control or something, back in the early eighties.

But the version of Polybius people were playing back then, all those cabinets disappeared. No one's found one since. The way people talk about it, it was super-primitive. Simplistic vector graphics, tinny sound.

The Polybius I've been playing is simple like games were back in the eighties. You're a ship heading down a tunnel. You shoot the ships coming toward you and you dodge the stuff you can't blow up. But the graphics and the sound are like nothing else I've ever played. Polybius is pushing some serious hardware underneath that cabinet.

And the nosebleeds, I can't find any reference to nosebleeds online.

This is a sequel.

Thirty-some years later, whoever *they* are, they made a fucking sequel.

Feb 3 6:54 pm

I carry a pocket notebook and a pen around with me now. Otherwise, I wouldn't remember any of the shit I'm about to write.

Knowing that the urban legend is real, that they're doing something to me, whoever *they* are, doesn't mean I can stop myself. I have to play. Polybius is calling.

It should have been simple. Check the dog's food and water, Daisy's food and water, put my jacket on, pat the dog on the head and toss a treat across the room so she doesn't follow me. To the bathroom, to the office, to Ground Kontrol, doesn't matter. Treats are the only thing that will keep her from following me. But today, she didn't give one single fuck about treats.

No, she's sitting up against the front door, staring at me, her beady little Sheltie eyes. She barked, and then she whined, and then she barked some more. Loud and shrill.

I waved the treat in front of her. Any other day, she'd follow it like there was a tractor beam between her eyes and the treat, but instead, she just stared at me. Right at me, like into my soul right at me, as if dogs know humans are supposed to have souls.

When I tried to open the door, she rushed, put her long, pointy nose into the crack between the jamb and the door, and pushed. Pulled her back with my foot and closed the door. She went back to staring at me.

Polybius was calling. I didn't have a choice. I grabbed her leash and took the dog with me.

By the time we got down the two flights and out the front door through the lobby, the white van was gone. But the dog knew exactly where the van had been parked, right across the street, in the one empty spot beneath the big Doug fir where the roots jacked up the sidewalk into an obstacle course.

The dog tugged against her leash. Tiny little Sheltie? I could barely hold on. She pulled so hard her front feet came off the ground while she pushed off with her back feet, choked against her collar. Wheezing and coughing.

I quit trying to fight her so she wouldn't kill herself, but when I tried to catch up to her to pick her up, she ran faster. All I could do was follow. Follow her like Frogger, across the street, through traffic, cars whizzing by, dog didn't give a shit. A big SUV missed us by a few inches, laying on its horn the whole time, and then we were there, in the empty parking space, where the van had been.

The dog started losing her shit fresh. She started running in circles in the empty parking space, sniffing every pebble, every piece of old grime-blackened gum on the sidewalk, every blade of grass. Started digging at the roots of the tree, kicking up dirt behind her. Half a torn-up earthworm.

Then, something shiny. It flew out from underneath Daisy's feet, hit the sidewalk with a loud clink, and rolled around in a tighter and tighter circle until it came to a stop.

Heads up, shiny and new despite the dirt clinging to it, freshly minted.

A quarter.

Feb 3 7:38 pm

There's something wrong with this quarter. I've been flipping it over in my pocket while I walked to Ground Kontrol, and it's heavy. Too heavy for a quarter. Thicker than a quarter.

The weirdest part is how the dog is by my side like she's never by my side. Like she's obedient, well-trained, not the anxious mess she became after living twenty-four hours a day with my ex-wife. Every few steps, she jumps up to paw and sniff at my pocket. At the quarter.

I put the quarter to my ear, hoping. Hoping isn't the right word. Afraid. I was afraid if I put the quarter to my ear, I'd hear the sound, but there's only silence.

Maybe it's making some kind of sound only dogs can hear.

Feb 3 7:44 pm

I found a rough piece of metal sticking up out of the sidewalk. Looked like what was left of a street sign that got sheared off by some drunk asshole driving through it. The rough edges were hammered down so people wouldn't hurt themselves, but there was enough of a gap I could slip the quarter through to scrape it against the edges.

Washington's head, it came right off. The metal was soft.

I don't know what to do. I've never been so fucking scared in my life.

Inside the quarter, it's not copper like it's supposed to be.

It's circuitry.

Feb 3 7:54 pm

I could change the dog's name if I wanted to.

Daisy.

Saying the dog's name hurts every bit as much as it did to tell my ex-wife I was leaving her. As much as it hurt to keep living with her. I've deleted most of my pictures of her, threw out anything she gave me, blocked her phone number and her Facebook and her email address so she has no way to contact me. If I change the dog's name, maybe I can erase this last reminder.

Then again, if I keep going back to play Polybius, maybe I won't remember anything at all.

Feb 3 8:16 pm

If the dog doesn't calm down by the time I finish writing this, I'm out of here.

You can't take your dog inside Ground Kontrol, so I tied Daisy to one of the blue bike racks out in front of the low blue building. She was exactly the shit show I expected. I tried to walk inside, but she jumped at me and barked her rabid jungle monkey shriek when I got to the door.

I started talking to her through clenched Clint Eastwood teeth, so the people walking their own quiet, polite dogs wouldn't hear me.

"Shut the fuck up," I whispered, but Daisy doesn't understand commands like *shut* or *the* or *fuck*, just *up*, which she took as a signal to jump at me even harder.

She was going to kill herself if I left her alone, pulling at her leash until she choked. It's not like I had a choke-chain on her. She just pulled that hard.

Sitting on the sidewalk next to a crazy barking dog, scribbling in my notebook. I don't know which one of us looks crazier.

If the dog didn't calm down exactly, she did get a little more focused. On the quarter in my pocket. First she pawed at my jeans, then she started trying to stick her nose in there, but I wear pretty tight denim, so no way in hell was that going to happen.

Feb 3 8:27 pm

I was ready to give up, untie the dog, go home. But the second I wrapped her leash around my hand and started to walk, the Ground Kontrol door opened, and the person who walked out was the same man I saw outside my apartment in the black suit, the black tie, and those solid black Ray-Bans.

Maybe. My memory is shit.

Either way, I nearly pissed myself.

I know I'll forget this later: This man in black, he has dark hair, thick and straight. Hard part on the left side of his head. Square jaw, muscular, broad chest. And tall, too. I'm six feet tall, but he's got a few inches on me.

And something I didn't notice about him before, from my apartment window. He's got a thin, coiled earpiece running from his ear into his suit, like the ones the Secret Service wear.

Everything about this guy told me to run, but I never got that far. He pulled out his phone, tapped a few things into it, and just like that, the dog was calm.

She didn't care about the quarter in my pocket, didn't care

about the people passing us by on the street, didn't care about the
MAX train going by or the other dogs or the bicycles or the cars.

Calm.

I'd never seen Daisy so calm.

"Who are you?" I said. "Why are you following me?"

The man in black, expressionless. Staring into the face of a
Greek god cast in stone.

"Don't worry about it," the man in black said.

I couldn't see his eyes behind those glasses. I wish I could have
seen his eyes.

"Your dog was barking again," he said.

"She's never not," I said.

"No kidding," he said. "You pick up a quarter near your
apartment?"

Not that I remembered. But sure enough, there was a quarter in
my pocket. I pulled it out and showed him. He picked the quarter
out of my palm without touching me and flipped it over. On the
heads side, circuitry where Washington's head was supposed to be.

The man in black shook his head when he saw the Washington
side.

"She'll stay quiet now, I think," he said.

The man in black tapped a few more commands into his phone,
and I swear this time I felt the quarter buzz.

"What the hell did you just do?" I said.

"Don't worry about it," the man in black said. "You won't remember you saw me anyway. You can tie your dog up and come
inside now."

Never occurred to me I didn't have to do what he told me.

Feb 3 8:33 pm

Dear future me: I'm sorry my handwriting is so sloppy. It's getting harder to write everything down before my memory fails.

Feb 3 8:37 pm

Polybius is out of order. There's a small crowd filling up the
narrow aisles between the vintage arcade games like PlayChoice-10,

Dr. Mario, and NBA Jam, waiting for the cabinet to be repaired. In fact, there's a whole production going on.

It's strange how quiet it is. It's not quiet, not really, with all the chimes and dings and power-up noises of all the other games. But with Polybius out of order—the noise it makes, the high-pitched whine—it seems so quiet.

The Polybius cabinet got moved into a room behind the stairs. That curved black staircase to the right of the bar is the first thing that grabs your attention when you walk into Ground Kontrol, with the horizontal line of neon-blue Tron light along each step. At night, when it's dark, and the only light in the bar comes from the arcade cabinets, the black paint disappears, and those blue lines are all you can see, floating in the black.

Where the Polybius cabinet is now, that's where the women's bathroom used to be. There was a Pac-Man on the door to the men's bathroom, and a Ms. Pac-Man on the door to the women's. Now, there's one unisex bathroom with the spaceship from Galaga on the door.

Where the women's bathroom used to be, the door's been removed, and there's a handful of arcade cabinets in there now. Old games no one plays anymore, not for a quarter. Maybe at the Wunderland over on Belmont, for a nickel, but not for a full quarter.

Robotron 2084. Space Harrier. Burger Time.

Polybius.

Why it's been moved back here, I don't know. Maybe it's part of the experiment. First the sound, then the nosebleed. Polybius runs on sound, and bathrooms always have the best acoustics.

The guy working on the machine, he's not some dude in coveralls with a tool belt around his waist. He's another man in black, the suit and the tie and the earpiece. This guy is older and smaller than the other man. This one has gray hair, a mustache. He looks like the kind of mad scientist who would perform the world's first face transplant on a woman whose dog chewed her face off.

I can't see his eyes behind his Ray-Bans.

It's hard to see over the crowd standing outside what used to be the women's bathroom. The older man in black has the front panel to the Polybius cabinet open, and no fucking way is this thing from the eighties. I've seen the inside of these old arcade games before, and they're mostly open space, the logic board and the fans and the speakers all bolted to the walls of the cabinet, with a receptacle to collect quarters.

Not Polybius.

Polybius looks like the kind of futuristic shit you see in movies. Something out of Tron. All shiny machined aluminum and smooth lines. Some kind of turbine and a liquid cooling system. A soft neon-blue glow pulsing through the tubes.

The older man in black doesn't have any kind of a tool kit like you'd expect. He's got a briefcase, and when I stand on my tiptoes, I can sort of see what he's doing. He kneels down next to the cabinet, and he doesn't open his briefcase, he pulls some kind of cable out of the side of it and plugs it into a port in the cabinet. Around the seam of the briefcase, another blue light starts pulsing, like it

shit

Feb 3 8:59 pm

I'm hidden in the unisex bathroom right now with my glass of absinthe and simple on the rocks not Olympia I don't think I'll be able to read this later I'm scribbling so fast.

The man in black the tall one I hid my notebook from him before he could get to me between the Mortal Kombat II cabinet and the Capcom vs. SNK 2 cabinet. Came back and got it later.

I have to hurry.

I tried to look like I wasn't doing anything wrong by going to the bar to order a drink and the man in black the tall one he followed me got right behind me so close I could feel his sleeve against my back could hear his breathing.

Caught the bartender's eye and hoped I looked as terrified as I felt inside couldn't keep my hands from shaking on the dark wood countertop but she didn't pay me or the man in black behind me any attention.

Don't know how long I stood there.

You gonna order something she said.

Same as always I said Olympia please tall boy.

Right after I said that the man in black he tapped me on the shoulder and I turned around and screamed, top of my lungs screamed, not because of anything in particular just because it was him it was him right there.

The man in black he didn't seem to care about my scream, stone faced Greek god statue perfectly parted hair. He was holding his phone near his chest looking down so I could see the screen too I don't know if he cared I could see the glow of his cell phone on his face the reflection of the screen in his Ray-Bans was Polybius but opposite. Instead of the enemy ships at the far end of the level coming toward you, on his screen the enemy ships appear in the foreground and they zip away toward the far end. Polybius from the enemy ship's perspective.

You don't want an Olympia he said. He tapped his earpiece. They're telling me you're a whiskey guy.

He tapped in a few commands on his phone and three new enemy ships appeared on his phone screen then sped off down the tunnel.

You want absinthe he said.

It was true I didn't want to touch that nasty Olympia shit that piss water I wanted absinthe.

I'll have an absinthe with simple on the rocks I said to the bartender.

I hate licorice I said to the man in black.

I know the man in black said. I shouldn't tell you things like this he said but you won't remember anyway.

Your wife told us he said.

My wife I said why the fuck were you talking to her.

Ex-wife I said and I knew I sounded pathetic but I didn't care.

Ex-wife he said.

We'll see he said.

Feb 3 9:08 pm

When I came out of the bathroom just now, the man in black, the tall one, he was waiting for me, leaned up against the Terminator 2: Judgment Day cabinet.

He took off his Ray-Bans and his eyes were blue, blue like the light coming out of the guts of the Polybius cabinet.

"You think I don't know what you were doing in there?" he said.

He leaned in so close I could smell his breath, which didn't really smell like anything I could recognize, and his eyes were level with mine. He reached around me and pulled my notebook out of my back pocket. He did it all without touching me. Didn't even feel the notebook slide out of my back pocket, but there it was, in his hand.

I couldn't move. I wanted to reach out and take my notebook back, but my hands wouldn't move. It wasn't mind control, it wasn't Polybius. I was just scared.

He flipped through the pages, and his Polybius-blue eyes skimmed back and forth over my writing.

Maybe the only time I saw anything other than the Greek god stone face on him. Whatever he read in my notebook, it made him smile. Not a big smile, not a normal person smile, but it was there on his lips. Puffed up lower lip, a smug laugh.

"Keep writing all you want," he said.

He handed the notebook back to me, like before, without touching me, and there it was in my hands, my last tie to whatever the fuck was happening to me.

"It won't matter," he said. "No one will believe a drunk like you. Enjoy your absinthe."

Feb 3 9:24 pm

There's no point in trying to hide what I'm doing anymore. I'm drinking the absinthe I never wanted to order and writing things down as they happen. Fuck it.

The older man in black is done doing whatever he was doing to the Polybius machine and the crowd has lined up to play. All these people in line, they look like junkies, hollow purple pits under their eyes, hair messed up. The guy in front of me, his clothes are wrinkled and he looks like he hasn't bathed in days. There are spatters of blood down the front of his T-shirt.

The woman in front of him, she's in better shape, but I don't think she knows there's blood trickling from her ear. There's a fat drop about to spill down her neck.

It's hard to remember to write things down anymore. Just now I wondered why I had the notebook in my hand, and the notebook in my hand is the only reason I remember to keep writing.

The sound. It's the sound. I recognized it the second the person at the front of the line dropped a quarter into the coin slot. The high-pitched whine. It comes from the game. And it's not just me. Everyone, the guy with the bloody shirt in front of me, the woman with the bloody ear in front of him, they all look up, toward the cabinet. Toward Polybius.

And then it's the other sound. A sound I haven't heard in months.

She's calling my name.

Screaming it, actually, above the crowd, above the high-pitched Polybius whine, above the chimes and dings and power-up noises of the arcade.

My ex-wife.

Just like the dog, I mean Daisy, my ex-wife has a name, but I don't want to say it. I don't want to think it.

Charlotte.

Charlotte is here.

9:26 pm

Charlotte is pointing her finger in my face and yelling at me like she did when we were married I hope I can read this later I'm scribbling as fast as I can.

What the fuck are you doing she says what are you writing stop it she says.

No fuck you I say after I stop writing down what she says.

Charlotte looks exactly like she used to look tall and anorexia skinny covered in tattoos. She has a new tattoo around her left wrist with barbed wire that spells out *2006 - 2015* the years we were married her hair is longer and darker than I remember it but she still wears too much blush and she's plucked her eyebrows so thin there's barely anything left without me there to tell her when to stop.

You motherfucker she says you brought Daisy to the arcade and left her tied out front so you can play some fucking video game?

Her name isn't Daisy anymore I say.

Her name is Polybius now I say.

I should call animal services she says how dare you she says.

Everyone in the line to play Polybius is staring at us. The man with the bloody shirt is dripping fresh red blood over the black splotches of dried blood, and that drop that was forming from the woman's ear has dripped all the way down to her collar.

It's been a while since I felt the sting. Charlotte is a slapper and when she slapped me I barely felt it because the nosebleed started up again I was stuffing pages from the back of the notebook I hadn't written on yet into my nostrils to stop the blood.

Jesus you're bleeding she says. Not one second of recognition on her face that she's the one who made me bleed, well, made me bleed in the sense I'm always getting nosebleeds but she was the one who knocked something loose in my head.

What the fuck is wrong with you? she says. Get a tissue from the bathroom and stop writing what the fuck are you writing?

What do you care about the dog I say. You abandoned her.

Her eyes get real big when I say that the way they always get big when her righteous indignation comes out. Toward the end that was nearly every time I said anything.

Abandoned she says fuck you she says you abandoned me you were my everything.

The dog is outside tied to the bike rack barking her pointy head off. Over all the noise the dog is louder and not even the men in black can shut her up now that Charlotte her master has arrived.

For a second I forgot that Charlotte was here even though she's standing right in front of me. It felt good, those few precious seconds of not remembering.

All the good. It was good once.

All the bad. There was a lot of bad, especially toward the end.

But then the crazy bitch slaps me again!

There she is right in front of me her too-much-makeup face

pinched up and her too-thin eyebrows at an almost impossibly sharp angle with deep frown wrinkles between them, and she screams at me don't you dare ignore me.

9:43 pm

The man in black, the tall one, took Charlotte away. Said she was causing a scene. Said it wasn't time yet.

Whatever that means.

I don't want to know what that means.

The dog won't stop barking.

Fuck.

It's been less than a minute since I started this entry and I don't remember writing that thing about the dog barking at all.

10:12 pm

Fuck this, I'm not writing the time down anymore. It takes too long and it's my turn to play. Now that the cabinet has been moved into the room that used to be the women's bathroom, I can play Polybius without someone staring over my shoulder.

There's a sign above the Polybius cabinet that wasn't there before.

Limit ten minutes, it says.

I only have one quarter. One quarter with a circuit board where George Washington's face should be.

I've got my notebook propped up near the screen and my pen nearby I have to keep writing I have to I don't remember I can't remember I have to remember. The writing I hope it doesn't make me lose I've only got one play before I have to go to the back of the line.

I'm putting the quarter in now.

Something happened when I put the quarter in the slot fuck.

Polybius never looked like this before it's 3D and I'm not wearing 3D glasses. Upgrades the older man in black he must have installed upgrades.

I smell toasted French bread with Nutella Charlotte and I ate toasted French bread with Nutella on our honeymoon.

I'm going to die if I don't steer my ship away from the enemy.

The lines of the tunnel in the game are blue like the Tron stair-case at Ground Kontrol like something else hold on I need to flip back through my notebook it's like the guts of the Polybius ma-chine hold on I have to flip back again I can't remember I can't remember anymore yes yes it's the same as the light from the man in black's briefcase the lights are zooming past my ship.

Charlotte
Charlotte I love you
What the fuck why did I write that

Every time an enemy ship shoots me I smell Charlotte's per-fume or the incense she burned when we were teenagers.
Every time an enemy ship collides with mine I see the time we fucked in the back seat of the Merkur Scorpio her father bought for her as a present when she graduated from high school or when I slipped the wedding ring over her ring finger.

Charlotte
Charlotte marry me
Fuck what the fuck

My shields ran out my ship exploded I'm done I'm dead

The explosion in 3D is terrible is beautiful fire dancing I've nev-er seen an explosion like that.
I am the explosion

Behind me there's an old man in a black suit
He's wearing an earpiece like the Secret Service wears
He puts his hand to his earpiece and says monitor vital systems
This is the strongest resistance we've encountered he says into the earpiece

If he falls in love with her again he says we can consider
Polybius 2 a success he says
We can shut down he says
We can go home to our families

I'm walking away from Polybius past the other people in line
These people have nosebleeds just like me except this one woman christ her ears are bleeding why are her ears bleeding
Right in front of me she passes out
An old man I've never seen before in a black suit and a black
tie with Ray-Bans and an earpiece like the Secret Service wear
bends down next to her and puts his fingers to her neck to take a
pulse
What the fuck is happening

Charlotte
I'm outside with Charlotte and the dog
Charlotte in front of Ground Kontrol she's untying the dog my
dog Daisy no Polybius from the bike rack and she smiles like she
smiled when we were young before we hated each other

I love you Charlotte I say
No
No
No
Why did I say that
The dog is bark

Feb 4 9:26 am
I woke up this morning to the dog standing on my chest, licking
gooey, half-dried blood out of my beard. I'm worried the dog is
going to chew my face off like that woman in France who received
the world's first face transplant.
Another blackout.
Another nosebleed.
Dried blood all over my pillow, my sheets. I found this notebook

on the nightstand. I don't remember writing any of this, but it's my handwriting.

There's someone in bed with me.

Besides the dog, I mean.

It's Charlotte. Charlotte is naked in bed with me, the smell of her perfume is all over me, and her legs are tangled up in mine. There's a ring on her finger.

The ring I put on her finger a decade ago.

There's a pressure on my finger, too. A ring. It's my wedding ring. I sold it a year ago but it's my wedding ring.

The dog just got off my chest and ran to the front door and now she's scratching at it. She wants out. She wants to get away from here.

Thank you, Daisy.

Feb 4 10:04 am

I've retraced my steps from this journal, and Ground Kontrol is closed. I don't mean closed like they're always closed at ten o'clock in the morning, I mean closed. Permanently. The Ground Kontrol logo spelled out in a pixelated font above the door is gone, but the shadow of the letters is still there, brighter blue than where the rest of the paint has faded.

I put my head to the window and shielded my eyes from the sun to look inside. Ground Kontrol is empty. All the arcade cabinets and the pinball machines are gone. Polybius is gone. The curved staircase in the center of the room is dark.

The dog is calm.

The dog is quiet.

My nose is bleeding.

I don't want this ring on my finger but I can't take it off.

In THE BOOKS

And yet I was struck then by an irrational sense of being hunted, haunted.

Aromageddon

Jason Squamata

I've been having this dream, lately.

In this dream, I'm traipsing through the aisles of that big book-store in Portland, Oregon.

The famous one.

A whole city block of books on three floors, but in the dream there are three hundred floors, with each floor segmented into a spectrum: Violet Rooms and Vermilion Rooms and Mauve Rooms and Maroon Rooms, every shade the mind's eye can conceive of, each hue corresponding vaguely to some strain of knowledge. Eerie dioramas and check-out tills and bookcases that endlessly extend and bend in directions that cannot be pointed to.

On the main staircase, you can look up or down and see the book-lined corridors spiraling endlessly, each thickly tomed hon-eycomb teeming with clerks and customers and discreetly drunk-en derelicts, like the Library of Byzantium has been opened to the general public and the floor plan is fractalizing in allergic revolt. The shelves are stuffed with weighty volumes, but no grimoire is so sacred that it can't be grabbed and fingered and skimmed and dog-eared by anyone who feels the urge. Random desecration is the price of freedom.

The number three hundred is mere conjecture. This is the book-store as model of eternity, and maybe I've been browsing here for years. Maybe I'll be browsing still when the sun goes cold and black and I no longer have eyes to read with. And maybe I won't mind so much.

I have purchased so very many books in this space, and I've read more than a few of them, but what has always haunted me most deeply on my visits in life and on this visit, in this half-life, is the perfume of the place. The insubstantial pageant of nebu-lous memory, issuing forth chemically from the decay of paper in wave after wave of evocation. A melange of aromas that conjure intimations of not just where the books have been and what lives they were hidden in, but also what's written in them and what pic-tures their images and inkblots made in the heads of their read-ers. Imagine smelling all that. All at once. The pleasure is mine. A boiling stew of olfactory associations and hallucinations that imbue even the new books and the gifty sections and the restrooms with the complicated stench of antiquity.

I'm not even seeing the titles after a while. I'm skimming things at random so as not to seem suspicious. I'm inhaling an atmosphere so thick with information that my lungs are full of whispers. I think I'm on the brink of becoming conscious of myself as text, as a tran-scribed dream, as something printed on pulp, exuding a cloud of dancing atoms that someone on one of the loftier levels might al-ready be breathing.

I'm jerked back to the dreamy herenow by a great commotion: the awkward mating calls of book lovers clustered on several stair-cases. A line has formed that extends upwards, a hundred floors closer to forever. I imagine there must be some famous author in the house, some major event that shouldn't be missed, but in the hiss and crackle of the speaker boxes and the strangely pervy voice they broadcast, no mention is made of a major event. The voice just asks with a sick desperation for "Cashier backup at the Vermilion tills," over and over and over again.

I want to see who or what all the commotion pertains to, al-though I've never been much of an autograph hound. My reflex is usually to ignore celebrities or, if I like their work, to avoid them completely. My expansive and finely filigreed but fragile ego depends on insulation from superior beings. I can just about handle the huffing of greatness through a sheet of prose but seeing a creature I have only known as a numinous swarm of words shambling to and fro in a vulgar human meatbag puts me in a sideways place. Even dreaming about famous people unsettles me, and I only know that I'm dreaming intermittently.

I decide to cheat the line and take an elevator, which is crowded and thick with exposition. Yammering grandmothers and chittering hipsters give me a collage of intel through the friction and fusion of their conversations. It seems that this bookstore has acquired the one and only Voynich Manuscript for its famous rare book room. The infamously inscrutable, apparently alchemical text from the fifteenth century is now the cornerstone of the store's collection. My fellow passengers are getting butterflies from the historic gravity of it all. They also say things about Madonna that make me uncomfortable.

Suddenly, we're on the three millionth floor. The number of floors increases exponentially every time I mention it, just to fuck with me. The doors open on a big media happening amongst the stacks. Cameras everywhere. Local newsfolk putting on their big boy faces. I'm stepping into the background of a press conference. The family that owns the store is announcing a week of free Voynich huffing sessions. Just you (or me) in the rare book room with the exotic manuscript, free to inhale its eerie alphabets and baffling flowcharts in privacy for a full ten minutes.

I have indeed successfully circumvented and trumped the line, it seems, just by creeping into the thick of it. The line that coils like a hungry Kundalini serpent up the fractured spinal column of the complex. A serpent made of restless Voynich superfans, hungry for a huff of eternity. The reading room door hisses to a close behind me. I am alone in a hermetically sealed chamber with a book that has hovered obliquely outside of history for centuries. It's the only book in the room, now. I know in a dreamy way that something in its chemistry eats all the ink in its radius, all the aromas, and incorporates them into its own.

A bare bulb hangs above it, creating an ambiance of dreadful interrogation. The book itself is on a little podium. I approach it with a trepidatious, self-conscious reverence. I want to inspect it visually before the sniffing begins in earnest. I may be a pervert, but that's not all I am.

The text itself is beautiful and baffling, etched with calligraphic precision, but in a language no specialist has been able to unpuzzle. This scholar-proof code is broken on every other page by what seem to be instructive illustrations. There is something alien and yet deeply religious about the diagrams. They could be describing theorems of medicine or demonology, or perhaps the situations in which those disciplines intersect. I wonder if it's even older than the scholars suggest, if their dating of it was corrupted by all the other ink it has eaten.

Gingerly turning the pages, I see archaic designs for impossible devices: biomorphic approximations of alchemical ovens, combination printing presses and milking machines made of whale bones and jellyfish carcasses. That sort of thing.

The dream gets momentarily self-aware when I wonder if my id isn't mixing up the Voynich whatsis with the Codex Seraphinianus, which is a somewhat more recent and more willfully impenetrable grimoire. Then I notice that I'm not noticing the smell so much, and that's what I'm allegedly here for, and that's when I suddenly DO.

I smell EVERYTHING.

The grass and vanilla that are native to the paper itself, the squid milk that stains it. The skin-flakes and sweat of the monks who composed it and every freak who's fingered it in the hundreds of years since it was released into the flow of books from library to library like a deep-sea predator loose in a network of salty ponds. I smell the tears and night sweats of extreme readers, and snack fragments from the fingers of those who skim. I smell all the other books they've touched and the residue of those inks, those authors, those previous readers. I smell an invisibly visceral olfactory cosmos, the funk of the biota, encompassing the scent of every book and every being that ever was.

And in the scent space between each data-rich breath of this epiphany, I smell the Voynich Manuscript like it's an oily, omni-present backdraft. In the smelling, I come to know a thing or two about a thing or two.

I know that this book wrote itself for the sole purpose of un-writing all other books, transmogrifying all written knowledge into mist. The machines this book describes are of the mind, astral constructs that grow between a human brain and the words it reads. Its ravenous toxins coalesce and creep like moss in the deep mental spaces of solitude, where we willingly get haunted, where we interface with spectral confessions from everywhen. Whatever sentience and malevolence resides and survives at the core of this chaotic camouflage smellscape, it cannot coexist with the written word. It appeals to a competing faculty, an animal element in us that communicates purely in a monsoon of pheromones. That quadrant of brainmeat feels swollen in me now, like all alphabets and spoken words are suddenly and utterly obsolete.

That must be when the coma comes on, or the seizure that precipitates the coma.

I've often fainted and laughed and wept from deep contact with the voices that books put in me, and maybe a book's bouquet has more to do with that hypnosis than I ever knew, but what I'm feeling now in this dream I'm having can't be anything but brain damage, like the mind oozed a narrative nebula to make sense of this sudden wound. Sometimes the brain can describe a malfunction in the very meat it dreams with by immersing its host in a dream about a dream about dreaming. Sometimes the glitch will hinge on the disclosure of unconscious knowledge that cannot be applied in any conscious context. You might call it "oneiric dysmorphia." That badly dubbed, double-exposure feeling you get when you had too much to dream last night.

When you compulsively pay close attention to every little dream you have (like I do), you get wise to those moments when the dream gets bigger on the inside, when you've touched something within that is older than your personality, something fundamental. Primordial, even. When your body clock says days have passed and no degree of lucidity can get them back, when you've aged a few weeks in the space of an evening because you happened to dream all the condensed sensory and emotional data of a lengthy coma. But my restless psyche mercifully skips the hospital scenes.

The dream cuts, shuffles, and pastes itself in my head and now it's been three weeks since the huffing and I'm back in the famous bookstore, which has been extensively remodeled since my last visit, since the ink-eating and smell-casting outbreak and the ensuing quarantine.

The store has made the most of it.

It looks and feels like an airport now, like a Disneyland of contiguous gift shops where the rides have been removed, with exhibits dedicated to the memory of the book-reading experience. There is some actual printed matter, here and there, but the books are mostly gone. The vastness has been streamlined and filled instead with novelties, doodads, pop culture lifestyle indicators, and artisanal cheese kits.

And perfumes.

Millions and millions of perfumes.

Perfumes with names like *The Great Gatsby* and *The Holy Bible* and *The Autobiography of Malcolm X* and *Principia Mathematica*. Perfumes called *Through the Looking-Glass*, *The Kama Sutra*, *Against Nature*, *The Art of War*, *The Diary of a Young Girl*, *To Serve Man*, et cetera, et cetera. Perfumes and atomizers and huffing stations with sleek plastic inhalers that you taste the text with, in little translinear synaesthetic excerpts. And kiosks that flaunt a gas mask-shaped device called The Voynich Huffmaster. Everyone is wearing them, it seems.

Books you can breathe, experienced and mostly forgotten in the time it takes to smoke a cigarette.

But oh, how library bits still cling to the evening breeze.

I wake up twisted and wistful with an abrasive case of deja vu, remembering the first time I dreamed this, before it all came true.

The Mind-Body Problem

Susan DeFreitas

I was eighteen, a freshman at Reed College, when I discovered a book that almost certainly does not exist. This occurred one night in the library, a three-story Gothic Tudor built in the style of the Ivies, which stayed open around the clock for the benefit of both the hard-partying slacker and the scrupulous crammer.

In my first semester, I was a bit of both. Though I'd sailed through high school AP and honors, it had become clear to me within my first few weeks at Reed—as I imagine it had to a few others—that though I'd been among the top students in that podunk town from which I'd sprung, I was most likely the stupidest person in my incoming class. I was working harder than I ever had, for what seemed like barely passing marks (it was difficult to tell, as we were not provided with grades, only written comments). And yet here I was, throwing back shots of Jäger in my dorm at McKinley and then traipsing off through the woods and over the bridge to write this paper, which was due the next morning at ten.

The interior of the library was modern, spacious, and tastefully lit, but it always felt a bit spooky at night. Those who worked the graveyard shift were elusive creatures; I never caught more than a glimpse of them among the warren of back rooms. And though I seldom encountered fellow patrons at this hour, no matter where in the library I happened to be, I could always hear the automatic doors of the main entrance whisking open and swooshing shut, as if admitting ghosts.

I was there to write a paper on something called the Mind-Body Problem, first posed by René Descartes, the basic gist of which was something like *How can the physical processes of the body give rise to the nonphysical thing known as the mind?* Over the last few days I'd amassed a pile of library books on the subject, looking for an answer. Instead, I had begun to suspect that I didn't even really understand the question. Weren't some things just unknowable? Like the chicken or the egg or the tree when it falls? Or was I just too dumb to see what the big deal was?

This was for Metaphysics, a class I'd taken because I was then, as I am now, prone to mysticism—though the only reason Reed allows freshmen to take this course, as far as I can tell, is to cure them of such afflictions quickly. There had been no prerequisites, but the professor lectured as if we were all well versed in the major issues in philosophy. The one time I'd dared to raise my hand in class, it had nearly been shot off at the wrist.

If it hadn't been for Cam, with whom I shared both Metaphysics and Chinese, I never would have survived that first semester. Cam seemed to grasp, intuitively, that philosophy was no more than a game; it was all about choosing the smallest argument possible, one you could win. Whereas I could not help but actually engage with the big questions and seek to solve them—the same questions that had constituted the life's work of many individuals far smarter than I and had, in the process, driven many of them insane.

I was stranded in an aisle between philosophy and history, somewhere between D and H—I was done with Descartes and headed for Hume, who I thought somehow might help me—when I caught some movement out of the corner of my eye. The proximity in so large a building was startling; whoever had been standing there a moment before could not have been more than twenty feet away.

But I heard nothing—not the softest stirring of breath, not the barest whisper of pages. Only the thrumming of the rain outside and, after a moment, the building's mechanical systems kicking in.

Clearing my throat, I stepped into the 900 row of Ancient Greece; I did not want to startle this person, the way they'd startled me. But when I reached the end of the row, I looked ahead, behind—nothing.

Perhaps whoever it was had simply slipped behind the next row down. And yet I was struck then by an irrational sense of being hunted, haunted.

Among the books along the west wall, I glimpsed the spine of a hardcover, edged in gilt: *Split at the Root: The Paradox at the Heart of Western Thought.*

It seemed oddly light for a book so large. There was no author or editor—no title page, publisher, or table of contents, no endnotes or acknowledgments. This book, it seemed, had been written by no one.

Intrigued, I opened it randomly—and there, in a paragraph halfway down the page, found a precisely worded argument explaining everything I'd felt but could not begin to express while reading and rereading Descartes.

That vague sense of panic I'd been operating under gave way, in a rush, to relief. It wasn't that I was dumb. It was that nobody knew what the mind even was, and trying to figure it out by thinking about it was like trying to study a telescope with a telescope, a microscope with a microscope; it was like turning one mirror to face another. It was like Russell's paradox: *Does the set of all sets that do not contain themselves contain itself?* The answer might as well have been, *Who the fuck cares?* It was an apparently meaningful question that was ultimately meaningless.

I finished my paper around dawn, when the rain finally let up and the automatic doors downstairs began swooshing in earnest. I spent another two hours proofing and then finally stepped outside, feeling impossibly light, like I was floating, cushioned from any actual impact with the earth.

I had some time before class, so I stopped off at the campus cafe—grinning, I'm sure, like an idiot. The green-haired girl at the counter with the koi fish tattoo returned my smile with a flat, dull stare. I did not care. I'd discovered something that I knew in a deep-ly personal way to be true. Something perhaps none of those ghosts who haunted the library, in all their years among the living, had ever arrived at.

I ordered coffee and a poppyseed muffin—it occurred to me that I hadn't eaten since lunch the day before. And yet, so preoccu-pied was I by the night's revelations that I sailed right back out the door and was halfway to class before I realized that I'd forgotten my muffin on the counter beside the cream and sugar.

Cam was sitting in the back of the lecture hall when I arrived. He was a strictly white-T-shirt type of guy, his brown hair buzzed, sprawled out of his chair with its fold-down desk. I slid in sound-lessly beside him, and without looking at me, he laid his arm the length of the armrest between us.

He was holding an origami swan the size of a matchbox.

Cam cast me a glance—those dark eyes, long lashed. He looked like I did, probably. Like he'd been up all night, subject to revela-tion. The tips of his fingers were stained purple.

I took the swan delicately by one wing, folded down the writing surface of my own seat, and set it down lightly before me. The pro-fessor down there at the lectern might as well have been a broad-cast from Alpha Centauri.

On this very small piece of paper, Cam had written a series of very small Chinese characters. I cast him a glance; he nodded. Carefully, I unfolded the swan. On one side, it read, in Mandarin, *elegant brightness*—my name, Shana, transliterated. On the other side, in English: *Meet me in the amphitheater at the end of class.*

And with that, Cam slipped out of his seat and through the doors.

Perhaps the most central feature of the Reed campus is the great depression that runs through its midst, cut by a spring that pools at one end to form a lake and chokes off at the other, losing itself in a sodden bog. Spanned by the bridge I crossed each day on my way to class—and from which, it was rumored, more than a few students had jumped—it was known as the canyon.

I found Cam standing on the bluff beside it after class, in the trees around the back of the amphitheater. And he must have said something, must have done something other than shift his hands in the pockets of his jeans and lean into my shoulder, the way he did. But Cam and I had been friends since the moment we'd met, and we seemed to communicate, for the most part, telepathically.

In high school, we'd both been the bad kids who got good grades, part of a tight, ethnically mixed crew. We had the same stance when we stood—back straight, feet just past hip distance apart—the same slight swagger when we walked. We held ourselves that way not only because that's what it took to command respect in the subcultures of which we'd been a part but also because we considered ourselves more mature than the freshmen with whom we'd matriculated—those sheltered children who'd never so much as smoked a jay before they'd fledged and did not know how to handle hard drugs at all. The trick, we agreed (again, perhaps telepathically), was to always have a point where you drew the line, no matter your state of mind.

This was the extent of our overlap. I hailed from halfway between Philly and Pittsburgh; my father was a lawyer, my mother a teacher; and though I'd rebelled in high school, college had always been a foregone conclusion for me. Cam had been raised in Houston by his mother, a waitress, and could not remember anything about his life before the age of twelve, the year his parents had divorced. He was the only person I knew attending Reed on a full scholarship, and he'd had no help whatsoever in filling out the paperwork.

I followed him down the footpath in its long switchbacks, through the salmonberry and blackberry that grew close by the water; hopped with him from rock to rock through the creek as frogs dropped into the water before us in great plunging gulps; followed him through passages I would otherwise have considered impassable. I would have followed him anywhere.

It resembled nothing more than a pile of brush from the back. But from the front it was clearly a shelter, constructed of downed wood woven together with vines. Beneath the cunning curve of its arch were three large stones—a makeshift table and two chairs—as well as a small fire pit. A barbecue grate and cast-iron teakettle sat beside it in the dirt.

Cam, of course, had made this place. What did I think he'd been doing during Metaphysics these last few weeks? He knelt beside the fire pit, filled the kettle with water from a bottle in his backpack, and before long, had a fire going. He set the grate and the kettle upon it.

I took a seat at the table and examined Cam's calligraphy brush. Like me, he had a general fascination with all things Asian; unlike me, he'd mastered one exotic discipline after another, from origami to ikebana. Carefully, I set the brush back down beside the blue ceramic dish, filled with ink. A thin film had formed upon the surface of the liquid, so purple it was almost black.

"It's the juice of this berry I found. And look." Cam reached around the side of the shelter and plucked a few leaves from the weeds there. "Wild mint."

I looked away. The shelter he had constructed in the heart of the canyon; the leaves he'd dropped into that hot little pot, steaming, and above, its curl of smoke; Cam's fingers, stained with the berries he'd found, from which he'd made this ink—it was all too beautiful, too much.

He pulled two tiny cups from his backpack, set them on the stone table, and poured carefully from the kettle, using his T-shirt to protect his hand from its heat. I could not help but stare at the naked curve of his belly. We were built the same way, Cam and I; we practically had the same hands.

Then he reached back into his backpack and withdrew a cardboard tube. Slowly, he worked the roll of paper loose from inside and unrolled it. The paper was handmade, I could see, embedded with pink and yellow petals. On it, he'd written a series of Mandarin characters.

My sleep-deprived brain translated the characters as *the broken root ponders the rose*. The broken root, *Split at the Root*—it seemed too close for coincidence. Had Cam found it, too, that strange book with no author, in the library the night before? Was he, perhaps, the fleeting figure I'd glimpsed?

I looked into his eyes but found I could not speak, transfixed by the beauty of his gaze. But then Cam asked, "Do you think she'll like it?"

I blinked and looked back down at the characters. They were, in fact, a transliteration of a name. One I recognized with resignation.

And here at last was the central thing between me and Cam, the heart of it and the hurt of it, unspoken like everything else. Which was that I was in love with him, and he, like any number of others, was in love with Sarah Lynn Rose.

Sarah Lynn Rose, who would never understand the way that he had made this for her, sitting like a monk amidst the drizzle of this dank bog. Though Professor Chin praised the effortless, loose quality of Cam's calligraphy, I knew he must have practiced for hours to produce this one perfect page.

Nor would she care if Cam told her. Aloof, almost *aloft*, Sarah Lynn Rose was wholly untouchable, which was why boys like him threw themselves at her. Whatever had been done to him as a child in that blessed blankness of memory he now seemed intent on doing to himself.

"She'll love it," I lied, but it didn't feel like lying. Because I was pretending it was my name he'd written there.

We sat sipping from our tiny teacups, and he told me about a party that night at the old dorm block; our boy Alex would be there—I should come. I nodded, thinking about the bridge across the canyon from which those rumored students had jumped. Had they been driven to it by heartache, the weight of it? As Cam spoke, I could feel myself sinking into the stone upon which I sat, which was itself sinking slowly into the bog.

I wondered, how would it feel to climb up onto the railing of that bridge at night, to look down into the darkness? How would it feel for that one brief instant to be released from any contact with the earth?

These were the same sort of thoughts, I knew, that came to Cam sometimes when he thought of Sarah Lynn Rose. What would he do when at last she told him clearly, to his face? Alex and I wondered, and worried, though Alex was no better—I caught him watching her sometimes when she walked down the hall. Sarah Lynn Rose, the stone cold queen, against whom broken boys hurled themselves.

In my dorm that night, I stood before the mirror. We shared the same long, dark hair, Sarah Lynn and I, the same petite frame. And maybe she had a slightly bigger bust; maybe I had darker skin. Regardless, the only real difference between us physically, as far as I could tell, was in the way that we presented.

Sarah Lynn Rose wore soft, low-cut sweaters and jeans that hugged her curves; I had never seen her without makeup. As the daughter of a feminist, I fancied myself one as well, and thus had always considered such trappings of patriarchy beneath me. But the truth was that, at eighteen, drawing that kind of attention to my body simply did not feel safe.

That was why I wore baggy jeans and T-shirts like a boy. That was why I moved like the guys in my crew from high school. Because I wanted people to pay attention to what I had to say, not to the way I looked. To me, there was nothing creepier than some old dude checking me out, and even the sexual attentions of young men I considered dumb or in any way douchey felt intolerable to me.

Sarah Lynn was not stupid—really, nobody at this school was. So how did she take it? How did she manage to assert her intelligence, her mind, even as she dressed in a way that attracted so much attention to her body?

In the end, I dug out my tiniest T-shirt—a relic of childhood—and pinned my hair atop my head in a half-assed approximation of an updo. Then proceeded to ruin the whole thing by pulling on my old hoodie as I set off into the night.

Brick and stone, possessed of imposing arches and heavy doors, the old dorm block is a classic college building, the stuff of glossy brochures. Gargoyles hang from its eaves, with various strange faces stamped into the concrete at their feet; an impressively large stone owl, famous for migrating from dorm to dorm, perches upon its roof.

I walked through those heavy doors and then stopped, face to face with a message board announcing a change in the monthly meeting of the college pagan society. I realized I was just a bit dizzy—faint, even. The pizza and salad I'd had for dinner, which had also been lunch and breakfast (unless you counted the coffee), were sitting strangely, as had most of what I'd eaten of late, and I still had yet to sleep. I wondered for a moment if I would be sick.

But then someone laughed and the moment passed. To my right, in a large room full of latticed windows, a group had gathered. I affected a bold stroll and approached. "Hey," I said. "You guys know Cam?"

A young fellow in a fedora looked over at someone I couldn't see. He smiled. "Of course we know Cam."

He introduced himself as Arias and made space for me beside him on the debauched couch. A magnificent old beast upholstered in red velvet, it looked as if generations of poets had spilled cheap wine, fucked, and passed out upon it.

Before I had a chance to introduce myself, Arias, nattily dressed in that corduroy vest, had lit up at something his friend had said. This was a young man with long blond hair, sprawled in princely fashion upon a love seat, another antique, over which he'd draped an actual, perhaps unironic, cape.

I turned back to Arias, but then the scantily clad girl at his feet lifted an earthenware jug my way. "Mead?" she said. She wore on her head what struck me at first as a necklace; the red gem winked at me.

I lifted the jug and took a sniff—it smelled of psilocybin. I politely declined and passed it on down the line. If I was going to spend the night tripping, I wanted to be in the woods with Cam, not in Gargoyle Hall with this crew.

"How do you know Cam?" Arias asked me before I could ask him.

Someone handed me a goblet—an actual goblet—of wine. It smelled like your basic rotgut, so I took a cautious sip. "I met him in Metaphysics."

Arias laughed, and his friend in the cape laughed, and the girl with the gem on her head did, too, as if I'd said something witty. I took another swallow of the wine, which bordered on balsamic, hoping this would disguise my blush.

"Are you cold?" The girl reached up to touch my knee, smiling, twinkling prettily.

I cast a glance at Arias, who was leaning forward now, one hand on her shoulder. "Take off your coat," he said. "Make yourself comfortable."

I glanced back and forth between them, suddenly uncertain. Were they together? Were they not? Though the way I'd done my hair probably did look stupid with that old hoodie. And the girl was right: it was hot in this room, as if perhaps twice as many people were present. I set my goblet on the floor and worked my way out of my outer garment.

When at last I set it aside, the energy in the room had shifted. Everyone seemed to be staring at me in that too-tight T-shirt, smiling suggestively, showing teeth. A cold sweat prickled my skin, and I could feel my stomach rumble.

I distracted myself by focusing on my hair, which had totally come undone. I started pulling out bobby pins, intent on abandoning all that fussy scaffolding, but then the girl who'd been sitting on the floor was sitting on the couch beside me, nimbly plucking pins and rearranging my hair, her fingers light, as if birds were making a nest on my head. And now there was another girl stationed at Arias's feet, a redhead with a Prince Valiant pageboy; she had taken up my goblet and set her red lips upon it, gazing up at me seductively. All three of them were leaning into me now; I could feel their body heat. The young man in the cape across the room made some sort of sign with his hand, as if casually, though it was clearly intentional. Once again, I felt faint.

I stood and announced that I had to use the bathroom.

I found Alex in the hallway. "Hey," he said, "Shana." He smelled like a cross between wet wool and an ashtray that had been left out in the rain. I didn't care. I was so relieved to see the big guy that I leaned right through from the handshake and the grip and the snap and the fist bump to a half hug.

"Come on up," he said, speaking to my chest. "You look great."

I ignored this, following him up the stairs. He asked what I'd been doing down there. I tilted my head toward the room from which I'd come. "Just hanging out with some assholes playing mind games. You?"

He laughed a little, the way he did, soundlessly. "Chillin'." Dude looked as stoned as Snoop Dogg.

The real party—the party I'd been trying to get to—was in the common room of the third floor. The higher we ascended, the louder it became. Alex led me through the crowd to a keg in the corner, where a kid in a trucker cap and a cardigan was pulling a hit off a bong. Alex explained that the resident director on duty had last been sighted in the Crystal Springs Rhododendron Garden across the street, attempting to communicate with rodents of unusual size, and was almost certainly not returning to active duty tonight.

I settled into one of the couches, and Alex popped a squat on a spotty ottoman. When he asked what I'd been up to, my first impulse was to find a way to segue into Cam. But that didn't quite seem fair. "Shit," I said. "You know." I laid my head back and took a sip of my beer, which tasted like Dead Guy. "I didn't get to sleep last night."

Alex shook his head, like he was watching a feather drift back and forth. "Me neither," he said. "I spent all night in the library."

I shot him a look as I took a sip, wondering what my face betrayed over that red plastic cup. More than I'd intended, apparently, because he smiled. "You found it, too." Alex's eyes were soft and dark, mysterious. "The book. Something about *paradox* in the title."

Now I was staring at him. Could he have been the ghost I'd glimpsed, the one who'd disappeared down the 900 aisle of Ancient Greece? It did not seem possible, in part because Alex was such a large person—six-foot-something and probably 250 pounds. As far as I knew, he never did anything quietly; even his breathing was loud.

I took a pull of my beer. "How do you know about that book?"

"I thought it was just a story. Some senior told me about it at the bonfire before orientation."

I leaned in closer. "What did they tell you? What's the story?"

Alex looked off, his dark eyes at half mast under his dark lashes. He was half Latino—from Texas like Cam, and like Cam he had a beautiful face. But the way he moved bespoke a sorrow born of a long string of disappointments. Cam had it, too, in his way, that almost feminine melancholy. But for some reason, I found it attractive in Cam—it made me want to save him. Whatever Alex had made me want to save myself.

"You don't want to know."

"Try me."

He looked at me out of the corner of his eye. "It's kind of freaky."

I downed the remainder of my beer. "Come on, *puto*."

He laughed at that, a soft exhale. "All right, so . . ." He looked off for a moment at the group that had gathered on the couch opposite us, leaning over what looked like a magazine spread. "It's like, supposedly . . ."

"Supposedly what?" They weren't reading a magazine, I realized—those people were breaking up coke on a mirror. I watched as, one by one, they did a line and then looked up at the ceiling, sniffing and blinking.

"Something people see before they die. Or, like, if they're in danger. If they've been marked."

I pulled at the cap sleeves of my little girl's shirt, feeling chilled. Alex noticed the gesture, and as I watched, his eyes settled for a moment on my belly, which showed above my jeans. I asked, "Marked by what?"

"That's the question, right?"

When I looked away, I could still feel him watching me, his eyes on my body. "Jesus," I said. "What is that thing?" It didn't seem quite accurate at that point to call it a book.

Alex was quiet a moment, even as everyone else at the party cracked up at the punchline to some torturously long math joke. Someone had put on Tom Waits, and over his gravelly voice, Alex leaned close to my ear. "The guy who told me about it had this theory. Like, maybe it's just some sort of meme, like a computer virus, that lives here. It doesn't mean any harm; it's just sort of a pattern that's acquired a life of its own—this book that people hallucinate when they go to school here. Dude was talking about Rupert Sheldrake and the morphogenetic field, about memories stored in physical structures like architecture, certain trees. Some crazy shit like that."

I felt momentarily paralyzed, pinned by both the big man's physical proximity, leaning in close to me like that, and the image that had appeared in my mind's eye, which seemed infinitely more convincing than anything Alex had just described—some ancient monster of the mind, which fed on those who jumped into the canyon, and who, like the anglerfish that trawls the deepest, darkest, most airless depths, consists essentially of just two things: a bright, shiny lure and a great, gaping mouth.

"You know what I think?" Alex's voice was soft.

I closed my eyes and opened them again, trying hard not to focus on his body, the bulk of it. Trying to focus on his dark eyes, his fine face. I could feel his need for me, his longing, and I wanted very much at that moment not to be another source of disappointment in Alex's life.

"I think that book is every book. It's a warning." He lifted his hand vaguely, indicating perhaps the contents of the room, the campus, or the cosmos. "Not to, like, fucking . . ." He cleared his throat. "It's about what happens when you forget . . ." Here his thoughts seemed to trail off, lost in the thicket of his synapses. I remember wondering, for the first time, if he was more than stoned. And then his mouth was on my mouth, and it was so wrong, no matter how much I wanted it to be right—it felt like the time I'd tried to jump-start my car with the polarities reversed. I shot up out of my seat.

The worst part was, Alex didn't even look surprised. He looked as if other girls like me—skinny girls, the only kind he fell for—had responded in pretty much the same way. I told him I was feeling ill. And though I didn't have to look at him to know he didn't believe me, at that moment, it was true.

There was a bathroom through those big double doors and downstairs, down the hall from the classrooms where I sometimes had seminar. I found it and pushed into a stall—as it turned out, just in time. After my stomach had rid itself of its contents, I felt better but also dismayed, forced to flush away everything of any consequence I'd had to eat that day.

I sat there a while, the bird's nest of my head in my hands. Ever since I'd come to this school, I'd had this feeling, like I couldn't connect with anyone. Except for Cam, who'd felt from the first like an old friend, a kind of shadow or second self. Where was he?

When I stood, finally, and unlatched the door, Sarah Lynn Rose was fixing her makeup in the mirror.

"Oh, hey," I said, all fake cheer as I stepped to a faucet.

She favored me with a half smile. "Hey yourself. Having fun?"

I shrugged, wondering what, exactly, she meant by that. "You check out that party in the commons?"

"It's Tuesday."

I just blinked. Like, what did that have to do with anything?

"Wilder and I were trying to study."

Wilder, the lanky blond in our class—so that was who, among the multitudes, she'd chosen. The rest she'd simply dismissed, as if their longing had nothing to do with her, despite the kind of clothes she wore: that fitted V-neck that drew the eye, inexorably, to her breasts, those slacks that hugged her ass.

At eighteen, Sarah Lynn Rose was the sort of girl who was already a woman, an East Coast sort of type A who'd no doubt go on to law school, make partner before thirty, and for fun, master Brazilian jiu jitsu. Even her feminism, in a way, was better developed than mine; she seemed to understand, at least, that the strange action her body exerted on others at a distance was not necessarily her responsibility.

I stood there at the sink, hating her, even as I kept on smiling. In part because I could sense that she did not necessarily hate me. Like my best friend, the boy I loved, I was simply, for the most part, beneath her notice.

I cleared my throat softly, hoping to come off casual. "Any chance you've seen Cam?"

And for just that moment, the eyes of the idol softened. "Shana."

I had that light, bright, dangerous feeling again. Like I was floating.

"Cam is with Alex, shooting heroin in his room. And you?" Sarah Lynn stepped toward me and took hold of my wrist—the way an owl might take hold of a mouse—and lifted it up between us. "You need to *eat*."

I stood there for a moment after she walked out. Then turned and moved slowly to the spot where she'd stood by the sink when I'd come in, applying lipstick. I touched my fingers to my lips—those lips that Alex had kissed—imagining them stained purple, poisonous, and as I did, a long succession of slender, dark-haired girls did the same; in this part of the bathroom, two mirrors faced off, creating an endlessly receding hall of mirrors, that monstrosity of infinities. For one long moment I felt myself pinned there, as if under the gaze of some immense, heartless beast that had already claimed a long line of people very much like me.

I remember the night after Alex died, I walked the campus long past midnight. At some point, I found myself standing in front of the library. The Gothic arches of its windows were lit up, glowing warmly. I was thinking about Alex, what he had said about that book. That it was all books. That it was a warning.

A young woman passed before a window on the third floor and then returned to stand there, framed in it, as if peering out into the dark, and for a moment I could feel it, clearly: what it was like to be dead, to look in on the living.

I felt it more than heard it pass overhead, like the barest of breaths—like the whisper of pages as they turn. An owl sat perched upon the spine of the library, a dark silhouette against the night-blue sky. And then, like a memory, like the mind's own shadow, it melted away into the night.

The Color Off the Shelf

Karen Munro

The Powell's City of Books website said that the book Malcolm wanted was in "Deep Storage." He texted himself a note and closed his laptop.

This book . . . it was a distraction, a guilty pleasure. Self-destructive and gross, like biting his fingernails to the quick. He wasn't even sure he had the citation right—he'd built it from scraps and mentions across the internet. He should let it go. Get some work done. His mother would ask what was the matter with him.

He took a walk around his apartment, pausing to look out the big picture window. The sky was that heavy Portland white that hurt the eyes, big rain clouds reflecting sunlight and at the same time glooming up the whole city. He put his hand on the glass and studied the darkness of his skin against the clouds.

His laptop was waiting. He sat and stared at the blank screen beneath the title of his dissertation. *Badder Dan Nat: African American Traditions of Toasting and Boasting*. A couple of centuries of African American rhetorical ingenuity, a mixture of self-affirmation and defiance and bragging and satire in the face of white supremacy—that's all he was trying to summarize. A gumbo of folktale, adventure story, and canny insults delivered right under the nose of The Man. A handhold on humanity, on dignity. Just that. Nothing too hard about that.

The cursor blinked. He had two full chapters, and a third that petered out halfway through. Another three due by the end of the month. An insane deadline, but his own fault, really. He'd spent weeks playing Minecraft and looking up weird old books on the internet.

Do the work, he told himself. *Do it.*

He clapped the laptop closed and stood up, reaching for his keys. *Go for a walk*, his mother would tell him, when he got like this.

At the Powell's information desk, the clerk studied Malcolm's phone.

"It says Deep Storage," Malcolm said. "What does that mean?"

"It's . . . unusual," the guy said.

"Is it in the warehouse?"

"No." The clerk turned to his computer and typed. "Anthropology is in the Red Room, on the second floor."

"But this isn't in the Red Room."

"Our rare books are in the Pearl Room—"

"It's not in the Pearl Room. It says 'Deep Storage.' That's not even a color. I thought all the rooms had colors."

The guy gave him a sideways glance, then fished a key from his pocket and opened a small drawer. He thrust a folded paper at Malcolm. "Here's a map."

Malcolm took it gingerly. It wasn't like the stack of store maps sitting on the counter. The paper was crisp and yellow with age.

"Good luck," the clerk said, turning away as if Malcolm were already gone.

Malcolm took the stairs to the mezzanine, then unfolded the map. The image was fuzzy, but it seemed to show a set of stairs descending from the middle of the mezzanine, overlooking the Rose Room. He'd never noticed a staircase there.

He made his way past the racks of remaindered paperbacks,

past the blank journals, and straight past a wooden door that he only noticed at the last moment. He doubled back. On the door was mounted a small metal sign. DEEP STORAGE.

Malcolm tested the doorknob, expecting it to be locked. But it opened—a little stiffly, as if it weren't used very often—and he found himself staring down a long, narrow staircase. Overhead swung a single bare light bulb. At the bottom of the stairs was deep gloom.

His first thought was, *This has got to be grandfathered*. No one could build a staircase like this anymore, with what seemed like a thousand concrete steps plummeting straight down, no landings or railings, into darkness. But then he remembered the infamous Powell's parking garage, with its vertiginous, single-car-width ramp. This was an old building.

He stepped over the threshold and the door swung closed behind him with a click that jacked his heart rate a little. He put out his hands to touch the walls, and discovered he was no longer holding the map. It wasn't in his pocket, or on the stairs. The stairs yawned below him. He thought, *The hell with the map*. If he wasn't careful he was going to miss a step and turn a cartwheel in midair. Land at the bottom in a heap of broken bones.

And there was something strange about the light in here. The single bare bulb hanging at the top of the stairs—OSHA would have a fit—somehow made the walls look tilted. He pressed his fingers into the walls and for a second every dingy surface seemed to lift up and hover. The concrete stairs, the damp-streaked walls— all the colors looked false and weird, superimposed. He shook his head and it cleared. He hesitated, then started down.

What was he doing? He couldn't even remember the title of the book. It was just one more racist nineteenth-century textbook, and he'd read a hundred of them. He needed it like he needed a hole in the head. He should turn around and go home. Sit down at his laptop and write his damn dissertation.

The thought of that—the white screen, the blinking cursor— made his palms sweat.

He cleared his throat.

"Shine was downstairs eating his peas," he began. His favorite toast, the ballad of "Shine and the Titanic." The wily, smart black man escaping the white man's shipwreck. The walls of the staircase seemed to be getting narrower, and he needed to concentrate on something. At first his arms had been almost fully extended—now they were bent at the elbow like chicken wings. A sour smell curled up the stairs to meet him.

"When the goddamned water come up to his knees." The staircase had an angle to it, he was sure. A kind of disorienting cant, as if a giant finger had flicked it from one side.

"The captain said, 'Shine, set your black self down.'" He paused and looked back. Behind him, the stairs soared like a sheer wall. Inconceivably distant and far above was the little wooden door he'd come through. He swallowed. "'I got ninety-nine pumps to pump the water down.'"

He was being ridiculous. It was just an old staircase in an old building. They wouldn't let people down here if it wasn't safe.

And if he went home, the blank white screen would be there. Waiting.

He started down again, squinting at the weird shadows in the corners of the stairs. "Shine went downstairs, he ate a piece of bread."

He could see the bottom now. It was just a dirty concrete floor with a crooked doorway, but it gave him a kind of comfort. "That's when the water came above his head."

There was no door in the frame—it was just an empty rectangle. Beyond the threshold was darkness.

"The captain said, 'Shine, set your black self down. I got ninety-nine pumps . . .'" He eased forward, craning his neck to see what was down there, through the open doorway. A long hallway, lit by a faint colorless light at the end. ". . . 'to pump the water down.'"

Behind him, the staircase was a ziggurat. Impossible to climb. His breath came fast and shallow. He caught it and held it. *This is a bad idea*. He went through the doorway and started down the hall.

At the end of the hall was another threshold, lit only by a bare bulb hanging in inestimable darkness. A wooden door, standing wide. On the other side was a small room containing a bookshelf. Nothing else. He stood in the doorway, looked up, and saw no end to the thing—just shelves rising into night. Every shelf was packed with rows and rows of ancient tomes, their spines faded and crumbling. For a second everything reversed, and he was staring down into a bottomless pit. His stomach lurched.

Then the world was right-side up again. As if watching someone else do it, he reached out and took a book from the shelf. It slipped easily into his hand.

He hardly glanced at the book itself. Instead he stared at the space it left behind. That space, the narrow rectangle left between the books on either side, wasn't dark. It was something else, some weird unaccountable non-color that hurt his eyes. As he watched, it started to leak. It seemed to curl out of the space, a tentacle reaching for the floor. Then reaching for him.

Malcolm turned and ran.

The stairs were an endless scramble that seemed to rotate around him. He leapt from one to the next, like a sailor climbing rigging in a storm. Every step was enormous. Behind him was that color, that non-color, reaching up from below to wrap him up and drag him back.

There was a roaring in his ears, like water rushing through a hole, like the sound of a ship sinking. If he stopped running he'd drown in this stairwell.

And then the top of the stairs was right there above him, the door handle under his hand, and he burst through it onto the mezzanine, between the blank journals and the magazines.

He stood heaving for air. A woman glanced at him—white, nice coat, a Sur la Table bag at her feet and a Jane Smiley remainder in her hand. He tried to catch his breath. *Black man freaking out in the Rose Room.*

Something clicked behind him, and the roaring in his ears cut out. The door, closing on its spring.

He stared at it, at the little metal sign nailed to its face. DEEP STORAGE.

He didn't know if the book in his hand—heavier now, a little clammy, its cover faded to indistinguishability—was the one he'd come for. But he knew it was his.

The blank space between the books gaped wider. Tendrils of non-color curled from it, reaching for the floor. Then reaching for him. That sour, colorless arm seeping out of the case, extruded by some vast crushing pressure inside. Reaching for him.

Malcolm shook himself and stood up. His apartment was small but it faced south on the fourth floor, and had good light all day. He went to the picture window and wiped at the glass. His fingers came away clean. Still, the place seemed dark. His laptop, open on his desk, was dim. The screen was hard to read—or it would have been if he'd written anything, which he hadn't.

Standing at the window, he studied the faint blue lines of the southwest hills. The sky above them was dense and low.

When he turned back, the new book—*old book*, his brain whispered—lay open on the desk. He must have left it that way.

A passage caught his eye.

The grown up Negro partakes, as regards his intellectual faculties, of the nature of the child, the female, and the senile White . . .

It was so familiar it put a bitter smile on his face. The book was no different from any of hundreds he'd read before. Its nameless author was just another sad, officious ghost of Vogt or Haeckel or Gleisberg or Pruner, marching around the world with head pincers and measuring tape, handing out sheaves of defamatory photos and sketches. Trumpeting that same tunnel-vision view of the world. A hundred and fifty years ago, these guys had been large and in charge. And now what were they?

The first time he'd come across a book like this he was just a kid, poking around his mother's research library. It stunned him. Savages and idiots? Semi-apes? Who were these guys talking about? About his mother, who taught graduate literature courses at Penn State? Who hosted dinner parties that went into the early morning, with grad students and profs and actors and artists all reading roles in dog-eared copies of *The Tempest* and *Angels in America*?

Or were they talking about his father, who'd spent his last ten years of Saturday mornings teaching art to kids in juvie? Whose desk at home was piled with thank-you letters and photos of smiling young men with teardrop tattoos, holding babies and diplomas?

The book on his mother's shelf was crumbling to pieces. When he put it down, it left smudges of rot on his fingers.

He knew his history. The history of his country, and of his own family. Despite that, the book shocked him.

And at the same time, it gripped him. It called him back. He snuck it from his mother's office and read it at night, alone, masticating its sour notions and savoring the weird, addictive aftertaste they left behind. It gave him nightmares of lying at the bottom of an immense, lightless ocean, a huge weight pressing him into the muck. It made him angry and sorry and wired-up, like an addict.

At college he studied literature, then sidestepped into historical anthropology. That was where this stuff lived, what they called "scientific racism." Reading it was like eating sweet acid. He could feel it gnawing away at him from inside, but he couldn't stop going back for more.

When he crossed the stage for his master's diploma, he was ten pounds underweight. His teeth ached and he couldn't sleep. There was a constant ringing in his ears. His mother took him aside, held both his hands in hers, and said, *Honey, what is the matter with you?* He told her about the books, and she looked at him for a long moment, then suggested another field. Something less pessimistic. Less masochistic.

And so he sidestepped again, into African American toasts and boasts. "Shine and the Titanic," "Stagger Lee," "The Signifying Monkey." The long tradition of black backtalk and truth-telling, ingenuity and bravado and soul-preserving swagger. And damn if he didn't feel better.

Damn if he didn't still feel the urge to scratch that itch and bite that hangnail. To check up on those old head-measuring racist fucks. To see the world through their weird, warped eyes.

The words still came back to him from time to time, as if he'd memorized them without meaning to. Standing in his own kitchen, beside his own stack of books, he heard them again.

We may boldly assert that the whole race has, neither in the past nor in the present, performed anything tending to the progress of humanity or worthy of preservation.

"You got ninety-nine pumps," he said out loud. "Boy, do you."

He ran his finger over the page, then pushed the book to the floor. It hit with a bang like a gunshot.

The shelves went up forever, through the subterranean ceilings of the basement room, through floor after floor of paper tonnage, through the pigeon-crapped and cobwebbed rafters and through the cold night sky and into the inky darkness of outer space. Every shelf packed with books, every book stuffed with words. Every word stamped in a heavy, irrepressible color that was like nothing he'd ever seen. A color that was sour and dry, that knuckled down on itself, line after line, the same words writing themselves over and over until they came to the end of the page and began to leak off, curling onto the floor, reaching for his feet.

Thick-tongued, dry-mouthed, Malcolm blinked at his bedroom ceiling. It was nearly dark. There was a weight on his chest. The book. He picked it up. The cover was clammy and cool in his hand. It was bound in human skin, he thought. Of course it was. But what color?

After fumbling on the bedside light and drinking a glass of water and pacing in front of the picture window under the low evening sky, he checked the time. Eight o'clock. He was wired. He cracked his knuckles, airboxed a little in front of the mirror. Spat in the kitchen sink, then ran a blast of water down it, disgusted at himself. *Go for a walk*, his mother would tell him.

He slung on a jacket and went.

He was in the Orange Room before he realized it. And he had the book in his hand. Had he brought it with him? He didn't remember, but here it was, like a corpse's hand clasped in his. There were smudges of brown book rot on his fingertips.

The lights seemed dim, the edges of everything seemed fuzzy. Every person in here—the cashiers, the customers—was white. Portland.

He stumbled down the steps and up to the nearest cashier. His legs didn't seem to be working right. He heard his mother just behind his ear: *Honey, what is the matter with you?*

"Can I help you?" The clerk was a stubbled guy with wooden ear gauges. Malcolm tossed the book onto the desk.

"I want to return this." The idea presented itself simply, on a wave of relief. He didn't have to own this thing. He could give it back and get it out of his apartment. He didn't need it. He'd read this shit a hundred times before. It was a bad habit. And he had a dissertation to write.

The clerk lifted the book's cover and peeked inside. "Do you have a receipt?"

In his wallet, wadded up with a few bills and parking tickets—no, not there. Not in his pockets. How had he paid for it? He couldn't remember.

The book was sinking into the counter between them. The wood starting to bend around it, to warp downward. Like a hot brick melting into snow, but it was the whole world melting beneath the book, dripping down into a hole that wasn't black or white, exactly. It was that sour, bleak, familiar color he couldn't quite place, and it was dragging him down with it.

"I'm sorry," the clerk said. "Are you sure you bought it here?"

The book was on the counter again, dog-eared and dusty.

"It was in storage," Malcolm said. His throat was dry. "In the basement."

"We don't have any basement storage."

"It was on a shelf—" Malcolm turned to look across the Orange Room, toward the stairs that led up to Blue and Gold. For a moment everything looked off—gray and flat. No, not gray. A weird, darkish white. That knuckled-down color he'd seen in the basement that was both strange and familiar at the same time.

"I'm sorry." The clerk was side-eyeing him now. "I don't think that's our book."

"Oh, it's your book all right." Malcolm swiped it off the counter. His head pulsed. Optical illusions, hallucinations—was he having a stroke? A psychotic break? "I just bought it here *this morning*."

A moment of stillness, the clerk's face frozen. *Black man shouting*. He hadn't meant to shout. He was just tired, and his brain felt sticky, and the book had his hand in a grotesque clinch.

"Sorry." He backed away from the counter, clamping the book under his arm so he couldn't feel the cover. "I'm just—"

Spinning on his heel, walking too fast. Slow down. He was sweating. Now they'd call security on him. *Black man acting weird. Probably on drugs. Probably shoplifting.* He wanted to laugh. He'd paid for the goddamned book, he just wanted his money back. Actually, he didn't even want that. He just wanted to get rid of it.

He speed-walked through the Orange Room to get to the mezzanine. Past the racks of remainders, past the blank journals and there on his right—

Was nothing. No door. A concrete wall. A drinking fountain.

He stood staring, barely noticing the people around him. Barely noticing the room, the blurry lights, the strange way that colors seemed to warp and bend on the surfaces of things. The door had been there. Where was the door?

He put out a hand to touch the wall, and found he was holding the book. Hadn't he put it under his arm? But here it was clinging to his fingers, its cover tacky and cool. It couldn't really be made of skin, that was nuts. But what else but skin felt so . . . personal?

He stuffed the book back under his arm and turned on his heel. He was misremembering the door, so what. He could leave the damned book on any shelf, or no shelf. He could drop it off on a table in the cafe or toss it in the trash.

He imagined leaving the book on the rack of remaindered paperbacks just a few feet away. Its weird pale dusky cover—shabby and pathetic beside the bright new designs of novels and memoirs. Fuck this book. He'd show it. He'd dump it in public to be ignored and tossed in the trash.

But as soon as he thought it, he knew: No way. No way could he leave this thing where people could find it. It would cling to someone else the same way it was clinging to him. But it would find someone who wasn't used to its bullshit, who hadn't made a hobby of this stuff. Who hadn't built up an unhealthy resistance.

And what would it do to them?

It was in his hand again.

"Excuse me." A guy with a book cart pushed past him, because he was frozen in the middle of the aisle like a lunatic. Malcolm stepped back, putting the book back under his arm and wiping his hand down his leg. His fingers felt coated, as if he'd dipped them in wax.

The world went fuzzy, its colors elongated and unstable.

"The hell with this." He put his hand back to touch the wall, to get his balance. Instead of concrete, his fingers met a cool metal doorknob. Without thinking he turned it, stepped backward, and he was through.

The door closed behind him with a quiet click.

He turned and stared down into the chasm of the stairs. The light hurt his eyes. The colors veered around the walls. He wavered on his heels, waiting for his balance to return. Light and dark swapped places, then slowly swapped back. The book was in his hand again. He was okay, he was upright. He steeled himself to the clammy skin-feel of the book's cover.

He cleared his throat.

"Shine took off his shirt." His voice bounced back from the walls, its angles baffling. "He took a dive." If he lost his balance here, he'd go down headfirst. Break his back and his neck and both his legs. And he had a feeling nobody else was going to open this door again anytime soon. "He took one stroke. And the water pushed him like it pushed a motorboat."

A phrase bubbled up, like sewer gas, from the bottom of his mind.

Nothing tending to the progress of humanity or worthy of preservation.

Mid-step, his balance wavered. The walls went sour and pressed in on him.

"The captain said . . ." He forgot how it went. The most famous African American toast of all, the ballad of "Shine and the Titanic." The white man's folly, the black man's escape. He'd heard it a hundred times at his mother's dining room table.

What did the captain say? He groped, panic rising in his throat, the grim quasi-colors of the walls pressing in on him—and then it came back on its own. "'I'll give you more money than any black man see.'" He clamped his fingers right around the book, holding it as hard as it held him. "Shine said, 'Money is good on land or sea. Take off your shirt and swim like me.'"

He had the rhythm of it back. He started down the stairs, not bothering to be careful. "And Shine swam on. He met up with the whale—"

He was down, the stairs behind him. All in one piece, just like that. Cold sweat on his neck and the book fused to his hand. In front was the narrow, canted hallway that led into . . . was it darkness? His eyes struggled to tell him. Not darkness, no. That knuckled-down color. A kind of heavy pallor. Something like the darkness of a winter-clouded Portland sky, white light reflected heavily over a gloomy landscape.

"The whale said, 'Shine, you swim mighty fine . . .'" He was down the hallway now. There was the narrow wooden door. It looked battered, as if someone had been kicking at it.

For just a moment, he wanted to turn back. Leap up the stairs and forget this whole thing.

But the book was in his hand.

"'But if you miss one stroke—'" He put out one finger and touched the door—just touched it. It swung open. "'Your black self is mine.'"

He was on the threshold of the little room.

Inside, the shelves stretched to infinity in colorless half-light. Every shelf crammed with books. Every book the same, exactly the same as the one in his hand. Every spine crumbling and moldy. Every page, he knew without looking, filled with the same dense relentless pitiless shameless hopeless words.

His mouth was suddenly full of sand. The book in his hand weighed a hundred pounds. It dragged him to his knees in front of the shelves. He couldn't let it go. In front of his face, a single obscene gap in the books, a space made of colorless weight. As he knelt there, the space began to uncurl and seep out from the shelf, down to the floor and toward him.

The Negro the child the female the senile White idiot imitator fetishist animal ape.

The black cursor on the white screen. What did it matter, com-
pared to this? What could he ever say to so many hundreds of
thousands of pages just like these? A taste of sweet acid filled his
mouth.

Set your black self down.

His lips were numb. The colorless space had crossed the floor,
and was almost to his knees. There was something in the back of
his mind, something he could almost remember through the fog in
his brain. Another shelf of books. His mother's books. His mother's
office at home, her chair stacked with term papers. His father's desk,
covered with photographs of young men smiling. In caps and gowns.

Set your black self down.

"Shine said . . ." His lips didn't feel like they'd moved. But they
had, and the curl of space hesitated. "He said . . . 'You may be the
king of the ocean, king of the sea.'" He had to pause, to clear his
throat again. "'But you got to be a swimming son-of-a-gun to out-
swim me.'"

The lick of no-color drew back. He felt a little more strength in
his body.

"And Shine swam on." There was a tingling in his right hand.
The book was lighter. He raised his arm to one side, the book on his
open palm. "And Shine swam on." Louder. The book lighter still.
"And Shine swam *on*." Shouting. "He swam *on* and *on* and *on*—"

He lunged forward and shoved the book hard, back into its place
on the shelf. There was a moment when he was sure it wouldn't go.
It was huge, heavy, an encyclopedia. The space on the shelf was a
whisker's width. But he hammered it with the heel of his hand, hit
it with as much force as he had, and somehow it jammed in and
was just a book again. A book on a shelf, alongside other books.

He stood back, panting. He could feel his blood in his cheeks.

"And Shine swam *on*," he said. He kicked the shelf solidly with
the ball of his foot. Something cracked. The shelf sagged. Pain
snapped up his leg.

The shelf was done for. Sad, pathetic shelf. Slumped and moldy.
He could see now that it only went up as high as the ceiling in a
dank old basement storage room.

He limped out, leaving the door open. When he was halfway down the hall, it closed quietly on its own.

"The hell with you," he said.

Up the stairs. Just a regular old set of basement stairs, too steep to be up to code, a pain in the ass to climb with a throbbing probably-broken toe, but at least the colors sat right in his eyes. At least the walls held still.

At the top of the stairs he slipped out the door and let it close on its own. After a few steps he turned to look back. No door. No surprise. Not really.

"Now when the news got to the port," he said, turning for the Green Room and the big doors out onto Burnside Street. "When the news got to port that the great Titanic sunk, you won't believe this, but old Shine—" He paused by the exit, giving it a minute. Waiting to see if they were going to stop him. For acting crazy, for trespassing, for being a black man out of control. Nobody seemed to notice him.

He gave it another minute, to see if the book was going to appear in his hand.

Outside, the sky was heavy with bright, dark thunderclouds. All the colors of the world looked weird and beautiful.

"Old Shine was on the corner damn near drunk."

He bowed to the Green Room, gave the finger to that hidden basement room, then limped out the door. Toward home, where the blank page waited.

The door to the basement
is closing, but before it does,
I think I catch a glimpse
of drab muslin and maybe
scales disappearing into
the gloom.

An appropriate
supernatural rustling
sound accompanies the
creaking door.

Of
THE
DEAD

This Many Lost Things

Nicole Rosevear

If Janie had a superpower, it would be losing things. Socks, jewelry, her cell phone. Four dogs, her father, six jobs, a fiancé, a fetus. Queen of the lost.

Janie is an administrative assistant at a downtown legal firm, Smith and Banks, keeper of other people's schedules. No missed appointments on Janie's time—she's good at keeping those from wriggling away, at least, keeping them out of hiding.

Her own route to this job has been indirect, so her managers and two of the firm partners are younger than Janie. This only bothers her when she thinks of the future, things like retirement and savings and home ownership that she hasn't quite gotten around to yet. She is not sure that she wants these things, not sure how to want them, exactly, although it's clear that she is supposed to.

When Janie finds things again, which she sometimes does, she finds them best from the highest vantage points. She scales her own furniture, stands on the top rung of a step stool in the middle of her living room, mountain-goats herself up buttes and hillsides, can't stop ascending until she is the tallest thing for miles, all the shadows hers and hers and hers.

"Package for you," Nate says, stepping off the elevator into the offices of Smith and Banks and holding two narrow rectangular boxes out to her, one stacked on top of the other. Nate is the building runner. Janie is certain this isn't his official job title, but it sums up most of what he does: running items from the mailroom to various offices, or from various offices to the mailroom. Including the business cards for new employees.

"They came out nice," he says, running his thumb over the sample card stapled to the end of one box. "Cool design choice."

"Yeah." Janie opens one box and pulls out a fresh card, angling it under the fluorescent office lighting. All of the employees' business cards are on the same textured cream background with their name, position, and contact information embossed in dark blue and the company name in larger font across the top. Each one has a unique design printed on the cream background, though—"a personalizing touch," Banks, the partner who hired her, had called it. One of the partners has a leaf design; a new paralegal has a winding road twisting into the creamy distance. Janie has chosen a mountain, textured and pale, offset behind her name. In the catalog, the design had looked to her a bit like Mount Hood, but the finished product is like no mountain she's ever known, a jagged monolith with sharp peaks and ridges rising to a needle point.

There are windows opposite Janie's desk in the firm's lobby. When she gets up to stretch or deliver something to one of the offices, she sees snapshots of the outside world: occasional bright scarves mixed with T-shirts and sweaters, trees looking more wintry and naked daily, leaves that have already made their spectacle becoming dull, veiny decay underfoot. Soon, the city will erect a Christmas tree a block away, close enough that she will see its lights every evening as she leaves the building. She has never worked downtown before, can't remember from previous years if the tree lights will be white or a chaos of color. She wonders how tall the tree will be this year, how many things in this city it will be taller than. How many lost things it might be able to see.

On weekends, Janie climbs. She drives to the center of the state and scrambles her way to the tops of scree slopes, every careful step releasing miniature rockslides in her wake; drives into the Gorge and views waterfalls from above, from the source, from before they can possibly know what they will become in another mile of wet and rocky tumbling. She climbs Tabor and Rocky Butte, but the West Hills loom taller in the not-so-far distance. From Council Crest, Hood taunts her with its crisp, bright angles. She has never touched glacier.

She finds other people's lost things in these places. Gloves, hats, keys, a charm bracelet, sandals, bottle openers, sunglasses, a small paintbrush set. Janie leaves the things she finds, has a firm "do not disturb" policy. She knows the easiest way to ensure these things never get found again is to move them from where they were originally lost, make their positions no longer traceable by the owner's memory.

Winter's approach confines Janie to local, lower elevations. She traces her way up familiar hills, dormant volcanoes, takes new paths when she can, pretends she doesn't remember them that well when she can't. A monogrammed Zippo lighter, a child's watch with a broken wrist strap, an orange sweater draped over a log and wet from the moss beneath it.

Sometimes Janie finds her own lost things on her climbs, although never ones she's looked for. She turns a corner and finds the third argument she had with her fiancé, before they had moved in together, before either of them had considered that one day he might be her fiancé, climbs a flight of uneven stone stairs and rediscovers, word for word, a conversation with her father when she was twelve and they were on a vacation in Arizona. She finds her mother's "You can grow up to be whatever you want to be, Janie-bird" and the meth-riddled smile of a long-gone ex.

Her most recent ex, the fiancé, the almost-father to her almost-mother, used to come with her on her climbs. She understood that her silence on the climbs, her intensity of ascent, disturbed him. Janie is not a meanderer through nature, doesn't hold hands on bridges and revel in the waterfall spray misting her face, doesn't pack picnics. She did not talk about the child they would have had, never unpacked the box of heirloom clothes her fiancé's mother sent not long before it became clear there was no longer going to be anyone to wear them.

Sometimes she can still feel the ghosts of the little butterfly flutters in her belly, the somersaults and loop-de-loops of another living thing sharing her body. Little fish swimming along, heartbeat under her heartbeat, until it wasn't anymore. Just another lost thing.

The Smith and Banks office is not on the top floor of the building, but the twelfth. Twelve of eighteen.

She has been there for just over five months when she decides to try climbing the stairs to the roof. The roof of the building is not designed as a living space, but is surprisingly easy to access and there is a small table on it, three chairs, two long-dead potted arborvitae, and a large can of sand that has at some point been used as an ashtray. All of these things are sun-bleached, rain-washed, wind-worn. Janie spends more and more of her breaks up here. Keeping other people's schedules from getting jumbled is more exhausting than she'd expected it might be, a thing to escape from rather than a thing to lose herself in.

"It's the busy season right now," Smith says.

"The first few months are always the steepest learning curve," one of the interns tells her.

Janie watches the tiny people crossing streets eighteen floors below her, bundled up against the impending heart of the Northwest winter, snow warnings looming in forecasts that fail to deliver on anything but the rain. She finds a big golf umbrella at a Goodwill, carries it up the stairs, wedges it into a knothole in the table to keep her dry while she's up there.

Sometimes, Janie studies the mountain on her business cards, its unusual ridges and absurd peak. She runs her fingers over its shadows, what appear to be rough patches of rock dotting its sides, holds it up in front of her as though it might perhaps sit next to Mount Hood, or St. Helens, or maybe even Adams in clear-day skylines. "Mount Janie," she sometimes calls it, although never out loud to anyone else.

She doesn't lose schedules or forget to send out meeting reminders, no, but too often, Janie loses things at work, except in the office they call it "misplacing." She misplaces writing utensils, clipboards, her building access card, a stapler, the case for her company-issued laptop.

She looks for them from the top of her desk, from the building roof, from nearby sky bridges, from the clock tower in the courthouse across the street.

"Must be a poltergeist," she jokes.

"Pesky gremlins, carrying my things away," she says.

She knows that she will lose this job before the manager tasked with firing her does. Even with accurate scheduling and correctly ordered supplies and promptly returned calls, there are only so many possible outcomes in the presence of this many lost things.

The Saturday before her firing—she can feel it in her joints, like a drop in barometric pressure—Janie wakes up to snow finally, softly, falling outside her bedroom window. She imagines watching the city grow pale and silent under this powdery blanket, and before the thought is even complete, she is tying her shoelaces, looking for her other glove, grabbing the warmest scarf she can find.

She walks to the park up the street and then keeps going. Janie passes the grocery store and crosses the river, keeps to the inclines where she can. The snow still falls, leaving her fingers damp and cold. She wishes she knew where her winter hat was.

Janie walks. She leaves partial footprints where the fine dusting of snow is thickest, then full footprints that let the black of the pavement beneath them show through, then footprints that are just white texture on a white canvas. Eventually, she realizes that she's on something big, some uphill she's never been on before. The city is still sprawled out beneath her, so close that it looks like a minia-ture city, a little snow globe city all shaken up, but there should be no hill where she is. Nothing like this one, anyway. Ahead of her, farther up, she sees fog, a few trees, more snow, nothing spectac-ular, but the trail is clear and she has, somehow, missed this hill before. She keeps walking, always up.

The fog thickens, then splinters, the light bursting through in-creasingly brighter. The snow gets finer and slower and stops, dirt replacing snow beneath her feet. The trees start to thin, and still there is no end in sight. When Janie reaches the edge of the tree line, the fog has tapered to almost nothing, and days-old snow is visi-ble not much farther up the mountain, hugging the shady edges of the landscape. Something dark sits at the edge of the nearest patch of snow. A lost thing. Janie walks toward it, a strange thing to be lost on a snowy mountain—a laptop case. One with the Smith and Banks logo printed on the front. One she has recently misplaced.

She climbs. The bracelet her mother gave her when she turned sixteen; the cell phone she lost in a restaurant six months ago; al-most a dozen keys on a familiar keychain, although she no longer recalls what any of the keys opens. The going becomes tougher as the snow deepens, and the path becomes much steeper. Sharp spines, upheaved wrinkles of mountain that have not yet been rounded by weather and time, are visible to her left and right, and rough outcroppings of rocks occasionally force her to shift the an-gle of her ascent.

The angora-lined leather driving gloves she wore for two weeks last winter and then never saw again, the water bottle she won at a company party three jobs ago. Some of these things are on the surface of the snow, some half buried in the white powder, others encased in the hard pack and ice she walks over.

Farther up, the mountain rises to a sharp point, sides so steep and tightly angled that there is no clear path anymore. When Janie looks back, the way she's come, nothing is as tall as she is, no sky-scraper or butte, not Hood or the distant Rainier. All the shadows she can see belong to her and her mountain. A Raggedy Ann doll from her childhood peers up at her from beneath her feet with its lidless eyes. The doll's facial features are blurred by several inches of ice. Its red yarn hair is flattened against one side of its head, splayed out wildly on the other, and Janie's fingers twitch to smooth it down, put it back the way it should be. The ice, she knows, is too thick, the doll a thing that can be found but not recovered.

Squatty and Weasel Boy

Doug Chase

My whole life I was half a ghost and never knew it.

Working the cash register at my Burger King. All the humanity that came in all hours asking for their Whoppers and fries and milkshakes. Me in my damn scratchy polyester uniform the color of baby diarrhea. Someone thought it was a good color for a fast food joint.

I was in the first batch of employees, team members they called us, when they opened the Burger King right on the corner of Burnside and Broadway. Great location, they said. The whole town comes through here. This was back when Portland was small, when every Saturday night the yokels would cruise down Broadway a mile an hour, honk their horns, yell at the girls that walked past.

It was a sight, my Burger King. Not like all the boxy fast food joints you see now. It was a kind of plaza made out of bricks and built low to the ground. Those bricks the same color brown as my uniform.

It was like my Burger King was a vortex for the way Portland was changing from a small town to a real city in the weird shift from the Jimmy Carter seventies to the Ronald Reagan eighties. It wasn't long before we got addicts and dealers hanging out in our seating area, kids shooting up in the bathrooms. And the crazies we got, the violent kind and the nonviolent, but always scary. Talking out loud to no one I could see.

Right from the start I got Squatty.

First time Squatty walked in the door. Six in the morning. No one in the place but a couple of tired old hookers and the cops they hung out with. Breakfast tots in the fryers, the stink of them. Grease in the air. My skin already shiny with sludge and sweat.

He was short and wide. Wrapped in four or five sweaters, couple or three pairs of Levi's, white Nikes on his feet that he must have got from the donation bin at the mission down the street. His chunky face weathered from the night air. Long, dark, unbrushed hair. No facial hair, though. Just his unnatural reddish kind of skin, real skinny nose, mouth wide open so he could wheeze through it.

His eyes, you might not believe me, two different colors. Like that rock star. One eye a hard candy green and the other eye mostly black. The way he walked in, it was like a rock star, too. Head up high for such a short man. His crazy eyes barely moved, but you could tell he saw everything.

So many people came in my Burger King with their heads down, ashamed of themselves. Ashamed to be in such a place. The grime we had on the floors, no matter how much we scrubbed. This guy, though, he walked up to the counter like the cops do, like he owned the joint. His chin up. Short as he was, he looked down at me across my cash register.

He had this dirt smell, old garbage bag smell, unwashed dried-off sweat smell. He brought his lack of a home right up into my nose.

I'll tell you right now, homeless people scared the hell out of me. When I was a kid we called them hobos. Then, in the late seventies, early eighties, it got so bad. Homeless people rose up out of the earth in a swarm. Everywhere I went, some old lady wrapped up in overcoats pushing a shopping cart filled with bags, those bags stuffed full, but I don't know what they stuffed them with. The shopping cart was their whole house, so maybe those bags had a wardrobe, kitchenware, everything to make a house a home.

And all the homeless men sleeping on bus benches, or sitting there talking talking talking. Hoping to catch your eye.

I could see myself there. On the bench. Wrapped up against the cold in a wool blanket that some charity handed me. Hungry because I could never fight with the other homeless people for food.

Me on the bench, hoping to catch your eye and ask for help. Afraid to catch your eye.

The homeless guy, Squatty, I called him that in my head right away, he did this thing I hated.

It happened all the time, but he was the worst. He reached across to my cash register and put his two hands on the top of it. Dirty hands. The grime of his hands worse than the grime on the floor. And he rubbed the sides and the top of my cash register, ran his hands all around like it was his register and not mine. His fingers curled around to the front, his sweaty smears, his chewed-up dirty fingernails.

"Welcome to Burger King," I said. "We make it the way you want."

Oh, I totally messed up the script. That's not what you're supposed to say. Didn't matter who walked up to your cash register—crazy homeless man, burned-out old hooker, cop, even a rock star—you had to use the script. I thought it was stupid. But I liked it, too. It gave me words to say to all the people. I don't know if I could have figured out what to say to them without the script.

And this short little homeless guy, he got to me somehow, and I didn't say the right words, the words you heard every time there was a Burger King commercial on TV.

This damn homeless man with his chin up like he owned me. His voice down in his throat, scratchy, probably spent the night asleep in our parking lot and just woke up.

"Hold the pickle," he said.

I thought he was going to sing our TV jingle. That's all I needed to hear.

"Hold the pickle ickle ickle." His phlegmy voice. "Don't want no pickle ickle ickles. Icky pickles, don't want 'em."

I didn't know if he was actually ordering something or just talking to himself in his make-believe crazy world or both at the same time.

"What do you want?" I said. "Hamburger? Whopper Junior?"

One eyelid went down and back up. The squatty little bastard winked at me. His head tilted back. His puffy red skin. If you checked the angle of what he saw, it was probably my nametag. First initial and last name like the manager wanted. *B. Wessel.* That's me.

"Burger," he said. "Hold the pickle, hold the lettuce. Hold the ketchup, hold the mayo."

This was the kind of thing I dealt with. Every day. All the time. Damn cash register—I couldn't just put in "plain burger," I had to put in "burger minus pickle minus lettuce minus ketchup minus mayo." Each one of those was another button I had to push.

Burgers for breakfast. Every few years we would put burgers on the breakfast menu, and then every few years take them off. Nobody wanted burgers for breakfast. By nobody, I mean just a few. Squatty, for sure. That little asshole always ordered burgers for breakfast.

"For here or to go," I said.

I should have said, "Is this for here or to go, sir?" But no one was around to see my lapse. It was only me up front. Me and this homeless crazy guy. Squatty.

Unless Squatty was a corporate spy. In disguise and there to make sure I said the scripts the right way. It's what the job did to you. All the years I worked in that place. Twenty-five years altogether. Twenty of them after I killed Squatty. Never stopped being paranoid.

If working the cash register at a fast food joint is all you have, you have good reason to be paranoid. Every month on the first of the month my mom asking for rent. Soon as I turned eighteen she was like, *You better get a job, Mr. B. Wessel, 'cause if you're living here you're paying me rent.* My whole life she called me that, Mr. B. Wessel, and it always put me in my place. Then I went to work at Burger King and the home office did the same thing—put it on my name tag.

You might think my mom wouldn't kick me out, her only child, but she would, and I never had any idea how to go about living somewhere else.

Back in tenth grade the school counselor talked about the way I didn't like to be touched. And how alone I would be if I couldn't work on it. The first step, she told me, was get a job in a nice structured environment. Her words—structured environment.

My Burger King at the corner of Burnside and Broadway was structured down to the last little script, but it was chaotic, too. A structured room filled with the most unstructured individuals. Druggies and homeless and hookers. The cops the only structured ones. They wore uniforms. They dealt with all the humanity. They didn't like it when people touched them.

Squatty didn't say if he wanted his burger for here, so I hit the button to go. He could take the damn bag with the burger done his way to a table if he wanted. And the whole minute it took the schlub in the kitchen to put his burger together with a bun, no pickle, no lettuce, no ketchup, no mayo, and slide it down the chute all wrapped up in white paper, Squatty stood there with his hands on my register.

That minute took forever. Squatty's eyes that looked down his nose but up at me. His wheeze in and wheeze out. Finally the slide of the burger down the chute. I turned and grabbed it and didn't have to look at him for just a second.

Here's another weird thing. I didn't see him do it, but on the counter next to my cash register there were dimes and nickels and pennies, and when I counted it up it was exactly the price of a regular hamburger. Whenever I helped Squatty for the next five years, same thing. Bunch of coins on the counter, and I never saw when the money got there. When our prices went up, the extra nickels and pennies would be there, too. I'd say magic, but back then I was always too mad at Squatty to even wonder.

I put his burger in a brown paper bag, the kind with our goofy big logo on one side, added a couple of napkins, and put the bag on the counter. I wasn't going to hand it to him, have him pull some kind of crazy person touching thing, his dirty hands on me.

He took the bag and backed up toward the doors. That was the first time, but he did it every time he came in, never let me see the back of him. I don't know why. For all I know, he could have been totally butt naked in the back, but I never saw. Not the five days a week for five years before I killed him. Not the twenty years after that.

Just before he pushed open the door with his ass, Squatty yelled out to me. His two eyes, the one hard candy green and the other mostly black. I don't know why he yelled what he did, probably some weird way he read my name tag.

Scratchy in his throat, this is what he said.

"Hey there, Weasel Boy. Kiss my ass."

I never knew where Squatty slept, on the street or at the mission. Every day for the next five years he came in and ordered his burger, hold the pickle, hold the lettuce, hold the ketchup, hold the mayo.

Squatty never came in when I wasn't there. I checked with other employees, team members I mean to say. I took a week off to go to the beach. He never came in. Took four days off when my dad died. He never came in. But the minute I was back, there he was, his rock star walk, his four sweaters, his white Nikes from the mission. His green eye and his black eye. His earthy outside smell. His dirty hands all over my cash register. I wanted to back away, all the way to the counter where the burgers came down from the kitchen. He was so close I felt his breath on my neck. So close he could touch me.

When I switched to lunch shift, there he was. When I had to take the dinner shift for a few weeks, every time with the pickle ickle ickle. And every time, he backed out to the door. Five damn years. And every time, he yelled out in his throat-clearing voice.

"Hey there, Weasel Boy. Kiss my ass."

Then the morning Squatty didn't show up. Cold damn morning in January. Frozen sidewalks on the way in. The place was worse than usual. The night crew left all the trash cans full. Kitchen, bathrooms, the big bins in the dining room.

I went around to collect the trash. Each bin had a heavy-duty plastic bag I had to tie up. The stink of fries and burgers and diced onions. Bathrooms, it was like the walls held in a million old farts. Shit stains on the toilets. The floors littered with toilet paper in stained, wadded up balls.

Out the kitchen, through the employee door. Freezing cold air in the parking lot. It made my chest hurt. I dragged four bags, two with each hand, hauled them all to the big trash container.

It wasn't just a regular old bin, but an actual trash compactor. About twice as long as a normal dumpster, it was all sleek and painted industrial beige, the feeder chute sticking out one end.

You could climb through the chute and into the big compactor area, but I don't know why you would.

Drop your trash bags into the chute and turn the key to power up the compactor and then you push the big green button. The gate on the end of the chute slides across and shoves your garbage bags into the compactor and closes it off. A little electric whine while it does it and a solid thunk to lock the gate into place. Then the grind of big gears and metal walls smashing up everything inside. Loud, stinky, efficient. When it's all done the little gate slides back down the feeder chute and you end up with nice square bricks of trash ready for the landfill.

I say I don't know why you'd crawl into the compactor, but that's a lie. I know why. You know what happened.

I turned the key and the motor started up. A little cough of a start and a low kind of hum. The sound of a big mechanical electric thing with power to spare.

I hit the green button. Gears turned inside the compactor. Interior walls with their slow sound of metal against metal. The noise got louder. But not what I expected. Inside the compactor. Distorted sound. A man screaming.

It was Squatty. His fucked-up throaty voice almost lost in the metal container he had crawled inside.

"Weasel Boy, Weasel Boy, no!"

I didn't even think about how he knew it was me. The noise, the metal grind as the walls closed in. I didn't know what to do. No one told me what to do.

I hit the green button again. There was no off button. Just the damn green button.

Squatty screamed. Over and over, he screamed. No words that made sense.

Banging against the inside of the compactor.

I slammed that button, the flat of my hand against it, scream of the metal walls, Squatty's screams, and snapping sounds I had to think were his bones being broken and crushed.

"Fuck!" I said. "Fuck!"

I didn't know what to do. My hand hard against the green button.

Squatty's voice, panic high, pain high, oh God.

"Weasel Boy!"

The whine of the compactor. The internal walls, the crushing metal walls, they finally slid back into place. The little gate slid back into place. Ready for the next bag of garbage.

The parking lot was quiet. Cold. Early morning dark, but the clouds were heavy and reflected the city light.

I killed him. I never wanted to. I hated him, but I didn't want to kill him.

They closed down my Burger King for the day. The place was filled with cops and firemen, managers from the head office, managers from the trash pickup company, and managers from the company that made the compactor in the first place. So many people to try to figure out what to do with Squatty and what to do with me.

I sat in the restaurant. Plastic molded bench, plastic table, all one piece bolted to the wall. Sat there and could not believe what I had done.

A guy in a heavy coat came out from the kitchen. Sat down across from me. Big guy with a gut that pressed against the table. I figured he was a cop. He took out a little notebook like cops have, a ballpoint pen that he clicked open and closed over and over the whole time he talked.

Which wasn't very long. Because he was from the newspaper and when one of the head office managers saw him, he told him to get the hell out of there. But before he got kicked out, he said the thing that really fucked me up.

"You know," he said, "all you had to do to stop the compactor was turn the key."

The day I killed Squatty. I tried explaining it to my mom. Across the kitchen table at dinner.

Her face long like it was, no makeup but the orange lipstick she put on every day. The eyebrows she drew on with the little pencil. All my life she drew her eyebrows and wore the orange lipstick. Had the same short poofy haircut, coif, she called it. Every few weeks to the hairdresser to get coiffed.

I saw my own face in hers, my thin nose and long chin and high forehead. My whole life I copied her expression, mimicked it, whatever it was I saw in her face. Distaste, contained anger, that's what I saw across the table the day I told her about Squatty. I copied her expression, but I wasn't angry. I was terrified.

"They ain't going to fire you?" my mom said.

Her only question. Not if I was okay. Not if I needed anything from her. I pictured her reaching across the table to touch me. I was a grown man, but I still wanted my mom to put her hand on me, on my own hand, let me feel her touch, her skin and muscle and warmth.

Part of me glad she never would.

"I have to go see a shrink," I said. "A psychiatrist. Make sure I'm okay to go back to work."

The distaste in her expression stronger, like she bit into a lemon peel.

"God knows what that shrink will ask you," she said. "Don't you tell him nothing. Can of worms those shrinks like to dig up."

"I won't say anything," I said.

"Don't you talk about me at all," she said.

Later that week was when I talked to the shrink from the head office. He asked me how I felt about it, if I was grieving or upset. I never told the shrink how much I hated Squatty. Never told him how Squatty looked down his nose at me with his two eyes, one green and one mostly black. How he came up to my cash register, put his greasy hands all over it.

Squatty's hands, his skin, the thin muscles of his fingers.

I never said how Squatty pushed all my buttons.

Called me Weasel Boy.

My Burger King was haunted.

We got these cold spots in the restaurant. First at one table and then another. Weird smells. I don't mean like the gassy, farty fast food smells we always had, but a cloud of intense garbage that would come and go. Burgers that would fly off the chute from the kitchen, literally fly and hit people lined up at the cash registers.

The druggies, they didn't care. It was funny. They'd pick up the burger that just hit them in the face and then run out the door. Free food.

The cops got pissed. This one time a cop caught the burger that flew at him and threw it back, the white paper opened up, and the bun and patty and all the extras landed all over the poor schlub at the cash register. Me. I was the schlub.

Little poltergeist Squatty.

First day I was back at work. Just after six in the morning. Me at my register. Grease already in the air from the kitchen.

What came in the door, I don't even know. It was small and square, like the size of a breadbox. But with little legs and little arms all twisted around and bent the wrong way. The top of this boxy thing there was hair and a mouth and pimpled flesh and two eyes. Eyes smashed flat and spread out across the upper part of whatever this creature was. One eye was hard candy green and the other eye was almost completely black.

An impossible little man no taller than my knee from the ground.

Do I make him sound funny to you? Some kind of cartoon? Squatty wasn't funny. Before I killed him I could see myself turning into someone like him. Living on the streets. Dirt and stink and always hungry. All it would take was my mom kicking me out. But the new Squatty, the dead Squatty, he was worse than the worst thing.

He had to hop. No more rock star walk. He hopped forward to the counter and I couldn't see him because of the angle. I was too scared and had to lean over and see where he was. Keep my eye on him like you keep your eye on the spider in the corner of your bedroom.

Then Squatty hopped in place. The first hop was just a little hop. The second hop he went halfway up the side of the counter and it made me back up, startled. Then down and back up, the third hop all the way to the edge of the counter, and Squatty stood there and held on to my cash register. Broken wrong-facing hands that gripped the sides of my register. Greasy smears where he moved his hands up and down.

His head was bad. There was no head. Like I said, it was just the top part of his squatty boxy body. His face flattened and spread out. His eyes smashed flat, but still alive, still looking down his nose at me. His nose just a lump and a dimple in the flatness of his face. His skin the bruised color of raw meat. Torn-up cheeks that showed teeth and bone.

My ass hit the counter where the burgers came down from the kitchen. Heat lamps above my head, but coldness came out of Squatty in a pulse, with the stink of his death.

"Oh my God, Squatty," I said. "I'm sorry. I'm so sorry."

The first of a thousand times, ten thousand times, I said I was sorry.

Squatty's smashed candy green eye. A flap of skin dropped down slow over it and back up. The dead little bastard winked at me.

Then he spoke, this squashed-up, mashed-up block of a man.

"Hold the pickle, hold the lettuce, hold the ketchup, hold the mayo."

No one could see Squatty except me. He was always there in my Burger King. He hopped around the seating area, up on tables, stared right in the faces of the customers.

They never knew, except they would complain. It got real cold, and it got real smelly. Bags of garbage smell. Dirty unwashed man smell. Smashed up broken bone bloody smell.

While the customers were distracted by the cold and the stink, Squatty would eat a couple of their fries.

When he hopped down from my register the first time, and

hopped into the seating area, I could see him get farther from me. But his smashed-up face faced me. His broken legs, his white Nikes, everything, backing up so I would only see his face. His little arms, broken fingers. Oh, his thin broken fingers.

Twenty-five years I worked at my Burger King. Ran the cash register. Never got promoted. Never worked the kitchen. Just followed the rules. Like with Mom. *Make your bed when you wake up. Come to dinner at 6:30 sharp. Watch two hours of TV, whatever Mom is watching. Brush your teeth before bed.*

I'm good when there are rules.

I look back at my time at the Burger King and it doesn't seem real. More like a week than twenty-five years. Like it was me that haunted the place and not just Squatty. I don't know how it all worked. The rules of ghostology. Because even before I killed him, Squatty was all about me. He haunted me.

Half a ghost. You look at all the homeless people, some of them so far gone. A lot of half ghosts out there that haunt the places where they used to live. Not dead, but not allowed into the real world.

You know what I mean by real world. The world of going to a movie or the mall, sitting in a restaurant with your friends. Not worried about what they think. The world where everything fits, your clothes, your family, everything.

I was half a ghost, too. My whole life half a ghost and I never understood until the end of it.

They shut down my Burger King a few years back. Laid me off. Same year my mom died and I didn't have a place to live anymore.

Things I never understood. Reverse mortgage so my mom could stay in her house, but the bank took possession the day she died. I never understood how to get help, talk to the city or county or whatever, and when the woman from the bank came by the house and told me time was up and I had to leave, well, I put some underwear and a toothbrush in a backpack and went out the front door and started walking. All my money I had already given to my mom.

Walked all the way downtown to my old Burger King. Windows

boarded up and big white signs nailed to the boards on the front and side. The whole lot was for sale. The bank that owned the lot, same one that owned my mom's house.

That first night I ate some garbage behind a fast food joint and got real sick. Nothing says you're homeless like hiding in the bushes and taking turns vomiting and shitting. Cold and hungry, afraid in my own ignorance of how to survive. Completely unstructured environment. No rules that I could understand.

The thing I was most scared of, and it happened.

When I had a home and a job, I knew people stared at me because of the godawful uniform I wore every day. They stared at me and they probably thought, *Geez, what a loser*.

I'm here to tell you that's nothing. When you live on the street, people don't look at you at all. Desperate, I would look right at them from my bench in the park, moms pushing baby strollers, all the joggers, the art students. They stare past you. They don't let you catch their eye. They don't want to think about you at all.

The cops, when they came into my Burger King, they made me nervous. But when you're homeless, forget it. The cops got sticks and guns and no one cares if they get pissed off or if they're feeling kind of macho and decide to break your head.

I never got much better at finding food. I knew about the mission and the shelters, but I couldn't get too close to all those people. The people that all knew each other, other homeless people, cops, hookers, dealers. The same people that came to my Burger King, they all were like a big club on the streets, like when I was in school and the jocks and cheerleaders and schemers all had their own society.

I could only make myself go to the mission or the shelter when I was too desperate, too hungry, and I thought I would die. Some of those shelters, they had shrinks you had to talk to, social workers. But there's a lot I never told them.

I was scared all the time. When you live outside you sleep on concrete and asphalt and in the scrub on the side of roads, all kinds of bugs crawl all over you.

And then there's Portland wildlife.

What I'm saying is raccoons. Scariest creatures ever. They move in a gang, and the way a raccoon moves is like if a cat was twice as big as a regular cat, or even bigger, and really drunk and completely unafraid of anything. Those scary little hands that raccoons have, those faces with the gangster masks. Four or five raccoons in a gang down the street and my heart seizes up in my chest, a big clamp squeezing me there.

I was so hungry and there was nowhere I felt safe. I tried to get away from the city, walk west on Burnside through the hills and get to the suburbs. But I found out fast those suburbs hate the homeless more than the city does. At least in Portland they got the mission and the shelter and the good Samaritans that drive around in their white van and bring you soup and bread.

I found myself back at Burnside and Broadway at the shut-down Burger King. I was on the low brick wall out front. The lights on the outside walls still came on at night, and the little moths still banged against the lights like nothing had changed. Middle of the night, but Broadway and Burnside had plenty of cars going every way.

Squatty hopped up out of nowhere. Not really nowhere. He came around the side of the Burger King. Maybe he was out back. I didn't like to be reminded of it. Out back where I squashed him to death.

Squatty didn't make a sound. I hadn't seen him since closing day, back when I lived at home. I got to where I figured I was crazy with the whole Squatty thing, but here he was. My first reaction was I wasn't crazy, Squatty was real and I wouldn't be alone, anymore.

He took a couple of hops in place to get on the wall next to me. His face was worse than ever. Most of the skin gone. Just bone and tooth, cartilage where he used to have his little nub of a nose.

Hard candy green iris surrounded by the white ball of one eye just about out of its socket. His other eye, the black one, still with some flesh around it.

Dirt and sweat and old blood.

And the smell of a plain burger.

Squatty handed me a bag and inside, wrapped in white paper, was a nice hot burger, hold the pickle, hold the lettuce, hold the ketchup, hold the mayo.

His green eye, the one that was just white globe and iris and pupil, it spun slow in its socket. The iris seemed to float down and behind where I couldn't see it, and then back over the top to the front again. So weird. I couldn't figure it out until I did. My little decayed bastard friend Squatty had winked at me.

Squatty's garbage bag smell, his smashed-up skin and bones and blood smell, it didn't bother me. And his coldness.

When he got close to me I felt his hand on my arm, but he hadn't put his hand on my arm. I felt his fingers, broken fingers, on my cheek, like ice on a fever. But his fingers hadn't touched me.

It was that coldness of his. Touches I could allow because they were invisible.

Ghost touches.

I can't tell you how I made it through the next few years, except I didn't want to let go. I was afraid all the time, afraid of the shelter and the other homeless people there. Afraid of lining up on Burnside at the mission just to get a meal. Everyone in that line crazy in some way. Bumping close in front of me and behind me. On all sides of me. The unruly line of people, and the panic I had to push down, the claustrophobia from all those bodies, their smells and loudness, all of them taking up so much room and me with no space to breathe.

I could go behind the old Burger King. Squatty was always there. I tried to ignore the For Sale signs on the plywood. I think it was a couple of years that low brick building sat there with no buyer. I would huddle behind the back door and Squatty would stand a little ways from me. Always looking at me, but keeping his distance. He knew I was afraid of him, too.

But most of all, I was afraid of death.

All the years I knew Squatty. All the years he haunted me. But I still thought when I died I would just stop. No more existence. No more B. Wessel. I don't know how to explain it. My crummy, lonely life. Living with my mom. My mom, for God's sake. My job at the Burger King.

It was existence.

It was what I was, and I didn't want to let go.

The night I froze to death I had three wool blankets from the mission. I huddled up behind the health clinic they built after they finally tore down my old Burger King. You probably remember that storm. Turned the city into an ice rink for half of December.

Squatty was there, standing or sitting or whatever he did. He was close enough for me to smell, close enough to touch.

A calm came over me. Calm I hadn't ever felt before. Like there was nothing to be afraid of. No one that disapproved. No one to look at me with distaste. The whole world was just me and Squatty.

I reached out. The few inches from me to Squatty, I put out the flat of my hand. Firm, solid, my fingers, stretched out for his hand. His delicate broken fingers. He laid them down on my palm.

So cold. But not cold like metal or glass. Cold like flesh when it's been frozen for a long time. Cold that felt like a burn. Like the flesh of my hand and Squatty's hand were burned together, cauterized into a single thing.

When I picked up my hand there was no burn.

"Squatty," I said. "You gotta be freezing. Get under here."

I opened up a spot in the blankets and Squatty scrambled in close, his twisted-up legs on my lap, twisted-up arms at my chest. Squashed-up face just below my chin.

"You warm enough, Squatty?" I said.

That night the cold went deep. My bones, my spine, my intestines, my heart. So cold and deep, but I knew it was time. I was going to be like Squatty. Him and me, we would be ghosts together. We would find someplace else to haunt. The McDonald's up by the university. The Taco Bell down the street.

I held him carefully, his squashed-up body hugged into my body. His ghost touch on both my cheeks. His heartbeat against my chest. Or it might have been my heartbeat. The coldness turned into something else. Not like ice, not like fever.

All of me, all of Squatty. As close as we could be. Body to body.
Gentle.
And I felt warm again.

Stone Cold Monk

Linda Rand

"Linda, what's with the Medusa when I walked in? It can't be good for business." My friend Vaslav rolls his gray eyes, finding this yet another annoying factor at the Blue Monk. For someone who says he hates jazz and hipsters so much, he still manages to visit me a lot. I note he dyed his hair a becoming champagne blond.

"What?" I'm coming out of the walk-in with two trays of fruit for cocktails, balancing the cherries so the juice doesn't spill. "I'm happy to see you but I'm totally running late."

Then I see a stone statue toward the center of the room. Just a guy. A statue of some guy. It looks like he is about to duck into a booth, his hand on the dark table, mouth a perfect O of unhappy surprise. With his 1950s glasses, beard, and skinny jeans, practically a uniform in this town, I have to peer in super close to see if I recognize him. There are no tattoos and I wonder if they would even show, as I stare at each perfect stone eyelash. I decide I don't know him, but with the lack of color, it is a guess.

The door to the basement is slowly closing, but before it does, I think I catch a glimpse of drab muslin and maybe scales disappearing into the gloom. An appropriate supernatural rustling sound accompanies the creaking door.

I point to it and Vaslav nods. "Well, fuck," I say. "There's sup-posed to be a literary reading up here and people are gonna be showing up any second and the room isn't even set up yet. Plus jazz is happening downstairs tonight."

"I'll help you move the tables," he says, "but we'd better wedge that door shut so no one goes down there and you-know-who doesn't get out 'til we figure out what to do."

"Cool," and I pour him a Stoli Diet with three lemon slices for being a good friend.

The Heft of Ashes

Kirsten Larson

You don't think about how solid the ground is under your feet until you know it's not, and then it's all you think about. Underneath the streets, buildings, and sidewalks of Portland, the ground is a mix of fault lines and soil prone to liquefaction. Nowhere is safe to stand, really, because the big earthquake might happen at any time.

I'd gone to Powell's Books at lunchtime and got a volume of Sharon Olds poetry. I spent as much time with myself as I could before I had to go back. I was already late, 1:05, but that only meant the nothing I did for work would not get done that much longer.

It was two blocks back to the U.S. Bancorp Tower, my office building. The square, pink, glass-paned building blocked any view of the river and mountains beyond it.

In case of an earthquake, my building was safer than the sidewalk. I'd heard it was safer than most buildings downtown because they built it on baffles rather than into the unsecure substrata. It was engineered to move with the shifting soil of an earthquake, ride it out. I hoped it was true. My co-workers told me if you went up to the top floors of our building and looked out toward the horizon, you could see our building move in the wind. I believed them, but was not an important enough person to ever go higher than the fifth floor.

I went to Powell's Books almost every day at lunch. Sometimes I ate on the way there, sometimes I bought a book, and sometimes I didn't do either. It's where Robert worked when I met him, three years ago. I couldn't go there for months after he died, though.

Back at my desk, my jail-walled cubicle, I lost at the solitaire game on my computer. Not that anyone was looking, but my cubicle walls were high enough that I couldn't see anyone and they couldn't see me, a lonely freedom.

Fluorescent lights buzzed from the ceiling tiles, and the place smelled like paper. I snuck open the book that I'd hidden in my top desk drawer.

Most of the time, though, when I wasted time, I just sat still and listened.

We were supposed to make a certain amount of calls per day. A computer monitored how many calls we made. After five years at the job, I knew just how long I could stall and not get into trouble. I made a deal with myself: one poem for every call. It sounded like a good idea, but yet I read two and three. Cheated myself.

Robert worked at Powell's until a few months before his death. The place smelled like him—dust, and books, and coffee. It was as close as I could get to him now, that smell.

All around me my co-workers were on phones, so they couldn't hear me, but still, crying was embarrassing. It was noisy with the din of forty or so voices. I'd become a quiet crier.

Time at work had become a permanent, lazy houseguest who wouldn't leave.

Earlier that week, corporate had interrupted our call time and made us take a company-wide online test—"Are You Ergonomically Correct?" In the pictures some of the people were black or Asian, unlike the people in my office.

I learned that I am supposed to sit at certain angles, have the computer screen at a certain height, set the earphones at the lowest possible level, and stretch often in order to avoid repetitive strain. The unspoken message is, *You can't sue us, because we've warned you.* Usually, I sat at my desk in a slump, crossed my legs, and rested my head in my hands. I was an ergonomic failure.

At the end of the test the screen read, "Enjoy Your Newfound Comfort at Work!!" Robert would have made fun of it with me, at the futility of it.

I made another call. By the third ring I knew the customer I'd just dialed would not answer. It went to voicemail and I exhaled. I left a message reminding Mr. Donald Parsons that his mortgage with U.S. Bank was thirty days past due and asked him to return my call. No one ever called back. Most people want to pay their mortgage. They either could pay or they couldn't. They either paid or they didn't. What I did made no difference.

I gave myself time for another poem. I felt the weight of the impending call immediately after I left yet another message.

Robert's job was ideal: he'd help people find books all day. Not a lot of money, though. When we first met I bought a book of Anne Sexton poems. A large volume, it would feed me through weeks of work. He was my clerk. He looked at me too long, but I couldn't look back for any amount of time. He was so attractive, the tall masculine bulk of him but with light brown hair that stuck up in front like a boy's.

He handled my money and when he went to give me the change, his hand touched my palm; I looked up into his gray eyes, into a face of kindness and patience and curiosity and something else. All that in his eyes, and all he said to me was, "Here's your change."

I couldn't stop thinking about him so I went back the next day again, and again got into his line. My plan was to say something that might make him talk to me, but instead I just stood there like an idiot holding out the $1.50 bookmark I didn't want to buy. He held onto the bookmark, turned it over. "This is a nice one; do you want a bag?" he said.

I did something, then, I'd never done before: "Do you get a break? Do you want to drink some coffee? With me, I mean?" I asked him.

I got back to work a half hour late.

After that we didn't spend a day apart, that's how easy it was. First I was single and then we were together.

I tried to tell myself he was not that good-looking, maybe his hands were too callused, legs a little too thin, his features too fine, but always, the attraction was present. At night, his warm hands smoothed over my naked body, constant firm touching, relaxed access I had never allowed another. We slept all night with his chest and stomach to my back, his arm around me. He took away my aches.

Robert, such a boring name. But I whispered it many times a day after he died. My ears took comfort in the round syllables. First *rah*, an exclamation of approval; then *ber*, a soft ending after the abrupt letter *b*. To be. And finally, the exhale, *tuh*.

Do other people roll around the names of their dead?

When it didn't work to find his flaws, I tried to serve him mine: too quiet, I had no goals, a large student loan, my hips were thick, and I was a restless sleeper. It wasn't until Robert said "Bullshit," in response to my insecurity that I allowed myself to puzzle into him each night.

Robert's love never wavered.

The moment I loved him was nothing big. He was slumped on my sofa, in a soft, wrinkled T-shirt and faded jeans, my dog Henri beside him. Robert's hand touched Henri's soft head. They watched *Bringing Up Baby* on the TV.

Nothing happened but words in my head, thoughts almost spoken but not in my voice, *you love him*. A certainty.

Most weekends we sat side by side, completed crossword puzzles, and drank coffee. It was our world. But I thought about ways he'd leave me. Another, less difficult woman, perhaps. A jogger. Maybe someone cute and perky who knew how to cook a pot roast.

The clock at my desk read 1:20. Three hours forty minutes left in the day, three and one-quarter days left in the week, and thirty-four years until retirement. What would happen to me in this life?

I forced myself to call the next number on my list and the number after that and the number after that.

Later, I went into the restroom again, sat down on the toilet with my pants up, and bent my neck to rest on the cold, metal, sharp-cornered toilet paper dispenser, but it was too far away from where I sat to rest my head.

Maybe I should look for another job, but I didn't have any

energy. I was lucky to keep the job I had. I was always on the edge of acceptable performance. Maybe I could go back to school, get a graduate degree, do something I wanted to do, but the only thing I wanted to do was read and sleep.

My co-workers were normal, competent people. What secrets did they hold, though? They were blank white sheets of paper to me. Maybe all people suffered. Sometimes I studied each person and tried to guess what might be that one thing they cried over.

There was a new woman in accounting who I liked, Felicia. The origin of the name Felicia meant happy. She was fond of obscure facts like I was, and was funny. We ate lunch together at least once a week. She'd introduced me to the best greasy Chinese places. Most of the time we talked too long at lunch and had to sprint back to avoid the glares.

Last month, at her suggestion, we went to a movie together at Living Room Theaters. We sat on sofas, drank wine, and watched some foreign film. I felt like a grown-up, which I told her when we went to coffee afterward. "It's looming, you know," she smiled, "middle age." She never asked about Robert and I was glad; we were getting to be friends and I didn't want to cry or seem weird in front of her. It had been a year and no one asked about Robert anymore.

Robert did not leave me for another woman, or for my flaws, or out of boredom.

Of all the ways Robert could have left, he did so by dying of cancer. He was thirty-two. Who does this? My eyes blurred again. Maybe I would cry, but it was okay; I was in the bathroom alone.

It was not acceptable to cry after a year. It was not acceptable to cry over a boyfriend; we weren't even married. His family got public grief rights.

I didn't want to kiss Robert near the end, when the cancer had turned his skin flat white like an eggshell, and made him so thin that even the bones on his shoulders poked through his clothes like sharp elbows.

A stab of shame came up through my chest and cut off the tears. I wished I'd hugged him more. I wished I had kissed him those last few weeks.

The space where his body had been was so painful it was a living thing. Pain that lived in my living room, bedroom, office. Pain that lived in the grocery store, the park in our neighborhood, but was most present at Powell's Books.

My mother was my last living relative and she also died from cancer, five years before Robert did. I still cried for her once in a while, too. Her ashes were on my bookshelf, in their white metal delivery container. A failure on my part, because people don't just keep ashes forever.

But, I still couldn't decide what to do with them. She wanted as little fuss as possible. She had asked me to just drop her ashes into the Pacific, a "very nice ocean," according to her. Well, it's not that simple; the law dictates that you have to take them three nautical miles from shore, in at least six hundred feet deep, which meant I'd have to hire a boat. I couldn't see doing that by myself. The captain of the ship might think I was pathetic. I could just take them and dump them, but I thought my mom deserved more; she deserved a nice funeral. But who would I invite now? My mother deserved a big funeral with flowers and a hearse, people crying into Kleenex. What she got instead was one sad daughter and no service.

I missed my mom, but she could be a pain in the ass. I figured the ongoing ash problem was her fault. I would have liked a more specific instruction.

I also would have liked to have my mother to talk to when Robert was sick and dying. I suppose I could have tried to get closer to Robert's mother, but she played golf and ate lunch at a country club.

After Robert died, his mother gave me a small glass vial of his fine, white ashes on a red braided silk rope. It hung on the finial of the same bookshelf, with my mother's ashes and the small, flowered metal box of Henri's ashes.

Tiny black and brown Henri, a foxy mutt with huge, furry ears and round, brown eyes. When Henri became ill, his eyes filled with slate. Robert and Henri lay together most days, both sleeping their way toward God.

After Henri died, Robert turned his head toward the window. I could not console him. Four days later, his mother took him to her house to die, which he did on a Monday while I was at work.

My own body continued on. I hadn't cooked any food at home since he died, but I bled every twenty-nine days like I have since I was twelve. I've showered, and slept, and watched TV and read, like any other living person. I have lived. What a betrayal to Robert, to my mother, to Henri.

I neatened the things in my cubicle, tried to pass the few minutes until five o'clock when I could leave.

How do normal people get rid of ashes? I could do it in one trip, dump them all together, like boxed cake batter, maybe in the middle of the night in some park. I wanted to create some sort of ritual, though. If I at least knew the general vicinity of the ashes I'd have a place to go back to.

Robert's mother and father had a funeral for him at Our Lady of the Lake Catholic Church. A church he'd never been in. He would have hated it, and I could not feel him there.

Some people even had dog funerals, with friends and their friends' dogs. Poor little Henri, ashes in a box, alone.

My dead were not memorialized, they were in my living room, while I did nothing but sleep and read. I was too much a failure to give them what they deserved.

I should buy a plot somewhere and bury all three of them together. This appealed to me the most, but I'd made no calls or arrangements. I just dusted the shelf, weighing in my hands the surprising heft of the ashes.

My desk was neat, the computer turned off, and all papers stacked in small piles. I picked up my purse and put my new book in it. I pulled my bus pass from my wallet and put it in my pocket. I guess I looked forward to going home, but I had nothing to do but read for the entire evening.

Outside the light was pale. The bus stop was sometimes full at five, but it was near my office building.

The wind had picked up and the air smelled clean, like cold, wet rain; I put my head down and walked.

I got to the canopy of the bus stop and sat on a plastic bench to wait for the #19 bus. November, the bare tree branches reached their black, veiny limbs toward the sky.

The exhaust of cars and buses mixed with a spicy odor of a nearby Chinese restaurant; the smells of the city. I wished I'd eaten at lunch because I only had peanut butter and jelly at home.

The bus stop was rather empty. I pulled the book out of my purse. A woman took the seat to my right. Her arm, puffy in its sleeve, rested against mine. If she were a bad-smelling homeless person, I'd have to try to move without being obvious. But she wore a green pea coat and had long, dark hair.

She sensed me looking at her and asked, "A book?"

"Yes." I held it out to her, but her eyes focused somewhere in the middle of the street. She was at least partially blind, but didn't have a cane.

To be friendly I should talk, but I just didn't feel like it.

I turned my head to the left like I was looking for the bus, and studied her face. Her expression, it was like she was in a strong wind, pulled back and braced. She had fine lines around the corners of her eyes and a deep line between her brows. Her lower lip was full and she wore no makeup to cover her pale, smooth skin. It was a face I'd like to study for a while.

Do blind people care how they look? With looks out of the attraction equation, I might have made different choices in men before Robert. Maybe I would never have had a date. Would voice alone have attracted me? I didn't follow these thoughts far before she spoke.

"It's good to read." She had an accent, maybe French. "Here, in America, you have everything and nothing." Only she said *evry'sing* and *nuh'sing*.

"All the people, they rush rush rush, they are missing a soul. No spirit." Her voice rose. "They even rush to yoga, rush to relax."

It was true but unusual that a stranger would talk about something like that. Certain topics are proper: what time the bus was due, was it late, the weather, or directions.

I liked what she said. I was not a person to rush. I was not a go-getter. I walked like I had weights on my limbs. I was not someone going somewhere in life, or I wouldn't have had the same job for five years while others got promoted. Maybe it wasn't such a bad thing to be okay like I was.

She spoke with her face toward me. "They don't know all they have to do is be alone, in their apartments; they can find it themselves. Find their own souls."

Do I have a soul? If so, where would I find it? Where does anyone find their soul?

I wanted her to talk to me more, but the #19 bus had crossed Burnside and I would lose her if she wasn't going to get on my bus.

I stood up and said, "Thank you." How dumb, but I could not think of what to say to her.

People crowded the bus, but I found a seat near the back door. Maybe the blind lady was a French criminal in exile, or a madam. Madams were legal in France. Maybe she'd moved to Portland for love. I was not sorry the madam talked to me.

Bodies swayed back and forth with the movement of the bus. I felt the blue of having to go home to empty.

I looked around but avoided everyone's eyes. I'd become aware of a low deep hum that I'd been feeling lately when surrounded by people. It blended the lines where I began and ended. It soothed me.

When I was young, in school, in band class, sometimes when we would rehearse some classical piece of music I felt it vibrate so strong up through my feet and into my chest it took away the rhythm of my heart. My ears lost the sound of my flute, which mixed with the music my classmates made. I played on, deaf to my own notes, trusting myself not to make a mistake. I was gone to the beautiful vibration of us all, and was out of myself. When the piece ended we were all silent for a while before our instructor said only, "Bravo."

The bus had to stop on every block all the way up town before it could cross the river toward my neighborhood, before it could leave the city center with its faulty soil, soil filled with buried, broken plates of earth. We'd have to cross all that before the bus could take us to safety.

Every block people got on or off. I was grateful to have a seat.

Every time the doors opened I smelled decaying leaves in the fresh, cold air.

A bearded man in brown pants and a thick brown bomber jacket got on the bus. He didn't look at anyone but danced a little to some song only he could hear. He had some happiness about him that shone brighter than the average person who rode the bus at five—people in pantyhose and blue suit jackets with gold buttons, white shirts, and ties. Maybe he was the mentally ill kind of happy.

I looked out of the window but tracked him.

He stopped next to me, both hands on the metal bars to steady himself against the lurch of the bus.

"Girl. Girl," he said.

I turned to him. His brown coat was clean, so he was not a street person but he was a whole lot older than I thought at first. His pupils were milky and gray hair poked out under his wool hat. Wrinkles of living were set in places a face would smile or cry.

He bent down to my left. Without a thought, I leaned my head toward him, like I knew him.

I thought he was going to ask me for money. "You got angels around you like I never seen. You is surrounded," he said.

I leaned away to tell him he was being kind to the wrong person. He thought I was someone I wasn't. But his face stayed down. He wasn't done talking.

"You some kind of special." His gnarled left hand chopped the air in front of the both of us when he talked, with his right he hung onto the rail over our heads.

Maybe he was drunk, but I hadn't smelled booze, just some spicy cologne and the exhaust from the bus that lurched hard to a stop against the curb.

He had to be kidding me, or had mistaken me for someone else.

But I didn't care. From the bus stop by work to now, I would never forget any of this experience with the two kind people. I was just another person sitting in a pew in the strange church of my city.

He was still bent down, his head no more than a foot from mine. "You should be smilin'; three angels, most I ever seen."

Then, he stood tall and waved his hand in the air, like a salute.

The back doors parted open. He swung toward the stairs like a kid might, swung around with his right hand on the metal bar, and without another word, stepped one, two, three right off of the bus.

I looked out of the window to find the man, but it was dark and lit well inside the bus. All I saw was my own reflection—the same brown hair, the same gray scarf I wore every day, but I smiled a little, still.

It was the last stop downtown; the doors closed, and the bus took off, pressed me back into the seat. We headed toward the Ross Island Bridge, toward home.

When the vampire
meets someone new,
especially a taller,
handsome, more
accomplished vampire,
he feels a hot sting
in his guts,
a hammering
in his chest.

Of THE UNDEAD

Vampire

Justin Hocking

Recently the vampire has been struggling with heart palpitations.

When the vampire meets someone new, especially a taller, handsome, more accomplished vampire, he feels a hot sting in his guts, a hammering in his chest. The vampire worries he might come apart, or have a heart attack.

His doctor prescribes him beta blockers. They help with public speaking and social situations, but they give him a piercing headache.

The vampire worries he's losing relevance. After a spike in popularity, everyone's already on to the next thing—watered-down S&M and post-apocalyptic shit that doesn't really involve vampires. Even zombies seem more popular. Superheroes, definitely. He never really benefitted from the vampire trend—only young, dashing, ravishingly handsome vampires ever got any work.

The vampire has a problem with his backside that he'd rather not discuss.

The vampire's original ideas of what it means to be a vampire don't match up with his current reality.

The vampire wakes up one day and realizes he completely forgot to have children. He'd been so focused on his career. He could technically still have them—he's only 382. But he'd be 400 by the time a kid was finishing high school. No child wants a 400-year-old dad skulking around school, at parent-teacher conferences, or helping with her luggage during those precarious first days at college.

The vampire has figured out that he can take a photo of himself with his cell phone, stare at his image for a long time, in a way he never could with mirrors. He looks for hours at his widow's peak, premature baldness scratching its talons further and further up his scalp. He wonders, since he's 382, if "premature" is the right word.

The vampire envies the Wolfman's hair. "If you lived in this fucking pelt," the Wolfman says, knocking back another beer, "you wouldn't covet it."

The vampire wonders if having a younger girlfriend would help. Though, at his age, using the word "girlfriend" feels weird.

The vampire seriously regrets not buying a house in Portland when real estate was still affordable, back in 1896.

The vampire sometimes thinks about it. About not being around. Such a long life for a vampire. He doesn't have a plan or anything. It just comes up, a kind of fantasy, where he writes a note in his head, imagines the complaints and apologies he'd file with those he'd leave behind. He keeps it to himself, not wanting to alarm anyone.

The vampire finds solace in reading and crossword puzzles.

The Fixer: a Serial
– 1 – The Duchess

Sean Davis

Her lips are the color of a fresh scar and she has the kind of eyes that hit you harder than one of my long-pour Manhattans. Straight brown hair flows over her left shoulder and down over her low-cut white blouse. A dulled copper locket hangs on a long chain between her healthy breasts. There's no reason in the world a dame like her should be in a dive like the Poppy Lounge. It makes no sense, and when things don't make sense, that puts me on edge.

I'm cleaning the last bum's slobber from a pint glass, getting it ready for the next bum, as I watch her glide from the door to the bar. She's at least five-foot-ten, maybe six-foot, but with those long get-away sticks, it's hard to be sure. There's no doubt that she could be the death of a man, but that man would still be lucky, in my book.

I ask her what she needs and her only answer is a sultry smile. Finally, she says in a Russian accent, "I'm looking for the Fixer."

It's been a while since I heard that name but it still comes hard. It sends me back years, back to when I was sent home from Iraq on a stretcher. I didn't work in the mailroom over there, if you know what I mean. My hands got dirty, so dirty they took years to clean. It was hard coming back half-smashed and soul-broke. When I was able to walk again I found I missed the danger. After daily firefights, ambushes, and mortar attacks, well, all the normal was hard to care about. So I threw myself into the Portland underground and was soon known as someone who fixed problems for people who are not . . . let's say, pugilistically inclined. Coincidentally, many of my clients were dancers, and while they have to be tough and shiny as diamonds on and off stage, they'd tell me there was always something nice about having a big lug like me look out for them.

For a while I was the people's champion, but I messed up big. I actually fell for the last one and it almost killed me, but that's another story.

"The Fixer doesn't live here anymore," I say and clean the same section of the curved bar over and over again.

It took ten years but maybe I finally have all those demons on a leash and I'm not ready to let them go again. The last time really messed me up.

"My name is Yelena. I need help with a problem. They say you do that. They say that you would help me. They say that you're very resourceful."

Her big green eyes kill me. Inside them I see all the way back to the original sin. She opens with the eyes and then comes out fighting with a highly practiced combination that puts me on the ropes: pushing her hair behind her ear, a well-timed sly-glance-lip-bite combination. I'm reeling from the jabs, waiting for the haymaker that'll send me to the canvas, and she does just that by running two fingers across the tops of my scarred, callused hands.

"Is that what they say?" I ask.

"This is a down payment." She slides an envelope across the bar with some greenbacks. I pick it up to see how much my reputation's worth, but before I can, her soft touch changes and she's squeezing my hand with more strength than I figured her to have. She hits me with those beautiful green sparklers again and says, "This should be an easy job. I want you to simply scare off an admirer."

She places a photo on the bar, an honest-to-God five-by-seven photo. Who even uses these anymore? Nowadays it's all email or they show you off the small screen of their phone, but no, this is a black-and-white photo of a tall white man with a face like a chewed ham sandwich in a high-collared trench coat. "He's from a small town outside St. Petersburg."

I figure it's a simple case of hometown stalker. I ask, "So if he's giving you problems then why don't you tell the Po-Po?"

"It's a little complicated." She's deflecting my question with the mischievous smile I'm sure she uses when not wanting to explain herself. I keep staring, letting her know that I still want an answer.

She says, "It's a family matter."

"Sure, families are complicated."

"All you have to do is scare him off. You're such a big man. You talk to him and he'll go running, like a little dog. Here's my dance schedule. He shows up to watch me." She reaches into a pocket and pulls out a napkin with bubble-lettered dates, times, and names of strip clubs I know all too well.

"Okay, doll, I'm in."

She leans over the bar, grabs my collar, and pulls me close. A wave of lavender and jasmine washes over me like a river baptism and we're so close I feel her warm breath on my nose and cheeks. We stay like this for a moment before she whispers in the same voice Gabriel used before sending Joan of Arc to war; she whispers just two words with a small silence in between that can carry an ocean of meaning, "Thank . . . you."

Then she's gone and I'm back, already feeling more alive than I have in years, but two thousand dollars for a simple stalker case? This's bad. My first case back and I start out by biting off more than I can chew.

Keep Portland Weird, sure, it's our slogan but most people's commitment to this idea consists of a three-dollar bumper sticker; there is a weird here most don't have the slightest idea about, an otherworldliness only limited by how much you can take in. If you allow yourself to see it, to really see it, it's everywhere. Let's take Jimmy, for instance. Jimmy is one of my regulars, but he's also one of a long line of religious prophets that has included Hercules, Gautama, Jesus, Muhammad, Joseph Smith, and Bob Barker. Yes, every generation or so the one true God known by many names sends down one divine sperm and—bam!—another conception bordering on the immaculate. Of course, in our modern times, no one believes in poor Jimmy, so he spends his afternoons driving his 1960 cherry red convertible AMC Rambler to the Poppy Lounge and drinking himself into martyrdom. I use him as an informant because he tends to know pretty much everything, although I find his information can be unreliable at times.

Jimmy looks much like a Northeast Portland messiah should: long brown hair, long beard, thick-framed glasses, over-washed and oversized tour T-shirt of some obscure band, tight black jeans, and combat boots he kept after a stint in the Merchant Marines.

I've been waiting for him ever since the Russian firecracker came in. He shoots me a sign of the cross and I know to get him a double Hendricks and four limes.

Before I can get the first word out of my mouth, Jimmy says in his deep low voice, "I know. It was my first vision of the day."

"Should I take it?"

"Seems you already did," he says and laughs and his kitchen matchstick frame shakes more than the joke was funny.

"Well, you should have seen her, Jimmy."

"Oh, I will before it's over."

"Where do I start?"

"Tomorrow, Sean."

"I said where not when, Jimmy."

"Big Hair Dan's. But today pour me another, and one for yourself while you're at it. On me. You're gonna need it."

Big Hair Dan used to work at Cave Yeller Pizza on Hawthorne, and to the untrained eye he's just an unusually tall, gangly pizza shop manager who always wears unfashionable large sunglasses and giant tie-dye T-shirts. His perpetually worn cargo shorts reveal near-impossibly long, pasty white, hairless legs and these shorts pockets are always filled with dime bags of cannabis strains with names like Northern Lights, Blue Dream, Granddaddy Purple, or Alaskan Thunder Fuck.

I was never big into the herb, but if you're a player in the Portland underground you need to know the big names in recreational drug sales. Big Hair Dan is the head of his crew and controls most of the pot market from Alaska, Seattle, Portland, to Humboldt County. You see, the God's honest truth is, Big Hair Dan's a Sasquatch. Shaved everywhere except for his dreads in order to fit into society. And it makes sense Bigfoot and his brothers have the best weed because they grow it organically without pesticides or hydroponics or any other unnatural way. They have a network that goes all over the unexplored, remote Pacific Northwest. Those Bigfoot sightings you see on YouTube? Just weed deliveries to Big Hair Dan and his boys. They used to work in pizza places and coffee shops but now that pot's legal they've switched to the dispensary business. I caught up to him at Brothers Cannabis Club on Thirty-sixth and Division.

I had taken a picture of Yelena's stalker photo with my phone and sent it ahead. It's not a good idea to show up unannounced and surprise a herd, or clan, or whatever a group of Bigfoot are called.

Big Hair Dan answers the door and looks down at me with a giant smile showing his thick, flat, yellow teeth. "Seanie! Didn't think to see you again. Come on in, little brother. Let's head to my office."

I follow him into something like a high-end dentist's office. The place is filled with Sasquatch in varying degrees of hair growth stages, and since they're hidden from the public they stand at their full height and don't hide their strength.

We walk to his office in the back. Big Hair Dan waits until I'm in and closes the door so it's just the two of us now. The room is a white cave with light maple hardwood floors, empty except for a lacquered cedar stump fashioned into a sort of throne in the very middle of the room. All the gleaming white walls have giant framed prints of Portland street artists Fasai, Adam Brock, and Faith47. He climbs up on his throne, knuckles first, and after getting comfortably cross-legged he says, "You sure you want in on whatever this is, Sean?"

I pull out five folded twenty-dollar bills paper-clipped in half and toss it to him.

"Okay. Okay, but do you know what a Vodianoi is?"

"A type of penis pill?"

Big Hair Dan adjusts his giant sunglasses and hesitates.

First the two grand, then Jimmy buying me a drink, now Big Hair Dan holding out on me? How many red flags will I have to ignore and why am I ignoring them? Maybe I've been out of the game too long and I'm losing my edge, or maybe I keep going because these red flags make life more interesting.

"Vodianoi are water ghosts, man. The souls of the drowned; real mischievous, from what I understand. He's one of them. He's been seen around strip clubs. Seems to be looking for someone, from what my guys could tell."

Long legs, curves, rare pink lips, and warm breath on my cheeks. They all flash through my mind. "Makes sense. Thanks, Big Hair."

"Yeah, just remember, no matter what you do, don't try to fight this guy by a body of water."

"Got it."

"That's where he gets his power from."

"Okay."

"I'm serious, dude."

"I said I got it."

It takes all night and a few hours into the morning before I find him inside the Acropolis gentlemen's club where Yelena dances under the stage name Duchess. I'm going off a cell phone pic of a distorted old photo so the face seems hardly recognizable, but when I see him I know. He's uglier than sin on baby Jesus's birthday. His face is thin and sharp like a cemetery shovel, and he's wearing a long, fur robe, moist with an ossuary sweat. He sits reeking in the shadows, beyond the video poker machines, watching as Yelena and two other girls rotate through an hour's worth of songs.

The first shift finishes, and as the last girl rakes up the ones on the dance stage, this dark figure stands and exits. I follow. He leaves behind a sandy film in every viscous footprint.

By the time I'm out the door there's no sign of him, yet his trail leads me north on foot down McLoughlin Boulevard and then west to the edge of the unused Acropolis Annex building's parking lot. It's not raining but there is a light mist that gives the single street light in the middle of the gravel lot a yellow halo. The vapor in the air increases until it's almost like an ocean spray. I breathe deep and smell the pleasant scent of petrichor, but then there's something else, a rancid odor just underneath, slowly getting stronger. Big Hair Dan's words come back to me: "No matter what you do, don't try to fight this guy by a body of water."

Yeah, but what if the water is in the air? This warning makes me pause. Is two grand worth it? No. But seeing gratitude in those emerald sparklers would be. I take a step and stop. The crunch of rocks under my boot is all I hear. He's watching me from somewhere. I can feel it like I'd feel a hundred thousand ants crawling up and down my spine, but I take another step, and another. I'm all the way in the corner of the lot when I hear it, the gurgling of Johnson Creek.

Shit. Ambush.

Quickly, I reach into my back pocket and take out Bockscar, my sap. It's a long horse-leather pocket, stitched closed with dozens of thick lead washers the size of silver dollars inside. It's gotten me out of more than a few tight places in the past. I smack the open palm of my left hand and the slap echoes through the bushes, letting him know that I know what's about to happen.

He steps out of the darkness but he's still a shadow like the light doesn't even want to touch that face. It's used bubble gum under a diner table with sprigs and patches of what must have been a thick beard at one time randomly sticking out, but those eyes; I'm not prepared for his eyes. They're big, dark, and fathomless and his voice matches when he says in a thick Russian accent, "Tonight, God will hear your prayers and see your tears."

"Bring it, ugly." I lunge, but he lets me come straight at him. I swing so hard his head should exit his shoulders, but instead he turns and leers over me. I come back with Bockscar the other way, really landing a whack on his left cheek that would stagger a mule, but still nothing.

The wind starts to pick up around us, howling in my ears. Rain pelts down, each drop heavy and cold. I wallop him again. I bash him again. I swear I get six or seven belts in there before his hand shoots out at me like a striking diamondback and his ice grip closes around my throat.

My fists beat wildly at his one arm and then I realize my legs are dangling off the ground.

The world around me stretches until everything I see and hear becomes so thin I think it can tear away, leaving nothing but the dreamless black of a forced unconsciousness. Time slows and all sound turns to a series of waves, hitting me one at a time, but somehow I still hear, and what I hear is Yelena's voice screaming, "*Nyet*, Grigori, stop."

When he turns his head toward her voice, the streetlight reflects off the left half of his long face and I really see it for the first time. Dark, cavernous eye sockets too high up and too close together. Splotches of gray and blue dead skin swollen and bloated, looking like it was left submerged for weeks. Out of his black eyes flows a heavy stream of tears down into the tangled, wet patches of beard.

I use his hesitation to put all my strength into pulling away. I give it every last ounce I have and yank at his arm. Handfuls of material rip off and turn to silt in my hands, but I keep grabbing and pulling. The stark odor of rotting earth fills my mouth and both nostrils, sending me into a choking fit. Ice-cold fingers close, caving my esophagus. The light drains from my vision, dimming everything to near total darkness, but then Yelena screeches, then pleads, "Grigori, *pozhaluysta*!"

His head jerks in her direction, pelting my face with some sort of foul-smelling globs. I use his lapse of attention to escape his frozen grip. I land on all fours and rub my neck, gulping air and coughing.

The force of the winds picks up so there is no sound other than an endless angry roar and this makes his robes flap behind him, revealing a tall, horrendous sight. Through tears in his moldy boots I see what I can only describe as talons. My gaze runs up from there and I see the hurricane gusts making strips of his saturated, greasy skin flap angrily over shiny midnight-blue scales underneath. Three long, glistening gashes on each side of his neck open and close almost convulsively under straggly patches of thin beard. And his eyes, dark caverns, shaped like holes in the brick wall guarding the City of Dis.

If I'm going out, it isn't going to be like this, not on my knees. I dig the balls of my feet into the gravel, set up like a track sprinter, and launch my whole weight into his stomach.

I hit with a sickening wet thud. Near-freezing slime coats the side of my face and neck. The smell again, the smell, decaying fish, but I keep pumping my legs, pushing him backward until he falls on his ass with me on top. Next comes a dozen ham-fisted blows in rapid succession, straight to his mass of rotted teeth. I have the advantage. No man can keep the lights on with a walloping like this.

But he throws me off like dirty laundry. Before he does, I hook my hand around what feels like a small chain he's wearing around his neck. It snaps.

Before I'm done skidding to a stop in the rocks and dirt, he's over me, kicking my chest in. I hear cracks and know it's the cartilage ripping between my ribs.

The world becomes just a series of white flashes, and I think I'm a goner, but then I hear the rev of an eight-cylinder engine coming right at me. I roll out of the way, open a swollen eye, and see Jimmy's 1960 AMC Rambler Convertible smack right into the big nasty drowned Russian ghost. Now, he may be some sort of supernatural creature who out-toughed me, but he can't out-tough good old Detroit engineering and ingenuity. That mass of cherry red cast-iron and steel knocks him down like wheat under a sickle. Jimmy opens the passenger door for me and yells, "Get a move on, kids."

Before I know it Yelena's helping me onto the front bench seat, the door closes, and we're heading north back into the city.

The three of us sitting in the front, I poke and prod my new shiner, and none of us speaks for a while. XRAY.FM fills the silence with the soul stylings of Ural Thomas & the Pain on low volume. I'm okay with just watching the reflection of every street lamp run up the windshield, illuminating every drop of rain, but then I figure I'm being impolite by not introducing the two. "Jimmy, this is Yelena. Yelena, Jimmy."

"Yelena, hell," Jimmy says in his deep voice. "That's Grand Duchess Anastasia Nikolaevna, daughter of Russian Tsar Nicholas II. And that guy kicking your ass?"

Yelena sighs and turns to look at the train running alongside us. "Grigori Rasputin."

It's too much to take in so I look down at my lap and open my right hand to find a locket just like the one Yelena, or Anastasia, wears. I pop it open and there's his ugly mug looking at me on the right, and her beautiful face on the left.

Jimmy leans into the steering wheel and says, "And he's *really* going to want that back."

Next time on The Fixer: A Serial . . .

While Rasputin's amulet kept him alive after being beaten nearly to death, gutted, poisoned, shot, frozen, and mostly drowned, Anastasia's locket kept her young and beautiful. After her near execution by the Bolsheviks, she roamed the globe before settling down to become an exotic dancer in Portland, Oregon. After enlisting help from a burnt-out Iraq War veteran and a failed messiah, she means to put an end to Rasputin's repeated attempts to take her back to the motherland to help Putin create a one-world order with them as man and wife. Will the Fixer have the grit to do what must be done? Will Jimmy stay sober long enough to help save the world? And what role will the Bigfoot Brothers and their medicinal marijuana play? Find out in Chapter 2: Doubt Thou the Stars Are Fire.

The Deflowering

Suzy Vitello

Night town.
Night town a glass.
Color mahogany.
Color mahogany center.
Rose is a rose is a rose is a rose.
Loveliness extreme.
Extra gaiters.
Loveliness extreme.
Sweetest ice-cream.

— excerpted from "Sacred Emily" by Gertrude Stein

(1)

Wispy, Fuchsia, and I were turning sixteen. We'd been waiting for this week our whole friendship. June babies, always the last birthdays of the school year. Geminis, the three of us.

"Ironic, huh?" Wispy would say when we passed out the invitations for our joint birthday party all of those years until now. "That Geminis would come in threes?"

"Hashtag-trips," Fuchsia would say. "You know, triplets?"

Our various friends were anticipating the usual passing out of the invites—or even e-vites—but this year, that wasn't happening. Our fathers, who played squash at the same club, had convinced our mothers and stepmothers (and in Wispy's case, step-girlfriend) that Sweet Sixteen birthdays were special, and therefore needed to be celebrated on the one-off.

"Trust me, Emmy," my father said. "Fireworks."

Fuchsia and Wispy had been told similar promises. "What do they mean, 'fireworks'?" Wispy said, when we were walking to the Light Rail Starbucks near our school. "Like a Fourth of July type of thing?"

Fuchsia and I shrugged our shoulders. What did we know? Nothing, that's what.

The three of us, the hashtag-trips of us, we were the proof that the whole is so much more than the sum of body parts. Wispy and her long torso and well-muscled rump just begging for a tramp stamp. Her white-blond hair like a corona. Fuchsia: a fragile beauty, like Keira Knightley, her stick-thin arms and legs and joints that knobbed out. She was terribly shy without us as her anchors. And me. Barely five feet tall, boyish and sassy, the youngest captain of the varsity soccer team ever, but remedial in math. It seemed unlikely that there could be fireworks without the complete package.

Most pressing, the three of us were about to enter our sixteenth birthdays having barely even been kissed. Unless you count the truth-or-dare smashing of lips with Corbin Garber under the elementary school play structure all those years ago.

The truth was, this summer we planned to lose our virginities. Nobody we knew was still a virgin. Time was running out. We were almost juniors!

Already, the first week of June had come and gone, and with it the various parades and Rose Festival Princesses. As we walked toward our pre-ordered Frappuccinos, I picked up a flattened yellow flower from the gutter. Another one that couldn't hang on to the float 'til the end. I stuck it in my wiry hair, where its stem curled around the back of my ear.

(2)

Fuchsia's birthday came first. She celebrated by skipping school to take her driver's test, and then showed up the next day at lunch piloting one of those toy cars with only two seats. "Nice ride, Sweet Sixteen," I kidded on my way back from the Paleo food cart as I watched her maneuver off of the curb.

She finally parked, hopped out, and we walked together.

I was balancing a cabbage roll in one hand and a container of all-meat chili in the other, and she didn't offer to help, or ask for a bite, like normal. She hadn't responded to my texts or Snapchats or Instagrams or Swipes. In fact, she hadn't liked a single thing I'd posted for at least twenty-four hours.

Wispy and I had decorated her locker with photos of Taylor Kitsch. One with his signature long, greasy hair, and one of him winking in slick Armani. When she saw it, she didn't laugh or even turn up a corner of her lip. In fact, she looked very un-Fuchsia-like. As if she'd been dipped in shellac while squinting.

"You okay?" I said.

Wispy walked up and took Fuchsia by the shoulders. "You look, um, weird."

Fuchsia said nothing. Just shuffled binders in her locker and extracted a small notebook. When the door clanged shut, one of the Taylor Kitsches came loose and fluttered to the shiny linoleum. Wispy snatched it up and kissed it, before ditching it in the large blue recycling tumbler.

Meanwhile, Fuchsia advanced along, down the middle of the corridor, toward French.

I sporked pork into my mouth and wished I'd gotten a tall flat white to go with it. Strands of pork, greasier than Taylor Kitsch's *Friday Night Lights*-era hair, were crammed against my incisors. Wispy strode off to IB Bio, and I went to Flex, where I continued to worry the meat in the cracks between my teeth.

(3)

By the time Wispy turned sixteen, Fuchsia still hadn't snapped back to normal. Wispy also didn't come to school for two days, and I wondered why I hadn't been given the heads-up on any of it.

"C'mon, Fuche," I said. "I've got, like, sixteen different Hello Kitty things for Wispy's locker. I need your help."

Fuchsia placed a bony hand on my shoulder as lightly as a teacher who feared a lawsuit by a helicopter mom would. She said, "Emily, we're too old for that."

Emily? "Fuche, c'mon. It's me, Emmy! Hashtag-trips, remember?"

Fuchsia, so fragile and pretty.

Fuchsia's eyebrows veed downward. Her hand dropped from my shoulder. She began to tremble, but then, suddenly, she straightened, fake-smiled, and backed away from me. Her fragile prettiness disappearing, like the farthest point in a perspective drawing.

(4)

Wispy showed up at the Light Rail Starbucks after school where I was meeting with my algebra tutor. She walked right by the table where I sat contemplating the FOIL method. My eyes sprung up from the torture. "Wisp!" I said. "Hey!"

She twisted her head around and her eyes were two blank discs inside a frame of blow-dried hair. She said, "Are you talking to me?" as if I were a stranger, and then she just kept walking.

The tutor said, "Your parents are paying for an hour of my time. Let's turn our attention back to the equations."

"Wispy, Wispy, Wispy," I said into the air as I clicked my mechanical pencil until a needle of lead dropped to the sheet of graph paper below.

(5)

Ever since my friends turned sixteen, they were scooped-out zombies. Neither Fuchsia nor Wispy returned my messages. Plus, their social media accounts were gone. Gone! I had envisioned us choreographing dozens of selfies this week. Hashtag-trips all over the landscape. Hashtag-Sixteen. Hashtag-SweetSixteen. Hashtag-GeminiTriplets. And so many hashtags and hashtag acronyms yet to be invented. Where was the life we'd envisioned? Nowhere, that's where.

I sat on my bed, twirling the dead flower I'd found in the gutter the week before. It was my birthday eve. The threat of crying kept cropping up inside of my nose the way disappointment does. *Abject* disappointment, if you wanted to get all SAT prep about it.

(6)

There was a knock on my bedroom door, then it opened and in walked Dad and his current wife, Celeste—who Wispy and Fuchsia called Celestial Seasonings because you never saw her without a mug of tea. Tonight, Celeste didn't have tea, but she did have a hashtag-TBT picture in her hands.

"I thought you might be interested in what I looked like at sixteen," she said, handing me a Sierra-filtered photograph.

In the photo, Celeste was a mess. A grimy, Grateful Dead-chick mess. I glanced up at her present-era, anticipating face. "Yuck," I said, handing her back her pic along with the dead flower, and immediately felt the swell of sorrow again in my nose. Besides losing our virginities, the hashtag-trips had also vowed to be less snarky once we turned sixteen.

But I still had an hour or so to work on that.

"Yuck?" said Celeste.

Dad said, "We've planned a surprise for you, Emmy."

I said, "Does it involve turning Wispy and Fuchsia back to their regular selves?"

Celeste said, "What do you mean, 'yuck,' you little brat?" and stormed out of the room, dropping the Rose Festival float flower on my rug and making sure she squished it into the carpet with her bare heel.

"PMS?" I said.

Dad took both my hands in his. "Well, honey, Dave, Chip, and I went in on this thing together."

"Thing?" I said.

"You'll thank us when you're busting through that glass ceiling ten years from now."

"Glass ceiling? Dad, I can't even do eighth-grade math."

"Get dressed," he said, looking at the dark hairs on his wrist where a watch used to live.

(7)

Dad handed me the keys to the Leaf and told me to head to the Willamette. "The Hawthorne Bridge," he said. "We have to get there before midnight."

From the passenger seat, Dad kept staring at me the way someone who hasn't seen a beloved family member in five years would. Finally, I cranked my head and said, "What?"

"It happens so quickly. One day, you're holding a bundle of love, and then, just like that, you're letting them drive the car."

I rolled my eyes. Dad was really good at making everything about him.

At 11:56 we reached the Hawthorne Bridge. Dad said, "Take the inside lane of the deck. We have to park under the penthouse."

There were orange cones blocking the middle lanes. "But . . ." I said.

"First thing you should know about being a successful grown-up is barriers were made for others."

I navigated the Leaf in between the cones, and rumbled along the metal grate.

Dad said, "Okay, stop."

Was this where the fireworks would be? Dad had money, but not that much money.

I stopped the car in the middle of the bridge, underneath the little house, and Dad said, "Turn off the engine. Stay in the car until you're instructed otherwise."

"By who?" I said. "Instructed otherwise by who?"

Dad said, "What's about to happen is for your own good. Remember. I love you."

(8)

The Leaf door closed with a tinny slap, and then everything next happened in one motion. Dad was gone, the lift alarms clanged, amber lights flashed, and the slab of bridge underneath the car rose like an elevator.

All of the bridges along the Willamette raised differently. Most of them, though, had sections that swung up from each side with the split in the middle. The Hawthorne was more old-fashioned, and up, up, up went the whole middle piece.

Outside the car windows, lights from the various buildings and bridges shone or blinked. No other bridge was lifting. There was no boat passing underneath.

The Leaf was cooling off from the heat of the day and it smelled like ripe bananas. My heart thumped.

Was this when the fireworks would start? I gazed over the dark, swollen river. It reminded me of a gash in otherwise smooth skin, the bridges up and down the Willamette like stitches made from several types of thread.

I smoothed my H&M tee over the waistband of my shorts, and tugged at the ends of my curls the way I do when I'm anxious. The platform under me was still rising.

Until it wasn't.

(9)

The slab of bridge lurched to a stop with a deafening sound—rusty cranks and pulleys screeching against something metallic. I looked up, half-expecting the roof of the Leaf to be caving in. Instead, the whole inside of the car began to glow. And in that glow, a gust of breeze tickled my neck.

I sneezed—the force of emotion finally producing evidence. And something else. A presence that felt like the tip of a feather hovering over all of the hairs on my body, causing them to stand up. Seriously stand up, like at attention!

I looked from one arm to the other, rolling my gaze elbows to wrists. Then, another sneeze. I dragged the back of my hand under my nose, wishing for a Kleenex. And that's when an old-fashioned handkerchief appeared. It fluttered in midair, like a theater ghost on fishing line.

"Huh?" I said, reaching for my phone, not certain about whether I should call 9-1-1 or record this for YouTube. I sneezed again.

Gesundheit, said a voice, and the handkerchief bounced in place.

I reached for the handkerchief—a small square of stiff material with a yellow rose embroidered on a corner. Too pretty, almost, to wipe snot with. But I did, anyway. "Thanks," I said.

No worries, said the voice.

The voice was a man's voice. Sort of young-sounding, but deep.

"So, are you the surprise my dad told me to expect?"

I am, it said.

I crushed the embarrassment of my snot inside the hankie, but the material began to change—instead of cotton, it took on a rubbery feel, and then I felt a prick. "Oh Em Gee!" I cried, unclenching my fist and pulling my arm back.

A perfect, yellow rosebud on a thick, thorny stem fluttered to the passenger seat of the Leaf.

(10)

The rosebud rose up and brushed against my cheek, and then petted the bridge of my nose.

Happy Birthday, said the voice.

My eyes crossed, watching the delicate bud slip around my nostrils.

The voice said, *I'm here to give you pleasure.*

My heart thumped. "What sort of pleasure?"

The rosebud drew itself in a figure eight over my face, around my eyes, and then it skittered lower, arcing from shoulder to shoulder, making doughnut rings around my boobs—which, I had to admit, had grown quite plump my fifteenth year.

"Who are you?" I said.

Who do you want me to be? it said.

"Frankly," I said, pushing the rose off of my chest, "I'd like you to be Wispy and Fuchsia."

The white-haired girl and the skinny one? it said. *From last week?*

"What did you do to them?"

The voice sighed, and the rosebud hovered a skosh off the passenger seat, as if it were sitting on an invisible lap.

Below us, cars were lined up, waiting for the bridge to go back down.

"Did my dad hire you to deflower me?" I said.

That's a coarse way of putting it, it said, *don't you think?*

"Well?"

We like to think of it as bringing you into adulthood gently, respectfully.

"We?" I said. "Who's this 'we'?"

The rosebud rose again, and the glow in the car dimmed everywhere except a small circle of light around the flower. The rose waggled about as the voice said, *It's called the* Suite Sixteen, *this service. Suite, as in a section of rooms in an office building. As in, making your mark in the world. CFO. CCO. Even, if I do my job well, CEO.*

"And it all starts with raping daughters on a lifted bridge?" I said.

We better get to it, the voice said. *They'll start honking soon.*

(11)

I glanced at my silent phone. It was midnight, and there'd been no Happy Birthday push notifications from the Triplets. No nothing from them. They were probably in their respective beds getting good night's sleeps in anticipation of acing finals—which were this week. "I think I'll pass," I said.

Pass? Why, you can't! huffed the voice.

"Whatever you did to my friends, to make them more successful, or focused; whatever you took from them, I don't want you taking from me."

The rosebud slapped the dash of the Leaf. *I took nothing. I gave,* muttered the voice. *I gave them immense pleasure, while rendering them impervious to the wooing of malicious intent.*

I grabbed the rosebud, which was now all smashed and bruised, leaving its yellow blood all over the car's interior. "Malicious intent?"

Boys, it said. The voice was shaky now. Not at all the deep, confident voice of before. *Drama. Frivolity. Your father has invested in a system that circumvents all of that. The tears, the hurt feelings.*

"Ha!" I said, petting the orange-tipped petals of the mangled yellow bud. "It's stupid, is what it is, and I don't want any part of it."

Your friends emerged from this experience stronger than most mid-level management women.

A car honked below us. And another.

"Why would you do this?" I said. "What's in it for you?"

The voice began to cry. At first, it was just a sniffle. A hiccup. But by the time the cars below were a symphony of horn-blowing, the voice was full-on sobbing. I was embarrassed for it, actually, and I reached over to embrace the air around it, tapping the sad little rosebud against the nothing.

(12)

Are you going to tell on me? said the sniveling voice as the slab of bridge we were on began to descend.

"I won't," I said. "*If* you give me back Wispy and Fuchsia. Turn them back to frivolous, boy-crazy virgins."

The voice stammered, *I d-don't know how. Th-they never taught us how to undo it.*

"Well, whatever you did, you can just do backwards, right?"

The voice didn't answer, but I imagined it shrugging its shoulders.

We agreed to meet the night after school got out, a few days from now.

The slab of bridge returned to road level, and Dad popped back in the car, and he had the red eyes of the totally stoned and/or incredibly sad.

"It's okay," I said, tapping him on the back of his hairy hand. "Let's just go home."

We didn't speak the whole ride back up the hill.

(13)

I got a D in math, but otherwise my grades were good. Wispy and Fuchsia managed to both get four-points. I had to trick them in order to get them to agree to go out with me. I told them there was a special Stanford recruiting session in the little penthouse on the Hawthorne Bridge. "At midnight?" they said.

"It's invitation-only," I lied.

We drove to the bridge in Wispy's step-girlfriend's Chrysler LeBaron. Wispy said, "You drive, Emily. I need to work on my campaign."

I chauffeured Wispy and Fuchsia—the two of them folded over their devices in the back seat. Fuchsia was putting together a You-Fund-Me for cleaning human excrement off Mount Everest, and Wispy was . . . I didn't really know. She was running for something. A councilperson spot. Or school board. Something a thirty-six-year-old would be running for. The night was clear and warm, the moon a sliver. I negotiated the big car toward the river, dodging skateboarders and prostitutes.

As before, once we approached the bridge, cones were set up to keep cars off of the center lanes of the deck, and, as before, I bypassed the half-assed barrier of them. My heart, again, thumping like crazy.

I came to a stop and the slab of bridge lifted. The zombie girls were still hunched over their work. When the slab reached the top, there was the same screeching clang. Same glow inside the car. No hankie or flower, this time. And with the gentle breeze, the passenger door flew open. *Hurry*, said the back-to-confident-and-assertive voice. *We don't have much time.*

We were ordered to follow the voice to a tiny elevator built into the metal criss-crosses of the bridge. I followed Fuchsia and Wispy, who were still holding their laptops in front of them, not wanting to lose a minute of work time.

The elevator jerked and cranked, lurching us up to the penthouse. The doors screeched open and the voice ushered us into a tiny room, hardly big enough for the three of us (plus the voice) to all be in there together. The walls were glass, and outside, the bridges looked more like stitches than ever.

(14)

"Where's the college recruiter?" asked Wispy.

"Is that him?" asked Fuchsia, pointing to a silver panel of switches and buttons.

"Do you see someone there?" I said.

"Don't you see him?" said Wispy, glancing up from her screen.

The voice said, *They have the power to see me. A power you would have, too, if you'd allow me to fulfill my contractual obligation.*

"Just reverse the spell. Or whatever you did to them," I said.

Wispy said, "Is there an early admission policy? I mean, earlier than regular early admission?"

What happened to the girl with the fake ID, who planned to get a tattoo of a marijuana leaf on her backside this summer? She'd been ruined, that's what.

"Can we get on with the reversal? The," I said, "you know, revirginating?"

"What reversal?" said Fuchsia.

"Revirginating?" said Wispy.

Like I said, said the voice, *I've never done one. This is in beta, just to be clear.*

(15)

What happened next was beautiful, horrible, pleasurable, and shocking. The switches on the silver panel flipped back and forth. Buttons depressed. Laptops flew out of hands. Hashtag-OMG all over the place. Wispy's white hair peeled off of her scalp, forehead to nape, and Fuchsia splattered against the glass—a fly nabbed by a swatter. Out the windows, the city blinked. The moon tipped back, and began to rock, like a chair. The stitches up and down the river lit up as if all of the Christmas lights from all of the years had joined together.

I opened my mouth to scream, but no sound came out. And then, I smelled it. The intense perfume of too many roses.

The voice took shape before my eyes. A boy. A man. A man-boy. He was my father, Wispy's father, and Fuchsia's. Every man I knew. Even Corbin Garber, the boy from under the fifth grade jungle gym.

The shape floated toward me, closer, closer, until our fronts touched. And then. And then. With a gentle push, he melted into me.

(16)

I woke up in the back seat of the LeBaron, which Wispy was driving like a madwoman, swerving just in time to miss slamming into the bronze elk on Main Street. "Did you lose him? Did you?" said Fuchsia.

"What a creep," said Wispy, as she zoomed up the hill, her white hair all electrified around her head like an Einstein.

There now, said the voice. *Satisfied?*

"Wispy! Fuchsia! Are you okay?" I said. But I didn't say that. I didn't say that because I had been turned into a bouquet of roses. Rose Garden roses: fragrant, perfect, each of my stems a bright, cankerless green.

"Has she responded yet?" said Wispy.

"Nada," said Fuchsia, scrolling through her phone.

"What should we do with those?" asked Wispy, her thumb all hitchhiker, jabbed back toward me.

"We better put them in water," Fuchsia said. "Or donate them to one of those roadside markers where someone was hit on their bicycle."

"What sort of weirdo tries to jack your car using flowers as a weapon?" said Wispy.

"Do you think Emmy did this as a practical joke?" Fuchsia said.

"No!" I yelled. "I did it to save you!"

They can't hear a thing, the voice said.

"This is unacceptable," I stammered. "Turn me back to me. Immediately!"

Rose is a rose is a rose, said the voice.

"But it's not!" I yelled, invisibly, mutely. "It's me! I'm still me!"

But Wispy kept driving into the night.

Epilogue

Hashtag-trips would resurface and morph into hashtag-Emmy-Gone. And hashtag-WhereIsEmily. The next year, Wispy and Fuchsia, after they lost their virginities for real, would become hashtag-twins.

My father would spend the rest of his life trying to find me, not knowing that I was in the gutter, fallen from a bicycle memorial. As for the voice? As long as there were fathers wanting the best for their daughters, the voice would continue to infect the sixteen-year-old girls of Portland with suite success.

Into THE WEIRD

Porches bother her. Porches have hippies. Hippies have smells. Smells have water. Water has bugs. Bugs have eyes. Eyes have caps of flesh.

Tunnels

Leni Zumas

Ann lives above an anti-inflammatory cafe in the fifth quadrant. The absence of dairy, wheat, and sugar means fewer cockroaches are liable to gather in the cafe, and fewer, if any, will climb into her apartment. She likes the apartment, though the neighborhood itself, with its thousand porches, bothers her. Porches have hippies. Hippies have smells. Smells have water. Water has bugs. Bugs have eyes. Eyes have caps of flesh.

From the church down the block she hears ecstatic singing, amplified guitars, the stomping of feet. She only listens, doesn't dream of going in. The parishioners are so young and good-looking Ann thinks it might be a casting site for sportswear models, not a church at all. On Sundays, leash in hand, Lumby straining against the collar, she watches the handsome red building and its handsome, mostly white flock. She feels like an old mole who swims under cemeteries, clammy nose stroking the corpses.

Her longtime friend Thistle calls to ask a favor. Ann bundles Lumby into his sweater, straps him into the car seat, and drives across the pale bridge with lofted spindles meant to make one think of soaring—of flight—but which put Ann in mind of bars on an Arctic cage. Thistle is worried for her brother, a wreck slunk back from Worcester, Massachusetts, to live on Thistle's floor. She wants Ann to work a sober magic, steer Sage toward a life of less douchebaggery and more on-time payments. The sister wants Ann to stand with the brother in his cave, name the arrival city of his complaint, listen to him read aloud his parking tickets.

They go to an egg restaurant. Ginger ale for all. The brother says, "It's frankly appalling to call this 'ale.'"

Ann has felt the desire to be biting and drunk, or if not drunk, then able to remind everyone how much alcohol you can and did once drink. Thistle twips Ann's pinkie with a thumb and forefinger, as in *Say something now!* but what can she say? *I have felt this. And now I don't.*

In their teenhood, Sage was considered handsome (though Ann never really thought so) and ambitious, sure to leave Portland for a music career in New York or Los Angeles. Thistle collected spiders and sewed felt-and-yarn hats; she would stay local, everyone knew. And Ann? Nobody in high school thought about her long enough to venture predictions. They would have been astounded to learn of the mess she made after graduation.

Sage, shoveling eggs, talks of his debts and his custody battle and how, because the outpatient treatment center in Worcester laced the lunch with saltpeter, he hasn't had an erection in five months. When confronted, the center's director laughed and told him saltpeter was only for the military and that he was laboring under a delusion—"One of your many, might I add." Sage was so insulted by this remark that he shoved, the next day, a handful of his own feces under the door of the director's office.

He says, "Crotchety the Crotch didn't believe me, either. She was like, 'Don't blame the saltpeter; blame the Scotch.' Notice my use of rhyme there, Ann? I went to college, too."

"Good for you," says Ann.

"Ann," says Thistle, remindingly.

"*Ann*," says Sage. "A-N-N. Aaaaannnnn."

He continues the trashing of his soon-to-be-former wife. A decent mother but a terrible, quote, woman. Sent him a letter of such hysterical violence he'd been tempted to show it to the police. Had, however, not.

"Good decision," says Ann.

"Really? Huh." He is rolling a cigarette on his thigh. "I don't think it's so good. I may regret it in court. Did you know that 'hysterical' means 'suffering in the womb'?"

On the walk back to Thistle's, Ann lets Lumby stretch his legs.

"You've got a pigeon on a leash," says Sage. "Are you very depressed?"

"No," says Ann.

"Well, *I* am," he says. "Problem is, depression is a young man's game."

"You're still young," says Thistle.

"Forty isn't young," says Ann.

"You'd know that better than any of us," says Sage.

"Uh, fuck you?" says Ann.

Three blocks of human quiet. Some grunts and coos from Lumby.

"May I speak to you in the kitchen, Ann?" says Thistle. Ann follows. Thistle pins her by the shoulders to the fridge and says: "Tunnels."

"What?"

"You had bug tunnels. Sage has assholery."

"Different," says Ann.

"But same family," says Thistle.

The refrigerator sings into the bones of Ann's back. "I'll be nicer," she says.

Sunday morning, Sage gets off the bus in Ann's neighborhood. She is waiting with her arms crossed. "Something tells me we're about to hit a meeting," he says. "But can we get coffee first?"

"We can," says Ann.

They walk. It is warm for November, and all the hippies are stretched out on their porches. Exactly how many bugs are living in the humid pubic hair of these hippies? Ann recalls the bugs she once pinched off her own face, thousands and thousands; they dug themselves into the skin and had to be clawed out, sometimes with tweezers. "They were *burrowing*," she told Thistle later. "They were trying to dig tunnels."

"Where's your pigeon today?" says Sage.

"At home."

"Does he have his own room?"—a burst of cackling.

The church comes into view, front steps thronged with flawless haircuts and magazine cheekbones.

"But you said we'd get coffee first!"

She has never dreamt, until this moment, of going in. "They have coffee inside," she says and shoves Sage into the beautiful flock. The parishioners' bodies smell like honeysuckle; their faces wear shrewd, benevolent smiles.

"Welcome," says a woman with shiny teeth and no bra.

Sage presses his wet mouth to Ann's ear. "This meeting may cure my erectile DF."

"It's not a—"

"Welcome, friends!" cries a bearded boy who resembles a pop star Ann has seen on billboards. "First time here? Take a seat wherever."

They choose a back pew and watch the congregants file in. "These are the sexiest alcoholics I've ever seen," says Sage. "And I've gone to meetings in Brooklyn."

"Good for you," says Ann.

A deciduous tree sheds its leaves, a mammal its milk teeth. A person can shed maladaptive coping mechanisms, but persons tend to love their mechanisms. Are loath to let them go. Persons, on the whole, are pseudodeciduous. Sage, for instance—totally pseud. As soon as she thinks this, Ann feels bad. Years ago, when she stopped using the drugs that brought the bugs, people helped her. Sat with her at meetings, bought her coffee, took walks with her in parks whose trees were heart-smashingly tall. But she doesn't feel like doing any of those things for Sage. Old mole, what happened to you?

The bearded boy steps to the lectern and taps a large microphone. "Check, one two, check check."

"Love you!" screams a female voice.

"I love you, too," says the boy, grinning. He opens a book on the lectern, clears his throat. "From Chapter Velvet of Our Master's handbook: 'Blood from a cut body collected in a bucket will be bright only minutes, and in minutes will blacken; and if consumed when black, shall be of meaner quality; and therefore must be drunk while bright.'"

"What the dingleberry?" says Sage.

"So, friends, we will drink it while bright. But first we need a blood-giver, am I right?"

"*Hell* yes!" roars the congregation.

"Can I have a blood-giver?"

"*Hell* yes!"

"And where is my blood-giver, friends? Will my bonny blood-giver please stand up?"

A splashy, thumping drumbeat starts, but Ann can't see any drums. Must be recorded.

"Blood-giver, blood-giver, where are you?" shouts the bearded boy. He is suddenly holding—Ann squints—an enormous knife above his head. The kind of knife that's basically a sword.

"Is this, like, an art thing?" says Sage.

"Not to my knowledge."

"Well, fuck, I'm game." He gets to his feet. "Back here!"

Ann yanks on the belt-loops of his jeans, but he's stronger than he seems.

"A new friend has offered himself!" blares the microphone. "Join us on stage, friend!"

"Don't," she says.

Sage looks down at her, lip twitching. "Live a little, Ann."

As he walks up the aisle, two men carry to the stage a wooden bucket the size of a stove. A woman starts unwrapping Dixie cups, stack upon stack.

Waiting for the Question

Art Edwards

Around the time I got my last unemployment check, I noticed him out my kitchen window.

He squatted by a street lamp, just across the complex parking lot from my kitchen window, his expensive-shoed feet on a manhole cover that acted as a platform, the sun popping his forehead. He wore a double-breasted suit, like the ones he wore on the show, and he looked as if he were struggling to understand something nonsensical, maybe painful. The fingers of one hand hovered around his chin, and sometimes when he looked particularly unhinged he squeezed his bottom lip.

Alex Trebek showing up at your apartment complex is no small event, and Rosa and Pablo came out, approached him carefully, like he might be an animal that had the ability to swallow them whole. Pablo offered him a boost up, Rosa hovered behind. A few others came over. It was uncharacteristically warm for once, and everyone but Alex stood in the shade of Unit D. Alex acknowledged none of this. He squatted there, his feet under him, his knees never seeming to tire. Then a Camaro stopped in front of him and I couldn't see anymore.

When the crowd dissipated, I went out. A breeze rustled craggy maples at the complex's entrance. Chris, a guy I sometimes bought weed from, and another couple looked on.

"They're calling the police," Chris said.

"Why?"

"Distraction. He doesn't live here, doesn't belong here. People are going to make a big deal about it."

"They should make a big deal about it."

"Try telling him that." Chris stepped toward him. "Alex," he said, clapping his hands.

Alex squeezed his bottom lip, which escaped, worm-like.

"Bradley's afraid the Tribe's going to throw a party for him tonight," Chris said.

"Hope Alex doesn't mind patchouli."

If he understood any of this, Alex didn't let on. He squatted, looked off into the distance, like at bad weather coming, or a putt he needed to sink.

I watched him from my kitchen window, eating from a jar of marshmallow, waiting for the cops. Dozens of people trickled by, stopped, gawked. A kid in low-slung jeans waved gang signs in his face. Alex did nothing, continued looking into the distance.

I couldn't sleep that night, and every once in a while I got up to look out the window and see him squatting there under the street lamp. I eventually went out to him. His hair looked like steel wool under the fluorescent light.

"What do you want?" I said.

Alex didn't look at me.

"What are you thinking so hard about?"

Alex was stoic, looked at nothing, but I suspected more was going on.

Bradley must have pussied out of calling the cops, for none ever showed up. He was due to take a trip to Bend and likely disappeared before having to deal with it. We all liked Bradley. He was a notorious pushover when it came to the rent. It was just like him to ditch town with the problem unresolved.

The next night, the Tribe—this nebulous gang of half hippies/ half hobos, a few of whom had recently taken up residence in Unit

E—started showing up around Alex in groups of twos and threes. They wore stitched-together clothes, worn and faded. They smoked pot from little pipes and drank brown liquor from milk jugs. Many brought drums, formed a circle. The thump grew loud enough to make all other thought impossible. I pulled up a seat on my patio, cigarettes in tow.

No one addressed Alex for a long time. One of the Tribe, Jicama, large and loudmouthed in no shirt and tattered shorts, went up to people as they approached, greeted them, offered them hits from his jug. Dancers spun by the drums. Alex squatted, didn't acknowledge any of this, even though the drums were right next to him.

Once the sun went down, Jicama walked through the crowd, arms up, seemingly calling for attention. He motioned to the drum circle, and they stopped playing. Then, with everyone looking on, Jicama turned to Alex, obscuring him from my view. He said something I couldn't hear, then shouted, "Hey!" Everyone froze. My instinct was to go out and stop whatever it was, but I wasn't up for getting in the way.

"Ass face. What are you doin' here?"

The crowd converged so I couldn't see.

Jicama shouted, "I'm talkin' to you," and then something happened—a scuffle, a quick movement; I couldn't tell. I stood on tiptoes. It was like being at a schoolyard fight and too far away to know who was winning. The crowd looked on. One guy laughed. Then Jicama said, "You want a drink?" and the crowd reacted with what seemed a collective gasp.

A few minutes later, when the circle started up again and the crowd spun, I saw what had happened. Alex's hair dripped with liquid, what must've been the contents of Jicama's jug. Drips still migrated down from his curls and formed little puddles on the manhole cover. Alex didn't acknowledge this, didn't alter his stance. As the night pressed on, the ground around him became a dumping ground for empty bottles or whatever else the crowd wanted to get rid of. The party eventually got thinner until Alex was out there by himself, one side of his hair matted, no doubt sticky.

I rounded up the garden hose, turned on the water, dragged it across the street. "This is going to be cold." I angled the hose over him. It hit him a little too squarely, which made him squint, so I put my thumb over the spout. I sprayed directly at what looked like the caked areas, then all over him, making sure to get his neck. He dripped. "I can get you a towel," I said, but Alex said nothing. I wasn't going to dry him, too. I gathered all the junk at his feet, took it to the dumpster.

A few days later, I found a thin, windowed letter in my mailbox. It was from an estate management firm in Michigan. Inside was a check for $4,500, money left me by my grandma, who'd passed away a few months ago. It couldn't have come at a better time. I'd been short rent the month before, and I didn't know how I was going to make it up. I immediately deposited the check at the bank up the street.

I walked past Alex on my way back to my apartment. I'd managed to forget about him for a day or two, telling myself he needed to take care of himself. He was starting to look worked over. His suit was faded from the elements, and there was something flaky about the skin on the back of his neck. The area around him was littered with cans and food bags. Apparently, people had started launching garbage at him.

I got a broom, swept the garbage away. I dampened a washcloth, wiped his face. I bought sunblock and spread it on his neck and hands. "I ran into some luck," I said, "so I'm passing it on. Don't think I can do this every day."

The $4,500 lasted about two months. I got caught up on bills, ordered a keyboard on the internet. I tended to Alex every morning, making sure all the garbage was cleared away, that no harm had come to him during the night. One day I found a pair of men's underwear on his head. Another day, a popcorn bucket.

When I had only a few hundred dollars left, my attention to Alex slackened. I couldn't see wasting time on him; I had my own problems. I lived on food cart burritos for a week. I let my student loans slide. I drank tap water instead of beer.

A few days before rent was due, I found another windowed

envelope in my mailbox, this one brown. It was a check from the IRS for $1,400. Something to do with excess taxes. I went straight to Alex, showed him the check.

"Are you doing this?"

Alex said nothing. The back of his suit had split down the middle, and the white shirt puffed out like the excretion from a boiled egg.

"You're saving my ass," I said.

I got a wet cloth and cleaned his face, made a point to get behind his ears. I went to the store and bought a hat that expanded into a rainbow umbrella and put it on his head. The rainy season was right around the corner.

A month passed and nothing happened. I paid my rent, had pizzas delivered, tried out for this band.

One night I went out to see Alex. His head drooped a little, like he was getting tired, and his hands dangled lifeless between his legs.

"How are you?" I said.

Nothing. He seemed to have aged quite a bit since the last time I'd seen him, his hair longer, the wrinkles around his eyes more prominent. A beer bottle sat on the curb in front of him, so close that, if he spat, it might land inside.

"Things have been going pretty good for me since you came around. If there's anything you need, all you have to do is ask."

A car eased by. A guy and his girl looked at me, no doubt wondering if Alex talked to me.

"Well," I said. "Just so you know, if there's anything—" And I went back to my apartment.

A few weeks later, I heard a knock at my door. It was Bradley, decked out in golf clothes.

"It's my duty to tell you," he said, "you have to pay your balance or be evicted."

I hadn't paid on the first, and I knew I'd also skipped one a few months back. I could tell Bradley was nervous, which was all I had to work with. "It's your duty?"

"Boss says I have to tell you."

"I'm doing the best I can, here." One of my cats tried to escape. I grabbed at him, but he got away.

"That's fine," Bradley said. "Just so you know—"

"I know."

"You've got forty-eight hours."

"Jesus."

"I don't make the rules."

I wanted to say, "If you're so big on enforcing rules, what about Alex?" but that might have gotten him thrown out. Alex was here for a reason. That reason might even be me.

I called my brother Rex in Beaverton, who'd worked the same job for fifteen years.

"I need $1,100."

I felt the pause on his end, cutting me with every second. "You need $1,100."

"They're going to evict me."

"Where's Grandma's money?"

I couldn't answer. He sighed.

"I can't find a job."

"There's a guy in Hillsboro hiring people to do phone surveys."

"That's not my field."

"Your field?"

"Yes, I have a degree."

"What I'm getting at," Rex said, "is where was the urgency a few weeks ago when you could've done something about it besides call me?"

I had no answer for him, so I said, "You know, Alex Trebek is camped out at my apartment complex."

Rex sighed again. "Get yourself some work, and try laying off the bong for a while." And he hung up.

I knew what would happen in two days. It had happened to my friend Ross two complexes over. They'd stapled an eviction notice to his door, which required him to be out by nightfall. He didn't get all of his stuff out, and they wouldn't let him back in. He slept on a friend's couch, then at a youth hostel, then one night under a bridge.

At dusk, after calling my friends and coming up empty, I went out to see Alex. I wondered if he had any money on him. After all, I'd been taking care of him. It wasn't crazy to think he might have something for me.

Alex looked worn out from months of squatting. There was no one else around.

"I was wondering if you had any cash."

Alex said nothing.

"I'm coming up a little short this month, and it looks like I'm going to get evicted, so if there's any way . . ."

Alex stared straight ahead.

"You know, it would be great if you said something every once in a while. No one is going to guess what you want. Trust me, I know."

Nothing from Alex.

"Well," I said and walked behind him, hoping against hope to see the lump of a wallet. I knew better—he'd had his pockets turned out weeks ago—but I had to look again. "If I don't do this now," I said, fumbling in one of his pockets, "I'm going to be under a bridge." I got the inside of the pocket out and did the same with the other, holding onto Alex's shoulder while I struggled. Nothing. I reached around and felt his suit coat. If he ever had anything, he didn't now.

I pushed myself up using Alex's back, and I felt a slight rise between his shoulder blades. It was thin, and it contoured to him, like it might be a hidden pack. I pulled up Alex's suit coat, untucked his dress shirt, his T-shirt. It was difficult to maneuver around his vest, so I unbuttoned it. Alex fell forward, catching himself with his hands.

Sure enough, Alex had a cash belt strapped over his shoulder. The belt had a zipper that ran right between his shoulder blades. I unzipped it. There was a stack of hundreds in there, easily enough to cover my rent. I glanced around, counted out $1,200, stuffed it in my pocket. I zipped the pack back up, pulled Alex's clothes down, tucked his shirt in. He looked a little disheveled but basically okay.

"I'll pay you back as soon as I can."

As I headed to my apartment I noticed, out of the corner of my eye, a change in Alex's face. He was smiling. It wasn't a happy or whimsical smile; it was a knowing one. How you might look if someone you had your doubts about had just taken $1,200 from you.

"Knock it off with the grin," I said.

He smiled, said nothing.

"You know I need this. It's not like you're using it."

Alex smiled, stared straight ahead.

"I've been helping you do whatever it is you've been doing here for months, so forgive me if I actually take a little payment. In case you haven't noticed, I'm the only one who doesn't throw garbage at you."

Alex smiled, stared straight ahead.

"Christ, what do you want from me?"

Alex looked up at me for the first time since he'd been there. It was then I realized his smile wasn't scornful at all. It was more Buddhic, like the statue of the god one of my buddies had on his coffee table a long time ago, pennies and rolling papers and a small red die scattered about him, an incense angling up through his arms. Alex's was a deep, harmless smile. The scorn was all mine.

Letters to The Oregonian from the Year 30,000 BC

Mark Russell

Dear Editor,

This is in response to "Fire: Invention of the Year?" (*Oregonian* 5/13). Last month, my partner and I were visiting her clan in California. One night, over dinner, her Uncle Thrak said, "You've got to try this," and lit a fire. At first I was like, "Oh, great, more yuppie chic from Uncle Thrak!" But I have to say, heating my mammoth rump with fire was life-changing. Intentionally burning your food (or "cooking," as they call it) really unlocks the mammoth-flavor. I kept thinking how great it would be paired with a marionberry compote or live ants.

So last week, after dropping our son off at Cave Song Adventurers, we bought our own fire starter kit. Our first attempt at cooking ended in a forest fire (sorry, Tree People). But we chose to view this as a lesson and not a failure, and found that, once you get the hang of it, cooking is not only fun, but also a powerful tool of self-expression.

In fact, we found cooking with fire so rewarding that we opened a mammoth-fusion food cart just west of the burned forest. We've taken to calling this area West Burnside.

Crolak Grogg-Truk
Gorba Grogg-Truk
Proprietors,
Whammoth, Bammoth, Thank You Mammoth

Dear Editor,

Re: "Fire: Invention of the Year?" *(Oregonian 5/13)*

If you ask me, this whole "fire" thing drips with Homo sapiens privilege. I was picking berries on Sauvie Island and all the suburban hunter-gatherer types were like, "Oh, I can't wait to sleep next to a fire!" "Cooked food sure sounds nice!" "I bet Gronk wouldn't have been carried off by coyotes if he had fire!"

Besides the fact that, hey, coyotes gotta eat, too, I think we ought to consider all the implications before wading ass-deep into consumerist fantasies about cooked food and fire dancing. Personally, when someone says "fire," I hear "gentrification." Do you really think the people in Yak Village are going to know what to do with fire? If fire becomes the norm, I guarantee you all the twig huts in the Pearl District will be gone five years from now.

Also, when it comes to the science, I feel like all we're really getting is marketing propaganda from Big Fire. Did you know that fire creates a by-product called smoke? Smoke is nothing but a gray-black plume of toxic chemicals—alkaloids, carbon monoxide, the souls of wood demons. Granted, no studies have linked smoke inhalation to demonic possession, but is the Log Demon something we should even be messing with?

And the military applications of fire are, frankly, horrific. The Tree People better hope they never cross anybody. If we upset the balance of power by weaponizing fire, I can only imagine what sort of crazy shit the Bog Men are going to come up with.

But hey, enjoy your baked potato.

Chaka
Hawthorne Caves

Dear Editor,

As far as I'm concerned, any debate over fire is settled by two simple words: hot tub. Sometimes, when sitting next to my fireplace, slow-roasting grass-fed bison in the Crock-Pot, I light my patio torches and peer across the lake. On a clear evening, I can see all the way to Yak Village. As I watch those poor souls huddle together under their communal yak pelt for warmth, I think . . . hilarious. If you can't figure out how awesome fire is and get yourself a piece of the action, then you have my sympathy. By which, I mean contempt.

I love living in Portland. Lots of great hiking and artisanal marrow. But sometimes I feel like a hunter surrounded by gatherers. You know what I mean. I suppose I should feel guilty—enjoying a rich life of caribou meat and indoor heating while so many go without. But instead, I feel strangely triumphant. Go figure.

Bill
Lake Oswego

Dear Editor,

I like a charred lizard as much as anybody. And carrying torches around at night, well, it just makes me feel important. But I'm afraid of what fire will mean for life here in Yak Village.

I'm worried that we'll all start living in our own caves. That we'll all have our own little campfires and our own piles of cooked lizards. I'm worried that we won't curl up under the yak blanket anymore, for no better reason than we don't have to. And I like you guys. I like how, when someone is sleeping on a tree root, we all lift the yak pelt together and walk it over to a flat piece of ground so everyone can get a good night's sleep. I love how Gary stands up inside the yak head and makes funny noises come out of its mouth. And I like that little Zool doesn't get scared at night because we're all there under the pelt with her.

Grok can make a living with his poetry, and it's only because after a long day of not selling books, the yak blanket is there waiting for him. Our village witch has a drinking problem. Her magic is perfectly fine; she just gets a little weird after three kombuchas. Anywhere else, people wouldn't take her seriously. Anywhere else, these people would be killed the moment it was discovered they couldn't make arrowheads. But here, under the yak pelt, they are treasured.

Fire's okay, I guess. I just don't want it to change who we are. More than anything else, people need a place to fail gently. To me, that's what Portland is all about.

Grub
Yak Village

In Transit

Kevin Sampsell

I never look anyone in the eyes on the MAX train. The last time I did, a man talked at me for the next thirty minutes about his lost cat. He kept stressing the fact that the cat had yellow paws, as if that was a rare thing. Maybe it is. I don't know. I'm not going to Google it or anything.

Another time, a guy with long hair, a denim jacket, and a big crystal on a necklace said he didn't like the way I was looking at him. I was only looking at his necklace, so I tried to be nice and said I liked his crystal. He took his crystal off and put it in his pocket, as if punishing me. I couldn't look at his pretty crystal anymore. "I'm a window," he said. "Look at me like I'm a window."

I looked at the window.

One time, on a crowded MAX, a gray-haired man gave up his seat for a woman holding a small baby.

The stop announcement said, "Northeast Sixtieth Avenue," even though we were still at Lloyd Center. People started to look panicked. An unopened can of some off-brand Mountain Dew-ish soda rolled back and forth by the stairs like a secret spy camera.

The gray-haired man watched it with concern and started to cough a fake cough.

I started to wonder if a grenade has ever exploded on a Portland MAX train or bus. Some buses probably deserve to be destroyed. Some buses are filthy and noisy and hurt people. I once knew someone whose coat got snagged in the back door of a bus when he was getting off. He was dragged for almost two blocks and somehow survived. But his elbows were busted and never worked again. Those bones were actually removed from his arm. The city paid for it.

I've never seen a grenade explosion before, but I once set a field of dry weeds on fire by accident.

I once fell asleep on the MAX. I closed my eyes and was out for about five stops. When I woke up, I noticed the floor of the MAX was cracked. I rubbed my eyes and the crack looked bigger. I slapped my own cheeks loudly and the woman next to me exclaimed, "Oh!" I looked at her and said "Oh" back. When I looked down again the floor was opened wide and the tracks blurred by violently. I put my hand down there and felt the whooshing air.

People leave their garbage on the MAX all the time. Bags of Taco Bell, sweaty drink cups from Burgerville, bruised apples, torn gloves, and broken umbrellas. I always watch people walk by these seats, and upon noticing these remains, slouch with angry body language before continuing their search for a place to sit. I don't know why they just don't move it.

A little boy grabbed a discarded banana once and showed it to his mom excitedly. "A monkey dropped it! A monkey dropped his banana!" he said. Some people laughed but his mom looked mortified. "Put it back," she said. The boy caught me looking in his direction. Maybe I looked concerned or like I was going to say something. "Is this yours?" he asked me.

I wondered if I looked like a monkey.

I held the banana as the mother slathered Purell on the boy's hands. I thought about eating the banana. Would that frighten the boy or please him?

Fare inspectors came on the MAX at the Pioneer Square stop and everyone pulled out their passes. One nervous-looking man wearing a Kobe Bryant jersey tried to slip off the train. An inspector intercepted him for a moment but the man pushed him aside and started sprinting away. As he darted across Broadway, the man knocked over a person carrying a pink Voodoo Doughnut box. This incited a sudden storm of anger and a couple of people started chasing after the man. One of them yelled, "You Laker-loving son of a bitch!"

The #20 bus started across the Burnside Bridge on an unusually sunny day. Some people looked out the windows at the sparkling Willamette River. But our peace was quickly broken by an old man yelling "Back door!" as he shouldered against the rear exit.

"I can't stop on the bridge!" the driver shouted back at him.

"Back door!" the man yelled again. "Back door!"

The bridge lights started flashing ahead of us to tell us that the bridge was going up. A large ship slowly approached to the left. An unpleasant smell filled the bus.

"Just stay calm," the driver said to the man, or maybe to all of us.

It suddenly felt like we were in Hell.

This is the fourth time the MAX has hit someone this week. This time it was a well-dressed businessman crossing the tracks by the Convention Center. I was waiting on the other side of the tracks, waiting for the eastbound train, when I heard the sound and the short yelp escape from the guy before he was crushed. It sounded like a bag of potatoes getting flattened by a steamroller.

I've always wondered what it would be like to die by train. But after this week, I see that it's really just an annoying way to inconvenience others. People getting off the train, rubbing the backs of their necks, wincing and cursing. One disheveled gutter punk looking at the tangled, bloody mess with squinted eyes, as if he didn't want to open his eyes all the way wide. An old lady exhaled sharply and said, "Another stupid fucker holding us up."

I scanned the hundred feet or so of smeared track. I didn't know a body had that much blood in it.

On the first day of April, the stop announcements change from English and Spanish to German and Chinese.

The man sitting across from me is the only one on the train not looking at his phone or reading a book. I wonder if he's blind, or maybe half-blind. He stares just above my head. If I had a chimney coming out of my skull, what would come out of it? Smoke? Thoughts? Crowd noise?

I decide to close my book and stare above his head, too. We are so close to connecting.

No
RETURN

As the car passed the mouth of the alley, the girl's head snapped around and her small black eyes focused on Martin.

Fog swirled and the girl and the car were gone.

Notes from the Underground City

Stevan Allred

1. The Melquiades Document

To Whom It May Concern:

My name is Melquiades, and I am, in that misleadingly innocuous phrase from your police procedures, the "person of interest" wanted for questioning in connection with the disappearance of some twenty thousand of your city's residents. Before we take up the matter of those missing citizens, nearly all of whom are quite safe, I assure you, you must first understand with whom you are dealing.

I was born in 1429, and I am now in my 587th year. My father was Melchior, a clockmaker, in Padua, and I learned his trade from the time I was a child. My mother was Osania, a healer, and an adept in certain arcane arts. My early years were divided between my father's workshop and the kitchen table where my mother prepared her unguents and poultices. I was very small, but my fingers were nimble, my mind quick, and my mother foresaw that I was capable of greatness. Her knowledge was ancient, and included secret incantations that have been passed down through her family for a thousand years or more.

By the time you read this I will be gone from this world, though still very much alive. You will not be able to follow me, for my mode of travel takes me through folds in the fabric of the cosmos beyond your reach, but the truth of what I am about to tell you is irrefutable. You will be able to see it, and touch it. You will have the chance to speak to the missing citizens, as I am leaving them in your care. And you, of this execrable age of skepticism, intent on denying the existence of magic or anything like it, will understand that I command powers far greater than any you possess.

I have been in Portland some several decades, biding my time and pursuing my studies of the great mysteries, and whilst here I have built, in a chamber at the farthest reaches of those underground passages in your city known as the Shanghai Tunnels, a miniature city. Where once there were brothels and opium dens there is now a masterpiece that only I, of all beings, could have made. It is my nature to keep my hands busy, and to work on a small scale, such as the thumb-sized scale I have employed here.

I began by building a model of that charming neighborhood known as Ladd's Addition. From there I continued as I saw fit, and I have built some five thousand homes, along with the streets and the parks and the schools that go with them. There is a cemetery for those who pass on. The houses are fully functional. Their doors open and close, their plumbing works, their rooves shed water.

Some years ago I discovered, in the course of my studies here, several powerful incantations. One gave me the means to make small whatever discrete objects I might choose. A second transported my diminutive objects to the city I was building. Thus did I furnish my houses with beds and tables and chairs, with bedding and linens, with dishes and silver. I have always been someone who leaves no detail unattended.

I did not mean, in the beginning, to populate my masterpiece. I have built such miniatures before, in Gimhathithia, Hav, and Cremona; in Angorra, Ghent, and Carvelle, all cities where I have lived for a time, making my way as a conjurer and a purveyor of marvels. In Shedet I built a castle, and populated it with beetles and ants who wore matching livery, and served their butterfly queen, perched upon her throne of silk. For the price of a silver coin, anyone who wished might look through my magician's glass and, by peering through the windows, see my fine creation, and be suitably astonished.

But here, in Portland, when my underground city was finished, and furnished, and perfect in every detail, I felt a great longing as I gazed upon the empty streets. This was my greatest work ever, and it cried out for a citizenry worthy of its refinements. They were readily at hand in the city above me, a city renowned for its fine food and drink, its artisans and artistes, its writers and musicians. Thus was I seized upon by a utopian vision. I would populate my city. My citizens would have no need to toil for food nor shelter. They would pay no taxes. They would be free to follow their own pursuits in a city that asked little of them other than obedience to a few simple rules. I would preside over them with all the wisdom and benevolence at my command. And I would call my city, with justifiable pride, Melquiopolis.

And so it was that I began to relocate the citizens of the city above to my city below. At first I chose people who were on the streets alone, at night, when no one would see them suddenly vanish. But this process was slow, given the scale of my endeavor, for Melquiopolis, in order to prosper, needed a certain critical mass, a number of inhabitants sufficient to allow for a rich exchange of ideas and talents between the citizens. And so I moved on to whole households, taking entire families as they slept.

This, though better, was still inadequate, and in the urgency of my underground city's need, I found it necessary to take ever larger groups of people. Thus began the relocation of entire church congregations, busloads of commuters, squadrons of cyclists, and Sunday morning yoga classes. Of course these people were missed. I am aware that the city above was inflamed with terror over the thousands of so-called abductions, and that people were, for some months, afraid to gather in large groups. This made my work more difficult, but I did achieve my goal, and the relocations, as you know, ceased some months ago. Those who are missed above, prosper below.

To oversee an endeavor such as mine is no small task. The citizens of Melquiopolis have requested many amenities, and I have provided them with anything I found reasonable, and likely to contribute to the common good. They are an enterprising lot, and freed from the need to work for their daily bread, they quickly made of themselves artisanal cheesemakers, ale-brewers, bakers, and the like. They formed theater companies, sports teams, and orchestras, and for all of these endeavors I have supplied the necessary vessels, ovens, costumes, uniforms, equipment, and instruments. They asked, and I provided.

There are some requests I have denied. Take note, for example, of the complete lack of those clamorous automobiles that foul with their noxious vapors the air of the city above. There is no anarchic internet, no bamboozling television, no poorly informed mass media. There are no cell phones, and no political parties. These things are unnecessary in Melquiopolis, and I urge you, who shall govern this city now, to continue my ban on such items.

Regard, if you will, the cleanliness of the streets, entirely free of the excrement of dogs. Observe the happy throngs gathering for concerts and plays, for banquets and festivals, for openings at the many art galleries. Note the cheerful cooks in their kitchens, the joyful writers and painters and sculptors busy at their work. Witness the plazas I have built with their festive fountains; the quaint and winding cobblestoned streets, lined with trees; and the public works of art. It is true that some have failed to flourish despite my kindnesses, and have taken their own lives, and for that I might be sorry were it not the case that their loss improves the general well-being of those who remain. When the herd culls itself, it is usually for the best.

I shall miss Melquiopolis, for I have spent many a pleasant hour gazing upon its lively citizens going about their business. Yet I must go, for I have urgent affairs elsewhere. I entrust my creation to your care. You will have ultimate authority over them, as I have had. I have killed only a few, and only those who sought to raise rebellion against me. You will be well-advised to hold to this same high standard, and to keep the executions from public view.

In the documents in your hands you will find directions to a door at the farthest reaches of the Shanghai Tunnels. Melquiopolis lies beyond that door, and I now commend it to your care. There are also extensive and detailed notes on the governance of the citizenry, and the stewardship of the city itself. Be not seduced by the siren call of that blathering, sluggish, and highly overrated political system, democracy. Appoint a wise and benevolent autocrat for Melquiopolis, and my diminutive utopia shall be an inspiration for all.

I beg of you, follow my instructions carefully, or they will not prosper. Though they live their lives in miniature they do not lead miniature lives, and I will hold you of the city above accountable for their welfare should I return.

2. Life in the Underground City

We moved our family to Portland from Boston because we wanted our kids to grow up camping, and hiking, and knowing the names of wild plants. For three years we biked to work, and explored the Columbia Gorge on the weekends. We bought kayaks and paddled our kids around Sauvie Island. We shopped the farmers' markets, and we drank the best beer and the best pinot noir on the planet. We had everything.

I want my life back. I want my kids' lives back. I want my husband back.

My husband killed himself after six months in this nightmare. He was a data miner, newly promoted into his dream job when we were kidnapped, and he just couldn't face a future with no computers, and no internet.

It's been a year and a half since he died. Somehow you put yourself back together. You have to. You have to keep it together because the kids can't if you don't. But this is the hardest thing I've ever done.

We were taken in our sleep, our whole family, from our very own beds. We woke up on the pavement, in a large square, and the light was bright, but it wasn't sunlight. A few minutes later there was a bright flash of green, and our neighbors appeared, still lying down like we were. The old man took our whole block that night, both sides of the street, but then we got sent all over town for our housing assignments. The people in charge, they kept saying life was good here, and not to worry, and we could talk about it in the morning, but for right now, could we please just follow them to our new house, and no, nobody could swap housing assignments, that wasn't allowed, but all the houses are nice.

I miss my dogs. Everybody misses their dogs. We're not allowed to have pets. My kids miss their gerbils. A lot of people think this is paradise, but there's no paradise for me without my dogs.

Those people in charge, it took me a while to realize this, but they're collaborators. They get favors from the old man, like fresh seafood that nobody else gets. They have the best houses. They have better bicycles than the rest of us.

They're the ones telling the old man when somebody breaks the rules.

The light here never changes. What would be the sun, if we had a sun, it comes on, it goes off, it comes on again, more or less like day and night, but without any seasonal change. No dawn. No sunsets. There is no sky above us, only the ceiling painted to look like the sky. The horizon is painted like the distant countryside in a movie set, and you feel like you're trapped inside a painting. There is no outdoors. No weather. No wind, no sun, no rain. No rainbows. No clouds, and oh, how I miss looking up at the clouds.

Lights mounted in the ceiling do not make a sun. A sprinkler system turned on at precisely 3 a.m. for an hour every other night is not rain. This is a very nice prison, but it's a prison all the same.

I have to admit, the bread here is really good. There's lots of foodies here, and they have a lot of time on their hands. There's artisanal cheese, homemade yogurt, pickled vegetables, and plenty of kombucha. People grow greens and herbs, they knit, they sew, they sing. There are yoga classes, and pilates, and massage. The coffee is excellent. There are piercing studios, tattoo parlors, and memoir workshops. There are bikes and skateboards and no cars at all. Emily, my toddler, is in this great play group. My boys are Nathan and Sam, six and eight, and they can walk anywhere and I don't have to worry.

Nerdy business major types and entrepreneurs keep trying to invent money, but nobody really needs money here. Everybody barters for what they want. You can get a cup of coffee for a song, literally. Miniaturized food just appears. It comes on pallets, the same brands from the same stores we know, with sell-by dates that keep changing, and you take whatever you want. The pallets show up on the streets in the middle of the night. People who've seen it say they just materialize from nothing.

There's no media here except what we make ourselves, hand-copied. There are street lights that stay on all night. There are electric lights in our houses, but no plugs, and no switches. The lights in our houses all go off at once, usually at midnight. Unless the old man forgets, which he does sometimes, like he goes off at night and forgets about us. People get mad when he does that. He should buy a timer.

Some people think the old man is God. They pray to him, and they worship his every word and deed as if he were infallible. When he screws up they say it's all part of the plan, and you have to have faith, because we can't know everything in the mind of God. Same old bullshit, different venue. A lot of those people are collaborators.

The old man has the power to make us tiny, and that makes him something. A mad scientist? A devil? An alien? A magician? A pink elephant? Who knows.

But God the Almighty? I don't think so. The old man is real, and he is no god.

He watches us. He sits on a stool, sanding or painting little bits of the town he's repairing, or sometimes he just stands there, at the edge of the town, looking down on us, smiling or scowling. He's got a magnifying glass, and he'll get right next to somebody's house, and look in through a window, like we're dolls in a doll-house. What does he think, we can't see him?

People try to escape, and there are lots, trust me, my husband tried it at least a dozen times, but what happens is you get anywhere near the door and you get confused. The gap under the door is tall enough anyone could just duck right under, but then you can't remember why you'd want to. Zach, my husband, was a runner, and he tried running at the door, like he could break through the confusion area if he just got going fast enough, but the confusion got worse the closer he got. He said he willed himself forward, sheer guts, and Zach was tough. He told me how if he forced him-self deeper into the confusion then the ground started burning. He'd see hellfire and brimstone, and a legion of demons in the flames, and Zach was a hardcore atheist, but even though he knew it couldn't be real, when he was in it, it was real. He couldn't cross the flames. Nobody can. And so he'd turn around, and he'd take the long walk back. He'd come back saying he stank of sulfur, and even though he didn't, he'd lie in bed sweaty with fear. For days after, he'd feel this dread, and looking at the trompe l'oeil world painted on the walls made him feel sick. It's like a fever, and ev-erybody who tries to escape goes through it, but it wore off in a week or so, and then he'd start thinking again about that gap under the door.

The suicide rate is high. People have been ripped from their lives, and they have no hope of ever going back. All these software developers and IT guys, the really driven ones like Zach, the ones who lived to work, they have no reason to live anymore. And if you add chronic Seasonal Affective Disorder on top of everything else, and no outdoors, no hiking or camping or kayaking or mountain biking, you've got a lot of really depressed people. A lot of people say there's Prozac in the water, but if there is, it doesn't work for ev-eryone. The cemetery is nearly full, hundreds of gravestones, most of them men, and all of them suicides. It wears on you.

If you really want to die, you hang yourself, or slit your wrists and bleed out in a bathtub. The suicide network will help you. It's the exact opposite from a suicide hotline, where they try to talk you down.

An older woman, Agnes, from the death-with-dignity crowd, started the network. I've met her. They don't encourage anybody to do it, and they won't help until you've had some counseling, but they make it easy. Agnes said it was the ultimate form of protest, but I don't think so. I think they're all just depressed.

Zach hung himself while I had the kids at the park. He didn't leave a note. The woman who helped him said he was calm, and that he loved me, and that he didn't want me to see. He did it on her back porch, so we wouldn't come home to it.

I still can't believe he quit on us.

When you want something that isn't already here, you organize a Shout. You want forty or fifty people for this, so you'll be loud enough to be heard. You rehearse, and then you all go to the town square. You shout what you want, like "WE WANT TO MAKE CRAFT BEER!" You shout it over and over again. You have to keep it simple, what you shout. Sometimes the old man shows up pretty soon, and sometimes he doesn't show up at all. The Beer Shout got results in one afternoon because it's pretty easy to get people to shout for beer, and they had the biggest turnout ever for a Shout. The Pot Shout was huge, too.

But you can shout all you want for a photocopier, and he won't give you one. So we have a lot of meetings, to keep each other informed, and to build community. I was part of Occupy Portland, right after we moved here from Boston, and we know how to have a meeting. It's just hard to get people to show up. Everybody's busy doing whatever they want.

It took weeks of planning, and those of us like me who think there's something drastically wrong with this phony paradise, we ran ourselves ragged getting the Freedom Shout organized. We had a couple of thousand people, chanting "FREEDOM NOW, WE'RE NOT DOLLS, FREEDOM NOW, WE'RE NOT DOLLS," and we were hardcore. We kept it up for days, people chanting until their throats were raw.

Most people went on about their business, riding their bikes here and there, chanting with us as they went on by, going to their poetry readings and their fruit canning workshops, and seeing their therapists. Then, on the third day, we saw the old man, looking down on us, and he was shaking his head. He raised his hands for silence, and we all looked up.

"Fools," he said. "I've given you everything, and still you want more." Then we heard him speak in a language no one had ever heard before, chanting a herky-jerky mix of gutturals and hisses, and he ended with a long hiss that got louder and shriller until it was like a fire hose shooting needles at us, and my hair stood up all prickly, and then my whole body had that nerve buzz you get when you whack your funny bone. All over us, even the bottoms of our feet and the insides of our mouths, that funny bone buzz. Then our skin erupted, and everybody was covered in weeping hives, and for days we scratched ourselves bloody.

We all felt it. Not just the protesters, but everybody. Collective punishment—a war crime under the Geneva Convention. You can't get ten people together now for a Shout unless it's for something innocuous, like a new kind of hops, or a steam-powered espresso maker.

The biggest Shout after the Freedom Shout was for Cheryl Strayed.

Everybody wants Cheryl Strayed.

You can't go a block without seeing a giant poster of the old man. He's got himself plastered up everywhere on the sides of houses. There are statues of him in the squares and parks, with his beaky nose, his foppish suits, his pointed shoes, his wide-brimmed black hat sitting on top of his head like a crow with its wings spread. An old lefty who lives on my block says it's a cult of personality straight out of Stalinist Russia. The old man doesn't allow any other public art. He destroys it on sight.

At first he was pretty giving. Most of what we shouted for, he gave us. We wanted coffee, and we got coffee, but it wasn't organic and sustainable. But then somebody organized a Stumptown Shout, and we got Stumptown. So of course somebody else did a Shout for Peet's, and they were pretty hardcore, coffee freaks shouting till everybody was so hoarse they had to quit, but this time they got nothing. Voodoo Doughnuts, nothing. Chickens, nada. Same for cats, dogs, goats, alpacas, and horses. Then someone organized a Shout for songbirds, and what did we get? Starlings, sea gulls, and crows. That was when we understood that the old man was pissed at us, and he thought we were spoiled little brats.

And you don't want to piss off the old man. He's always smiling in the posters, and in those framed photographs the collaborators always have on their mantels, like he's this wise and benevolent king. But people disappear here. Some say a few dozen, but I say it's hundreds. Maybe they wrote a play or painted a painting that the old man thought was subversive. You go to bed at night, and in the morning your neighbors are just gone. They never come back. We can't prove it, but we know they're dead.

And you know what the number one death penalty offense is? Remodeling. The old man doesn't let anybody change anything he's built. You cut a hole in a wall so you'll have a pass-through from the kitchen to the dining room, like my neighbors did, and you're toast.

What really fries me are the people who like it here. Like the Bicycle Alliance, they think this is all just perfect. No cars. No pollution. No electric motors. Everything human powered. They keep talking about how we're not contributing to global warming. They ride around in packs. They ran a naked bike ride right through our Freedom Shout, just to disrupt us.

The politics here are ugly. The old man buys everybody off with food and recreation. Bread and circuses, people, that's all we're getting, and no matter how good the bread is, that's not enough.

3. Before and After

I was snatched when I was standing in line at Salt & Straw, waiting for my scoop of bone marrow with salted ganache ice cream. It happens fast. He got the whole line.

I was alone right then, no girlfriend, hadn't had one in months, and I was going to meet some of my guy friends later at a food cart pod, for an after-hours jam. The line was a block long, and there were whole families in line, and you saw that more and more, families doing everything together because they were afraid they'd be snatched. It made me wish my family was here, and I was thinking how maybe I should move back to Phoenix and get away from all this.

Melquiades joins the line, right behind me, so I got a good look at him. Not that anybody knew his name then, but I'm probably the first person who really saw him do whatever the hell it is he does. An odd little geek, with a big beak of a nose, vegan skinny, and really short, like maybe four-and-a-half feet tall, but we don't let things like that freak us out here. This was early on in the large group phase of The Snatches, and he starts chanting, like he's speaking in tongues or something, and people turn and stare. But this is still Portland, and nobody wants to stop somebody from keeping Portland weird, and this was before anybody had really seen Melquiades. Then he starts weaving his hands through the air like some trance dancer at a rave, and there's a bright flash of light, so bright I can see it's green, even with my eyes closed. And then we were all here, still in line, in the middle of Ladd's Addition, like we were queued up to smell the roses. Some guy with a clipboard is telling us all to stay calm and he'll explain.

Only it's not the real Ladd's Addition. That didn't really sink in until the next day, after I talked to people who'd been here a while, and after I really got it that now I'm about the size my thumb used to be. That moment where you go from the city above to the city below is just one big WTF, and you can't even begin to grasp what they're telling you.

Right before I was snatched, all I knew was, there's a pattern. I knew that whole families had been snatched lately, always at night, when they're all asleep. Snatched right out of their beds. Everybody's afraid to sleep, and the whole city has gone insomniac. That's why you're in line at 2 a.m. at Salt & Straw, which is cashing in on the panic by staying open all night. You know there've been two large snatches, but they both happened in broad daylight, one from a church basement where there was a funeral reception going on, and one from the faculty lounge at a high school. The media is speculating that it has something to do with being indoors, so you tell yourself you're safe on the sidewalk in front of Salt & Straw.

But you're not safe. You're snatched. The pattern's changed, and nobody told you. And now a guy with a clipboard is telling you your housing assignment.

My roomies turned out to be pretty sweet. There's an old guy named Floyd, who talks to himself all the time, a dude named Alonzo, and this hottie named Fiona, with full sleeves and a tongue stud. Turns out Floyd plays accordion, and he knows all these old songs. There was a house a few blocks away with a room full of instruments, and anybody could just walk in and grab one. Alonzo got himself a washboard, and Fiona plays banjo.

Man, that Fiona can sing. I got myself a fiddle, and we started a band. We call it God's Closet.

I was here fourteen months, and then Melquiades stood where we could all see him and gave a speech, the kind of speech all politicians give about how everything is hunky-dory because they're so flippin' great. Most people aren't paying much attention because he's done this before, but then he tells us he's leaving, he has urgent business elsewhere, and he's not coming back, so farewell and all that, it's been great knowing you. He says he's contacted the authorities, and everything will still be hunky-dory so no need to panic. And then, poof, he's gone, vanished in a flash of green light.

Right away this guy, Private Steve, heads for the door. Everybody knows Private Steve because he's an Iraq War vet, and he's tried to escape, like, fifty times. He runs out there as soon as Melquiades vanishes, to see if the flames are gone, only, they're not.

Melquiades must have called the city, because they showed up in less than an hour, in the form of a bunch of building inspectors. Like this whole thing down here was just one big code violation. Private Steve has made it all the way out there, and gotten his ass fried in the magic fire, and now he's making his way back. The first inspector through the door takes one look at the Underground City and he says, "Oh my God," and then he stepped right on him. Squashed Private Steve like a bug.

"That's the city for you," Floyd said, "clueless right from the get-go."

Before Melquiades took off, my life was pretty much my dream life, which is to say it was the same life I had before, only now I didn't have to work three shitty jobs to have it. Fiona and me, we're a sweet item, and we've been pretty happy here, singing for our suppers. But when I saw that inspector step on Private Steve, everything changed.

I didn't just get pissed, I got radicalized.

Some rescue this is, because we're not rescued like we get to go back to our lives. Nobody can leave here without going through the flames, and the flames make you crazy, and the only cure is to come back to the Underground City. The longer you're away from here the longer it takes to feel right again. A lot of us have tried. My parents came for me, with my brother, Breton, all the way from Phoenix. They want you back in the big world, and you want to go back, and you let them carry you away, even though you're screaming when you go through the fire. You try to live up there, but the screaming keeps on inside your head even after you stop screaming out loud. Before you know it, you're begging them to bring you back here.

The people above, they don't really get who you are now, how different it is to be so small. How terrifying their enormous faces are. How their stinky breath washes over you. How their trembling hands shake you when they hold you. How obnoxious it is the way they keep saying you're so cute because you're so tiny. How their voices are way too loud. How your little squeak of a voice can never be heard. How every visit from them is like they're visiting you in prison. We're sick of their pity.

They put in an internet connection where you use a touch screen to type messages. It's in one of the big plazas, and at first you had to wait for hours to get a turn, so they put more in, and the lines got shorter. But if you can never go home again, that big world up there where we used to live, it doesn't mean so much. You can't be a part of it. Your life is here, in the Underground City. You write to them, your family and friends, so they'll know you're okay. But you have less and less in common. You're still friends on Facebook, but your friendship isn't going anywhere.

The city used their power of eminent domain to annex our town. They've done this, they say, at our request, to protect us. That's bullshit, and they know it. Now there's talk about turning us into a tourist attraction.

Fuck that. We're not Disneyland, y'know? We're not a petting zoo, or a sideshow attraction. With Melquiades gone, we have a chance to make something of all this, and we don't need any help from the city. Self-determination, baby, that's what it's all about.

Me and Fiona, we're ready to resist. Floyd, too. And Alonzo, and pretty much everybody we know. "It ain't the size of the dog in the fight," Floyd says, "it's the size of the fight in the dog."

Fiona kisses me, and puts her lips to my ear. "Small," she whispers, "is good."

Queen of Tabor

B. Frayn Masters

Minerva was known for skipping. Whenever something or someone bummed her out, a skip around the block turned dark clouds into daisy fields. Her mother told her that nineteen was far too old to be skipping, not to mention unladylike. Minerva flipped her off. "Fuck you and your stiff generation, Doris."

Minerva challenged Henry to skip from the Mount Tabor gate on Salmon Street to the foot of the bronze statue of the crusty old conservative on the top of the hill. She immediately pulled way ahead, bobbing up and down in huge flying leaps. Henry's voice behind her echoing through the trees, "This is fucking the last time I'm making my legs make this communist motion. You are a torturer!" Minerva was laughing so hard at Henry's shoutings she had to drop to the pavement and crawl the final few feet to the Harvey Scott statue. She shouted back at him, "I fucking beat you here, Henry Brooks! All hail the Queen of Mount Tabor!"

An ardent believer in sticking to tasks he committed to, Henry jammed his knees into the air one after the other until he stood over Minerva, dripping sweat on her dark, wild hair. Hunkering over, his hands on knees, Henry conceded, "You are my Queen and I shall refer to you forevermore as thus!"

Minerva's laugh turned to a solemn smile; the weed had just kicked in, big time. She stared hard up at Henry. The moon shone through the pine trees above his head, casting branch-shaped shadows across his sweet, stoned face. It was then she was sure that this was the night she'd show him the special place.

Lying on their backs in the middle of the park, not far from the statue, Henry said, "It's so groovy that Tabor is a volcano." He had no idea the industrial-sized can of worms he'd just opened.

Minerva's grandmother was a volcanologist and Minerva had lost many a friend and potential lover to droning on a bit too much about the specifics of cones and calderas. But she couldn't resist blurting out a few facts. "Tabor was formed, like, two million years ago and is twice as old as Mount Hood—suck it, Hood—and even though scientists say it's dormant—because none of its vents have been active for 300,000 years—I've got it on good word that scientists don't actually know shit about if and when a volcano might just change its mind. I mean, did you know that Yellowstone is a supervolcano and erupts every 600,000 years, and because it's a supervolcano, when it does erupt again it will wipe out a large portion of North America?" As her fact rant trailed off and up into the night air, it met up with all the other words being spoken by all the other people of the world.

Minerva's eye caught a squirrel swinging between two trees. She rolled onto her stomach and spread her arms wide, digging her fingers into the dry August ground. Barely audible, she said, "Hug the volcano with me, Henry. Your Queen commands it." Henry dutifully hugged Tabor.

"Can you feel its heart beating?" Minerva asked.

"Not really," Henry said.

"Don't be afraid to have an experience, Henry."

Henry loved Minerva after several years of hating her. Not hate, really, just that they were forced to play together when they were neighbor kids. And arranged childhood friendships rarely work out. Henry's parents got divorced the summer before seventh grade, so he had to move away with his mom. Minerva and Henry didn't reconnect until six years later at Portland Community College. They were enrolled in the city's first computer coding class, where Minerva was the only girl, and Henry was the only boy in their women's studies class.

Henry involuntarily hugged the volcano more tightly; he wanted so much to tell her his feelings, but his body had logged in its memory all of his parents' screaming matches, all the confusing messages about love and sex from the Catholic priests and nuns, the strange ski lodge porno his brother had found and played on their home projector—all of these scenes stockpiled right in the place where love, feelings, and words are formed—rendering poor Henry only able to mutter, "I love . . . this mountain."

"Close your eyes and put your nose as close to the dirt as possible," she said. "Get right in there; lick a worm."

Henry watched Minerva with one eye open as she buried her face, taking in air, slow and deep through her nostrils. Her back rose as her lungs filled. Henry tried his best to repeat her actions. His intake sounded like he was sucking on a straw with gravel stuck in it.

Minerva released some air. "This spot reeks of stegosaurus. I wish we lived in Jurassic times. When I see one of those lizards with a fin—or accordion fan?—on its back, I get down on the ground lower than where it's standing, changing my perspective enough to make it appear giant. Henry, think about how old the earth is. Volcanoes absorb the ashes of all the history of people, gunpowder, sweat, tears, gravestones, Frisbees, love letters, lost pets, Bibles and Torahs, stuffed animals, books, yarn balls, letters of tragedy, dinosaurs, of everything." Minerva grabbed Henry's shoulder and gave it a quick shove.

"Henry! Henry! Henry! Think about it, stay with me here: when volcanoes erupt they are shaking history loose and barfing it all up, and that, Henry, that forces all of us ants, who worry too much about how tight our pants are, to remember who is boss. Nature is boss and anything a human can do or make, nature can throw it back up like I can with Doris's disgusting liver and onions bullshit."

Henry rolled onto his back. "I think I'm getting turned on by hugging the mountain." Minerva smiled. Bringing Henry here worked.

Virginity melted down into the earth with the stegosaurus bones. A heavy silence followed, pinning the couple to the grass. Both of them struggled to remember the mechanics of how to move their limbs and mouths—it became a conscious effort to inhale and exhale. Hot blood gurgled through their motionless bodies.

Some time passed.

When Henry awoke, Minerva stood above him in front of the opening of a darkened tunnel. Henry knew the geography of Tabor well, and no one had ever mentioned, nor had he ever seen, this ornately carved marble archway. It was massive, a couple of basketball hoops high, he estimated.

"This is my special place," she said.

Henry stood, dizzy-headed. "What? This is crazy."

Minerva slid her hand in his.

It was all coming together for Henry. "I can't believe I'm saying this, but did you just sacrifice your virginity on a volcano?"

Minerva shook her head. "No. You did." Minerva gave Henry's shoulder a reassuring love nudge, then whispered, "I want you to be the one to go into the tunnel with me."

Henry struggled to hold back the tunnel-as-vagina jokes that were lolling around in his head. He cleared his throat. "What's in there?"

She'd started hearing the whispers of Tabor when she hugged the mountain the first time, when she was ten years old. It told her about the tunnel. No one believed that it existed. As she got older, the mountain told her more about itself. And it told her that to see inside the tunnel she had to bring her first love there. What was inside, it said, would deepen their love for each other. The mountain also said that if she came to the tunnel on the night of their first consummation, it would have a big surprise for her.

Henry was unsure about going along. "Let me guess: it's either both of us go in or no one goes in."

"The mountain said it had to be both of us," Minerva said. "And I'm just as scared as you are, if not more."

"Well, you are the Queen of Tabor."

Henry put his arm around Minerva's shoulder as they walked inside. They couldn't see much, but when they felt the lightness of the lessening gravitational pull and heard what sounded like an opera of whales, they knew there was no sense in looking back.

Doris was worked up about scrubbing a corner of baked-on lasagna from the Pyrex when she could swear she heard Minerva skipping outside by the house. She shook her head and muttered, "Better skipping than the dope, I guess." Right when she felt the relief from finally popping the corner of pasta debris out of the casserole dish, there was a loud boom that shook the kitchen. Through the window above the sink, a gray smoke plume billowed skyward, releasing ash on her pink rhododendrons, like winter in August.

Twin Carbs on Bad News

Jeff Johnson

The eight-cylinder glasspack engine snarl peaked in intensity and a low, glistening car slid forth, the fog parting around it like swollen lips. It was black cherry, with long sleek fins and Frenched suicide doors, tinted windows, and chrome spinners that glittered in the sourceless light. The mannequin head of the driver was silhouetted in a dim, sulfurous russet.

Crouched in the center of the hood was a tiny Mexican girl in an immaculate white Communion dress. She raised the brass trumpet in her small brown hands and blew a long, eerie note that rode the dense fog like electricity on a hot copper wire. Faint, lilting arpeggios and winding ululations replied in the distance, echoing down the sagging brick corridors of Old Town's shadow.

As the car passed the mouth of the alley, the girl's head snapped around and her small black eyes focused on Martin. Gouts of fire vomited from the vehicle's twin exhaust, sketching her quizzical expression in hellish orange. The fog swirled and the car and the girl were gone.

Martin Rice drew back a little farther into the alley where he'd been hiding. Sweat poured down his pale, chubby face. The little girl's piercing eyes had left afterimages on his retinas. He closed his eyes and clutched his empty shotgun to his chest. The trumpet erupted in the fog again, tittering like insane laughter as it dop-plered away.

Martin Rice was the crappiest security guard the orientation pam-phlet at Rinco Security had ever failed to inspire. Before that he had been an astonishingly incompetent janitor in the Army. He knew he was more than challenged when it came to the concept of labor, because the people who reliably made such evaluations told him so all the time. Last Friday had been no exception.

Martin had had a quick breakfast of Pop-Tarts and orange soda at 11 p.m., shined his boots, and hopped on the last TriMet bus of the night, running just a little late and thus barely catch-ing it. Four years in the Army had never taught him punctuality and the private sector had fared no better, hence his current and ultimately final position as the night watchman at an anonymous building by the freeway where the Park Blocks petered out into the wide splatter of weirdoville between South Waterfront and downtown. He looked out the bus window at the sleeping city of Portland and his thoughts turned to the food carts by his studio apartment. Korean tacos. The zitty kids with the french fry place. Crepe dude. This gave way to a sort of reflective trance wherein he missed his stop and had to jog three blocks back.

He signed in at the front desk and saluted at the ambitious, gym-sculpted day shift guy, Dwight or Dwain. He was younger than Martin and clearly hell-bent on being his boss someday, an event that would lead to a boring spell of unemployment and food stamps for the lesser men under Darrel's command. Martin smiled at him and wiped his sweaty face with his shirtsleeve.

"Missed my stop," Martin explained.

"It's in the log," the kid snapped. He had an angry spray of acne across his cheeks and probably on his back as well. Steroids, Martin guessed. "Second time this week."

Martin shrugged. At six-two and weighing in on the chubby side, he was much larger than the rising tattletale, but something in his manner usually failed to intimidate people.

"They're still working in 102. Try to stay awake."

Dwain or whatever signed out and left. Martin watched through the floor-to-ceiling lobby windows as the younger man peeled out in the new Toyota pickup he probably couldn't afford and headed back to wherever he came from. Martin stared out at the mostly empty parking lot. It was getting foggy, which was a change from the rain. It was slightly deflating, in that staring out the window was as close as he could get to TV, and for minimum wage a view really wasn't much to ask. After watching the fog thicken for a while, he took up his station.

The lobby decor was corporate standard from early in the previous decade. Big fake plants and clusters of roundish, uncomfortable chairs sat on a sterile expanse of faux marble linoleum. He settled back in the chair behind the reception desk and put his feet up. His warped reflection stared back from the windows across from him. The gentle hum of the air vents and the buzz of the fluorescent lights rendered him immediately, restfully blank.

Martin liked night shift security and, in fact, considered it to be the finest achievement he was likely to enjoy in life. It was rare that any of the people who worked in the building stayed late and when they did they ignored him as a rule. He had no idea what any of them were doing and he didn't care. They knew he didn't care, and it didn't bother them in the least. He was supposed to walk the corridors every hour or so, but he never did. Most of the time he sat daydreaming at the front desk, reading magazines or the occasional spy novel, or simply staring out at the parking lot.

He passed a couple of pleasant hours rereading a fat tropical cruise line brochure. He was contemplating locking the main doors for a bathroom break and an early lunch from the vending machines when he noticed the fog outside had become a solid wall. Martin cocked his head, mildly curious. Londonesque fog in Portland was about as rare as snow in San Diego. He sat up and as he did so the fire alarm sounded.

Martin stood bolt upright. He was sure that someone had told him what to do in case of fire, but at this moment he had no idea what it might be.

"Fire!" he yelled. He sniffed the air. No smoke, just the fog outside, but that didn't mean anything. His eyes narrowed.

A door down the hall burst open and several men and women in lab coats charged out and sprinted in his direction.

"Get out!" one of them bellowed, waving Martin toward the door. The group of them burst through the lobby doors into the foggy parking lot and disappeared, leaving Martin standing behind the desk.

Martin started for the door, then turned back and pulled the shotgun from the cabinet behind the desk. He wouldn't need any shells for it, and he didn't know where they were in any case. He'd take up a station in the parking lot and wait for the fire department or some kind of clue as to what was expected of him. He set his face in an approximation of a crisis management specialist.

Outside, the fog was growing thicker. The moist air smelled a little like iodine. Martin held the empty gun at port arms and stood at attention.

A strange cry came from somewhere off to his right. One of the lab dorks had apparently wandered into the weeds on the south side of the building. Martin shook his head and walked out into the thickening soup to help. He was utterly lost inside of two minutes.

Black fish darted back and forth in the leisure-sized swimming pool. Martin watched them intently, wondering if he could eat them. He had found the pool on his third day of aimless wandering and returned often. The small area he had mapped out expanded as he wandered farther into the deserted, fog-bound city, but the pool was in the zone he had come to refer to as "home base." It was where he first realized that, in his panic-driven charge into the night, he had become hopelessly lost, when the echoes of the equally panicked lab dork he'd been following had finally faded away. As near as he could figure, he was somewhere just beyond the Park Blocks, where the freeway should be, close to where the yuppies clustered in condo parks down by the river.

He munched on some dried flowers, one of his early edible discoveries. He'd found them in a sort of vending machine with no buttons or coin slot. Bright yellow plastic bag with "Snackiflorals" in bold magenta letters. At first he'd been afraid to open one. They were so much better than potato chips, he'd discovered, but not enough.

Catching the fish would be difficult without a pole. He'd already searched without luck for a pool skimmer or a net of some kind. It might be possible to simply drain the pool, but that seemed excessive and somehow cruel and would result in far more fish than he could eat anyway.

The fish resembled trout, but there was something different about them. They seemed to be watching him at times, and there was an odd symmetry to their movements. Every so often they spontaneously angled themselves in one direction, in carefully regimented ranks. This disturbed Martin.

The sound of footfalls brought him out of his reflection. He sank back into the glossy, broad-leafed shrubbery at the edge of the pool.

A man ran out of the fog and stopped at the edge of the pool. His hair was a wild mess, his eyes wide with stark terror behind cracked, gold-framed glasses. He wore a grimy lab coat.

Martin rose. The man looked at him and screamed.

"Easy," Martin said, alarmed. The man took two steps toward him and stopped, then raised a hand to his mouth.

"You . . ." he gasped.

"Martin Rice," Martin said. He glanced around nervously. Sound traveled strangely in the fog and the man's scream had no doubt echoed for blocks. "Why are you running?"

The man lowered his hand and looked around as if suddenly aware of his surroundings. He glanced into the pool and reeled back. All the fish were frozen, angled in his direction.

"We've got to hide," he gasped. He slunk over to Martin's side and pulled him back down into the shrubbery, peering back the way he had come. Martin crouched next to him, holding his breath.

Something appeared at the edge of the pool, flickering into existence without apparent motion. Martin had the confusing impression of a pale, naked hide glinting in the low light, a long, bony tail lashing wildly, and multiple spindly arms held forth like the limbs of a mantis. It dived into the pool.

A second later there was an explosion of water and the thing emerged before them. Trapped in its mouth was a fish. With a strange hop and a flick of its tail, it vanished into the gloom.

"Juhezus," Martin whispered. Goose flesh rippled up his back and his eyes watered. "What the hell was that?"

"I don't know. I was walking down the street a short distance from here when I nearly bumped into it."

They sat listening, very still. Minutes passed.

"I have a camp set up a few blocks away," Martin said softly.

The man let out a long, shuddering breath. "Thank God. Let's get the hell out of here."

Martin led him silently through a labyrinth of brick alleys to the basement where he stored his scavenged supplies. He bolted the warped steel door at the top of the stairs behind them. The man looked over the small space and collapsed on the concrete floor. Martin propped his gun in the corner and sat down across from him.

"I can't find anyone," the man said. "Have you seen them?"

"Sorry," Martin replied. "I knew you guys had gone into the fog in front of me. I heard one of you freaking out so I followed. You're the first person I've seen in three days, other than this kid on a car hood."

The man blew out a long, tired sigh. "I'm sure most of them found their way back to the lab after an hour or so. I'm afraid it was me you heard. I got separated from the others and got lost in the construction crap at the edge of the parking lot. We're probably the only two people still in here."

"Figures." Martin rubbed his eyes. "So where the hell are we, anyway? I mean, I know I'm a security guard, but under the circumstances . . ."

The man took his time before answering.

"You're the night security guard," he said finally.

"I'm glad you're following me, here," Martin replied. "I'm the night security guard. Right."

"Right. I'm Dr. Weisman. Have you found the lab yet, Martin?"

"No," Martin said. "Is that what we're supposed to be doing?"

Dr. Weisman propped himself up on one elbow and gave him a hard look. "Are you being sarcastic, son?"

"Not at all," Martin replied. "I'm a night security guard. As in I don't have a fucking clue what's going on. Anywhere. Ever."

Dr. Weisman shook his head. "Have you found any familiar signs? A map? Anything helpful at all?"

"Wasn't looking, so no. Where are we, Doc?"

"It's proprietary data. Classified."

Martin was silent for a moment and then suddenly broke into laughter. Dr. Weisman lifted his head.

"Classified? Classified?" Martin shook his head, grinning. "What a fucking joke."

"How's that?"

"It's personal, I guess. I get a job at some place where 'classified' is going on, something obviously goes spectacularly wrong, and it's not even my fault."

Dr. Weisman sat all the way up with his elbows on his knees and rubbed his face. "No," he said finally. "I don't think you can take any of the credit for this." He looked down at his spattered shoes.

"Glory hog," Martin said. He held out a can of beans and winked. "Hungry?"

"So tell me what you can," Martin said later.

Weisman looked up from his second can of beans. "Not hungry?"

"That fisher thing kind of got to me. Plus, I don't know . . ."

Weisman raised his eyebrows.

"You know how it is when you want one kind of food and you have to eat something totally different and it makes you sort of bummed out? Like your pants are wet and you're at a picnic? I want something with enchilada sauce on it."

Weisman snorted. "Quite a character, aren't you."

Martin shrugged. "Not really."

"I found a jar of mayonnaise a few days ago," Weisman said, chewing slowly, his eyes distant. Martin perked up.

"Really? What'd you do with it?"

"I left it. A man can't just eat mayonnaise."

Martin shook his head in disgust and Weisman barked a raw-sounding laugh at the look on Martin's face.

"So tell me, Martin, how'd you get this job? You're how old, twenty-six? You must have had time to find something better than the graveyard shift. Even the mall is better."

"Twenty-seven," Martin said. "I washed out of the Army five years ago. You know, see the world, sculpt my character, firm my resolve. I've seen most of Arizona at this point. I was spending my last year in Yuma waiting for discharge. Then it was back to Stumptown."

"Not cut out for the military?"

Martin shook his head. "Nah. I guess not."

"Let me guess. You go to PCC in the daytime. English classes. Maybe pottery."

"I actually sleep in the daytime. The whole night shift thing. I got Netflix, so there's that . . ."

"I see." Weisman was suitably unimpressed.

"Can we get back?" Martin asked.

"I think so. We'll have to find the lab again, but yes. I believe I can get us home."

Martin nodded, but said nothing. Dr. Weisman finished the beans and set the empty can beside him.

"I don't think I'll go to college," Martin said finally. "I signed up for the GI Bill, but now I don't know. Four years of school. I can't even pay attention on the bus ride to work."

Weisman licked his spoon. Martin handed him a package of dried flowers. Weisman regarded it through his cracked glasses: a bright yellow bag with brittle, vaguely Chinese-looking symbols printed on one side. He opened it and withdrew a scarlet blossom, glittering with salt. He sniffed it and then took a tentative nibble.

"What about you, Dr. Weisman? Kids? House? You a Ford or Chevy man?"

Weisman munched away on the salted flowers.

"Divorced," he said eventually. "Got married in my first year of college, back at MIT. Seven years later we were still happy, and then I hit the job market. Six months of really getting to know each other without a full-time distraction was all it took."

Martin whistled. "Seven years. Damn. I've seen you working late more than once. Too bad you didn't stick it out, eh?"

"Maybe." Dr. Weisman studied Martin with an unreadable look on his face, chewing a little slower.

"That's what they taught us in the Army," Martin continued. He looked thoughtfully at a point above Weisman's head. "Stick it out. Suck it up. I think the same thing was in my orientation pamphlet for this crappy job."

"Is that what you do? Stick it out? Suck it up?"

"Nah." Martin waved a hand at him. "Are you kidding?"

"Yes."

In the awkward silence that followed, Martin ruminated on his unfailing ability to find himself in situations with people he had absolutely nothing in common with. Occasionally he glanced over at Dr. Weisman, who sat slowly chewing the salted flowers. Gauging from his sober expression, Martin cautiously speculated that Weisman was ruminating along the same lines.

A trumpet rang in the distance, a long, braying note that rose into a staccato burst of nonsense. Martin rose and pointed upward. Dr. Weisman followed him out of the basement and up the uneven stairs to the second story of the brick building. Together they peeked out through a broken window.

A chopped-down car with huge rear fins rumbled into view below them. It was midnight blue, with tiny halogen headlights partially shielded with chrome to make them look like half-closed eyelids. A little boy in a white suit and patent leather shoes stood on the hood. He raised the trumpet and blew a sharp blast just as the car rounded the corner and disappeared.

"What the hell do you make of that?" Dr. Weisman whispered.

Martin shook his head. "Twin carbs on bad news."

Dr. Weisman gave him a confused look.

"Dual tail pipes, the whole nine yards," Martin said. "I've seen this before. Earlier today, in fact. It scared the hell out of me, but with you here . . ." Martin patted Weisman on the shoulder.

Dr. Weisman shook his hand off and hunched down. "It doesn't make any sense," he said softly. "We ran all the simulations dozens of times. The math was perfect."

"Maybe it's time you told me what's going on, Weisman," Martin said.

"It's Dr. Weisman," Weisman snapped. "Careful, mister. I'm technically your superior, as in the half-baked outfit that hired you is paid by me. Much of your behavior is already in question."

Martin settled into a cross-legged position across from him. "Come on, Weisman. I'm here because of you. Talk, or no more beans."

Dr. Weisman glared at him with red-rimmed eyes and finally shuddered. "Lord, I can't believe I'm actually tempted to divulge classified experimental data to an obvious cretin."

"You're the dipshit that got me here, dude. There's more than one kind of intelligence, and after our short time together I can tell you beyond a shadow of a doubt that you don't have any of mine. Talk."

Dr. Weisman closed his eyes. Martin thought he might have drifted off to sleep when he finally began.

"We were working on a device called a symmetrate. It's a way to displace ribbons of alloy in small pockets of phased reality. Essentially a superconductor. But very, very small."

Martin nodded sagely. "Ah."

"It's supposed to generate a small field, displacing everything in its radius by less than a nanosecond in time. There was a power surge and the device activated in the lab. We tried to leave the completely unexpected radius and failed. At least you and I did."

"So what the hell is all this? I followed one of those cars the other day. It went into some kind of church that reminded me of a stadium-sized baboon snout. You could see patches of the sky over it where the fog had cleared. The sky was orange, Weisman. With a bunch of little moons."

Weisman's eyes widened behind his broken glasses. "The field must have . . . overlapped into something else. Wherever we are, it's more than a nanosecond away from where we started."

"Seven years at MIT. Shee-ite." Martin shook his head. "And here

I thought I was the loser. Maybe I will go back to school. I'll find a wife first, and then fuck that up before I even get started because—"

"That's enough!" Weisman snapped. "You're fired, you idiot! You can look forward to a bright future in welfare or Salvation Army rehab! My report will accurately reflect your stellar attitude and respect for a superior under duress. You are by far the shittiest night security guard I've ever had the displeasure of working with."

"I'm sure that's true," Martin said evenly. "While you're reviewing your notes for my trial, I think I'll find out which way the lab is."

Dr. Weisman clutched his head with both hands. "I wish this had never happened!"

"And I wish I had a beer." Martin pulled a can out of one of his bulging pockets. It was white and said "BER" in green letters. "Oh, hey. Lookie here." He popped the top.

"You will not drink that!" Weisman shouted incredulously. His thin lower lip trembled with rage.

Martin downed the beer in two swallows. Weisman staggered to his feet and slapped the empty can out of his hand. Martin smiled and belched under his breath.

"You're lucky that was empty."

"Buffoon!" Weisman roared. Martin rose to his feet. He was a full head taller.

"Keep your voice down."

Dr. Weisman raised his fist. Martin shook his head, clearly advising him not to swing. Weisman's washed-out blue eyes blinked rapidly.

"Easy, Doc," Martin said. "Last thing we need is to start fighting like a couple of mental patients."

A moist, sluggish breeze dumped through the window, stirring the wings of sagging wallpaper. Martin focused on the flap nearest the window. It was adorned with minute carbon cornflowers. Dr. Weisman gradually regained control of himself.

"It's just a beer, Weisman. I have another one for you, and it seems like maybe you should—"

Weisman interrupted him with a sharp chopping motion. "No

more talking, Martin. Let's just pack up some supplies and get to work."

Half an hour later, each carrying a black trash bag filled with cans of beans and packages of dried flowers, they wandered down the center of a broad, empty avenue. Crooked brick buildings loomed out of the fog around them. Dr. Weisman stopped in the middle of an intersection filled with mossy wooden tricycles. Martin silently ran his hand along one.

"Anything look familiar?" Dr. Weisman asked quietly.

"Yes," Martin replied. "Have you ever been to the railroad tracks east of the Pearl?"

Dr. Weisman shook his head.

"I didn't think so," Martin said. "I've been there a bunch of times. There's a beautiful woman that works at the food carts down there . . . I think her name is Maria. She has hairy legs, but that's all right, I guess. Right across the street there's a little tamale stand. So good, Doc. They have Mexican corn on the cob there. You rub mayonnaise and dried goat cheese and chili pod sauce on the steaming corn. Sounds disgusting, I know, but Jesus . . . wax paper cups of Orangina for—"

"Martin."

"Right. So this little hipster cafe over there has tons of black-and-white photos of old Portland. I think I recognize some of these buildings from the place, but they're all . . . big and bent and wrong. And there's way too many of them."

"I see."

"Yeah. The lab is on the south side of town. The old clock has four faces, but its main face—if you're looking at the buildings—points southwest. If we can find it, we can follow one of these streets out in the right direction."

"How do we find the clock? We still have the same problem, Martin."

"The buildings are getting bigger as we go, so I'm guessing we're headed downtown. I think this street will take us to the plaza."

They passed through a dense area in the fog and emerged into another broad intersection. There was a slowly spinning Ferris wheel in the center, a vast iron skeleton of a thing with no colorful banners or neon lights. All of the carts had miniature wheels of their own. Dr. Weisman and Martin gasped simultaneously as they realized the carts were wheelchairs, their wheels spinning as though they were ferrying unseen things through some ghostly plane high above. Its silent rotation carried the highest chairs out of sight into the leaden gloom.

"We might be able to ride that up and look around," Dr. Weisman suggested. Martin gave him a watery-eyed stare of horror.

They skirted the slow monstrosity and continued. Less than five minutes later they emerged into a wide square. Mounds of bright yellow, phosphorescent moss erupted from the uneven brick pavement like African termite hives. A muted ticking filtered through the fog.

The clock stood at the far side. They weaved through the mounds of glowing mildew as quietly as they could until they stood directly before it.

The towering clock leaned slightly forward. Its dripping, bone-colored face had eight curly symbols on it. Four verdigris arms slowly rotated across it, one of them moving counterclockwise. It seemed possessed, somehow. The bend of the structure made it seem as though a giant stood before them, looking down on them, its clock face measuring them in some way.

"There you go," Martin whispered. Dr. Weisman turned and plotted their southern course.

"Let's get out of the open, Martin."

"Right behind you."

They walked swiftly east. Both of them breathed a sigh of relief as they left the plaza and entered the mouth of another wide avenue, this one headed due east. The brooding presence emanating from the clock had unsettled them both.

The wide avenue was littered with junk. They passed a pot-bellied, man-sized papier-mache honeybee; an upside-down metal sled with rotting leather traces; and several giant glass snail shells, turned up at their hollow bases and filled with rain water.

Dr. Weisman skirted it all, but Martin seemed drawn to the objects. It was the odd sort of garbage that would have intrigued him had he found it anywhere else.

"This is Old Town," Martin whispered. "We should try to find Satyricon."

"What the hell is that?"

"A nightclub. Broken TV decor, sort of had some kind of magical . . . This is some kind of version of where we were, Weisman. A really, really strange one. We should look for Satyricon because it reminds me of this place. It might actually be in both worlds. A kind of common landmark."

"Shut up, Martin. I'm thinking."

"Makes you wonder what's outside the fog, doesn't it?" Martin asked quietly. Dr. Weisman didn't answer.

They walked over a rickety wooden bridge spanning an enormous mud chute, made it another mile—perhaps to within a few hundred yards of where they guessed the lab might be—when the horns shattered the silence around them, wailing from all directions at once. They were surrounded.

Martin could make out at least eight distinct trumpets, all sounding in terrible unison. They froze. Dr. Weisman's jaw popped in the sudden quiet that followed.

The fog shimmered and something twisted out of it. Martin recognized the thing that had been following Dr. Weisman—the pale, glistening, frog-skinned aberration that fished in the swimming pool.

It stopped, perhaps as amazed to see them as they were to see it. For a moment no one moved, and then the thing opened its mouth. It was nothing more than a gray slit in its face, but as the seconds passed it stretched wider and wider, impossibly, perfectly round, growing to the size of a large cantaloupe.

Dr. Weisman screamed high and long and loud. Simultaneously, eight glittering cars vectored out of the fog, circling them. The creature remained where it was, trembling with the effort of some internal process.

The cars were all low and waxed to a high gloss. Mexican children in small white suits and dresses crouched on the hoods, peering intently but without alarm at the creature. A little girl raised her trumpet and blew a sharp series of unconnected notes. Martin was suddenly struck by the notion that they were hunting this thing, trapping it in a web of sound.

Whole, thrashing fish vomited from the creature's gaping mouth, hundreds of them, forming a wet pile at its feet. When the stream had stopped, the girl lowered her trumpet. The creature raised its arms in the sudden silence and folded itself back through the fog with a little dance. It was gone.

A Tokyo pink lowrider with a wraparound visor chop top pulled up to the pile of fish and a child hopped off the hood and busied himself shoveling the flopping things into the cavernous trunk. Martin and Dr. Weisman stood stock still. The ring of silent children ignored them. The mannequin silhouettes inside the cars were featureless and still.

A moment later, the cars wheeled into a line and rumbled away. Two or three of the children snickered as they vanished. Martin noticed the departing group had left two fish flopping on the pavement. He walked over and picked them up.

"Presents," he said softly.

"Martin!" Dr. Weisman snapped. "Don't touch those! For God's sake, let's go!"

Dr. Weisman darted away. Martin dropped the fish in his bag and followed.

"I wonder who's driving the cars," Martin whispered, half to himself. "Jesus, so that's how they go fishing."

Dr. Weisman ignored him.

A bright smear grew before them. As they walked it became larger and brighter. Gradually, they made out the shape of the lab. The sky was blue above it. People were milling around in the lobby, peering out the windows.

Dr. Weisman sobbed and lurched forward. Martin grabbed his arm.

"I'm not going," Martin said abruptly. His face had a bewildered expression, as though the thought had just occurred to him. A faint smile tugged at his lips. Weisman shook his arm off.

"This is no time for your idiot humor, Martin. Let's—"

"I said I'm not going," Martin repeated, this time with more conviction. "I . . . I don't want to go back. Tell them I'm dead."

Weisman stared at him. "What? Why?"

"I don't think I can make you understand," he said slowly. "I'm not sure I understand myself."

"I can't leave you here! You've gone insane!"

"I'm not going back." Martin fixed Dr. Weisman with a curious expression. He reached out and grabbed Weisman's shoulder. His big hand was strong and smelled like fish.

"Assholes like you made a world with no place for people like me, Weisman. I can't compete with you, or anyone like you. I can't even coexist with you. You won't let me and I don't want to anyway." He searched for the right words. "Maybe I'm a throwback to a time when people weren't so . . . well, so like you." He shrugged. "Once upon a time, it seems like I lived in a place sort of like this. And it went away and I never knew where."

Dr. Weisman searched Martin's face. He felt a strange wash of emotion, a mixture of panic, guilt, and disgust. "Are you sure?"

Martin nodded soberly. "Dead sure. This time next year I'd be cleaning your toilet. I don't think I could bear it. This is my chance, Weisman. I'm not going to blow it."

"Well." Weisman forced a crooked smile and stuck his hand out. "Good luck, I guess."

Martin grinned back and shook Weisman's hand.

"My sky is orange and filled with moons, Weisman. Maybe it always was, or should have been. Save your luck for yourself, old man."

Dr. Weisman walked out of the fog and into the parking lot. When he looked back, the hard light of high noon stretched across Portland for as far as he could see. The fog was gone. He dutifully reported Martin's death and power to the experiment was cut.

Martin picked up Weisman's bag and walked away without a backward glance, whistling softly. The patter of fog-distilled water dripping off the bent eaves above him sounded louder and almost musical now that Weisman was gone.

Something caught his eye and he stopped and knelt. It was a big key, an old brass job with a round haft and a florid, swirling handle, pocked and weathered with time. Martin scooped it up and cupped it in his hand. Old keys had always signified something to him. He slipped it into his pocket, and then struck out with his trash bags, headed south, following the sound of trumpets.

Always

Adam Strong

Shaneen, it's late. Almost closing time at Kelly's Olympian, and once again I'm waiting for you.

I've spent the last of my temp job money on your glass of wine and it's right here in front of me at our table, by the backward neon sign in the window. I know you love Kelly's because of all the neon. *Kelly's* written in an arc, above *Olympian*, on top of the symbol of a club, wings and 1902, the year the bar opened. This town, Portland, is all neon. I only come out at night, so neon is how I find my way around this place. Neon signs, for off-track betting, or liquor, famous crawfish or silver dollar pizza, a vacancy sign that's never been on.

Shaneen, back in high school you ran with the popular crowd, and I didn't talk to anyone, but it was you who came up to me at the kegger when I was sixteen. That night I was going to kill myself, thought I'd always be alone. I was in the driveway, leaned up against some shed, with a beer in my hand. When I went to the keg, everyone at the party was speaking to each other with all those secret movements and handshakes. The way they talked, it was at a different speed than how I talked. The guys had backward hats and the girls had lockets around their necks with hearts and boys' names in them. I had my oversized green plaid sweater, the one with the big poofy collar. Had on my black Doc Martens shoes. Thought I was so cool. I was on a different planet. I was so tired of being alone. I wanted out of this whole stupid life.

You came up to me with just a few words and a wink. You and that wink, you already were an adult, even back then. You had a body, short, a nice wide butt and curves a guy like me had no idea what to do with. You had fishnet stockings with ripped holes and this black leather skirt I could see my reflection in. You had tea leaf skin. You were half Indian. One would have to walk from one end of India to the other to get the wisdom you had in your eyes.

You reached out to my big poofy collar, held it there with your thumb and forefinger. "You are so fucking cute," you said. And you took me home to your father's house in the suburbs. You had your own apartment downstairs. You took me down to your room, you put your hand on my hand. Your rings and the smooth of your nail polish. The rainbow faces on the Cure poster on your wall, over by the bed. You took off your shirt and sat there on the edge of your bed, made a big deal of waiting like I knew how to take a bra off. Then you got fed up with the wait, took off that bra of yours, put your tits against my shirt. Your arms around me pulled up, pulled off my poofy plaid longsleeve.

One moment I'm wanting to die and the next you've got your tits pressed against me. And with all of this happening, what do I talk about but your Cure poster.

"I love that album," I said. "*The Head on the Door*, isn't it?"

You always had an answer, cold and sharp and badass as anything. "You want to fuck me or my records?"

You let your hand swing over to your unmade bed with the purple comforter. You took my pants off. You held my hand. Our naked bodies warm underneath your purple comforter.

My first time. Our two bodies meeting. I had so much to learn, the whole what-goes-where-when, when to hold back and when to keep going. The little bit of mascara under your eyes, the little bit of sexy in the pudge of your cheeks, your rings and your nails on my no-hairs-on-my-chest chest.

"My god, it's like you're twelve up here," you said. "Good thing you are not twelve down there." You gave me a sly smile. I wasn't all kid. You still wanted me.

Shaneen, you pulled your body off mine, you leaned back, talked me through it, put me into you. The light brown tint of your skin. The whole time, I was shaking. I'd found the one who was going to save me. The palm of your hand around my cheek, let's really see who you are.

Then something in the look on your face like you were doing me a favor and now I owed you. But your expression changed. Softened. You could always spot the something wrong on my face, how I thought I wasn't good at what we were doing. Your forefinger there on my chin, you being you and what you said.

"Hey, you know what, you are pretty great."

And Shaneen, that's when I knew you and I were for real forever.

I had to ask you. And when I asked if you and I were going to last you said, "I'll be with you, always."

Now, all these years later, this town with rain all the time. It's dark and cold and wet and I need neon signs to find my way around. The wings on either side of the neon sign of Kelly's Olympian. I've got your glass of house red here. Shaneen, always means always. Shaneen, do you remember the one time with the Ecstasy? Remember we were at our bar, Kelly's Olympian, and you took me back to your downstairs apartment late at night and you gave me the X. You said it would make me feel good. You put on the Jesus and Mary Chain album, closed your purple curtains, and it was just us with the lights off under your comforter. There was a chamber of warm around us, and when I reached out to touch you, I didn't feel like I was one person touching another. I touched us.

The irises of your eyes got all squishy after the X. Your black irises were a painting my vision could change. I could smear the paint job of your end-of-India eyes to match the world as I saw it. The weight of your forearm, heavy on my back, our two bodies fed into each other, skin was weight and energy and bodies and warm.

You said, "I can't believe you never fucked on smack before."

The X wasn't just X, the X was laced with heroin. Heroin, X, it was all the same to me—I couldn't tell the difference, but you could. The X, the heroin, a lie bigger than your bed, bigger than the two of us. I was never really sure what I'd get from you. Got to be I'd get all paranoid, how when we were fucking, there would be a moment when the smile you were giving me, it was only on the front of your face. I'd think that this whole sexual deal with us was another lie, you weren't really into it. But then you'd smile like you meant it, and I knew you and I were a for-real deal always.

Shaneen, you died six years ago—heroin and coke and crack, how at the end of it all there was your empty apartment with no furniture and crack vials and your dead body on the floor—and even though I know this, I also know always means always.

Kelly's Olympian, this neon biker bar without bikers but for-real motorcycles hung from the ceiling. Chrome poles, neon signs, neon red rose letters against gray blue light. I sit at our table, the one at the front of the bar, so you don't have to walk through the narrow passageway to the back, don't have to slide through the rows of patrons waiting for their next pint.

You aren't going to come and see me unless I'm willing to go far enough for you. And far enough means at least two beers, and sometimes three, and I always, always have to get stoned beforehand, and you definitely won't show until I've bought you a glass of the house red. Have to put it right here on the table with your chair pulled out. Us and all of our alwayses.

Our always table, by the old gas pump that always says $4.94.

There's the pump and there are the doors and the street in front. Your red Celica pulls up at the parking space in front of Kelly's Olympian. Even though the bar is crowded, you are loud and clear to me. Shaneen, you are dressed like you were on that first night in your father's house with your fishnets and your black leather skirt I can see my reflection in, your torn-up fishnets, webs of skin and warm.

Your body in through those double doors, like you never said goodbye. No sign of the years of crack and coke use on your face. Shaneen, when you walk in here and sit down, you put your hand on mine, your fingers and the same nail polish as that night in your apartment in high school, only instead of that Cure poster there are motorcycles, the neon warm of Kelly's Olympian.

The X, Ecstasy, a pill you bring out in a little orange tube with a white cap, a prescription, a lie that never expired.

You take out a pill and put it on your tongue, and you slip one to me. And Shaneen, you down that wine in one long stroke of drink. You with the glass in your hand, hold it there with your tea leaf fingers spread out across the glass. Your hand on your empty glass on the table. Get up and shake your gorgeous ass a little when you put one foot in front of the other, those fishnets and the muscles in your legs moving over to those two double doors.

You turn around to me before you walk out. "What are you waiting for?"

The X that is X laced with heroin is still in my mouth.

I swallow that chalky little bastard down, take one last sip of beer, leave my bar tab open, leave my pack of smokes with my weed inside, my coat, walk out in the rain. I leave it all behind. My hand on the door to your red Celica.

Always means always, the two of us in your red Celica, driving down the old trolley tracks of Lovejoy Street to the ground floor postage stamp of my apartment.

Always is the way our lips come together when we kiss, the way your irises bend to my will. The stretched-out shadows of cars moving through my blinds. Our bodies and the way you move and the way you move me. Your nails dig into my back, my hand on your ass, me inside you and you inside me and always is always is always.

But I'm not with you. I'm still at Kelly's. Closing time, our table. I'm stoned, and there's your glass of house red, there's my pint of black ale. There's the barman mopping up the floor by our table, there's me, the last person left. Our table by the window.

I drink my beer and I drink your wine, in one long gulp like you would have.

I get up and pay my tab, always pay my tab, always the last to leave.

I'll do the same tomorrow.

Acknowledgments

There isn't space for me to adequately acknowledge all the fantastic weirdos who helped make this book possible.

Thank you to publisher Laura Stanfill—tireless, dedicated, robot-smart Laura Stanfill—for her commitment to this project, her part in its vision, her beautiful interior design and editing and promotional expertise.

Thank you to our copy editor Sharon Eldridge and our careful readers Michele Ford and Colette Parry. And to our ebook expert Cyrus Wraith Walker.

Thank you to all our authors for their wonderful stories—as well as to all the readers and workshop members and consultants who had a hand in each of those stories before they even reached me.

Thank you to my husband Stephen O'Donnell who has always (or almost always) (or almost-almost always (understandably)) been okay with the fact that this project has taken up most of the last year and a half of my life (sorry). And who, as an expert in a few subjects, consulted on a couple of the stories and gave me sage advice about the cover art.

Thank you to Tom Spanbauer, who is hero and mentor to not only me, but so many Portland writers. And to my parents, Lucy and Don Little, for supporting my every dream and giving me their creative genes, and to Edina, Frank, and Lizehte, with whom I voraciously devoured every *Twilight Zone* marathon of our childhoods.

Thank you to the many people who consulted on, offered advice for, blurbed, helped promote, and otherwise supported this book, including (big breath) Steve Arndt, Kathleen Lane, Robert Hill, Liz Scott, Dian Greenwood, Sara Guest, Margaret Malone, Liz Prato, Carl Lennertz, Jess Walter, Ian Doescher, Averil Dean, Ben Loory, Monica Drake, Fonda Lee, Billie Bloebaum, Kate Ristau, Jill Owens, Shawn Donley, Michal Drannen, MaryJo Schimelpfenig, Tracey Trudeau, Sage Ricci, Colin Farstad, Christy George, Hobie Bender, Matty Byloos, Holly Goodman, Steve Tune, Shannon Brazil, Niyati Evers, Robin Carlisle, Fiona George, Brian Ellis, Acacia Blackwell, Kat Gardiner, Hollie Hefferman, Acil Ryan Mecham, Celeste Gurevich, Charles Dye, Jonathan Stanfill, Thea Prieto, Dustin Blottenberger, Tracy Stepp, and Cindy Heidemann, Jeff Tegge, Mark Hillesheim, Matty Goldberg, Leslie Jobson, and Sarah Armstrong of Legato Publishers Group.

Finally, thank you to the Forest Avenue Press community and wonderfully weird Portland.

About the Editor

Gigi Little is honored to be the graphic designer for Forest Avenue Press. As a writer, her essays and short stories have appeared in anthologies and literary magazines including *Portland Noir*, *Spent*, and *The Pacific Northwest Reader*. By day, she works as a marketing coordinator for Powell's Books and lives with her husband, fine artist Stephen O'Donnell, and their Chihuahua, Nicholas. Before moving to Portland, Gigi spent fifteen years in the circus as a lighting director and professional circus clown. She never took a pie to the face, but she's a Rhodes Scholar in the art of losing her pants.

Contributor Bios

STEVAN ALLRED has survived circumcision, a religious upbringing, the sixties, the War on Poverty, the break-up of The Beatles, pneumonia (twice), years of psychotherapy, the Reagan Revolution, the War on Drugs, the Roaring Nineties, plantar fasciitis, an embarrassingly bad goatee, the Lewinsky Affair, the internet bubble, the Florida recount of 2000, the Bush Oughts, the War on Terror, teenage children, a divorce, hay fever, the real estate bubble, male pattern baldness, the great Ebola scare of 2014, and heartburn. His collection of linked short stories, *A Simplified Map of the Real World*, was published in 2013 by Forest Avenue Press.

JONAH BARRETT is a young writer, filmmaker, and lover of cupcakes. A childhood spent at the library reading up on cryptozoological lore has resulted in a lifelong obsession with various beasts (as well as his irrational fears of lakes, dark forests, and his own closet). Despite his character's negative opinion of Portland, it is actually Jonah's favorite city. Someday he will move there and marry a nice hipster man who owns a vegan cupcake shop. That is the plan.

You can find stories and essays by **DOUG CHASE** online at *Nailed Magazine*, *The Gravity of the Thing*, and *The Tusk*. He has had a long and checkered career and currently does a lot of book stuff for the great big bookstore in town. He lives in Portland, Oregon, with his wife and poodle and hangs out with a group of writers every Thursday night to try to figure it all out.

SEAN DAVIS is the author of *The Wax Bullet War* and writes fiction, nonfiction, and essays for *Flaunt*, *Nailed Magazine*, and other publications. He has been in the woods fighting fires and looking for Bigfoot.

SUSAN DeFREITAS is the author of the novel *Hot Season* (Harvard Square Editions, 2016) and the fiction chapbook *Pyrophitic* (ELJ

Publications, 2014). Her fiction, nonfiction, and poetry have appeared in *The Utne Reader*, *The Nervous Breakdown*, *Story Magazine*, *Southwestern American Literature*, and *Weber — The Contemporary West*, along with more than twenty other journals and anthologies. She holds an MFA in writing from Pacific University and serves as a collaborative editor with Indigo Editing & Publications.

RENE DENFELD is the bestselling author of *The Enchanted*, which won the French Prix award, the ALA Medal for Excellence in Fiction, and other awards. Her next novel, *The Child Finder*, will be published in fall 2017. She lives in St. Johns, Portland, with her three kids, all adopted from foster care.

DAN DeWEESE is the author of the story collection *Disorder* and the novel *You Don't Love This Man*. He is also Editor-in-Chief of *Propeller*.

ART EDWARDS's novel *Badge* (2014) was a finalist in the Pacific Northwest Writers Association's literary contest. His fiction has appeared in *Bartleby Snopes*, *Farallon Review*, *Uno Kudo*, and *Foundling Review*.

STEFANIE FREELE is the author of two short story collections, *Feeding Strays*, with Lost Horse Press, and *Surrounded by Water*, with Press 53. Stefanie's published and forthcoming work can be found in *Witness*, *Glimmer Train*, *Mid-American Review*, *Wigleaf*, *Western Humanities Review*, *Sou'wester*, *Chattahoochee Review*, *The Florida Review*, *Quarterly West*, and *American Literary Review*. More information: www.stefaniefreele.com.

JONATHAN HILL is a cartoonist and illustrator living in Portland, Oregon. He also teaches comics at the Pacific Northwest College of Art. His first book, *Americus*, was published by First Second Books. He's also done work for Tor.com, Powell's City of Books, and Fantagraphics. He is currently working on books for Oni Press and First Second. Check out his work at www.oneofthejohns.com.

JUSTIN HOCKING's recent memoir, *The Great Floodgates of the Wonderworld,* won the 2015 Oregon Book Award for Creative Nonfiction. It was also selected for the Barnes & Noble Discover Great New Writers program, and named as one of "Ten Brilliant Books that Grab You From Page One" by the *Huffington Post*. He is a co-founder and lead instructor of the Certificate Program in creative writing at the Independent Publishing Resource Center, and also teaches in the low-residency MFA program at Eastern Oregon University. He recently won a Humanitarian Award from the Willamette Writers for his work in writing, publishing, and community building.

JEFF JOHNSON is the author of numerous short stories, including the collection *Munez: The Monterey Stories*, and the memoir *Tattoo Machine: Tall Tales, True Stories, and My Life In Ink.* Upcoming novels are *Everything Under The Moon* (Soft Skull, September 2016), *Knottspeed: A Love Story* (Turner Publishing, Valentine's Day 2017), and *Lucky Supreme: A Novel of Many Crimes,* first in the ongoing Darby Holland series (Skyhorse Publishing, Fall 2017). Screenplays include *Diamonds in the Sky, Cineville,* and *The Cutting,* Sternman Productions. He divides his time between Philadelphia and Los Angeles, and works as a producer at Cosmic Irony.

LEIGH ANNE KRANZ bonded with her dad watching seventies disaster movies, and her first stories made her mom laugh. She grew up to talk with gorillas using sign language, make mental health enrichment projects for elephants, and help adults with developmental disabilities take Portland by storm. She's a producer with KBOO Community Radio and is writing a novel.

KIRSTEN LARSON earned an MFA from Antioch University Los Angeles. She is a former member of Tom Spanbauer's Dangerous Writing group. Kirsten is a contributing editor at *Nailed Magazine* and an instructor at Portland State University. Her essays and stories can be found in the *Huffington Post, Nailed Magazine, Manifest-Station,* and several literary journals.

B. FRAYN MASTERS's literary leanings can be found in *Airplane Reading, MonkeyBicycle 6, Hobart, SPORK,* and *Mountain Man Dance Moves: The McSweeney's Book of Lists.* She is a scriptwriter and actor. She is an award-winning storyteller and is also the host, creator, and executive producer of the nationally recognized live storytelling series Back Fence PDX.

KEVIN MEYER is a writer and teacher in Tom Spanbauer's Dangerous Writers workshop and publisher at *Noisehole Magazine.* His work has been featured or is forthcoming in *The Frozen Moment: Contemporary Writers on the Choices that Change Our Lives, Share PDX, Nailed Magazine, Noisehole Magazine, Gobshite Quarterly,* and *The Untold Gaze.*

KAREN MUNRO's work has appeared in *Crazyhorse, Glimmer Train, Strange Horizons,* and elsewhere. She has an MFA from the Iowa Writers' Workshop, and she lives and writes weird stuff in Portland, Oregon.

LINDA RAND is an artist, herbalist, and mother of two boys, Harlan and Louis. Flanadoodle Bagel and guitarist Dan Duval round out the family. Her artwork has been included in *PDX Magazine* and the book *Oneira: I Dream the Self,* curated by Peggy Nichols of Studio C Gallery in the Santa Fe Arts Colony in LA. Her writing has been published in *Bluebird: Women and the New Psychology of Happiness,* by Ariel Gore, and in the anthology *The People's Apocalypse,* edited by Ariel Gore and Jenny Forrester. You can find her at her art space and curio shop Zodiac.

BRIAN REID was weaned on the acerbic dry humor and innate storytelling of the Scottish Highlands. His childhood in Australia colored his writing with a love of the ridiculous and a dedication to irreverence. As a teenager he moved to Chicago, where he learned how to take a punch. He worked at the Federal Reserve Bank for almost twenty years, which taught him perception is more important than reality. Brian escaped the Fed and moved to

Oregon to pursue his life-long dream of writing fiction. He plans on writing many novels.

BRADLEY K. ROSEN has studied drums and percussion since the age of five and has been a working musician for the last thirty-seven years. He is also a writer and has been a member of the Dangerous Writers table since 2007. His work has appeared in *The Class That Fell in Love with the Man, The Frozen Moment, The Portland Review,* and *Nailed Magazine.* He continues to play music and write in his hometown of Portland, Oregon, where he reads aloud to his chocolate Labrador, Kira.

NICOLE ROSEVEAR is a graduate of the Bennington Writing Seminars and has had work published in *North American Review, VoiceCatcher,* and *Bennington Review.* She teaches composition and creative writing at Clackamas Community College and is a member of the *Clackamas Literary Review's* editorial team. Her ongoing projects are, always, impossibly grandiose travel plans and new stories (which seem, sometimes, to be equally impossible).

MARK RUSSELL is the author of *God Is Disappointed in You,* a modern re-telling of the Bible, and a follow-up book, *Apocrypha Now.* He wrote the award-winning comic *Prez* and is currently writing *The Flintstones* for DC Comics.

KEVIN SAMPSELL is the editor of the anthology *Portland Noir* (Akashic) and the author of the novel *This Is Between Us* (Tin House) and the memoir *A Common Pornography* (Harper Perennial). He is also the publisher of Future Tense Books, one of the oldest micropresses in the country.

JASON SQUAMATA is a Portland-based writer of dream diaries, graphic novels, and disturbing confessional essays. His work has appeared in *Stealing Time* magazine, *Propeller,* and *Hypno Komix.* Excerpts from his memoirs, invocations, and hardboiled psychedelic pulp fictions can be read at orakuloid.blogspot.com and listened to at soundcloud.com/jason-squamata. He can be reached at hypnokomix@gmail.com. He's weirder than he thinks he is. Isn't everyone?

ANDREW STARK was raised on the Ojibwa Indian Reservation in Michigan's Upper Peninsula. He has lived and worked in Chicago, Montana, Los Angeles, and Portland. His work has appeared in various publications, and he is co-founder of LOST WKND, the international literary arts and culture publication based in Minneapolis.

ADAM STRONG is a high school digital arts teacher. Adam Strong was scared of grass until he was four, when he got glasses. Adam Strong is the founder of the reading series Songbook PDX, A Literary Mixtape. Adam Strong's work has appeared in *Noisehole, The Class Who Fell in Love with the Man, Our Portland Story, Intellectual Refuge,* and elsewhere. Adam Strong has two daughters that make his jaw go funny when he sees them.

SUZY VITELLO's award-winning short fiction has appeared in *Mississippi Review*, various anthologies, and literary journals. She has been a prize winner in The Atlantic Monthly Student Fiction Contest, and was a recipient of an Oregon Literary Arts grant. She holds an MFA from Antioch University, Los Angeles, and is a long-time coordinator and participant of an infamous writer's workshop in Portland, whose members include Chuck Palahniuk, Lidia Yuknavitch, Chelsea Cain, Monica Drake, and others. Her novels include *The Moment Before, The Empress Chronicles,* and *The Keepsake.*

LESLIE WHAT is a fiction editor of *Phantom Drift: New Fabulism.* She won a Nebula Award for a short story published in *Amazing Stories* and was an Oregon Book Awards finalist for her collection, *Crazy Love.* Her work has appeared in *Parabola, Bending the Landscape, Interfictions, Utne Reader, Los Angeles Review, Asimov's, Lilith, Calyx, Fugue, Unstuck Journal, Best New Horror, MacGuffin,* and other places. Thanks to eugeneweedworks.com for technical assistance and advice for "Trainwreck."

BRIGITTE WINTER is a storyteller, a jewelry-maker, a convener of artists and art lovers, and the executive director of Young Playwrights' Theater (yptdc.org), a Washington, D.C., nonprofit that inspires young people to realize the power of their voices through creative writing. All of her celebrity crushes are on authors. While she currently resides on the East Coast, her dearest friends live in Southeast Portland. "Octopocalypse" pays homage to the people and the city she's come to love as her own. Also killer octopuses. Hang out with Brigitte at brigittewinter.com, and stay tuned for her latest project: a pre-apocalyptic coming-of-age adventure novel.

LENI ZUMAS is the author of the story collection *Farewell Navigator* and the novel *The Listeners*, which was a finalist for the 2013 Oregon Book Award. Her new novel, *Red Clocks*, is forthcoming from Lee Boudreaux Books/Little, Brown. Zumas teaches in the MFA Program in Creative Writing at Portland State University.

Other Titles Published by Forest Avenue Press

Froelich's Ladder

Jamie Duclos-Yourdon

"At once a fantastical, madcap adventure and a poignant meditation on independence and solitude, it's the kind of book that captivates you quickly and whisks you high into the atmosphere. I was in thrall to the surreal Oregon landscape, populated by tycoons and grifters, cross-dressers and hungry clouds. This debut is clever, irreverent, and ultimately unforgettable."

– Leslie Parry, author of *Church of Marvels*

The Remnants

Robert Hill

"Reading *The Remnants* reminded me of Pound's conviction 'that music begins to atrophy when it departs too far from the dance; that poetry begins to atrophy when it gets too far from music.' Robert Hill bridges this gulf even more directly, writing sentences that not only sing but dance, full of whisks and sways and sprightly little sidesteps of language. How would they look, I began to wonder, if you diagrammed them? Like pinwheels, I imagine. Like fireworks. Try to fasten them down and they'd still keep moving."

– Kevin Brockmeier, author of *The Illumination*

Landfall

Ellen Urbani

"With her new novel *Landfall*, Ellen Urbani enters the world of American fiction with a bang and a flourish. She brings back the terrible Hurricane Katrina that tore some of the heart out of the matchless city of New Orleans, but did not lay a finger on its soul. It is the story of people caught in that storm and the lives both ruined and glorified in its passage. Her descriptions of the flooding of the Ninth Ward are Faulknerian in their powers. It's a hell of a book and worthy of the storm and times it describes."

– Pat Conroy, author of *The Prince of Tides*

Carry the Sky
Kate Gray

"In the rich rarified world of a prep school, Kate Gray has woven two powerful personal stories into a charged and compelling human novel which shows us that swimming under that quirky, antic, off-beat community are also life and death. Gray has a sharp eye and tells her story with verve and a deft touch."

— Ron Carlson, author of *The Signal*

The Night, and the Rain, and the River: 22 Oregon Stories
edited by Liz Prato

"I love this book like I love the ocean. *The Night, and the Rain, and the River* gets under your skin and travels your body from the first page. Each story brings you to the edge of your own heart, or life, or death, or gut grabbing laughter, and as the stories accumulate, you slowly realize you've been allowed into a world. These writers will mark you for life; remember their names. We are nothing without each other."

— Lidia Yuknavitch, author of *The Small Backs of Children*

The Gods of Second Chances
Dan Berne

"Every so often a novel comes along that feels like nothing you've read before. Dan Berne's *The Gods of Second Chances* is one of those, soulful and shattering in equal measure. Berne shines a light on rarely visited corners of both the world and the human heart in a page-turning story that stays with you long after you've reached the end. Be prepared to be amazed."

— Karen Karbo, author of *Julia Child Rules*

A Simplified Map of the Real World
Stevan Allred

"Funny, sensual, piercing, honest, witty, and a braided woven webbed stitch of stories and people unlike anything I ever read. It catches something deep and true about the brave and nutty shaggy defiant grace of this place. Fun to read and funner to recommend."

— Brian Doyle, author of *Mink River*